Patricia Burns is an Essex girl born and bred and proud of it. She spent her childhood messing about in boats, then tried a number of jobs before training to be a teacher. She married and had three children, all of whom are now grown up, and she recently became a grandmother. She is now married for the second time and is doing all the things she never had time for earlier in life.

When not busy writing, Patricia enjoys travelling and socialising, walking in the countryside round the village where she now lives, belly dancing and making exotic costumes to dance in.

Find out more about Patricia at
www.mirabooks.co.uk/patriciaburns

Patricia Burns

We'll Meet Again

MIRA®

First published in Great Britain 2008
by Harlequin Mills & Boon Limited, Eton House,
18-24 Paradise Road, Richmond, Surrey TW9 1SR

WE'LL MEET AGAIN © Patricia Kitchin 2008

ISBN: 978 0 7783 0217 9

58-0408

Printed and bound in Spain
by Litografía Rosés S.A., Barcelona

To Dorothy Lumley,
who never stopped believing in this book

CHAPTER ONE

January 1953

IT SEEMED to be a day like any other. Windy, certainly, but at Marsh Edge Farm they were used to almost constant wind, exposed as they were. It swept over the Essex flatlands with increasing power that day, the last day of January in the year of the new Queen's coronation. It came howling across the low grasslands that had once been part of the sea, raced over the snaking sea wall and buffeted the grey North Sea into angry white-topped waves.

It whipped the skirts of Annie Cross's old grey mac round her frozen legs as she brought the dairy cows in for evening milking. She pulled her muffler more snugly round her neck and looked round anxiously at her small son. Bobby was plodding behind the last animal, stick in hand, the clinging mud nearly to the top of his wellingtons. His small face was pinched and his nose was streaming. In the gap between his raincoat and his boots, his bare knees were bright red with cold. Annie forced an encouraging smile.

'Nearly there, darling! Grandma's making us some scones for tea. That'll be nice, won't it?'

Bobby nodded and sneezed, and wiped his nose on his

sleeve. Annie's heart contracted. He shouldn't be out here in the wind and the cold. He should be indoors in front of the kitchen range, being cosseted by his grandma. But cosseting was out of the question at Marsh Edge Farm.

Her father was waiting for them in the yard. A small man, Walter Cross watched their arrival from beneath the peak of his cloth cap, his eyes hard in his narrow face.

'You took your time. What's the matter with you? Having a holiday?'

Annie shook her head. It wasn't a question that required answering.

'You'll have to do the milking. I still haven't got that blasted tractor to work. Don't know what you've gone and done to it,' her father said.

'Right,' Annie said.

It was no use pointing out that the tractor had failed while he'd been driving it. After all, everything that went wrong round here was her fault. Hers or Bobby's.

'And make sure that brat of yours helps. Cold, indeed! I never heard the like. Never got colds in my day. Get the little bastard working. That'll soon cure him.'

Walter glared in the direction of the child, who stood in the yard entrance, his frightened eyes flicking from his mother to his grandfather. Walter grunted.

'Bad blood,' he muttered.

Annie's self-control snapped. 'He's your grandson!'

Her father's mouth stretched into a grim smile. He had provoked her. Satisfied, he turned to trudge across the yard to where the tractor stood under an open-sided shelter.

'Make sure it's all scrubbed down proper after. No skiving off early. I'll be checking to see you've done it right, mind,' he warned over his shoulder.

Annie said nothing. Walter stopped and slowly looked back at her. Behind her, Annie heard Bobby give a small whimper of fear.

'You heard what I said?' he demanded.

'Yes, Dad.'

'Good.'

His absolute authority assured, Walter walked on.

'Pig,' Annie muttered under her breath. 'Bully. *Schweinhund*.'

She had learnt that one from the pictures. It gave her particular pleasure. She repeated it with as guttural a German accent as she could manage.

At least the milking was inside. Annie and Bobby went about the well-worn routine—feeding, washing udders, fixing on the cups. Without Walter there criticising their every move, they could almost enjoy it. Bobby sniffed and sneezed but worked manfully. He was only seven, but he was a well-seasoned assistant.

'When I was little,' Annie told him, 'we did all this by hand. It took ages, even though we didn't have so many cows then.'

Like Bobby, she had had to help from an early age. She could hardly remember a time when she hadn't laboured on the farm.

'Did they like you doing it by hand?' Bobby asked. 'The cows?'

Annie thought about it.

'Yes. I think so. But you had to do it properly, or they'd kick you, or knock the bucket over.'

'I bet *he* didn't like that.'

'No, he didn't.'

The long day wasn't yet over. The cows had to be turned

into their pens and the dairy scrubbed down. Then there were the pigs to feed and hens to shut up for the night. By the time they had finished, Bobby's teeth were chattering. Annie fished a handkerchief out of her pocket and held it over his nose.

'Blow,' she told him.

He blew.

'That feel better?'

He nodded.

Annie put an arm round his shoulders and gathered him to her. He hugged her hips, nestling his balaclaved head against her. She glanced over to where her father was still leaning over the tractor engine with a spanner in his hand. She knew better than to go in without clearing it with him.

'We're finished, Dad,' she called across the yard.

He didn't let them go in straight away, but that was normal. Instead he found fault in their cleaning of the milking parlour. But when that was finally done to his satisfaction, they all went inside.

Marsh Edge farmhouse was a square plain brick building with a parlour, large kitchen, a scullery and an outside toilet downstairs and two large and two small bedrooms upstairs. The only room in the house that was heated was the kitchen, and it was there that they lived. It was hardly a model of comfort. The floors were stone-flagged, the walls whitewashed. A wooden sink and some shelves were built under the window, a green-painted dresser and some deal cupboards stood against one of the walls, a plain scrubbed table occupied the middle of the room with four stick-back chairs round it, while two Windsor carver chairs and a settle were set round the rag rug in front of the blackleaded range. The only clues that this was 1953 rather than 1903 were the big brown wireless on top of one of the cupboards, and the single electric light bulb under its red shade in the centre of the room.

Plain as it was, the kitchen seemed a haven of light and warmth after the raw cold of the yard. Annie and Bobby left their macs and wellingtons in the porch and washed their hands in the scullery. Edna Cross welcomed them in.

'You poor things; you must be frozen. How's my poor boy? That cold any better? Here, come and get warm by the range. I'll open the front up…'

Edna was an older version of her daughter, small and round-faced with a turned-up nose, but years of hard work, poor health and marriage to Walter had etched lines into her pretty face, and made her painfully thin rather than slender. Her narrow hands were red and rough and the hair that had once been fair and naturally wavy was limp and colourless. She had long ago given up any idea of being anything but a drudge.

'Is he coming?' she asked Annie, with a motion of her head towards the yard.

'I think so.'

'I'll do the toast, then. Can you make the tea, love?'

Annie shifted the big black kettle from where it was simmering on the side of the range to the hot spot in the middle, while her mother threaded a thick slice of bread on to the toasting fork. Bobby crouched on the rug, warming himself like a cat.

'He got that tractor fixed?' Edna asked.

'Not yet.'

Neither of them made any further comment. It went without saying that his failure would not improve Walter's temper. Edna's hand shook a little as she held the toasting fork.

Walter came in and the meal was put on the table—toast and dripping followed by scones and gooseberry jam, washed down by plenty of tea. The lack of conversation was disguised by the measured voices of the BBC announcers on the *Home Service*.

The evening passed like a hundred others. Annie put Bobby to bed and then sat by the range knitting him some socks. Walter read the local paper with the odd comment on the stupidity of one person or another while Edna hand-worked buttonholes in a rayon blouse for one of her customers. They listened to *Saturday Night Theatre* on the wireless. The weather forecast warned of continuing gales.

'There's a spring tide tonight and all,' Walter said.

Edna looked fearful.

'Spring tide and a gale? Will we be safe?'

'Don't talk daft, woman,' Walter scoffed. 'Wind's offshore. If anyone gets it, it'll be them Dutchies. Very low-lying, Holland is. Much more'n here.'

Annie made cocoa and put the porridge pot to simmer on the range, then there was the ritual of locking up before they went upstairs. Annie undressed as quickly as possible in her freezing bedroom and put on a flannelette nightie that came up to her neck and down to her ankles while on her feet she wore woolly socks.

Before getting into bed, she held back the curtain and took a quick peep outside. Way across the fields was the dark line of the sea wall, the place where she had met Tom, all those years ago when they had both been hardly more than kids. She pulled her mind away. It was no use dwelling on Tom. Under the sea wall, a light shone in a window, bringing a smile to her face. The light meant love and cheerfulness and hope. It came from Silver Sands, the little wooden chalet where her dear friends Reggie and Gwen lived, surrounded by the half dozen caravans that they insisted were going to make their fortune one day soon. While Reggie and Gwen were there, her life had a bright spot in it. She sent them a goodnight blessing. Then she climbed into the iron bedstead with its lumpy mattress and curled into a ball round her stone hot water bottle, gradually extending her feet down the bed as it warmed up.

Tired out from a long day working in the cold wind, she fell deeply asleep, only to be woken some time later out of a confused dream. Somewhere out in the yard, a door was banging. It was still a wild night out there. Wide awake and anxious about her friends, Annie slid out of bed and padded across the dark room to the window. Gwen was expecting a baby any day now. What if it had chosen tonight to arrive? What if Reggie's car, never very reliable, refused to start? She drew back the thin curtain and looked out once more. The sky had cleared and a bright moon shone down, silvering the marshes, glinting off—water! Annie caught her breath, not wanting to believe her eyes. There was a lake where the lower meadows should be. The fields were flooding.

She stared through the night, trying to make out what was happening, trying to distinguish the solid bulk of the wall, their only protection from the North Sea. She could see the pale glimmer of Reggie and Gwen's caravans crouching under where it should be.

'My God! Gwen!' she cried out loud.

If the water was coming over the wall, Reggie and Gwen were right in its path.

She blundered for the door, feeling for the light switch. Nothing happened. She flicked it up and down. Still nothing.

'Damn, damn.'

She stumbled across the landing and banged on her parents' bedroom door.

'Dad, Mum! Wake up! The water's coming over the wall! There's a flood!'

It took a few minutes to get her father awake and to make him understand what was happening. Once he did, his thoughts were for the stock.

'Get dressed. We got to get the store cattle in. The dairy herd'll be all right. The water won't reach as far as here.'

'But, Dad, it's already over the lower meadows—'

Her head rocked sideways as his heavy hand caught her round the ear. Through the ringing, she heard him shouting at her.

'Don't argue with me, girl. Get some clothes on. Quick.'

Annie knew better than to say any more. As she hurried into sweaters and trousers and felt her way downstairs in the dark, anxiety about her friends gnawed at her. How could she warn them? If only they had a telephone. Her father was in the kitchen, cursing as he lit the hurricane lamps that they kept for emergencies. The warm glow only made the shadows in the corners of the kitchen look darker. He thrust one into her hand.

'Come on.'

Annie hurried after him into the night. Once out of the protection of the farmyard, the full force of the gale hit her, nearly knocking her off her feet.

'Shift y'self, you useless mare, it's not even high tide yet. It'll get worse,' her father yelled.

'Who said it was all right because the wind was off-shore?' Annie muttered, but she did not dare say it out loud.

They struck out across the fields, leaving the gates open as they went, Annie almost running to keep up with her father as he strode ahead. The wind was pulling at her rain-coat, buffeting her face, making her ears ache and her eyes water. She did not look ahead, just kept her eyes on her father, a darker shape in the surrounding night. When they got close to the drainage ditches, where the water usually flowed sluggishly along the bottom, she could see by the moonlight that it was lapping over the edges. And there was another thing—something wrong. She could not put her finger on it at first, what with the wind and the dark and the effort of keeping up with her father, but then it came to her. The water in the ditches was running the wrong way. It was not draining away to the sea, it was coming in. Soon it was spreading out into wide puddles. She slid and floundered on the waterlogged ground. She fell on her knees and stag-gered up again. The journey took on the quality of a night-mare, going on and on, with her father looking back occasionally and cursing her for not keeping up.

Then at last they were at the field nearest to the sea wall. The young cattle were huddled at the gate, already up to their hocks in floodwater.

'Get round behind them, you stupid slut!' her father bawled.

She tried to obey, wading round the uneasy herd, mov-ing with difficulty as the floodwater came over the tops of her wellingtons and filled them up. She started yelling at them. The wind tore the sounds from her mouth. She thumped and pushed the animals' rumps, her feet sliding and squelching in the thick mud. Already upset by the storm, they started lowing and milling about. She could only hope that one would have the sense to get going, and then the oth-ers would follow it. To her relief, some instinct for survival seemed to get hold of them. One went through the gate, then another. Knowing where to go now, they went plodding into the next field. Already that was awash as well, the gale whipping it into miniature waves. Over the next field and the next they went, gathering up more stock, herding the frightened animals towards each gate, forcing them through. The water seemed to be racing ahead of them, turning each field into a lake before they reached it. Annie's throat was raw with yelling at the beasts, every muscle in her body ached, her legs felt like weights, dragging her back, slowing her down. But ahead was the farmhouse, silvered in the moonlight. They were in the home field.

She paused in her own battle to spare a thought for her friends, staring through the night towards Silver Sands. With the electricity out, there were no lights showing, no way of knowing whether Reggie and Gwen were awake and saving themselves.

'Don't stop now! Get on!' her father shouted.

'Reggie and Gwen—' she yelled.

'What? What now?'

'Reggie and Gwen. At Silver Sands—'

'Too late. Get on.'

If only they had a telephone. Or a boat. If only the tractor were working. If she could just know what was happening. How deep was it down by the sea wall now?

Then, above the howl of the storm, she heard, or rather felt, a rumbling roar, and there, coming towards her across the flooded fields, was a wall of water that seemed as high as a double-decker bus. Terrified, she turned and tried to run.

She staggered forward, fear giving her a new desperate energy. Ahead of her the farm buildings loomed, blacker in the surrounding darkness, promising safety, but her way was blocked by a solid rank of frightened, bewildered cattle. She shrieked and beat at them, trying to get through. She glanced over her shoulder. The wave was getting nearer.

The first cows reached the farmyard and waded inside, fanning out into the wider space. Annie lashed out at the ones behind, swinging the hurricane lamp at them, screaming. Then the water hit her.

Icy and black, the whole weight of the North Sea behind it, it knocked her off her feet. Helpless, she was carried along, her arms and legs thrashing uselessly in the swirling current, knocking into bony rumps and sharp horns. There was a roaring in her ears. Her lungs were bursting. Then, just as she thought she could not hold her breath any longer, she crashed into something solid and held on with both arms and all her strength. She found her feet and dragged herself upright. Her head surfaced. Choking and gasping, she sucked in the blessed air.

She had fetched up against a tree. For several moments she just clung on to the slender trunk, shaking, gasping, thankful simply to be alive. Around her she could hear the cattle still lowing in fear, but now her only thought was for herself. She had to get to the house. The water was up to her shoulders and still rising.

'Ann!'

A croak in the darkness. Her father. At first she couldn't see him in the swirling confusion.

'Ann! Help me!'

The moonlight caught his head. His hat was gone, his face was twisted in fear. He was being washed towards her, the tyrant reduced to a helpless rag doll by the raging force of the flood. Annie could see him trying and failing to get his feet to the ground, his arms flailing. An odd disconnected thought slid into her head. He hadn't called her by her name in years.

A chance eddy brought him near to her, nearer—

'Ann!'

There was terror in his voice, desperation in his face. His hand stretched out to her. He was three yards away, two. The events of her life seemed to whirl before her. She was six years old again, was cowering before him as he grasped her arm, his heavy hand beating her again and again. She was eleven. Her teacher said that if she worked hard, she could pass the exam for the grammar school. But her father sneered at the very idea. Grammar school was not for the likes of her. She was needed on the farm.

'Please, Ann—!'

He was her father. He couldn't swim.

'Dad?' she croaked.

She had only to let go of the tree with one hand and reach out to him.

She saw Bobby cowering, Bobby terrified at having failed to do some task way beyond his years and strength, Bobby called nothing but 'that boy' and forced to call his own grandfather 'Mr Cross'.

'Ann, for God's sake—'

He was close enough for her to touch his fingertips. But she did not. And a moment later he was gone, swallowed up into the black water.

'Dad!' she screamed.

She let go with one arm and strained after him. The hungry current got her in its grip, tugged and sucked at her.

'Dad!'

Frantically, she flailed about, trying to find him, to catch hold of him.

But it was too late.

CHAPTER TWO

July 1940

'NO MORE school, no more books, no more teacher's dirty looks!' Annie's friend Gwen chanted as she danced along the road.

Annie followed with a heavy heart. This was her last day of freedom, the last day she would walk towards home with Gwen, the last day of laughing and chatting to her friends at break time, the last—

'Let's go and look at the beach!' Gwen called over her shoulder. Her freckled face was pink with excitement, her girlish plaits and her white ankle socks contrasting oddly with the woman's figure beneath her cotton frock.

Annie glanced down at her own woefully small breasts. That was something else that Gwen had more of than her. It wasn't fair.

'All right,' she agreed.

Anything to put off going home.

Gwen waited for her to catch up and threaded an arm through hers.

'I'm never going to open another book again,' she vowed.

Annie sighed. 'I probably won't be allowed to.'

'Oh, you—' Gwen pushed her away and pulled her in again. 'You're such an old swot. Mr Clifton's favourite! Teacher's pet! What did he say to you, when he called you up to his desk?'

'He wished me luck and told me to keep going to the public library,' Annie admitted.

She was going to miss Mr Clifton, Annie decided. He had stuck up for her when her dad had refused to let her take up her scholarship to the grammar school. He'd offered to go and speak to her dad about it. Not that it had done any good, but at least he had tried. And he'd always been kind to her and encouraged her reading, getting her to try new authors and discuss what she had read.

'No need to tell you that,' Gwen said. 'Oh, isn't it lovely? We're grown-ups now. We're not kids any more.'

'It's all right for you; you're going out to work. You'll have money of your own. I'll just be stuck on the farm, day in, day out,' Annie said.

School had been her escape. Her father didn't see the point of her going, but it was the law that children had to attend until they were fourteen, and even he had to obey that. He flouted it as much as he could, keeping her back when they were busy on the farm, but still Annie had been able to get away most of the time. But from now on, she was going to be tied. It was like a prison sentence, stretching away ahead of her, with no let-off for good behaviour. Already, her father had given notice to the elderly man who had worked for them for the last ten years. She was cheaper, and available seven days a week.

'But you'll get time off, surely?' Gwen said. 'He won't have you working in the evenings. We can go to the pictures together.'

'Yes—' Annie tried to be optimistic. 'He can't keep me in all the time, can he? We'll go to the pictures Friday nights.'

'Cary Grant…' Gwen sighed. 'Humphrey Bogart…'

'Clark Gable…' Annie responded.

'Who would you like to be, if you was a film star?' Gwen asked.

'Judy Garland.'

How wonderful to be Dorothy and meet the Tin Man and the Cowardly Lion…how wonderful to escape from your farm and land in Oz. But of course you had to live in Kansas for that to happen to you. Whirlwinds didn't tear across Essex.

'Judy Garland? Oh, no. I want to be glamorous. I want to be Vivien Leigh.'

And meet Rhett Butler.

'Oh, yes…' Annie sighed.

Both happy now in their fantasy world, the girls marched arm in arm along the dusty summer streets of Wittlesham-on-Sea. The neat terraces of guest houses leading to the sea front still had 'Vacancies' notices hopefully displayed in their front windows, but many of the gardens had their roses and geraniums replaced by lettuces and peas as people answered the call to dig for victory.

When they reached the sea front, they stopped automatically and looked towards the pier.

'Quiet, isn't it?' Gwen said. 'My mum says it's hardly worth keeping open.'

Gwen's mum ran The Singing Kettle, a tearoom fifty yards from the pier entrance. The previous summer, the last summer of peace, it had been a little gold-mine, and Gwen had been kept as busy as Annie, running from kitchen to table with trays of teas and cakes and sandwiches, and back again with piles of dirty crockery. This year the visitors were few and far between. People were reluctant to go on holiday when invasion forces were threatening just across the Channel.

'Blooming Hitler,' Gwen grumbled as they surveyed the sprinkling of holiday-makers and the barbed wire entanglements running the length of the beach. 'Gone and ruined everything, he has. That's what my mum says.'

'Yes,' Annie agreed. 'We've had to plough up the fields by the road because of him.'

Digging for Victory had meant that her father had had to change some of his farming practices. He hadn't liked that at all, and she and her mother had been the ones to bear the brunt of it.

The girls turned away from the pier and strolled along together towards the southern end of the promenade. Even fewer businesses were open here, and the locked doors and boarded-up windows gave the prom a forlorn air.

'D'you really want to go and work at Sutton's Bakelite?' Annie asked.

Gwen shrugged. 'It's good money, and it's all year round,' she pointed out.

Year-round jobs were at a premium in Wittlesham, where seasonal work was the norm.

'Yes, but Sutton's—Beryl's dad,' Annie persisted.

'I know—' Gwen said.

Both of them thought of Beryl Sutton, their sworn enemy.

'—but it is war work. I'll be making parts for aeroplanes and stuff. Wirelesses, that sort of thing,' Gwen said.

'I s'pose so. But Toffee-nose Beryl—'

'Swanky knickers—'

'Posh pants—'

They giggled happily, dragging up every insult they'd

ever thrown at Beryl. But it still didn't help with the deep jealousy Annie harboured, swilling like poison in her gut. Beryl had been allowed to go to the grammar school, when Annie had always beaten her in every school test they ever did. On top of that, they shared a birthday. Somehow, that made it much worse.

'She won't be there,' Gwen pointed out.

No, Annie thought. She'll be at school, for another two years. Lucky cow.

'And her dad's all right.'

'Yes.'

That was another thing. Beryl's dad was all right. He was nice. He was big and cheerful and adored Beryl. But then Gwen's dad adored her, too. He called her his little princess and slipped her money for treats with a wink and a 'Don't tell your mother.' Annie sighed. It wasn't fair.

The closed up souvenir shops and cafés dwindled into bungalows as the cliff ran down towards the marsh at the edge of the town. As the sea wall joined the end of the prom, there was a no man's land of nettle-infested building plots and little wooden holiday chalets on legs that was not quite town but not country either. The roads here were just tracks and there was a temporary feel about the place. On the very last plot, a field under the sea wall that took a corner out of Annie's father's land, was a holiday chalet called Silver Sands. It belonged to the Suttons, who let it out to summer visitors.

'Looks like they're opening it up,' Annie said.

She was right. The windows and doors were open and the net curtains were blowing in the breeze. Rugs hung over the veranda rails. From inside came the sound of someone banging around with a broom.

'Trust the Suttons to get lets when no one else can,' said Gwen. 'There's a lot of people in this town don't know what they're going to do if this war goes on much longer. My aunty May's desperate. She's only had two families so far this summer, and lots of her regulars have cancelled. And my uncle Percy, he can't work, not with his chest. And, like she says, rates've still got to be paid, and the gas and electric and everything, and the rooms kept nice, whether there's visitors or not. She was talking to my mum about it the other day. Went on about it for hours, she did.'

'Yes,' Annie said.

Her eyes were on Silver Sands. It was a trim little place, painted green and cream with sunray-effect woodwork on the veranda rails. Around it was about half an acre of wild ground with roughly cut grass, a few tough flowering plants and a swing. Positioned as it was, right next to Marsh Edge Farm, it had always held a special place in her imagination. When she was little, she liked to picture herself creeping in and living there, safely out of the way of her father, her own small palace where she could order everything the way she wanted.

'I wish it was mine,' she said, without really meaning to let it out.

'It's only a holiday chalet like all the rest,' Gwen said. 'I dunno why you make such a fuss about it. You wasn't half mad when the Suttons bought it! I thought you was going to burst a blood vessel!'

'Well, why should they have it? Them, of all people? That Beryl...'

Annie's voice trailed off. There, on the track leading to the chalet, was Beryl. It was as if she had been summoned like a bad genie by Annie's speaking her name. Annie took in her grammar school uniform, the green and white checked dress, the green blazer, the straw hat with its green ribbon and green and yellow badge. Her guts churned with jealousy.

'Ooh—' she jeered. 'It's the posh girl. Look at her soppy hat! What're you wearing that hat for, posh pants? Looks like a soup plate!'

'Soup plate on her head!' chimed the faithful Gwen.

Beryl glared at them. She was a solid girl with brown hair cut in a straight fringe across her broad face and thick calves rising from her white ankle socks. The school uniform that Annie envied so much did nothing for her looks.

'Common little council school brats,' she countered, her lip curling into a full, cartoon-sized sneer. She glanced behind her. 'Come on, Jeffrey. Mummy doesn't like us talking to nasty little guttersnipes. They might have nits.'

It was only then that Annie noticed Jeffrey Sutton, Beryl's younger brother by a year, sloping up along the track towards them. He was also in grammar school uniform, his leather satchel over his shoulders, his green and black striped cap pushed to the back of his head. It was unfortunate for Beryl that she took after her mother while her three brothers favoured their father, for the boys had the better share of the looks. Jeffrey caught up with his sister and threw Annie and Gwen a conciliatory grin. You never knew which way Jeffrey might jump. His loyalties depended upon the situation.

'Wotcha!' he said.

Beryl rounded on him. 'Jeffrey! Ignore them.'

Jeffrey shrugged and walked on, opting out of the situation. As he went, he said, 'Bye!'

It was difficult to know who he was speaking to, but Annie leapt on the one word and appropriated it.

'Bye, Jeffrey,' she said, as friendly as could be.

She was rewarded by a look of intense annoyance on Beryl's face.

'So you're going to be one of my father's factory girls, are you?' she said to Gwen, breaking her own advice of ignoring Gwen and Annie.

'I'm going to be earning me own living,' Gwen retorted. 'Not a little schoolgirl in a soup plate.'

'You are so ignorant, Gwen Barker,' Beryl said, and stalked off up the track and in at the gate of Silver Sands.

'Ooh!' Gwen and Annie chorused and, linking arms again, marched after her, past the gate and on towards the sea wall. As they dropped arms to take a run at the steep slope, Beryl's mother came out on to the veranda, her face set in lines of disapproval.

Annie couldn't resist. She gave a friendly wave.

'Afternoon, Mrs Sutton!' she called cheerfully and, before Mrs Sutton had a chance to reply, the pair of them raced up the grassy bank, over the bare rutted path at the top and slid down the other side. They landed in a heap at the bottom, giggling helplessly and scratched all up their bare thighs from the sharp grass blades.

'Did you see her *face?*' Gwen chortled.

'Sour old boot!' Annie gasped.

It was warm and still at the foot of the sea wall, for the wind was offshore. There was a smell of salt and mud and rotting seaweed on the air. The very last of the Wittlesham beach was at their feet, a narrow strip of pale yellow sand and shingle that dwindled to nothing fifty feet to their right where it met the marsh.

Annie wrapped her arms round her legs and rested her chin on her knees, staring through the barbed wire entanglements, out across the fringe of grey-green marsh and wide expanse of glistening grey-brown mud to where the waters of the North Sea started in lace-edged ripples. It was friendly today, in the height of summer, the sunlight glinting off the gentle green waves. She let the peace steal into her with the heat of the sun. A curlew uttered its sad cry. She felt safe here.

'Jerries are over there, across the water,' Gwen said.

'Mmm,' Annie said.

That was what they said, on the wireless. It was difficult to believe right here, sitting in the sunshine.

'My dad's out every evening, drilling with the LDVs. No, not that. The Home Guard, it now is. Mr Churchill said.'

'My dad doesn't hold with it,' Annie said.

But then her dad didn't hold with anything that meant co-operating with anyone else. And her dad would be expecting her home soon. She didn't own a watch, so she had no idea of the exact time, but her dad knew when school ended, and how long it took to walk home. Reluctantly, she stood up.

'S'pose I'd better go,' she said with a sigh.

'You got to?' Gwen asked. 'It's the last day of school. It's special.'

Gwen's mum had promised her a special tea, and then they were all going to the pictures—Gwen, her sister and her mum and dad.

'Not in our house, it isn't,' Annie said. 'Have a nice time this evening. Tell me all about it.'

They scrambled to the top of the sea wall again. Gwen set off towards the town. Annie stood for a moment watching her, then turned and ran down the landward side and up the track beside Silver Sands. She couldn't help glancing over the fence at the little chalet in its wild garden but, though the windows were still open, none of the Suttons were outside. She skirted round the back of the garden and struck out across the fields. The newly expanded dairy herd grazed the first two. Then there was an empty field that had been cut for silage. Ahead of her across the flat land, she could see the square bulk of the farmhouse and the collection of sheds and barns round the yard. Marsh Edge Farm. Home. It gave her a sinking feeling.

One field away from the house, Annie climbed over the gate and on to the track that led from the farm to the Wittlesham road. She looked at the yard as it grew steadily nearer. Was her father there? She started counting—an odd number of dandelions before she reached the hawthorn tree meant he was there, an even number meant he wasn't. Nineteen—twenty—twenty-one. Bother and blast. Try again. If she could hold her breath as far as the broken piece of fence he wouldn't be there...

She reached the gate into the yard. In winter, it was a sea of mud, but now, in summertime, it was baked into ruts and ridges in some places and beaten to dust by the passing of cattle hooves twice a day in others. Hens strutted and scratched round the steaming midden in one corner, the tabby cat lay stretched out in the sun by the rain barrel. A gentle grunting came from the pig pen. Annie started to relax. Perhaps he was in one of the fields on the other side of the farm. She could go in and have a cup of tea with her mum.

Then there was a sudden flutter and squawk from the hens, and out of the barn came her father. He stopped when he saw her and fixed her with his pale blue eyes.

'You're late,' he said.

CHAPTER THREE

ANOTHER long day of work was done and the last chores in the farmyard were finished. Annie looked in at the kitchen door. Her mother was sitting at the big table, turning the wheel of her sewing machine. The needle flew up and down so fast that it became a blur, while her mother fed the long side seam of a green silk dress beneath it.

'Mum?' Annie asked. 'You all right? You need me to do anything?'

'No—no—' Edna Cross did not take her eyes from the slippery fabric. 'Just want to get this done before Mrs Watson comes for her fitting tomorrow.'

'I think I'll go out for a bit, then.'

'All right, dear.'

Annie slid out of the porch, ran across the yard and away down the track before her father could see what she was doing. Once over the gate into the first field, she slowed to a walk. She felt physically light, as if she might bounce along if she wanted to. For a short while, until it got dark and she had to go back indoors, she was free.

She headed automatically for the sea wall. It was no use looking at Silver Sands, for a big family had moved in two days ago for a holiday. Even from here she could see the two little tents they had put up in the garden because the chalet wasn't large enough to accommodate them all. But it would be all right the other side of the wall. That was one advantage of the barbed wire—it kept people off the beach. Nobody but her liked to sit on the small bit of sand between the wall and the wire.

It was a beautiful summer's evening, warm and still. Annie dodged the cow-pats and the thistles, singing as she went.

'Wish me luck as you wave me goodbye…'

The one big bonus of the war, as far as she was concerned, was that her father had gone out and bought a wireless so he could listen to the news each evening. Which meant that they could also listen to Henry Hall and Geraldo, and her mother could have *Music While You Work* on. Now she knew all the latest songs just as soon as Gwen did.

As she came nearer to Silver Sands, she could see the family there out in the garden. She felt drawn to study them. There were two women—Mum and Aunty, maybe?—sitting on the veranda knitting, together with a man reading a newspaper, while a bunch of children all younger than herself were running round the bushes and up and down the steps in a game of 'he'. Annie skirted the garden, wishing there was another way on to the sea wall, but you had to walk a long way away from the town before you got to the bridge over the wide dyke that ran along behind the wall. There were shrieks from the children as someone was caught, and then yells of, 'Joan's It! Joan's It!' Annie wondered what it would be like to have a holiday. It must be nice to be able to play all day long like those children. Not that she was wanting to run around playing now, of course. She was too grown up for that. But she would have liked it when she was little.

She ran up the sea wall, stopping at the top to look about.

'Oh!' she said out loud.

For there, just below her on the seaward side of the wall where nobody ought to be, was a boy a year or so older than herself with a sketch-book on his knee.

If he had heard her, he made no sign of it, but just kept on glancing at the sea then looking down at his paper and making marks. Fascinated, Annie looked over his shoulder. He was making a water-colour sketch. The sky was already done and, as Annie watched, he ran layers of colour together to make the sea, leaving bits of white paper showing through so it looked like the low sunlight reflecting off the waves. He made it look so easy, so unlike the clumsy powder paint efforts that she had occasionally been allowed to do at school.

'That's ever so good,' she said before she could stop herself.

The boy turned his head, screwing up his eyes a little to see her as she stood against the light.

'Oh—' he said. 'Hello. I mean—thanks. I thought you were one of my beastly kid cousins creeping up on me.'

He had an angular face with broad cheekbones, and very dark hair cut in a standard short-back-and-sides, but what struck Annie most was his unfamiliar accent—something she vaguely identified as being northern.

'No,' she said.

Now that she had started the conversation, she wasn't quite sure what to say next.

'You an artist?' she blurted out, and instantly curled up inside with embarrassment, because how could he be an artist? He wasn't old enough.

But, to her relief, instead of laughing, he took her question seriously.

'I want to be. But I don't know whether I'm going to be good enough.'

'But you are! That's lovely!' Annie cried.

He shook his head. 'Not really. The colours aren't right.'

'They are—well, nearly,' Annie said, sticking to the truth. 'And it's—' She stopped and considered, her head to one side. She'd never really looked at a painting before, not a proper one. She had no words to describe what she thought about it. 'It's like—moving. Yes—that's it. The sea's sort of moving—'

It sounded daft, put like that, because paint didn't move. But the boy's face lit up. He had an infectious smile.

'Really? You think so?'

Glad that she'd hit the right note, Annie grinned back. Without thinking about it, she came and sat down by him. He was dressed in a blue short-sleeved shirt, khaki shorts and plimsolls. His arms and legs were long and skinny. His nose was peeling.

'I do, honest. I think it's good,' she assured him. 'Are you going to put the pier in? And the wire?'

'When it's dry I'll draw the pier in Indian ink, so I'll be able to get all the little details. I don't know about the wire. I think I might do another one, without the pier, just sea and sky and the wire across it.'

Annie nodded slowly, seeing it in her head. 'Yes, sort of…like a prison—' The boy turned and gave her a long, considering look.

'Yes,' he said. 'That's just it. It's supposed to be keeping the Jerries out, but if you look at it the other way, it's keeping us in.'

'But if you look through it—sort of fuzzy your eyes—you know? You can pretend it isn't there at all,' Annie said.

Which brought on that dazzling smile again.

'Yes! That's what I'm doing right now! Just—making it go away. How did you know that?'

'I do it a lot,' Annie told him. 'Pretending things aren't there. Or people. It's better like that.'

'And how,' the boy said.

They looked at each other, breathless, startled by that heart-stopping moment that revealed a kindred spirit.

'I'm Tom. Tom Featherstone.'

That intriguing accent. The way he said 'stone'.

'Annie Cross.'

Self-consciously, they shook hands. Tom put down his sketch-book and brushes.

'Are you here on holiday?' she asked.

'Mmm. At the chalet.'

'Silver Sands?'

If it had been anyone else, she would have resented them being in the place she wanted for her own retreat, but with Tom it was different.

'S'right.' he said. 'You?'

'I live at the farm. Marsh Edge. Over there.'

She pointed her thumb over her shoulder.

'Oh—that farm. We can see it from the garden. I wondered who lived there.'

'I wondered who the family was at Silver Sands. I saw the tents in the garden. I thought—I thought it must be nice, to have a holiday, and lots of people to play with. If you're a little kid, of course.'

'They're pests, my cousins,' Tom said. 'They're all younger than me. My sister Joan's five years younger than me, and my cousin Doreen's only a year younger than her, so they're friends, and then the twins, that's Doreen's brothers, they're always together anyway. I came over here to get away from them.'

It was all falling into place.

'Who are the grown-ups? They your mum and dad?'

'My mam and Aunt Betty and Uncle Bill. My dad had to stay at home and mind the business.'

Mam. She liked that.

'Where're you from?' she asked.

'Noresley. It's near Nottingham.'

Nottingham. Annie pictured the map of England in her head. They'd traced it and put in all the boundaries and principle towns and cities in Geography a couple of years ago. Nottingham was just about in the middle. The Midlands.

'Where Robin Hood came from?'

'Sort of. We're not in Sherwood Forest, though. It's all pit villages round our way.'

'Pits? You mean coal mines?'

Miners were one of her father's many dislikes. They were all good-for-nothing commies in his opinion.

'That's right. We run a bus and coach company, in and out of Nottingham and Mansfield, and between the villages.'

Annie thought of being out and about all the time, driving from one place to another, talking to all the people getting on and off the bus.

'Sounds like fun. Are you going to drive a bus when you're older?'

Tom sighed. 'I suppose I'll have to. I can't really see my dad letting me go to art school. Depends, though, doesn't it? If the war's still going on by December next year I'll be joining up.'

'D'you think it'll go on that long?'

'Last one did, didn't it? It went on for four years.'

'Four years! I'll be eighteen then.'

Eighteen. It seemed a huge age. And where would she be then? Still here at Marsh Edge Farm, probably. Or... Annie looked at the barbed wire that was supposed to keep the Germans out and a dreadful thought struck her.

'Do you think they will invade?' she asked.

It had never really presented itself as a possibility before. It was something lingering on the edge of imagination, like a past nightmare. Now she saw waves of grey-uniformed soldiers coming ashore, cutting through the wire, marching over the fields—her fields—towards her home. Fear sliced through her.

'I don't know,' Tom said. 'We're winning the Battle of Britain so far. Our planes are shooting down more of their planes. We can't lose, can we? I mean—we just can't—'

'No,' Annie agreed. 'We can't.'

They both stared through the wire to the horizon. The fear subsided, but still lurked there.

There was a rustling and panting on the other side of the wall, and then two shrill voices broke through their reverie.

'Tom! Tom! Your mam says you're to come in, she's making the cocoa.'

Annie turned round. Two small boys with identical round faces, grey eyes and grubby knees were staring at her.

'Who's she?' one of them asked.

'Never you mind. Go and tell my mam I'm just coming,' Tom told them.

The twins stood and gazed.

'What's she doing here?' the other one asked.

'Talking. Now buzz off. Now! Hop it! Go!' Tom ordered.

Giggling, they went.

'Brats,' Tom grumbled.

'I thought they were quite sweet,' Annie said.

Their likeness was fascinating.

'Huh. You don't have to share a tent with them,' Tom said.

He washed his brushes, emptied his water jar, closed his paint box. While they had been talking, the light had faded. It was dusk.

'You—er—you going to be here at all tomorrow?' he asked, not looking at her.

'I've got to work. But I might be able to get away in the evening again. I might,' Annie said, knowing as she said it that she would move heaven and earth to do so.

'Come over this side again. Where that lot can't see us,' Tom said, indicating his family with a backward movement of his head. 'If you want to, that is.'

'Righty-oh. If I can,' Annie said. 'Bye, then.'

Tom looked at her now and smiled—a shy smile.

'Bye, Annie.'

She ran all the way home in the gathering dark, inches above the ground.

CHAPTER FOUR

THE sun was already warm on the roof of the small ridge tent. The twins, as usual, were sprawled over far more than their share of the space. The elbow of one of them was jabbing in Tom's ribs while the foot of the other was dangerously near to his face. They both had sleeping bags made of old blankets held together with large safety pins, but neither of them seemed able to stay inside them. But at least they were still asleep. Once awake, they were liable to start their favourite game of the moment—breaking wind in unison.

Cautiously, Tom moved his arm so that he could look at his new watch. Just gone half past six. He was wide awake now and, for the first time that holiday, filled with a sense of excitement. At last, somebody his own age to talk to, instead of being stuck in between the little kids and the grown-ups.

Annie.

Annie Cross.

A girl.

Girls were practically unknown territory to him. Since he'd been eleven, he'd been at an all boys school, and his sister was much younger than he was so her friends were just kids. Some of his friends had sisters, but they tended either to giggle and blush when he tried to speak to them, or were so adult and sophisticated that they might as well be on a different planet to him. Annie was different, though. He could talk to Annie, and she understood what he was about. And she was pretty. The artist in him appreciated her elfin face, her wide blue eyes, the wave in her fair hair, while the male wanted to reach out and touch the soft warmth of her skin.

Tom eased himself carefully from under the old pink eiderdown until he was sitting up. Still neither of the twins stirred. He reached for his clothes, in a heap by his feet, unlaced the first two eyelets of the tent flap and wriggled out into the morning.

The dew was still wet on the coarse grass of the wild garden, big droplets sparkling diamond-bright in the morning sunshine. A seagull wheeled across the blue sky, filling the silence with its raucous cry. Tom almost skipped as he walked barefoot across the grass to the wash house tacked on to the back of the chalet. By the time he got there, the ends of his pyjama legs were soaking and clinging to his ankles, but it was all part of the heightened pleasure of the morning.

His mood was knocked back as he studied his face in the small mirror above the basin. His features fell so far short of the mature, smooth, immaculately groomed look of all the film stars and band leaders that he couldn't imagine Annie being remotely interested in him. He couldn't even shave the night's sprinkling of stubble off his jaw since that would mean going into the chalet and risking disturbing his mother as he heated the water. Instead he resorted to what his mother referred to as 'a lick and a promise' of a wash and dragged on his clothes. After all, Annie wasn't going to see him now. She wasn't free till the evening, and even then she hadn't promised to come. As he went over this fact, how she had hesitated and said 'I might', he realised how very much he wanted to see her again.

Outside again, the heat of the sun restored his optimism. The chalet was still, so none of the grown-ups were awake, and the children slept on in their tents. Tom went out of the side gate and on to the sea wall. Usually the first thing he looked at was the sea, but today he faced the other way. Those fields belonged to Annie's farm. The house in the distance with the collection of barns and outbuildings round it was her home. The sheep and cows... And then he spotted a herd of cows all going in one direction, with a small figure behind them. His stomach tied itself in knots. It was such a weird sensation that he felt quite sick. Annie. That had to be Annie, driving the cows along. He and she were both out in the early morning while the rest of the world was asleep.

He waved, first one then both arms at her, but either she didn't see him or she didn't want to respond. Perhaps she was too busy making sure the cows were going the right way. He tried again. Still no response. He watched as she shut a gate behind them and turned away, then waved once more, not realising that he was practically jumping up and down as he did so. The distant figure stopped and, to his joy, raised an arm and waved back. He waved with all his might until she went off across the fields the way she had come. He watched her out of sight.

That must mean that she would come and see him again that evening.

The day seemed to go on for ever. It felt as if he were in a strange parallel existence, talking and acting as usual, yet separated from the rest of the world. He went for walks, played rounders with the children, did chores for his mother, and all the while his thoughts were centred on one thing. Annie.

At last evening came. He escaped from the demands of family and bolted over the sea wall to wait for her. The relief of it. He didn't have to pretend to be normal any longer.

He knew it was no use trying to paint. Instead, he wrote her name, over and over again, in different styles. Annie Annie Annie. After a while, he gave that up and just stared between the strands of barbed wire at the sea, waiting.

And then, just when he thought that she wasn't coming, there was a scuffling sound behind him and there she was. Tom was at once delighted and excruciatingly embarrassed. What was he going to say to her? What could she possibly want to say to him? He felt himself going red.

She paused at the top of the wall.

'Hello,' she said.

'Hello,' Tom managed to reply. 'You made it, then.'

And cursed himself for being stupid. Of course she had made it. She was here, wasn't she?

She didn't seem to think it was stupid. She just nodded and scampered down the wall to join him on the strip of sand at the bottom.

'He gave me extra chores to do,' she said with a backward motion of her head. 'I thought I was never going to get away.'

'Who, your dad?'

'Mmm.'

Her face was dark and brooding.

'Does he make you work hard?'

'He's a slave-driver.'

The edge to her voice shocked him.

'Don't you like your dad?' he asked.

'I hate him.'

She sat hugging her knees to her chest, glaring through the barbed wire. Tom felt at a loss. There were times when he hated his father, but most of the time he was all right. If pushed, he would admit that he loved him.

'Why?' was all he could think of to say.

'I don't want to talk about it.'

She picked up a stone and tossed it through the barbed wire. When she spoke again, it was cheerfully. It was as if a shadow had lifted.

'Tell me all about your family, and your house and where you live. I want to know everything,' she said.

Glad to be back on firm ground, Tom complied.

'Well, you've seen my mam and my sister,' he said. 'Mam looks after the house and us. She moans a lot about all this rationing. Our Joan's all right, I suppose. She used to be quite sweet when she was little, but now she's getting right bossy. And our dad, he works all hours—' He skipped over a description of his father, because it seemed like rubbing it in that his was nice when hers wasn't. 'And we live in this house on the edge of Norseley. Mam says she'd like to move somewhere nicer, and Norseley's just an ugly pit village, but Dad says we shouldn't be ashamed of us roots. And anyway Norseley's all right. It's just a bit mucky, that's all.'

'I wish I could see it,' Annie said. 'I've never been anywhere. Just Brightlingsea, where Gran and Grandpa live, and once I went to Colchester.'

Tom looked at her in amazement. Colchester was no distance. It had been the last main line town on their journey here, where they had changed on to the branch line for Wittlesham.

'Where's Brightlingsea?' he asked.

'Just down there a bit—' She flapped a hand southwards, away from Wittlesham. 'Tell me some more.'

So he told her about the rows of cottages and the fires that were always kept burning and the rattle of the winding gear, about the big house at Norseley Park and the family with their horses and their Rolls Royce, and about his school and his friends and the cricket club and the cycling club. And all the while Annie fixed him with her wide blue eyes, and asked questions and smiled or looked angry or sympathetic in all the right places so that he forgot all about time and place in the pleasure of talking to a willing listener.

'Tom! To-om!' His sister's voice shrilled over the sea wall.

Tom stopped in mid-sentence and put a finger to his lips. Annie grinned in instant understanding. Silently, they listened to Joan calling.

'Tom, where are you? Mam wants you. Tom—' She was puffing now as she climbed the grass slope.

'I'm just coming,' Tom called back. 'Go and tell her I'm coming.'

He looked at Annie.

'I've done nothing but waffle on about me,' he apologised softly.

'All *right*. But you've got to come right away,' said an aggrieved voice quite close to them.

'It's nice. I liked it. It's like seeing a different life, like when you go to the pictures,' Annie whispered.

'I said, you've got to come right away,' the voice insisted.

'All right. I am,' Tom repeated. He smiled at the thought of his life being like a film. 'I don't think they'd put me on the pictures. I'm right ordinary.'

'No, you're not. You're not at all ordinary,' Annie said.

Tom felt oddly breathless. His heart was thumping in his chest.

'Nor are you,' he said.

'Oh, *there* you are,' exclaimed Joan.

Tom could have killed her. He swivelled round to glare up at her in the twilight.

'Yes, here I am. Now clear off and tell Mam I'm coming, all right?'

He would never hear the last of this now.

'All right,' Joan repeated. 'And I'll tell her who you're with, shall I?'

With an irritating laugh, she made off.

'Blooming sisters,' he groaned.

Annie stood up. 'I got to run. It's nearly dark.'

'Will you—will you be back tomorrow?' Tom asked, the words tumbling out of his mouth.

'I'll try,' she said.

And that was all he had to live on for the next twenty-three hours.

The next day was broken up by a very different visitor. In the afternoon, Mrs Sutton, the lady who owned the chalet, arrived with her lump of a daughter and her small son. Tom heard them arrive, heard the mothers all talking together and the kid go off to play with his cousins. He kept very still in the sunny spot where he was playing patience, hoping he'd be forgotten. No such luck.

'Ah, now, here's poor Beryl with no one to play with,' he heard his mother say. 'Tom's in just the same position. I'm sure he'll be glad to entertain you. Tom! Where are you? Come over here!'

He ignored her, hoping she'd assume he was out of ear-shot, but again he was out of luck. Joan snitched on him and he was forced to make an appearance. The girl was standing there with a silly expression on her face while all three mothers smiled at them both.

'Hello,' he said, trying hard not to sound too put out about being interrupted.

'Hello,' the girl said, smiling for all she was worth. 'My mum was coming so I thought I'd come along too.'

'Oh,' Tom said.

There was an awkward pause.

'Well, run along, the pair of you,' his mam told them. 'Perhaps you'd like to show Beryl some of your paintings, Tom.'

'Not on your life,' Tom muttered. He caught his mam giving him a warning look. He suppressed a sigh. 'Come on, then,' he said to Beryl.

She followed him round the side of the chalet.

'Do you do painting, then?' she asked, in the same tone of cheerful politeness that his mam used with strangers she wanted to impress.

'Not really,' Tom said.

'Can I see them?' Beryl persisted.

'They're not good enough,' Tom stated. He wasn't sharing that with her. It was private. He stopped at the far side of the chalet from the grown-ups and the children, where his game of patience was laid out on a bare piece of earth.

'D'you play cards?' he asked to distract her.

'Oh, yes!' Beryl exclaimed, looking delighted. She studied the arrangement on the ground. 'Look—you can put that seven of clubs on the eight of hearts.'

'I know,' Tom told her. 'I was just going to do that.'

He squatted down and swept the pack up.

'Patience is no good with two. What else can you play?'

'We play rummy and happy families at home so that Timmy can join in too, but they're a bit babyish. My mum's teaching me canasta,' she said.

'That's no good with just two,' Tom said.

Snap and pelmanism were dismissed by both of them as stupid. Newmarket and chase the ace needed more players. Tom had an inspiration.

'Can you play poker?'

Beryl looked a bit shocked. She shook her head.

'It's easy,' Tom told her. 'We'll play for matchsticks.'

He explained about pairs and runs and flushes. Beryl nodded and said that it all sounded pretty straightforward. But she couldn't get to grips with the timing. She had no idea when to raise and when to quit.

'Shame it's only matchsticks,' Tom said as he swept her stake into his pile yet again. But there was no pleasure in it really. You needed really sharp competition to make it fun.

Tom shuffled the cards. If only Annie were here instead of this stupid Beryl.

'D'you know a girl called Annie Cross?' he asked suddenly. 'She lives at the farm over the fields there.'

The minute the words were out of his mouth, he regretted them.

'Yes,' Beryl said.

Tom said no more, but carried on shuffling.

'Why?' Beryl asked.

'Oh—no reason. I just met her the other day, that's all.'

He riffle-shuffled the pack, neatly layering them together, not looking at her.

'I was at school with her, at the elementary. I'm at the grammar now,' Beryl told him.

It was a safe subject, so he took it up.

'So am I, back home, that is,' Tom said.

'Annie stayed on at the elementary. She's left now. At fourteen,' Beryl told him.

Tom said nothing, hoping she'd drop it. He dealt the cards.

'So she's never done Latin or French or science,' she pointed out. 'Not like you do at grammar school. Not like us.'

There was an unpleasant edge to her voice.

Tom clamped his teeth together to stop himself from answering. He should never have mentioned Annie. Like his painting, she was something private, too special to share with the likes of Beryl.

He picked up his hand and studied it.

'You playing?' he asked.

He glanced at his watch. Only four hours till he might see Annie again.

Beryl and her family finally left. The time crawled round to evening. To his joy, Annie managed to get away from the farm. This time they decided to go for a walk along the promenade.

'Just in case my mam takes it into her head to call me in,' Tom said. 'Every now and again she thinks I shouldn't be spending so much time by myself, and makes me come and join them. I don't want that happening when you're here.'

They wandered along towards the town. The beach was deserted and there weren't the crowds about that there were during the day, but there were still plenty of people enjoying the warm evening, couples strolling arm in arm, girls in chattering groups dressed up for a night out, men on their way to the pub.

'I got good and caught today,' Tom admitted. 'That Mrs Sutton who owns the place came to call, and I got lumbered with her daughter.'

To his surprise, Annie stopped still and stared at him.

'Beryl? You've been talking to Beryl Sutton?'

'Well—yes,' Tom said. 'What's the matter?'

'Her, that's the matter. I can't stand Beryl Sutton. She's my worst enemy.'

'Oh—I see—you never said,' Tom floundered. There was so much he didn't know about Annie. 'What's she gone and done, then?'

'Everything,' Annie said. She started walking along again, her body stiff, refusing to meet his eyes. 'She's just such a stuck-up madam. She thinks she's so much better than me, just because her dad owns a factory and she goes to the grammar. I could've gone, you know. I was always better than her at school, but she got to go to the grammar and I was stuck at Church Road Elementary.'

'That's so unfair,' Tom said.

'And another thing, she's got the same birthday as me. Imagine that—having to share your birthday with your worst enemy. Her mum and mine met in hospital when they were having us, and now her mum comes over and has her clothes made by my mum—'

'Your mam's a dressmaker?' Tom asked. This was a piece of information she hadn't let drop before.

'Yes. And you should see the flap she gets into when Mrs High-and-Mighty Sutton is coming! The best china comes out and the embroidered tablecloth. You'd think it was the flipping Queen coming to tea. Makes me sick, it does.'

'It must do,' Tom agreed, though he couldn't really see what the problem was.

'And now you're seeing beastly Beryl behind my back!'

'It wasn't deliberate! I tried to get out of it, but Joan went and told Mam where I was and then I was stuck with her. It wasn't any fun, I can tell you. She's boring and stupid. Not like you.'

Annie flexed her shoulders and made a h'rmph noise in her throat.

'You're a thousand times nicer than she is,' Tom elaborated.

Annie stole a look at him. 'Really?'

'Cross my heart and hope to die.'

'If you really mean that—'

'Look, we don't want that great lump to spoil things, do we?' Tom insisted, tired of these games.

Annie tossed off her bad mood like a coat.

'No, we don't,' she agreed. 'Tell me what else you've been doing today.'

Peace restored, they ambled along as far as the pier, then turned to go back towards Silver Sands. At one point they swerved to go round a large group of young men spilling out of a pub. Their hands touched, and then, of their own accord, it seemed, slid into each other. The warmth of their joined palms, the touch of their fingers, glowed all up Tom's arm. The blacked-out promenade of a small seaside town was a place of magic.

Neither of them noticed a solitary figure behind them staring with outrage at those clasped hands.

CHAPTER FIVE

THE storm had been brewing all day. Annie could feel it in the viciousness of her father's criticisms. He always picked holes in everything she did, but on some days it was different. Instead of it being just the way he was, there was an added force behind his words, winding tighter and tighter until the inevitable explosion. The best thing to do was to keep out of his way, but it wasn't always possible. When the mood was upon him, he seemed to seek difficult jobs that needed both of them to complete so that he could feed his anger at the world and at her. Today it was replacing some fencing. Annie had to hold the posts while Walter hammered them into ground hardened by the summer sun. As they started on their task, planes droned across the sky—a formation of bombers. To the south, ack-ack fire started.

'It's them, the Jerries,' Annie said, gazing up and seawards at the dark shapes. Puffs of smoke were breaking around them, but they flew on unharmed. 'Where are our boys?'

Her father took no notice.

'Hold it still, yer useless bitch,' he growled. 'How can I hit it if yer waving it about like that?'

Head averted, eyes screwed shut, Annie held the post at arm's length as Walter smashed down with the sledgehammer.

From the west she heard a higher-pitched engine noise. With an accelerating roar, fighters swooped overhead. Annie squinted skyward. Spitfires! Her hands shook as she held the fence post.

'For Christ's sake, you stupid mare—'

Her head stung as her father caught her a blow with the back of his hand. She looked at the post. Straight, she had to hold it straight.

Gunfire cracked over the sea. The engines whined and roared and droned. Caught between fear of her father and of the approaching planes, Annie hung on to the post for all she was worth. Walter swung the sledgehammer. Each blow drove the stake a fraction of an inch deeper into the unyielding soil. The vibration kicked up her arms and felt as if it were shaking her brain inside her skull. Half a mile away over the sea, there was an explosion. Annie looked up. A bomber was going down in flames.

'They've got one!' she cried.

At that moment the sledgehammer descended again, out of true. The post split at the top.

Walter's hand cracked into her.

'I told you!'

'Sorry,' Annie gasped.

The life-or-death struggle continued in the air, the planes passing over the coast not half a mile to the south of them, but Annie dared not look up from her task. Her father was nearer than the invaders, and she feared him more.

Each fence post seemed to take an age; none of them went in entirely straight and it was all her fault.

As always, her mother had the meal ready dead on midday. Not even the possibility of a German plane landing on the farm would stop Edna from having dinner ready the moment Walter wanted it.

'Did you see—?' she started as Walter and Annie came through the back door.

Then she saw their faces, sensed the atmosphere and lapsed into silence. Her hand shook a little as she ladled out the stew and handed it round. Annie noticed that, as usual, most of the meagre portion of meat was on her father's plate, while she and Edna had vegetables and gravy. It didn't even occur to her to question this. Appeasing her father was the number-one priority.

Both women ate silently, covertly watching Walter. Faintly through the window came the sound of another dogfight somewhere in the summer sky.

Walter threw his knife and fork down. 'What d'you call this, then?' he demanded.

Annie held her breath. This was it. Fear throbbed through her.

'B-beef and vegetable stew,' Edna muttered, keeping her eyes on her own plate.

'Beef? There's no beef in this. It's nothing but carrot and swede. Swede! Flaming cattle food!'

Edna said nothing. Long experience had taught her that anything she said would be fuel to the fire.

Walter's hand slammed down on the table. 'Where's the meat in it?' he demanded.

The silence stretched, marked out by the ticking of the clock on the mantelpiece.

'Well?' Walter barked.

'It—it's the rationing,' Edna whispered.

'The what? What did you say, woman?'

Edna's lips trembled. Annie felt sick. She longed to intervene, but knew that it would only make things worse.

'Rationing,' Edna repeated, her voice barely audible. 'I got to m-make it stretch.'

'Rationing? Flaming government! Here I am, working my fingers to the bone producing beef and those flaming pen-pushers up in Whitehall think they can tell me how much of it I can eat? I'll give them rationing—'

Relief washed over Annie, leaving her limp and wrung out. It was all right. Her father's rage had been diverted. She and her mother sat silent, not even meeting each other's eyes. They ate, though neither of them had much of an appetite left, but the food must not be wasted, so they pushed it into their mouths, chewed, swallowed. All the while Walter's invective flowed round them, battering their ears, hurting their brains, and they were glad, for words directed at a distant authority were nothing compared to blows rained on them.

When the meal was over, Edna immediately started washing up, busying herself to deflect any possible criticism. Annie was left to follow her father out into the fields again.

As they trudged back to the half-finished fence, she looked towards Silver Sands. There it was, crouching under the sea wall. And there he must be. Tom. Tom, from a magic land called Norseley, far away from Wittlesham, where all families were happy and no one got hurt. In her daydreams now, she no longer got whisked over the rainbow to Oz, but ran away with Tom, hand in hand, to Norseley.

The afternoon went on for ever. To the north and to the south of them, distant gunfire could be heard, while white vapour trails and black balls of smoke scrawled across the sky. At first Walter worked silently, but as the sun beat down on their heads and the grinding labour began to sap his strength, the curses and the criticisms started again. The rant against the government had not been enough of a safety valve. Life itself was stacked against Walter, and someone had to take the blame.

'Look at that—that's not straight. For Christ's sake, can't you do anything right? All you got to do is hold it straight while I hit it. It's not difficult. A halfwit could do it. Jesus wept! Why are you so useless? Why was I given just one useless girl—?'

And so on until he was ready to hammer in the next stake, mercifully leaving him without spare breath for speech.

Annie held grimly on to each fence post, trying her hardest to hold it still, hold it straight. But she could not fight against the force of the hammer blows when they landed off-centre and drove the post out of true. Her head ached from the sun and her body ached from bracing against the sledge-hammer. She tried to cut her father out, centring her thoughts on the evening to come. She would walk across this very field, past Silver Sands, over the sea wall, and there Tom would be, waiting for her. And then everything would be all right.

When the posts were at last driven in, then the barbed wire had to be stretched between them and held with heavy-duty staples. Annie struggled with the coil while her father hammered in the staples.

'Keep it tight, can't you? No good having it sag like that. Beasts'll be through that before the week's out. Tighter, you stupid mare! Put some effort into it. Jesus—!'

At last the job was done. Now there was only afternoon milking to get through. It was like walking on the edge of a volcano. Annie knew it would only take one mistake to set off the eruption. Weariness and tension made her clumsy.

Only luck brought her through without making a serious blunder.

Teatime was another tense meal, the silence broken only by the *Home Service*. They all put their food down and stopped chewing to listen to the six o'clock news. Forty-two Allied planes had been lost, but they had claimed ninety of the enemy. In homes across the country there were desperate cheers for another day's holding on. At Marsh Edge Farm Walter merely grunted, while Annie and Edna said nothing.

Annie thought about the plane she had seen go down. One fewer to invade England. Later, she would talk to Tom about it, for he must have seen it too.

Annie ached to get away. Soon, soon the chores would be over and she would be free. Every fibre of her being longed to escape, to set off across the fields to the sea wall. But her conscience fought against it. What about her mother? Without her there, her mother would be sure to catch it. She was in a ferment of indecision.

They finished off the last tasks of the day and went back into the house. Walter dropped down into his chair.

'Pull my boots off, woman,' he growled.

Edna hurried to do as she was bid, kneeling on the rag rug in front of him. She fumbled the laces undone, then began to draw off the boot. It stuck. Edna tugged and caught Walter's bad toe.

'Aagh! You stupid—'

He lashed out with his other foot. The heavy boot smashed into Edna's shoulder, flinging her back so that her head cracked against the flagstone floor.

'Mum!'

For a vital few seconds fear for her mother overcame fear

for herself. Annie flew across the kitchen to cradle Edna's head in her arms.

'Leave her be, you interfering little bitch! Coming between man and wife—!'

Walter's boot thudded into her legs and buttocks, while Annie and Edna clung together and whimpered with terror...

The mothers were talking on the veranda again—his mam, his aunty Betty and Mrs Sutton. This time, thank goodness, Beryl hadn't come. The anticipation of seeing Annie filled Tom up, so that he felt as if he could almost burst with the excitement of it. There was so much to talk about, with the Battle of Britain happening right over their heads that very day. On top of that, he wanted to hold her hand again, and to walk along together with her as they discussed what had gone on in the sky. There wasn't much time left now, just this evening and tomorrow, for on Saturday they had to go home. So every minute counted. He slipped out of the chalet, checked that his sister and the cousins weren't looking, and made a run for the sea wall.

He was used to waiting. Sometimes Annie didn't manage to get away till quite late. One evening, she hadn't come at all. When he'd asked about it, she wouldn't answer directly, wouldn't even look at him, had just said she had to help her mother. Something about her expression had alarmed him. That look of fierce hatred that came into her face when her father was mentioned.

'Why? What was so important that you couldn't get away?' he asked.

'I just had to stay,' she said.

'But what for?' he persisted.

'I just had to, all right? Don't you have to do things when your parents tell you?'

'Yes,' he admitted.

But he was sure there was more to it than that.

He slid down the wall and sat on the sand at the bottom. It was still warm from the day's sunshine. He had given up all pretence of painting now and just lay against the rough grass, looking out across the water and thinking. Soon, Annie would be here.

The minutes ticked by and turned into a quarter of an hour, then half an hour. Annie did not come. Tom heard the mothers calling goodbye to Mrs Sutton. Another five minutes went by, and then someone came over the top of the wall. It was his sister Joan. Disappointment kicked him in the stomach.

'Tom, Mam wants to see you.'

'I can't come now.'

'You've got to.'

'Tell her I'm busy.'

'But you're not. You're not doing anything.'

'Yes, I am.'

'No, you're not. You're just sitting.'

'I'm thinking. Now, go away.'

It took a bit more arguing, but in the end Joan went.

Where was Annie?

He didn't allow himself to look at his watch. He sang *Over The Rainbow* to himself all the way through, twice. That was Annie's favourite song. Still she hadn't come. Bursting with impatience now, he climbed up to the top of the wall and looked out over the fields.

'Tom!'

It was his mother, standing by the fence.

'Hell's bells,' Tom muttered.

'Tom, come down here, will you? There's something I want to speak to you about.'

Reluctantly, he went.

'Come and sit down here, dear.'

His mother was using her Very Reasonable voice. It was a sure sign of trouble. Silently, he sat down on the edge of the veranda with her. The children could be heard playing in the garden at the back. The other grown-ups were nowhere to be seen.

'Now, dear,' his mother began.

Tom looked at his watch.

Where was Annie? Was she coming across the fields this very minute?

'You know I don't like to interfere with your friend-ships—'

That wasn't true for a start. She never had liked his pal Keith, because his dad was a collier. He made a non-committal noise.

'But I have to say, I am a little bit concerned—'

Tom looked at her. What was she on about?

'What?' he said.

'I've just had a little chat with Mrs Sutton,' his mother went on. 'Such a nice woman. Very genteel. And very well-meaning. She has got your best interests at heart, you know, Tom.'

'Who—Mrs Sutton?' Tom said, puzzled.

'Yes, dear. That's why she thought she ought to speak to me. You see—' his mother hesitated, then went on '—you've been seen, dear, walking along the promenade. With a girl. Hand in hand.'

'What?'

Outrage flared through him. How dared people spy on him and Annie? How dared they? He felt as if something precious had been ripped open and exposed to the world.

'Who told her that? I know! It was that beastly Beryl, wasn't it? Great fat lump. She's got no right—'

'So it's true, then?' his mother asked.

Tom wanted to hit himself for being so stupid.

'Yes,' he had to admit.

His mother put a hand on his knee. He jerked his leg away.

'Well, dear, I have to say that I think you're still far too young to be having girlfriends—'

'She's not a girlfriend—!' Tom protested.

And then stopped short as he realised that maybe she was. What he felt about her was quite different from what he felt for anyone else, boy or girl.

'All right,' his mother conceded, though he could tell that she was just going along with him in order to gain a point. 'So she's just a friend. But you see, dear, this girl—she really isn't a very suitable friend for you. Mrs Sutton knows her, you see, and she says she's a very coarse, common girl. Not at all the sort of person that I or your father could approve of.'

Incensed, Tom jumped up.

'Oh, really? Well, that's just too bad, because I'm not asking you to approve of her. She's my friend and you're not stopping me from seeing her.'

He ran down the steps, ignoring his mother's protests. How dared she say that about Annie? Annie was—

'She's not coarse and she's not common,' he shouted back at her.

'Tom, dear—'

'She's better than Mrs Nosey Parker Sutton and Fat Beryl any day!'

'Tom—'

He bolted round the side of the house, across the garden

and out down the track, heading for Marsh Edge Farm. Anger propelled him across the fields, talking out loud to himself as his mother's words revolved in his head. That interfering old bag, Mrs Sutton. He wanted to wipe her face in one of the cow-pats he was jumping over. And his mam believed her! She had no right. Nobody was going to stop him from seeing Annie if he wanted to.

It occurred to him that Annie had told him never to come to the farmhouse. But this was important. This was their last but one evening. They couldn't waste it.

He slowed to a trot, and then a walk. The field he was walking across had a shiny new piece of barbed wire fencing down one side. That must be what Annie had been helping with today. He had seen two figures working while he'd watched the battle in the air. He opened a gate into the track leading up to the farmhouse and closed it carefully behind him. The edge of his anger had dulled now. He just wanted to see Annie.

And then there she was, coming out of the farmyard. Joy glowed inside him, lighting a great big smile on his face. He waved his arm above his head.

'Annie!'

She came trotting down the track towards him. Tom broke into a run and, as they got nearer to each other, he noticed that Annie was limping. She stopped before they met. Her face looked different. Pinched. Distressed. Anxiety threaded through his delight. Something was wrong.

He came up to her and put his hand out to touch her arm. She flinched.

'Annie—what is it? What's the matter?'

'What are you doing here? I told you not to come.' Her voice was sharp, not like her ordinary voice at all.

'You didn't come,' he explained. 'I wanted to—'

'You can't stay here. He'll see you, and then everything'll be spoilt.'

'Who?' Tom asked. But, even as he said it, he knew. 'Your father? Is it him? What's happened?'

'Just go! Now!' Annie was frantic. 'Please. I'll come and see you tomorrow. I promise.'

And she turned and hurried away from him, still limping.

'But, Annie—'

He took a few steps after her, his arm reaching out. Then he stopped. She was in deadly earnest. Whatever the trouble was, she thought his being there would make it worse. Slowly, reluctantly, he made his way back.

He got very little sleep that night.

CHAPTER SIX

ON THE very last day of the holiday, Tom's family went out to lunch at the Grand Hotel. It was far too stiff and starchy a place for Tom or the children to find enjoyable, but the grown-ups seemed to like it, and talked a lot about keeping up standards despite there being a war on. In the afternoon it rained and Tom was dragooned into playing an interminable game of ludo with the others. And then they had a visitor, or, rather, two visitors. Beryl and her little brother came tramping on to the veranda in their macs and wellingtons. Tom's heart sank when he heard their voices, but the mothers greeted them kindly.

'Beryl, dear, how nice to see you. And Timmy too. Is your mother coming?'

'No, she's gone to the Whist Drive, so she asked me to look after Timmy. He wanted to come here so much that I had to bring him. I hope you don't mind,' she said.

'Of course not. The children love playing with Timmy,' Tom's mother said.

'Perhaps you'd like some lemonade,' his aunt offered.

'I'd rather have a cup of tea,' Beryl answered.

And so it was that Tom found himself sitting with Beryl and the grown-ups drinking tea. He glowered at her across

the table. How could she sit there so calm and po-faced
when she'd gone and told on him and Annie?

The two mothers chatted on about Wittlesham and holidays.

'We've enjoyed it so much here at Silver Sands that we're
thinking of coming back next year,' Tom's aunty Betty said.

'That's nice. My mother will be pleased to hear that. Not
many people are going on holiday this year, on account of
the war. We haven't got any more bookings for Silver Sands
this summer. My mother thinks you're all very brave to be
coming away,' Beryl said, looking at Tom.

Tom looked away.

'We're not going to let that Hitler stop us from having our
usual family holiday,' Tom's mother said. 'That would be
giving in to bullying.'

'Lots of people are letting him stop them. It's really quiet
here this summer. Of course, we don't depend on the lettings.
My father has a factory, you know, making parts for the ra-
dios in bombers—'

Both women looked suitably impressed. Tom did not.

'So Silver Sands is just a sideline. My mother says it's her
pin money project, but it's a good thing it's within walking
distance as we can't run our car any more. My father's stood
it up on bricks in the garage. For the duration, he says.'

Tom could see why Annie loathed her. She was out to impress them at every turn. When his mother mentioned the
Grand, Beryl had been there too, and went on about only
going to the best places. What was more, she seemed to be
directing it at him. She was for ever looking at him as if to
see what sort of an impression she was making. It was time
to put her in her place.

'The rain's stopped. Coming to the top of the sea wall?'
he asked the moment tea was over.

As if pulled by strings, Beryl sprang out of her chair.

'All right,' she said, and trotted after him as he ran down the steps and strode out of the garden. Once outside, he didn't make for the sea wall, but instead skirted one of the other chalets, so that nobody at Silver Sands could see them. Then he stopped so suddenly that Beryl nearly cannoned into him.

'It was you, wasn't it?' he demanded.

Guilt was written all over her face.

'W-what?' she said.

'It was you who was spying on me and Annie. Prying into other people's business and then going and telling.'

Just talking about it made him furious all over again.

Beryl tried to make her face look blank.

'I don't know what you're talking about.'

'Oh, yes, you do. It was your mother who came and told my mother, and someone must have told her. You're the only person who knows both of us, so it must have been you. Made you feel good, did it? Sneaking on other people?'

Beryl went red. 'It wasn't me! I didn't do it! It was—it was my brother, Jeffrey. He's always doing things like that. He's a real little snitch. He likes getting people into trouble—'

'I don't believe you. I've never met your brother Jeffrey. You're a liar as well as a sneak,' Tom accused.

'I'm not a liar! It's true!' Beryl cried. 'He—he came up here a couple of times and watched your family through the fence. Spying. He likes spying. And then he saw you the other evening, with—with—her, and he went and told my mother. She thought she ought to tell your mother, because Annie Cross is such a common girl, but *I* said she shouldn't. *I* said it wasn't fair and Jeffrey shouldn't go round telling tales and *I* said it wasn't right that my mum should tell your mum and get you into trouble for being with a little guttersnipe like her. But you know what mothers are. They stick together. She went and came up here and told—'

Tom was staring at her, trying to see inside her head.

'You'd better not be lying,' he said.

'I'm not, I'm not! I tried to stop her—honest!' Beryl squealed.

Still Tom wasn't convinced.

'Now you listen to me,' he said, 'and you listen carefully. First, Annie Cross is not common or a guttersnipe. She's a thousand times better than anyone in your family. Second, you tell your brother to keep his nose out of my business, or I'll have his liver and lights and hang them up to dry. Have you got that?'

'Y-yes,' Beryl stammered.

She looked terrified. Shame nibbled at Tom's anger. He shouldn't be shouting at a girl like this; it wasn't right.

'Right, now go and get your other brother and clear off.'

'Y-yes, right—but it wasn't my fault, Tom. Really it wasn't. I tried to save you—'

'All right, all right, so it wasn't you. Just tell your brother.'

'I will, really, I will—'

He didn't want to hear any more. He turned away and ran back past Silver Sands and up the sea wall. From there he ran as fast as he could along the top, until he was out of breath. As he ran he looked out across Marsh Edge Farm. Somewhere down there was Annie, and this evening he would see her for the last time. No one—not Beryl, not his mother—was going to spoil that.

'You all right, Mum? Can you manage?'

Annie hurried to help her mother with the heavy galvanised bucket of water to scrub the kitchen floor.

'Yes, yes, I'm fine,' Edna assured her.

But she winced as she lowered herself on to her knees.

'It's not right. He shouldn't treat you like that, the bully. That's what he is, a vicious bully,' Annie burst out.

Edna looked frightened. 'Don't talk about your father like that, love. A few bruises don't matter. Men are just like that. It's their nature. They can't help it.'

'Not all of them,' Annie said.

Tom wasn't like that, she was sure. And Gwen never came to school with bruises on her.

'He's a good provider. That's what matters.'

Was it? Was that all that a man had to do—provide for his wife and children? Gwen's dad did that, and he was nice to them all as well. Beastly Beryl's dad was a much better provider, come to that, with enough money to run a car and send them all to the grammar. Did he beat Mrs Sutton and Beryl and the younger boys? She didn't think so.

Annie sighed. 'Right, Mum,' she agreed.

Because it was no good trying to discuss it with her. She'd tried it before, many times, and got nowhere. Her mother simply accepted the beatings as her lot. Sometimes she even claimed to have deserved them, because of her own shortcomings.

The one good thing about her father's explosions of temper was that for a few days afterwards he was always calmer and quieter. Annie had no trouble getting away that evening to meet Tom. She put on a shirt with a high collar to hide the bruises on her neck and shoulders and set off for Silver Sands, practising controlling her hurt side so that she did not limp. Last—day—last—day—her feet went as she hurried across the fields. Tomorrow Tom was going home, back to the magic land of Noresley, and she might never see him again. It didn't bear thinking about, so she pushed it to the back of her mind. Now—she would just think about now, and the next hour or two.

When she was nearly at the last gate, Tom suddenly appeared from round the side of one of the other chalets. He took hold of her hand and started pulling her along.

'This way,' he said, 'where they won't be able to find us.'

'Who won't—?' Annie asked, trying not to flinch as he tugged at her poorly arm.

'My beastly family. They know to look for us over the sea wall. And if we go along the prom that Beryl girl or her ferrety brother might be spying on us.'

'Beryl? What's Beryl got to do with it?'

Tom opened the gate to the chalet garden.

'This one's just right. I had a recce this afternoon. They can't see us from Silver Sands.'

He spread a raincoat on the wet grass and sat down in the shelter of a tall patch of willowherb. Annie eased herself down beside him, carefully arranging her bad leg.

'What's up? What's this about Beryl?' she demanded.

'Nothing, according to her, but I'm not so sure. She says her brother saw us on the prom the other evening, and he told his mother, and she told my mother. Then my mother said I wasn't to see you again.'

'Not see—?' Annie was appalled. This was a disaster. 'But why?'

The next time she saw Beryl and Jeffrey, she was going to give them what for.

Tom looked uneasy.

'Oh, you know what mothers are like. They get these bees in their bonnets. She went on and on about me being too young.'

'Too young?' Annie was mystified.

'To—er—to have a—you know—girlfriend,' Tom said gruffly. He could not meet her eyes for embarrassment.

Girlfriend? She was his girlfriend? Like people in the pictures? Annie could feel herself going all hot.

'That's stupid,' she said.

'Yes.' Tom looked relieved. 'Yes, it is, isn't it? If we want to be friends, then we can. Never mind what they say.'

'That's right,' Annie agreed, though her stomach sank with disappointment. Not a girlfriend then, just a friend.

'Not a good day, yesterday, was it?' Tom said. 'First my mam trying to put her oar in, then a problem up at your place. What was going on? You looked terrified. I was really worried about you.'

Years of covering up what went on in her household came into play. Part of her wanted to confide in him, but a larger part was ashamed to reveal what her family was like.

'Oh—nothing. My dad was in a bit of a temper, that's all.'

'Really? It looked like it was worse than that, as if you were afraid something dreadful might happen,' Tom said.

'No, no…it's just…like you said—they get bees in their bonnets, parents. If he'd seen you, he might've blown his top.'

'So you've not—' Tom hesitated. 'I thought, well, you were limping when you came out to see me, and I thought your dad might've hurt you. He didn't, did he?'

'No, no—' Annie shook her head to emphasise the point, and caught her breath as pain shot from her neck right down her bruised side.

'He did!' Tom's voice was filled with concern. 'Was it bad? Come on, show me.'

'No, really—'

Annie tried to move away, but Tom took hold of her hand

and carefully undid the cuff of her shirt. Dying of embarrassment, Annie watched his face as he drew back the sleeve. Horror was closely followed by anger as the ugly purple bruises were revealed.

'Annie, this is terrible—you poor thing—and this was your father? How could he? Are you hurt anywhere else?'

'No, really—it's nothing—'

Annie tried to move away, but Tom let go of her arm and caught her foot. He pulled back the leg of her working trousers, which she had kept on today in order to be covered up. He drew in his breath sharply as more injuries came to light.

'Annie, Annie, how can he do this to you? We've got to stop this. We've got to tell someone. The police—'

'No!' Annie squealed. You mustn't—my mum'd die of shame—'

'He hits your mum as well?'

Silently, Annie nodded.

'The bastard— Oh, I'm sorry, Annie, swearing in front of you, but—I want to go and tear his head off—'

Tom's hands were balled into fists. His face was contorted with anger.

'Don't—' Annie cried, seized with fear. 'Don't—you look like him when you say that—'

Tom looked ashamed. He took a deep breath and let it out slowly.

'I'm sorry—it just makes me so mad, to think of you getting hurt like this. I want to help you, Annie. What can I do to help, to stop it?'

'Nothing,' Annie said flatly. 'There's nothing. My mum says it's just the way he is and we have to put up with it because he's a good provider.'

'But there must be something.'

'No. Maybe one day I'll be able to go away. But till then... Look, it helps just to have you as a friend.'

'That doesn't sound like a lot of use,' Tom said gloomily.

'It is, really,' Annie assured him. She tried to put her feelings into words. 'It's been really...nice...coming to see you each day. It's made everything sort of...brighter...you know? Knowing I'll talk to you at the end of the day.'

Tom's face was glowing now. 'Yes! That's just it! It's made everything different, knowing you. Like—even very ordinary things like walking along the prom are special when I'm with you...'

He stopped abruptly, scarlet with embarrassment.

'That sounds right daft,' he muttered.

'No, it doesn't. It's—nice. It'll be a nice thing to remember when—well—things are bad,' Annie told him.

A phrase from the Bible came to her. *She treasured it up in her heart.* She would treasure up those words of his in her heart, and warm herself with them when life was cold.

'Look—we're not going to let them stop us, are we?' Tom insisted. 'It's like in *Romeo and Juliet*. They didn't let their families stop them.'

'Who are they? Were they in a film?' Annie asked.

'No, it's Shakespeare.'

Shakespeare. He'd written things, she knew that much. Plays. They'd never done them at the elementary, but she would get them from the library and find out what Tom was on about.

'Yes, of course it is,' she said, to cover her ignorance.

To her relief, Tom did not pursue it any further.

'We'll write to each other. Would you do that? Write to me?'

Delight bubbled through her.

'Oh, yes! That'd be wonderful. But...'

She thought through the difficulties. Her father always sorted through the post, since it was mostly bills and stuff for him. She could not explain away a personal letter to herself from Nottingham.

'…send them to my friend, Gwen, and she'll give them to me.'

'All right. Where does she live?'

Annie recited Gwen's address. Tom committed it to memory.

'What about your mum? Is it all right to send to your house?' Annie asked anxiously.

'I said I'm not going to let her stop me and I'm not. You write to my address,' Tom insisted.

Annie repeated it after him till she had fixed it in her head.

Satisfied that they had done all they could, they talked and talked until the light had drained from the sky.

'I've got to go,' Annie said reluctantly.

This was it. The last moment.

'I suppose so.'

A whole year till they saw each other again. It was so long that she could hardly bear it. Going back to life without seeing him at the end of each day was like a prison sentence.

Awkwardly, they got up. They looked at each other in silence. Then Tom swooped forward and planted a quick kiss on her lips.

'Remember—write to me!' he said.

'I will,' Annie promised.

And as she walked home alone with his kiss still warm upon her mouth, loneliness stalked beside her, cold and dark and bleak. She refused to let it in, pushing it away by holding on to the thought that she still had Tom as a friend, even if he was far away. It wasn't like having him at Silver Sands, but it was something. Whatever else happened, Tom thought she was special.

She began planning the first letter she would send to him.

CHAPTER SEVEN

'THOSE poor people in London,' Gwen said, as she and Annie snatched a few minutes' conversation outside Sutton's Bakelite before she went back in for the afternoon shift. 'Do you know they're sleeping down the underground now, because of the bombing? I seen it on the newsreel at the pictures. Hundreds of 'em, all lying on the station platforms. Must be horrible.'

'It must,' Annie agreed, though she found it difficult to imagine what it must be like. Unlike Gwen, she had never ridden on the underground.

'Still, the war's all right for some. Sutton's is expanding. Mr Sutton told us all this morning. We're doing such a lot for the war effort, we're moving to a bigger factory, out on the edge of town.'

'I s'pose that means the Suttons'll be richer than ever,' Annie said.

'Yeah, but who cares, eh? Would you really want to be old fattypants Beryl?'

Annie laughed. 'No, I would not,' she agreed.

'Coming to the pictures tomorrow?'

'If I can get away.'

'You must. Oh, look, everyone's gone in. Got to go. I'll get my pay docked if I'm late. See you outside the Roxy.'

Annie waved goodbye and cycled off to do her errands. She sang at the top of her voice as she bowled along. At this moment, life was good. It was a dull and damp October day, the heavy old bike would soon be even heavier with a load of shopping in the front basket and at home ahead of her there was her father, but for now she was happy. She enjoyed her Thursday afternoon buying provisions and delivering some of her mother's alteration work, and meeting Gwen was always a treat. But best of all, here in her skirt pocket, warming her thigh, was a letter from Tom.

She put her hand on her leg, feeling the outline of the envelope through the layers of clothing. It was a huge temptation to stop and tear it open, but she controlled herself. It was better if she spun it out. First the pleasure of just having the letter in her possession, then the anticipation all evening, knowing it was hidden under her mattress upstairs, then finally the delight of opening and reading it after her parents had gone to bed. Then she allowed herself a whole week of rereading and planning a reply before starting on the equal but different pleasure of writing back. The letters, together with her outings into town and meetings with Gwen, lit up the drudgery of her day-to-day life.

As she turned into the track up to the farm later that afternoon, she was surprised to see someone cycling down towards her—a man in a raincoat and trilby hat.

'How odd,' she said out loud.

They had hardly any visitors at the farm.

It was only when he got really close that Annie recognised him. It was Mr Sutton.

'Evening, young—er—' he said as they passed each other.

'Annie,' she told him. 'Evening, Mr Sutton.'

She longed to ask what he was doing at Marsh Edge, but he did not show any sign of stopping.

When she went into the kitchen with the shopping, she found her mother in a fluster.

'We've had a visitor. I'm so ashamed. If only I'd known, I could have at least made some scones. To have a visitor and not even be able to offer some cake! And the state of the place as well—'

'It looks fine, Mum,' Annie assured her.

Her mother always kept the kitchen scrupulously clean and tidy, however much mud was walked into it over the course of each day.

'Oh, but the Suttons have such a lovely house. All modern, with a gas stove and one of those geyser things for hot water. Imagine! This must look so old-fashioned.'

'It's nice,' Annie said loyally, though really she wished her mother could have modern appliances to help her. 'But what was he doing here—Mr Sutton? I was so surprised to see him cycling down the track.'

'Oh, I don't know that, dear. He came to see your father. Now help me get the tea on the table, will you? Or we're going to be late.'

They both bustled about getting the meal ready. Being late with Walter's tea was simply not an option. When he came in they all sat round the table in silence as usual, listening to the wireless. It was only when they had finished their last cup of tea and the plates had been cleared away that Annie dared approach the mystery of their visitor.

'I saw Mr Sutton as I was cycling up the track,' she remarked.

It was no use asking a direct question, but an observation sometimes got a reply.

'Ha.'

Walter got out his tobacco tin and began rolling one of the two cigarettes he allowed himself each day. Annie hurried to fetch an ashtray. Walter licked the paper, poked the protruding strands of tobacco inside with the end of a match, then lit up.

'I sent him away with a flea in his ear,' he said with satisfaction.

'Did you?' Annie said.

Edna looked mortified. Mrs Sutton's visits for dress fittings were as much a highlight of her life as Tom's letters were of Annie's. She didn't want any risk of spoiling them.

'Thought he could palm off his unwanted bit of land on me. Must've taken me for a fool. But I'm not. He might have that fancy factory of his, but I know a thing or two. Oh, yes. Showed him the door, I did.'

Annie stared at him. Silver Sands! He must mean Silver Sands. That was the only bit of land that the Suttons owned, as far as she knew.

'You mean the chalet by the sea wall?' she hazarded.

''Course. What else? Rubbish corner of scrub with a hut on it. He thought that just because it's running with my land that I'd want it. Must be off his head. Or think I am. I soon told him his fortune.'

'Summer visitors are nothing but a nuisance,' Annie said sadly, quoting his often-repeated words back at him.

To have had the chance of owning Silver Sands, only to have it thrown away! It was heartbreaking.

'Too right. Walking all over my land, leaving gates open and worrying my stock. Ought to be shot on sight,' Walter agreed. 'And he thought I'd be interested in holiday lettings after the war was over! I told him, flaming townies are like the plagues of Egypt. I won't have nothing to do with 'em.'

Walter went on for some time, telling them what he thought of holiday-makers and giving examples of the dreadful things they had done in the past. Annie just sat and made affirmative noises, her face carefully blank. It had never occurred to her in the past that there was any real possibility of their owning Silver Sands, however much she had wished it. Now it would have been even more wonderful, for Tom had said that his family were thinking of coming back next year. If her father had bought it, she could have been the one who got it ready for them and went to see if they were all right. She would have had the right to stroll in there and visit them, instead of hiding from Tom's family. And her father had thrown that all away. She felt quite sick with disappointment. Only the thought of Tom's letter waiting for her upstairs kept her going through the evening.

She needed the letters to get her through the following months. As autumn turned into winter and Walter Cross was forced to change his farming methods by the local War Agriculture Committee, it was Annie who bore the brunt of the extra work. One Saturday late in November, she was out cutting cabbages in the field nearest to the road. It was a foul afternoon with a wet wind coming in from the sea. The continual bending was making her back ache, the sticky mud clung to her boots, making it difficult to lift her feet and the cold was cutting into her exposed fingers and face. On top of this, she had left her mother in a flap about the Suttons. Both Mrs Sutton and Beryl were coming to order dresses for Christmas, and Edna was tying herself in knots trying to stretch the meagre sugar ration enough to bake a batch of biscuits for them.

'The government's giving us an extra four ounces of sugar each for Christmas,' she said.

'The Suttons'll have their own. There's no need to waste ours on them,' Annie pointed out.

'Oh, but I must have something to offer them,' her mother insisted.

The thought of biscuits hot out of the oven made Annie's mouth water as she toiled. And to think that they were going to be wasted on beastly Beryl.

She saw the Wittlesham to Brightlingsea bus stop at the end of the lane and three figures step down. Beryl's little brother Timmy went running up the track. Beryl caught sight of her and waved and shouted.

'Cooee! Annie!'

Annie didn't answer. She pretended not to see as they made their way to the nice warm kitchen, leaving her labouring in the wind and rain. With a bit of luck, she would be finished by the time they came out again.

But luck was not on her side. As the Suttons came out of the farmhouse she was just on the last row, by the fence that separated the field from the track. Once more, Beryl waved.

'Hello, Annie!'

At first Annie ignored her, but as Beryl drew level with her, she was forced to give up pretending she hadn't heard. She straightened up.

'Hello, Beryl.'

She knew she looked dreadful. She was cold, wet and exhausted. Her face was raw red and her ancient work clothes were spattered with mud. Beryl was warm and dry and still glowing from sitting by the range.

'Having a nice time?' Beryl enquired.

Annie wanted to push her face in.

'It's my bit for the war effort,' she responded. 'What's yours?'

'We're knitting mufflers for soldiers at my school,' Beryl said. 'They're so grateful, poor things. They send us lovely letters thanking us.'

Annie said nothing. The thought of sitting at a desk and learning things instead of cutting cabbages was almost too much to bear.

'I came top in French these exams,' Beryl went on. *'Je suis très fort en Français*. I bet you don't know what that means. It means I am very strong at French. My form teacher says that all educated people should be able to speak French, and she's a history mistress. *Tu es un cochon*. I bet you don't know what that means, either. That's the trouble with only going to the elementary. Still, I suppose you don't even need to know how to read and write to dig potatoes.'

'I'm doing something useful, not just sitting round all day getting fat. Our pigs can do that,' Annie retorted.

'And this year I'm starting Latin. I bet you don't even know what Latin is,' Beryl said.

'It's a dead language. You see stuff written in it in churches,' Annie said in a bored voice. 'What's the point of learning that?'

If she'd hoped to score a point, she was disappointed.

'Well, of course an uneducated person like you wouldn't understand. It's still spoken by doctors and people at universities,' Beryl retorted.

Annie gave a disbelieving laugh. 'And you're going to be a doctor, are you? Pull the other one!'

'We all know what you're going to be—a farmhand,' Beryl said.

Annie was actually glad when Mrs Sutton and Timmy reached them.

'Come along, Beryl, don't hold Annie up. I'm sure she still has plenty to do. Good day, Annie.'

'Good day, Mrs Sutton,' Annie muttered.

'Bye, Annie. Have a lovely time!' Beryl called as she walked off down the track.

Annie choked back tears of frustration and jealousy. Beryl had everything—a rich, kind father, brothers to keep her company, a place at the grammar school. It wasn't fair.

But then she remembered. Beryl didn't have Tom. That almost made it all worthwhile.

CHAPTER EIGHT

THROUGH the long hard winter of 1940 to 1941, the people of the industrial cities and ports of Britain suffered the terrors of the blitz while the bombers of the RAF carried out Churchill's promise to 'give it them back'. Stray bombs and damaged aircraft crashed into fields and villages and towns, and even the quietest village had its German spy scare. The convoys crossing the Atlantic were harried by submarines, making scarce commodities even scarcer. Britons tightened their belts, worked harder and ate more frugally. But they did not think of giving in.

Annie laboured through the cold days, learning how to work farm machinery from the pool of modern devices now available on loan to farmers, on top of carrying on with the day-to-day work of running a dairy herd. Harder than either of these was keeping on the right side of her father. Praise, or even recognition of the huge part she played in the increased productivity of the farm, was out of the question. But when Walter was in a neutral mood, he did allow her the odd evening off. They were occasions to be savoured to the full.

An April Thursday saw her hurrying to meet Gwen outside the Roxy in the High Street. Gwen squealed when she spotted her and rushed to take hold of her arm.

'You're so late! I thought you weren't coming.'

The two girls trotted arm in arm up the steps of the cinema.

'I know, I'm sorry. The bus was ever so late, and when it did come it was an awful old thing. I think they've sent all their decent ones up to London,' Annie explained.

'We need buses just as much as Londoners do,' Gwen grumbled.

They pushed in through the swing doors. Annie paused for a moment, looking around, making sure it was all just as grand as ever. She breathed deeply, taking in the smell of smoke and wet coats and the faint whiff of disinfectant. Yes, this was it. This was Life. Even in the dim wartime lighting, the entrance looked like a palace with its high ceilings, red flock walls, gold paintwork and shiny brass rails. Wonderful. It was like living in a fairy tale after the wet fields and the austere farmhouse. And it was all hers, for the price of a ticket in the front stalls.

'Come on, dozy!' Gwen was already at the ticket booth. 'We've missed part of the first feature already.'

They walked to the stall doors and were escorted into the smoky darkness by the usherette and her torch. Trying not to stumble over people's legs, they groped their way to their seats and subsided with sighs of pleasure. Settling back, they gave themselves up to fantasy. The sheriff's posse thundered across the screen, the baddies galloped up into the rocks on the side of the valley, bullets whined and ricocheted, horses reared and fell. The good guys won.

'That was good,' Annie enthused as the credits rolled.

'Yeah—' Gwen's accent had slid to somewhere in the mid-Atlantic '—sure was.'

A short cartoon came next. Tomcat chased Tweetie-Pie and failed yet again to catch him. The adverts rolled. Gwen elbowed Annie and offered a small paper bag.

'Here—have a pear drop.'

'Thanks, Gwennie! Can you spare them?'

''Course—go on.'

Annie sucked off the rough sugar coating and let the gloriously artificial sweet fruitiness fill her mouth. Bliss.

The newsreel followed. Victims of the latest blitz on Birmingham were seen clearing up and fixing 'Business as Usual' signs to their damaged shops while smiling and making thumbs-up signs at the camera. Much was made of the successes in Eritrea and the huge bombing raid on Kiel.

'I heard them going over the other night. They must have been heading for Kiel,' Annie whispered.

'They're so brave, the RAF boys,' Gwen said with a sigh.

That was quite enough reality. Now it was the big feature—a Busby Berkeley musical. Annie and Gwen were swept into a world of colour, song and dance. Time was suspended and nothing mattered but that the hero and heroine should end in each other's arms.

The whole audience stood for 'God Save the King', and then shuffled out, chattering and laughing.

It was strange being back in cold, dark Wittlesham High Street. At least half of Annie was still prancing about in satin and feathers. The contrast made her feel quite light-headed.

'That was just wonderful,' she said, sighing.

But it was no use staying in Hollywood with your head in the clouds. There were practicalities to obey. The last bus left in just five minutes. The girls hurried to join the line of people climbing on board.

Gwen dived into her bag and produced an envelope. 'Here,' she said, 'something to keep your pecker up.'

Annie took it and stared at the writing.

To Miss A Cross c/o Miss G Barker.

Tom. It was from Tom.

'Already?' she said, dazed. 'I wasn't expecting one for days…'

She stood still, gazing at the letter in happy disbelief.

'Come on, darling. You taken root?' a voice demanded from behind.

'Oh, sorry…' Annie shuffled forward to the head of the queue. She gave Gwen a quick hug. 'Thanks ever so, Gwennie. I don't know how I'll ever repay you—'

'I'll think of something. Come and see me as soon as you can! Toodle-oo!'

'Toodle-oo!'

Annie climbed on board and found a seat near the back. She sat staring at her letter. A night out and a letter from Tom. It was almost too much happiness for one day. Treats had to be hoarded up, brought out as rewards to herself. She thrust the letter in her pocket and sat staring out into the dark, reliving every detail of the musical.

Tom's letter was like a beacon, seeing her through the next day when the rain drove across the flat fields and it felt more like winter than spring. Her father was in one of his blacker moods and her mother went tiptoeing around trying to appease him. Annie hummed the tunes from the film to herself and kept picturing what was waiting for her under her mattress. It was like a protective charm around her.

The wireless went off at ten o'clock to conserve the battery, and Annie lit a candle to go up to bed. She slit open the envelope while her parents were still moving around, so that there was no danger of them hearing the noise of ripping paper. Then she tore off her clothes, pulled on her nightie and jumped into bed. Now, at last, the letter could be taken out.

There was Tom's familiar sloping handwriting in black ink.

Dear Annie
We've had a big bit of excitement here in Noresley. A bomber got lost on its way back from raiding Sheffield and dropped a bomb on us. Well, not quite on us. The way folk are talking round here you'd think the village had been flattened, but actually it fell on the playing fields of the Miners' Welfare. But what a bang! It blew all our windows out, which was pretty frightening. Our Joan was screaming her head off and Mam was yelling 'Are you all right?' and Dad was yelling 'Don't move!' and all the lights were off. Mam wanted us all to go and sit under the stairs in case it was a real raid, and Dad said that was potty because who'd want to bomb Noresley? So he and I went off to see if the neighbours were all right, which they were except for old Mrs Jackson on the corner, so we brought her back for a cup of tea. Luckily the gas was still working and by then Mam had swept up some of the glass though it was still all over the place. It sort of crunched under your feet. So we sat round the kitchen table and drank tea and cocoa with extra sugar and brandy in it because that's good for shock. You should try cocoa with brandy—it's jolly good. Worth having a shock for. Mrs Jackson got quite tiddly and started singing songs from the last war like 'It's a Long Way To Tipperary', so it all got quite jolly, almost like a party. I hoped I'd be allowed not to go to school the next day as there was such a lot of clearing up to do, but Dad said that would be giving in to Jerry, so off to school I had to go, but it was good because everyone wanted to hear all about our bomb from us Noresley lot. I went to see the crater after school and it was massive! The Welfare was pretty

well wrecked, but everyone's getting together at the weekend to repair it and so that's two fingers up to Jerry. (Whoops, sorry. That's rude. But you know what I mean.)

So that's my big news. Our house is all boarded up now until we can get hold of some glass, so it's pretty gloomy inside, but at least the electricity's back on again. Otherwise, it's same as usual—school, homework, football practice, cycle club, pictures. How about you? Have you seen the new Cary Grant film yet? It's going to be on in Mansfield next week so a gang of us are going over to see it. Has your dad been all right? I think of you a lot like you were after he did that. It makes me mad just to think about it. What does the sea look like now? Not all bright like it was in summer. Whenever I think of Wittlesham it's always sunny. It's quite strange when you say it's been cold and raining for a fortnight.

Sunday. Bad news, I'm afraid. Mam says the bomb has really shaken her up and she doesn't want to go far from home, so we'll not be going on holiday this summer. I'm really sick about it, I can tell you. I tried reasoning with her and saying that if she booked up Silver Sands she'd have something to look forward to but she wasn't having any. Honestly, parents! I'll be glad when I'm old enough to join up. I'm sick of being treated like a little kid.

Monday. I've thought of a way round the holiday problem. The cycle club are doing a tour round the Peaks at the end of July. I've already cleared it with the parents to go on that, so what I'll do is, I'll come down to see you instead. I can put my bike on the train

*and there's a youth hostel in Wittlesham. So I will get
down after all! Don't you think that's a clever plan?
I'm going to put this in the post now.
Yours truly,
Your friend,
Tom.
X*

Annie's hands were shaking. The bomb story wasn't
really frightening because Tom was obviously all right, and
the bit about the old lady getting tiddly even made her smile.
But the Featherstones not coming to Wittlesham! It was a
nightmare. It was the end of the world. The thought of Tom
being in that tent in the garden of Silver Sands this summer
had glimmered ahead of her ever since he'd gone away. His
alternative plan sounded feasible, but—there were so many
buts. Supposing his parents found out and forbade it?
Supposing he didn't have enough money? Supposing the
cycle club trip was called off and he lost his cover story? It
was a bleak prospect—a summer with no Tom to look forward to.

But then, that X at the bottom of his letter.

She stared at it in the wavering light of the candle flame.

He had never put an X on a letter before.

That had to be a good sign. It was a good sign. Annie blew
out the candle and fell asleep with the letter against her hand
under the pillow.

Spring turned reluctantly into summer and Britons learned
of the loss of the Hood and the abandonment of Crete while
the air raids carried on unabated. The one rousing piece of
news was the sinking of the battleship Bismark. And then

the Nazis invaded Russia. Though the ordinary people of Britain did not realise it at the time, the invasion pressure was off. What concerned them more was that first clothes and then coal were rationed.

At Marsh Edge Farm, Walter Cross finally gave in to pressure from fellow farmers to try sowing ley grass and cutting silage to increase the amount and quality of feed available to the greatly increased dairy herd. By June, a second-hand tractor replaced the elderly work-horse. Its variable reliability did not improve his temper, though even he had to admit that it could work faster and harder than the horse and did not need attending to each day. Annie's letters contained accounts of these innovations and of her trips into town to meet Gwen and her occasional brushes with Beryl Sutton, but mentioned nothing of Walter's eruptions of temper. After all, Tom could do nothing about it, and the thought of her being hurt obviously worried him. On top of that, she felt ashamed to admit, even to Tom, what went on in her family. Her letters always ended the same way, asking him if he was still coming to Wittlesham at the end of July. His answer was always the same—yes. But still she harboured doubts.

Her birthday came round. Her mother gave her a blouse she had made out of rayon hoarded from before rationing. It had square shoulders with little shoulder pads and was darted in to a narrow waist. A real grown-up garment. Gwen gave her a lipstick. Fifteen. She was now fifteen years old.

'We could get married next year,' said Gwen, whose birthday was a few weeks earlier than hers.

They both tried the lipstick, which was dark red. They tried to do each other's hair up in fashionable rolls around the face, though Annie's hair wasn't really long enough and

Gwen's was too fly-away. Neither of them looked very much like a film star or a dance band singer, but still they were quite pleased with the result.

'We do look a lot more grown up. That blouse is lovely, very fashionable. You are lucky, Annie, having a mum who can make you things like that,' Gwen said.

'Yes, I am,' Annie agreed, stroking the silky fabric.

'*And* you've got a boyfriend, you lucky thing.'

Two things to feel lucky about. Annie savoured the feeling. Usually, it was Gwen who had so much more than she did in the way of people in her life.

'He's not really a boyfriend. More like a pen-pal,' Annie said.

'Ooh!' Gwen teased. 'I've seen how desperate you are for a letter from him. And you never show them to me. I bet they're full of lovey-dovey stuff and kisses.'

'No, they're not. We just write about what we've been doing.'

'So you *say*. I wish I had a boyfriend. My mum and dad would go potty, but I'd really like to have one. I want to know what it's like, being in love.'

'Mmm,' Annie said.

She stared at her reflection in the mirror of Gwen's dressing table. She did look older, what with the lipstick and the hairstyle and the new blouse. No longer a little girl. Love. She imagined love being something all floaty and dreamy, like a romantic song in a film. What she felt for Tom was not like that. It was sometimes quite gnawing and painful and desperate. If he didn't manage to get to Wittlesham...

'Wakey wakey!'

Gwen was making faces at her in the mirror. Annie put

her tongue out. Gwen crossed her eyes. Annie put her thumbs in her ears and waggled her hands. They collapsed against each other, giggling.

'Some of the girls at work like John Sutton,' Gwen said when they had recovered.

'Ugh! Beryl's brother!' Annie squealed.

'I know but—wouldn't she be mad if he was my boyfriend. Supposing I married him! She'd have to be my bridesmaid—just think! And that boot-faced mother of theirs, she'd have to smile and be happy. It'd be wonderful!'

'Why not marry Jeffrey?' Annie teased.

'What, that little squirt? No, thank you!'

They both screwed up their faces and collapsed into giggles again.

'You will let me meet this Tom of yours, won't you?' Gwen said.

'If he comes,' Annie said.

'But you will, won't you?'

'I expect so,' Annie prevaricated.

She wasn't sure. If he did come, she wanted him all to herself.

'You'd better,' Gwen told her.

Annie changed the subject.

The nearer it got to the last week in July, the more she wanted to see him, and the less likely it seemed that he would actually arrive. And then, if he did make it, it wasn't going to be plain sailing. What was he going to do during the day, for a start? It was different when he was here with his family. Even if he did think the little ones were brats and the grown-ups were boring, still they were company. She could only get away in the evenings, and sometimes not even then. It was all so difficult. She turned it over in her mind all day. She lay awake at night worrying. She began to feel quite ill.

On the Friday, she was taking the cows back to their pasture in the evening when she saw a girl on a bike where the track met the Wittlesham road. As she looked, she girl waved frantically and Annie realised that it was Gwen. She waved back. Gwen made beckoning gestures. Annie shut the cows in their field and ran down the track.

'Gwen! What are you doing here? Whose bike is that?'

'I borrowed it off my friend at work. Look—I had to bring you this. It says "Urgent".'

Gwen flashed a letter in front of Annie's eyes just long enough for her to recognise Tom's writing, then whipped it behind her back.

'D'you want it, then?' she teased, dodging as Annie tried to snatch it from her.

'Yes—you know I do. Give it—please—!' Annie squealed.

Gwen was bigger than her and had longer arms. However hard she tried, her friend kept the letter just beyond her reach.

'Just give it, Gwen. It's mine!' she demanded.

She aimed a kick at Gwen's shins, but she leapt out of the way.

'Ooh! Kick donkey!'

Annie was practically crying with frustration.

Gwen held the letter with the ends of her fingers, a tantalising two inches too high for Annie to reach.

'Promise you'll let me meet him,' she bargained.

'Gwe-en—'

'Promise!'

'All right, then.'

Anything, just as long as she could get her hands on that letter.

'You promised, remember,' Gwen insisted, and handed it to her.

Annie ripped it open. There was just one sheet of paper inside.

Dear Annie,
Just a note to say that I'll be on the seven-twenty train
on Saturday. Hope you can meet me at the station. It's
going to be a terrific holiday.
Your friend,
Tom.
X

'Ooh,' Gwen said, breathing down her neck. 'Kisses! Who's a lucky girl, then?'

Annie didn't even care about the teasing. She flung her arms round her friend.

'He's coming!' she cried. 'He really is coming!'

CHAPTER NINE

'ALL RIGHT, son, it'll be safe with me. I'll make sure no German spy gets his hands on it,' the guard said, patting the saddle of Tom's bike as it leant against the side of the van.

'Thank you,' Tom said, forcing himself to sound properly polite.

Why did grown-ups have to patronise you like that? he wondered. He wouldn't do it when he was a grown-up. It was only a few months now before he would be able to join up. Then they would have to take him seriously.

He hurried down the platform, looking for a carriage with some space in it, but the train was packed. The one before had been cancelled due to lack of rolling stock, so everyone was crowding on to this one. In the end he had to make do with a space in a corridor. A group of soldiers piled on after him and soon he was wedged between khaki-clad bodies and bulky kitbags. It was all very different from the last time he had made this journey. Then he had been with his family and they had got a compartment to themselves. This time it was not exactly comfortable, but it was a whole lot more exciting. Around him the soldiers were laughing and joking and passing round cigarettes. He was on his own, making his way without anyone telling him what to do. The train started. This was it. The adventure had really begun.

By the time he got to London, Tom and the soldiers were the best of mates. Some of them were only a year or so older than him, and they had plenty to tell him about army life. They shared their cigarettes with him, he passed round the sandwiches his mother had made for the first leg of his cycle trip. Tom stopped worrying about whether his cycle club friends might inadvertently drop him in it. This was real life. He was no longer a kid. He was an individual, making his own decisions. Getting from King's Cross to Liverpool Street when he didn't know the way was going to be easy.

The journey took the best part of the day. He was starving hungry by the time he reached Colchester and wolfed down a pie and a cup of tea before finally boarding the Wittlesham train. Here he actually got a whole compartment to himself. At first it felt luxurious. Then he began to get nervous. Up till then he had had plenty of people to talk to. Everyone seemed very eager to talk to complete strangers these days. It was something about wartime. The journey across London had been easy enough, for people were more than willing to help a polite young lad and set him on his way. Now at last he actually had time to think about what he was doing.

Over the seats opposite him were two posters of Wittlesham, one showing the pier, the other the winter gardens. Wittlesham. All year, it had seemed like Shangri-La to him. Now he was actually going there. In between the posters was a small mirror. Tom stood up and studied his reflection. Was that a spot breaking out on his chin? He poked the place with his finger. It felt like it. Damn. He wanted to look—well—nice for Annie.

It set off a chain of anxieties. Would Annie still like him? Was it going to be like last time? She'd been working for a year now, up all hours looking after sick and calving cows, driving heavy machinery and the like, while he'd still been at school. Would he seem like a kid to her? He took out a comb and slicked back his hair. Was this all a big mistake? Maybe he should have gone on the cycle club trip after all, and kept it so that he and Annie were just pen-pals. But…he did want to see her again. He sat down on the stiff horse-hair-filled seat and tried to remember exactly what she looked like—the wave of her hair, the expression in her eyes, her smile…and then there was the feel of her soft skin, the way her fingers curled round his… Yes, he did want to see her again. Very much.

He recognised some of the landmarks as the train rumbled into Wittlesham. There was the rock factory. There was the back of the Toledo cinema. As they pulled into the station, he let down the window panel on its leather strap and stuck his head out. Was she there? He was sure she would come and meet him if she could, but maybe she hadn't been able to get away. Her father. Always there was her father, standing in their way. Tom understood. It wasn't her fault if she couldn't be there, but he really did want to see her waiting for him on the platform. It caught him by surprise, how much he wanted it. The lurch of hope clutched at his guts like a huge hand.

The train slowed to a halt with a squeal of brakes and a billow of steam. There were hardly any people on the plat-form. A mother and child, an old lady, a station official. Disappointment sank through him, sick and sour. Her bloody father. It was all his fault. Tom picked up his canvas knap-sack and hoisted it over his shoulder, then jumped down and went to collect his bike from the guard's van. He wheeled it after the straggle of passengers making for the exit and held out his ticket to the collector at the barrier.

'Tom!'

He looked up. There, just beyond the barrier, flushed and breathless, was Annie.

'Annie! You made it!'

Happiness surged up and spread a huge smile over his face. He hurried forward until they were standing within a foot of each other, each of them gazing at the other and smiling and smiling. She looked the same, and yet different. The same Annie, just as pretty, just as pleased to see him, but more grown up. Yes, that was it. More grown up.

Overcome with shyness, they shook hands.

'I'm so glad you managed to get here,' Tom said.

It sounded stupid even as it came out. He felt himself going red.

'I nearly didn't. I had to cycle like billy-o all the way,' Annie told him.

Her hair was longer. That was it. And done in a different way, except that the cycle ride had blown it about. It looked nice like that, all wild round her face.

She saw him looking at it. Her hand went to her head, smoothing her hair down.

'I look a mess.'

'No, you don't. You look very nice. Very…pretty.'

He stumbled over the compliment and felt even hotter. Why couldn't he be suave and sophisticated, like someone in a film? He fiddled with the gear lever on the handlebars of his bike.

'You look older. And you're taller, too. I have to look up more than last year,' Annie commented.

It was true. Sometimes he felt all legs and elbows.

'It's nice,' she added. 'I can't really believe you're here. I thought… I was really hoping you would be able to come, but when you said your family weren't…and then all this about the cycle club and coming here instead, and I thought you'd never be able to make it but…'

'Here I am!' Tom said.

'Large as life and twice as natural!' Annie cried.

And then they were laughing, and it was all right. It was just like last year. Tom knew he could say anything and Annie would understand, just as it had been then.

'I suppose I'd better go to the youth hostel first, and make sure there's a bed for the night,' Tom said.

'Right. It's up this way,' Annie told him.

They walked along together, wheeling their bikes, talking away nineteen to the dozen. There was so much to say, all the things that they had written to each other to be expanded and explained. A mother with a pushchair passed them. Tom moved to let her by and his hand touched Annie's. Her fingers clasped his. He stole a glance at her and saw that her face was pink with pleasure, and knew that his was just the same.

So much to say, and so little time to say it. After he had dropped his things at the youth hostel, Tom rode with Annie to where the farm track met the Wittlesham road.

'See you tomorrow, then. Where shall we meet?' Tom asked.

Annie considered. He watched the way she screwed up her face a little when she was thinking.

'Silver Sands!' she said. 'Where else?'

'Of course. Silver Sands,' Tom agreed.

He hesitated. He knew what he wanted to do. Then he took a breath and swooped forward, planting a kiss on her cheek.

'See you tomorrow!' he said, and jumped on his bike.

All the way back to the youth hostel, he felt as if he could conquer the world.

* * *

All the next morning, Annie was bursting with energy, despite the fact that she had slept very little the night before. Whatever her father asked her to do, she breezed through it with ease. His bad temper just slid off her. The only problem was appearing as if everything was just the same as normal when the whole world was glowing with possibilities. She caught herself singing as she washed her hands for dinner, despite the fact that her father was scowling and growling behind her. Her mother shot her a puzzled look.

'You're cheerful,' she whispered, when Walter was in the scullery.

'Oh, well…it's a nice sunny day,' Annie said.

She sucked in her smiles and helped her mother bring the food to the table. During the meal she kept her eyes on her plate and concentrated on eating. But it was hard, when what she wanted to do was to dance round the room.

Through the long afternoon, she wondered what Tom was doing. Was he all right? Was he lonely? It wasn't as if Wittlesham was much of a resort any more. At least it was nice weather, and he could be outside.

The evening chores had never seemed so lengthy. Annie seethed with impatience as her father checked that she had done everything right. As usual, he took issue with her over details and she had to do things again, but at last she was free.

'I think I'll just go for a walk down to the water,' she said, as offhand as she could manage.

'Waste of energy,' Walter growled. 'What about your ma? She want anything doing?'

'No, no. I asked her and she said not.'

'You sure?'

'Yes. Completely sure.'

'Go and check.'

Annie swallowed down her howl of frustration. If she let him see how much it meant to her, he would invent something for her to do, or even simply forbid her to go.

'All right,' she agreed, and went to see her mother.

At last she was released. At lightning speed, she washed, changed, ran a comb through her hair and smoothed on some of the new lipstick. And then she was off, running across the fields towards Silver Sands as if her life depended upon it.

And there was Tom, waiting for her by the gate.

'Seems funny to see the old place all shut up,' he said after they had gone over their news of the day.

They were sitting on the sea wall, but not in their old place, the sea side. This time they were on the landward side, overlooking Silver Sands.

Annie lay back on the long dry grass. It was lovely to rest after the day's work, to feel the last of the sun on her face, to have a soul mate to talk to.

'It's been shut ever since your family left. I was so mad when my dad didn't buy it from Mr Sutton. I don't even know who owns it now but, whoever it is, they haven't done anything to it. I suppose they're just waiting for the war to end before they can let it again.'

'Might have a bit of a wait, then,' Tom said.

'Yes,' Annie sighed. 'Nearly two years now.'

'At least we weren't invaded. Remember last year, when the Germans were just over the North Sea?'

'And the Battle of Britain was going on in the sky?'

'We won that.'

'We did. Good old RAF.'

'I'm going to join the RAF.'

'You said that last year.'

'I know. I meant it then, but it seemed a long way away. Now it's just over four months.'

'*What?*'

Fear jolted through Annie. She sat up and stared at Tom. He was still looking at the chalet, a long piece of grass between his teeth.

'Four months,' he repeated. 'Till I'm eighteen.'

Something seemed to be squeezing her chest, making it difficult to breathe.

'But…but…you're still at school,' she said.

'So?' Tom threw the grass stalk away and selected another. 'All the more reason to join up. Do something real. What's the point of studying if the country might be conquered? I want to get out there and do my bit.'

Annie cast about desperately in her mind for an argument.

'Well, of course you do,' she said, 'but—you don't have to go yet. I know there's talk of the call-up coming down to eighteen, but it hasn't yet. Why not wait? You're so lucky to be able to stay at school.'

'For heaven's sake! You sound just like my dad. I don't want to stay at school. What I'm doing there is irrelevant. There are people out there defending our country and what am I doing? Studying stuff that has nothing to do with real life. Look at you—you're doing your bit, you're doing a man's work on the farm, putting up milk production and helping feed the country. It just makes me feel useless.'

Fury swept through Annie.

'Do you think I'd be doing that if I had a choice? You don't know how lucky you are. I could've gone to the grammar, you know. I passed the eleven plus, but my dad wouldn't let me go. He says book learning is useless. He'd've had me working on the farm full-time when I was ten if he could've. That's all he wants me for, slave labour. And you—you get to go to school, not just till you're sixteen, but till you're eighteen, and you're going to throw it all away! You're mad. It's just a stupid, stupid waste!'

'It's not a waste,' Tom declared, just as angry. 'I'll tell you what is, and that's to go on going to school when I could be in the forces. If I wait till I'm called up, they'll have me in the transport corps, you can bet your life on it. Then I'll be driving stuff around when I want to be flying. If I go and volunteer, then I'll be able to say where I want to serve, and that's the RAF, and don't say that they're not doing a good job, because they are.'

'I know, I know they're doing a good job, but you don't have to go rushing off to join them. Not the moment you're eighteen; it's crazy.'

Tom flung his hands up. 'I can't believe you're saying this. You sound just like my mam and dad. That's just what they'll say. I haven't told them, because I know they'll make a fuss and try to stop me. In fact, I haven't told anyone, not even my pals. You're the only one I have told. I thought you'd understand, but it seems like I'm wrong.'

Annie was torn. She desperately wanted to be the one Tom told his innermost thoughts and ambitions to, but her whole being cried out against his going.

'I do understand,' she cried. 'But why do you have to go the moment you're eighteen? Why not—'

'No, you don't. If you understood, then you'd know why. I thought you'd be on my side, Annie.'

'I am, I am on your side!' Annie shouted. 'I just don't want you to go off and get yourself killed!'

'Oh, for God's sake!'

Tom jumped up and stood for a moment, glaring down at her.

'You're just like everyone else, treating me like a kid. Well, I'm going to join up, whatever you say. And you'll just have to lump it!'

He stormed off down the steep slope of the sea wall to where his bike lay in the yellowing grass. For fully half a minute, Annie could only sit staring after him, horrified that a leisurely discussion could have blown up into a full-scale row like this. Tom picked up his bike and began cycling off up the track.

'Tom!' Annie found her voice and the use of her legs. She jumped up and ran after him. 'Tom, stop! Come back!'

But if he heard her, he gave no sign of it, and went on pedalling away from her as fast as he could go.

CHAPTER TEN

WITTLESHAM sea front in the rain was a depressing place. It reflected Tom's mood. Just a handful of cafés and one amusement arcade were open and they were full to overflowing with the few summer visitors who had dared come on holiday. He didn't fancy going in all by himself. He decided to take a walk along the promenade, then go to the pictures. With a bit of luck he'd be able to sit there until it was time to go and meet Annie. If Annie turned up, that was.

The weather had kept practically everyone off the promenade. From where he joined it by the pier to as far as he could see in the driving rain, there were only three other people out walking. Tom's head and body were dry enough in his oilskin cycle cape and hood, but his feet in their plimsolls were soaked, so much so that he didn't bother avoiding puddles but just splashed straight through them. To one side of him was the rusting barbed wire that kept everyone off the beach, to the other, closed guest houses and gift shops.

Tom put his head down and his hands in his pockets. Where had it all gone wrong? He had arrived with such high hopes, but now the big adventure had crashed. It was as if he had been cycling happily along and a chasm had opened up at his feet and swallowed him up. He and Annie never quarreled; they always understood each other. That was what had made it all such a shock. He didn't know what to do.

He was so engrossed with his problem that he hardly noticed that the other people on the promenade were getting closer. He vaguely heard the sound of a child pretending to be a fighter plane, but it didn't register until a small boy cannoned into him and fell over.

Tom bent down to help him up. He was a skinny kid in a sou'wester hat too big for him. There was something familiar about him.

'You all right, lad?' he asked.

'I crashed,' the boy said. 'But it's all right; I've got my parachute on.'

'Jolly good,' Tom said, feeling old. It seemed a long time since he had been engrossed in a game of make-believe like that.

The mother arrived. With a sense of doom, Tom recognised her. It was Mrs Sutton.

'Thank you so much,' she was saying. 'I hope he didn't hurt you at all?'

'No, no, I'm all right.'

He hoped that with the poor light and his face half hidden under his hood, she'd not know who he was.

'All this promenade to run along and he has to run into you—say sorry, Timmy.'

'Sowwy,' the boy repeated obediently.

'It's nothing, really. He only bumped into me,' Tom insisted, dying to get away.

'Well, if—'

It was all right. He was going to get away with it. He started to walk off.

But then Beryl arrived.

'Tom! It is Tom, isn't it? Fancy meeting you here!'

'Yes, just fancy,' Tom muttered to himself. He almost opened his mouth to say that his name wasn't Tom, but Mrs Sutton was too quick for him.

'Tom? Oh—! Dear me, I didn't recognise you. But of course, you're the Featherstones' boy, aren't you? You stayed at Silver Sands with your family last summer.'

He was caught. Glumly, he held his hand out.

'Er—yes, that's right. It's Mrs Sutton, isn't it? How do you do?'

There was no stopping Mrs Sutton now.

'And are you still all staying at Silver Sands? No? Where are you, then—one of the hotels? The Grand is still open, but I'm afraid some of the others have simply given up. Of course, there are still lots of guest houses, and very good some of them are too, especially as you have small children with you. Your little cousins are with you again this year, I take it?'

'Er…no,' Tom said.

'No? It's just your mother and your sister this time, then? Or is your father able to take a holiday as well this year? So necessary for a man to have a proper break when he works hard, I think—'

Like a police interrogator, she extracted the information that Tom was without his family, on a cycle tour and staying at the youth hostel. At once, she invited him to join them for a cup of tea. Try as he might, Tom couldn't get himself out of it. Together, they turned and headed back along the sea front, with Mrs Sutton now questioning Tom closely about every member of his family. Back at the Suttons' house, Mrs S disappeared into the kitchen to put the kettle on while Timmy roared upstairs to get his model aeroplanes to show Tom. Tom was left with Beryl in the front room. They sat uneasily on the two armchairs, facing each other across the empty fireplace. The silence seemed to ring in Tom's ears. Years of being brought up to be polite could not be overcome. He had to say something. He cleared his throat.

'It's nice of your—' he began.

'What made you—?' Beryl blurted out at the same time.

'I'm sorry—'

'No, you say—'

Tom kept silent. Beryl was forced to carry on.

'What— I mean, you must have liked Wittlesham to come back here again. On your own, I mean.'

'It's a nice place,' Tom said.

'It was really strange, meeting you again like that.'

'Yes, who'd've thought it?'

'It's—it's a long way to cycle, all the way from Nottingham to here,' she ventured.

'Yes,' Tom said. 'At least—yes.'

He wasn't going to go into details about the train journey. The less he told her, the better.

'And you came here all by yourself?'

'Oh—no. I'm on holiday with some friends—cycle club. You know.'

It was no good admitting that he was here by himself. That would lead to all sorts of difficult questions.

'You got them all to come to Wittlesham?'

'Yes. Well, like I said, it's a nice place. It makes a change from all the places back home.'

It sounded a bit thin, but she seemed to accept it.

'You must all like cycling,' she ventured. 'Did it take you long to get this far?'

'Oh—a few days,' Tom said. He had no idea how long

it would have taken to cycle all the way here from Noresley.

'But wasn't it hard? Finding your way, I mean, with all the signposts down and everything?'

Tom shrugged. 'People tell us the way. We don't look like German spies.'

'It was quite an adventure.'

'Yes,' Tom said.

'Didn't your friends want to go out today?' Beryl asked.

'No—well—it was raining. But I wanted to see the sea front.'

At that point, to Tom's relief, Timmy came into the room with his collection of cardboard aeroplanes. Tom immediately switched his attention totally to Timmy, asking all about them and playing at dogfights with him. After that, Mrs Sutton came in with the tea tray.

'Ooh, cake!' Timmy exclaimed. 'Why are we having cake?'

His mother looked slightly embarrassed. Cake was a treat, what with sugar and eggs being rationed.

'Oh, well—we do have a visitor,' she said.

Tom made to go as soon as tea was finished.

'Won't you stay for dinner? You're very welcome,' Mrs Sutton said.

Tom had a horrible vision of being kept there for ever.

'Oh—no, thank you. I…er…I have to get back to my friends. The…the ones I'm touring with,' he said.

'Well, come back any time you like while you're staying here,' she insisted.

Tom thanked her, said goodbye to everyone and left. It had at least filled part of a very long day.

By half past six he was sitting on the veranda of Silver Sands with his back against the wall of the chalet. He shivered. It had stopped raining but the evening was damp and unpleasant. He was far too early, but he wanted to be sure that he didn't miss Annie.

What was he going to say to her? He shouldn't have flown off the handle at her like that yesterday. Suppose she didn't come this evening? He wouldn't blame her. If only there was some way in which he could get in touch with her. And now there was this visit to the Suttons. One thing was for sure, he mustn't say anything about that to her. If she found out he had been eating cake with her worst enemies, there would be hell to pay. He was worried too, about what he had said to the Suttons. Should he have told them he was here with friends, or not? Whichever, the lie was told now, but he couldn't help wondering if there would be some sort of repercussions.

He was just about convinced that Annie wasn't coming when he heard her voice calling softly from the other side of the building.

'Tom? You there?'

Tom jumped up. 'Yes! Round here!'

He hurried to meet her. She paused at the corner of the veranda, her hand on the rail, her expression guarded. As if she wasn't sure what to expect. As if— And it came to him with horrible clarity that she must look at her father like that, not knowing whether he was going to do something dreadful. He recalled the bruises on her that final evening last year and felt like a monster. Surely she didn't think he would be the same? Did she think all men were like that? He couldn't bear it. He rushed up to her and grasped her hands.

'Oh, Annie, don't look at me like that. I'm sorry I went off my head yesterday. I shouldn't have gone marching off like I did. I didn't mean to, it was just… Say you'll forgive me?'

Her face relaxed into a smile. ''Course I do. It was just thinking of you joining up like that, so soon—I didn't think you were going so soon…'

'I know, I didn't think…'

But solid and unmovable within him was the knowledge that, whatever she said, he was not going to change his mind about joining up.

'I'm so glad you came,' he said hastily. 'I was afraid you wouldn't, and I know you don't like me coming up to the farm, and there's no way I can get a message or anything to you.'

'I didn't know whether you'd be here, either,' Annie admitted. 'After you went off like that…'

'But we're both here now,' Tom said. They seemed to keep swinging dangerously close to opening it up all over again. The other pressing problem on his mind surfaced. He grabbed hold of it. 'For now, anyway. I've only got one more night at the youth hostel. They're meant for people touring, so you have to keep moving on. You can't stay in one for a whole week.'

'Oh—' Annie was immediately distracted. 'That's dreadful. What are we going to do? Well, there's plenty of guest houses. Gwen's aunty runs one, for a start, but it'll be more expensive than the hostel—'

'I've got some money saved,' Tom said, 'but I'm not sure if it'd be enough.'

'I know!' Annie interrupted. 'Oh, this is such a wonderful idea! Listen, you could stay here.'

'Here?' Tom couldn't follow what she meant.

'Yes, in Silver Sands, just like last year.'

'But—' Tom looked at the chalet with its drawn curtains and locked doors. 'You said you didn't know who owns it now.'

'That's just it. Nobody comes here any more. I don't even know if the new owners live in Wittlesham. I'm sure we could get in, and nobody would see you from this side. You've got a bed-roll with you, haven't you? And you could buy food with your coupons. It'd be such fun! Our own little house.' Annie's face was shining with pleasure and excitement.

'You mean—break in?' Tom asked.

'Well—yes,' Annie agreed. A little of the excitement dimmed as she was forced to look at it like that. 'But it's not like we're burglars. We're not going to steal anything, or damage anything—just stay here for a while. We wouldn't be doing any harm. In fact, we could clean it up, make it look nice.'

All Tom's careful upbringing urged against it, but it had no chance against Annie's enthusiasm and powers of persuasion. He put up a few arguments, but allowed them to be swept away. Together, they examined the windows. The third one they tried had a weak latch. It was all too easy. Tom lifted Annie up so she could get her arm through the fanlight and open the casement. With a bit of a thump, the window opened, and in they climbed. Silver Sands was theirs.

They tiptoed through dim rooms that smelt of damp and dust, Tom remembering last summer, Annie looking at the inside of the chalet for the first time. It felt strange, so quiet and still like this, such a contrast to last year, when the place had been overflowing with his family and shaking with the noise of the little ones belting round and shouting at each other. There were no swimming costumes hanging up to dry, no toys left about. Everything was ready for visitors, though, down to the last cup and cushion. The beds were stripped but had mattresses. The spirit stove just needed meths.

'I'll move in tomorrow,' Tom decided.

'Hooray!' Annie cried. 'It'll be such fun, you'll see. And I'll be able to look across the fields and know that you're here.'

It made him feel very odd to have her say that. It heightened the need he felt to protect and care for her, but it also gave him a twinge of alarm, as if he was being backed into a corner.

'Yes, that'll be spot-on,' he agreed.

The days passed all too quickly and the time they spent together was far too short. Annie managed to get away one afternoon to go shopping in town and deliver work for her mother, and the two of them went to a church fête where they had a go at all the competition stalls and Tom won a ring in the bran tub. It was a large sparkly glass affair, much too big for Annie's hand. She wore it on her thumb. They went to meet Gwen when she left work and Tom thanked her for being their postman. Gwen giggled a lot and kept elbowing him. Tom wasn't very taken with her, but she was Annie's friend so he made an effort to be nice.

Before they knew where they were it was Saturday and their last evening. They sat on the sofa in the little living room and ate Annie's sweet ration.

'I can't believe you're going already,' Annie said. Her voice was small and bleak.

'I know,' Tom said.

He hated leaving her here with that father of hers, but there didn't seem to be anything he could do about it.

'We must keep on writing,' he said. 'I really like getting your letters.'

Sadness was seeping into the chalet, bearing down on them, filling a big black pool inside them. Letters were nice, but they weren't like being here, talking to her, holding her hand.

'Will you be able to come back next year?' Annie asked.

Next year. It seemed so far away as to be out of sight.

'I don't know,' Tom said. It was too important to lie about. 'I'd like to, but…'

'You're going to join the RAF,' Annie stated.

'Yes.'

And there it was again, the insoluble problem.

'I'll have to join up anyway, sooner or later. Probably sooner. They're always changing the age limit. Whatever it is, I'm sure to get my call-up before next summer,' he pointed out. 'And if that's the case, then I might as well make sure I get in the service I want, mightn't I?'

Annie heaved a great sigh. 'I suppose so, but—the RAF, Tom! So many planes shot down—'

'I won't get shot down.'

He truly believed it. He wouldn't be killed. It couldn't happen to him.

'You wait and see. Once I'm up there flying over Germany, old Adolf'll give up.'

Annie tried to smile, but failed.

'I hope so,' she said.

Tom almost wished she'd be angry again and argue with him. It made him feel guilty to see her like this. He took her hand in both of his.

'It's just that I want to get away. Like I told you the other day, I want to do something that counts. I don't want to be treated like a kid any more. You understand that, don't you?'

'Oh, yes, I understand that. I long and long to get away from here,' Annie said.

He could hear the yearning in her voice, see it in her eyes.

'Why don't you, then? When you're old enough. They want girls to join the forces. You could be a WAAF. We might be stationed at the same place. Or you don't even have to wait till then. You could go now. You could get lodgings and work in a factory. They're crying out for girls.'

For a moment her face lit with longing at the thought, then it died. She shook her head.

'I can't.'

'But why not?' he persisted.

'It's my mum. She needs me.'

'She managed before, when you were too small to help,' Tom said.

It didn't seem fair, that Annie should be kept prisoner like this.

'You don't understand,' Annie said. 'I think she's having a baby. She hasn't said anything, but I'm sure she is. She's let out her clothes to disguise it, and she's wearing her blouses hanging over her skirts, and it's not just that she's getting fat. She's thinner than ever in her face and her arms. So you see, she's going to need me more than ever.'

'But lots of women manage to look after babies all right,' Tom argued. 'The colliers' wives are for ever having babies. My mam's always on about it, how they keep on having them—' He paused as he remembered that the bigger girls seemed to do a lot of looking after the babies and toddlers. 'And it'll only be one little baby. That can't make much work, surely?'

'I can't leave her. She's not strong, and my father…'

Her father.

'He wouldn't—you know—not when she's having a baby?' he asked.

'I don't know. I hope it's a boy. He wants a boy, to take over the farm. He always holds it against me that I'm a girl. If it's a boy, he might be nicer,' Annie said.

It was hopeless, he could see that. It was duty. He had

been brought up on duty. Duty to your parents, and to God, and the King and all the rest of it. It was his duty to go into the family firm rather than become an artist. He was going to use duty to his country to reason with his parents when he told them that he was going to join up.

It was getting dark inside the chalet.

'I've got to go,' Annie said. Her voice was rough with unshed tears.

'I've got something for you,' Tom said.

He handed her a large manila envelope. She brightened up a little.

'A present? For me? What is it?'

'Have a look.'

Annie opened the envelope and drew out a sheet of paper. It was a water-colour of Silver Sands, with part of the wild garden around it and the two of them sitting on the veranda steps. It was the best of the several attempts he had made at painting the chalet.

'Oh…' Annie breathed. 'Oh, Tom, it's lovely, it's the nicest thing anyone's ever given me. Look—that's us, on the steps! I'm in a painting! Thank you so much, I'll treasure it for ever.'

She sat studying it for a long time while Tom watched, aching with pleasure that he had managed to please her. Then she put the painting carefully back in the envelope and stood up.

'I really have got to go.'

He couldn't bear to see her like that, so small and forlorn. He almost blurted out a promise not to join the RAF. Anything, to see her just a little less unhappy.

Instead, he put his arms round her. He felt her slight body against his, her arms gripping him fiercely.

'I'm going to miss you something terrible,' he heard himself say.

'Me too.'

He touched her hair and she looked up at him. Her eyes were swimming with tears. As naturally as breathing, he lowered his head and their lips met. Her mouth was on his, sweet and soft and intoxicating. For a timeless space, they kissed and kissed again, and then pulled apart, breathless. They looked into each other's eyes, both bemused by the wonder of it.

Then a sob broke from Annie's throat and she tore away, across the room, out of the door and down the steps. Tom ran after her, but he knew it was no use. He stood on the veranda and watched as she ran off across the fields in the gathering twilight, the brown envelope still clutched tightly in her hand.

CHAPTER ELEVEN

ANNIE knew something was wrong the moment she stepped into the back porch. Though the wireless could be heard, there was an ominous quiet about the place. Foreboding wormed through her. She opened the back door. The kitchen was empty, which in itself was odd. Her parents always sat in there, every evening.

'That you, girl?'

It was her father's voice, from the hallway. Fear catching at her throat, Annie hurried through to find her mother sprawled unmoving at the bottom of the stairs, her eyes shut. Her father was kneeling beside her.

Annie stared at her, horrified.

'What—?' she began, then stopped. It was obvious what had happened. Hard on the heels of fear came guilt. If she had not gone out, it might not have happened.

Her father looked up at her, his face set in its usual grim expression.

'Get on that bike of your'n and fetch the doctor,' he ordered.

'The doctor!'

The doctor was never sent for, except in cases of dire emergency. The doctor cost money.

'What have you— Is she—?' Annie faltered.

She peered at her mother's face in the half light. She was deathly pale, but she was still breathing. Then she saw the blood and cried out in horror.

'Oh, my God! What's happened? Where's she hurt? Mum, Mum—'

She dropped to her knees beside her mother and took her limp hand in hers. Beneath skin worn rough and callused from years of scrubbing, it felt so fragile.

'She's miscarrying,' her father said. And there was more than his usual harshness in his voice. There was a real urgency. 'Tell the doctor that. Tell him she fell. Go on! What are you waiting for? Useless girl. Run!'

Annie ran. Whimpering with fear for her mother, she grabbed the bike and jumped on it, then pedalled for all she was worth. Her father had really done it this time. What if her mother were to…? She couldn't face the thought, shying away from it. That couldn't happen, it just couldn't. Down the track she went, with just a passing glance across the fields to where Silver Sands crouched, dark under the sea wall. To think that while she had been there with Tom, all this had been going on at home. If only she had come back sooner—or not gone at all. She might have been able to stop it. Her mother would be all right at this very moment, instead of lying so still on the floor, bleeding… Along the Wittlesham road she went in the half light with her legs aching, her lungs burning. A miscarriage. Sometimes the cows miscarried. They generally survived, but then they hadn't been knocked unconscious.

Never had the Wittlesham road seemed so long. After what felt like an age, she came to the outskirts of the town. Please, God, she prayed, please let her be all right. Please. She pedalled up the tree-lined street where the doctor lived and into the driveway of the bay-windowed house. Flinging the bike down on the front lawn, she rang frantically at the bell. When it wasn't answered immediately she banged the knocker. The door opened.

'All right, there's no need to rouse the whole neighbourhood. What's the matter?' The doctor's wife was staring at her with cool disapproval.

'It's—my mum—'

Annie could hardly speak. Her chest was heaving.

'It's all right, I'm coming.'

Dr Scott stepped round his wife. He was large and authoritative and already had his bag in his hand. He reached out and held Annie's shoulder with a reassuring grasp, looking into her eyes.

'Where are we going, young lady?'

Annie made a huge effort to control her breathing enough to speak.

'Mar—sh—Edge—Farm.'

She was aware of the relief of having part of the weight of responsibility lifted off her shoulders.

Events blurred. She was hustled into the front seat of a big black car. As they drove through the gathering dark, the doctor asked her about what had happened. Annie answered as best she could. Part of her registered that here she was, riding in a motor car for the first time in her life, but she could take no pleasure in it. She stared through the front window, leaning forward in the seat as if to encourage the thing to go faster. The doctor was saying reassuring things, but Annie couldn't accept them. He hadn't seen her mother's face, or the blood.

As they entered the back door, a groan of pain met them.

'Mum!' Annie cried and flew through the kitchen to the hall.

Her mother was no longer at the foot of the stairs. Another groan sounded. It was coming from above.

Dr Scott was right behind her.

'Good God, he's not gone and moved her, has he?' he muttered. 'These people!'

Annie ran ahead to the first floor. The sound was coming not from her parents' bedroom, but from the spare room next to it. Annie pushed open the door. Her mother was huddled on the unmade-up bed, her face sweating in the yellow light of an oil lamp. A blanket had been thrown over her and she was alone. Walter was nowhere to be seen. Annie flung herself on her knees on the bare boards beside her and cradled her hand in both of hers.

'Mum, Mum! It's all right, the doctor's here—'

'Doctor?' Her mother's voice was a thin rasp. 'No, no, not the doctor, I don't want—'

'Now, then, Mrs Cross, let's have a look at the problem, shall we?' Dr Scott cut in.

He took off his jacket and handed it Annie.

'How old are you, young lady?'

'Fifteen,' Annie said, puzzled.

He nodded. 'Old enough, and you look like a sensible girl. Helped with calvings, have you?'

'Y-yes—'

'Then you can act as my nurse. Go and fetch some old clean sheets and a large bowl of water and some disinfectant, if you have any.'

Glad to be doing something useful, Annie ran to obey. As she ran water into a tin bowl in the kitchen, her father came in from the yard.

'He here?' he asked.

'Yes,' Annie said. She did not even think of pointing out that he must have heard the motor car come into the yard.

Walter grunted. 'You making the cocoa?' he asked.

Something snapped inside Annie.

'Cocoa! You make your own cocoa. I'm helping the doctor,' she told him.

Half expecting to feel a hand smash into her head, she picked up the bowl and stalked out of the room.

Walter said nothing. Five minutes later he appeared at the door of the spare room. Annie looked up from easing a pillow under her mother's head. To her amazement she saw that there was something close to real anxiety in his weathered face.

'She going to be all right?' he asked.

Dr Scott was frowning over his examination of Edna's bruises.

'She's concussed. That doesn't help matters. What happened here, precisely?'

'She fell. Down the stairs,' Walter said.

'I see.' The doctor's voice was carefully neutral. 'Well, Mr Cross, I'm not going to be able to save the baby. It's far too late for that. As for your wife, I'm not sure yet what effect the—er—fall will have on her.'

Annie gasped. He knew. The doctor knew what had happened even though she had told him that her mother had fallen. She watched open-mouthed as her father thought this one through.

'You do all you can for her,' he ordered.

'That's what I'm here for, Mr Cross.'

'You mind you do.'

Edna moaned as another pain gripped her. Annie clasped her hand. Dr Scott put a hand on her shoulder.

'Don't fight it, Mrs Cross. You're going to be fine,' he assured her. Then, as the pain retreated, he asked, 'So what brought all this on, then?'

'I fell,' Edna whispered.

'You fell? Right down the stairs?'

'Clumsy. Always—so clumsy—'

Dr Scott sighed. 'If you say so, Mrs Cross.'

Annie looked across the bed at him. He understood. Here at last was an ally. Hope surged through her.

'She didn't fall. I'm sure she didn't. It was—' she began.

Doctor Scott held her eyes. 'It's what she wants to believe,' he said.

Hope died as quickly as it had been born. He wasn't going to help them. They were still trapped, she and her mother. There was no way out.

She helped the doctor undress her mother and get her into an old nightdress and make her as comfortable as possible, while Edna looked horribly embarrassed and kept apologising for all the trouble she was causing.

For the next two hours, Edna drifted in and out of consciousness as the labour pains got closer together. Distressed and afraid, she clutched at Annie's hand, while Annie, just as frightened, tried to soothe and reassure her. She found she was saying things that her mother used to say to her when she was a little girl and had hurt herself. It was as if she were the grown-up and her mother the child. The responsibility of it was terrifying.

'The baby's coming, isn't it?' she gasped. 'I don't want it to…it's too early…too early…it'll die…I don't want it to die…'

'It's all right, Mum,' Annie said. 'The doctor's doing all he can—'

'Doctor? You won't let him take me away?'

'No, no, of course not. He's here to help you.'

In the quieter moments, the doctor questioned Annie. Had there been any other miscarriages that she knew of?

Annie thought about it.

'Not like this,' she said. 'But, there have been times when she was ill and she said she had women's troubles— I don't know—'

Her mother didn't discuss that sort of thing.

'I see. No other babies, then? You're the only child?'

'There was another baby…'

Annie shivered as she remembered the time when she'd been quite small. She had woken in the night to the sound of adult activity and a strange woman's voice. When she'd crept out of bed to see what was happening, a big woman was bending over her parents' bed and her mother was crying out, the same way that she was now. The big woman— the midwife, she now knew—had ordered her back to bed, but Annie hadn't been able to sleep. The sounds coming from her parents' room had been too frightening. As soon as it was light, she'd got up again and slid across the landing. She had been just in time to see the woman put a small cloth-wrapped thing in a bag.

'Best you don't see it, dearie,' she was saying to Edna. 'You'll get over it quicker that way. There'll be others, you'll see.'

And then her mother's voice, barely recognisable. 'What was it? A girl or—?'

'A boy,' the woman said. 'Pity. A girl would have had a better chance. They're tougher, baby girls.'

'A boy? It was a boy? Oh, no—' Her mother dissolved into agonised sobs.

'My mum wasn't herself for a long time after that,' Annie told the doctor.

In fact she had never really been the same since. The woman who'd used to sing as she'd gone about her tasks had disappeared. Only occasionally did flashes of the old Edna surface, usually when Walter was away from the farm for some reason. Then they would rush through the chores and make time for a little treat together, a cup of tea and a special cake, perhaps, or the planning of a new item of clothing. Then her mother would laugh and chatter, the tense lines in her face would soften and she would open up, talking about things that she used to do in her family home. But generally she was quiet and subdued, holding everything inside herself, appearing to think of nothing but getting the chores done and keeping on the right side of her husband.

'I see,' the doctor said again. 'And she never sought any treatment? She didn't see my predecessor at the surgery?'

Annie couldn't recall her ever going.

'I don't think so. Mum's frightened of doctors.'

Dr Scott shook his head. 'If only people would come to me before things got serious, I might be able to do more to help.'

Some time in the early hours of the morning, the pains got closer together. Edna thrashed her head from side to side on the pillow, her mouth set in a grimace of pain. Groans and cries tore from her throat. Terrified, Annie could only hold her as she gripped her hand. Was her father listening to this? He had to be. It was his fault. He had done this.

'Won't be long now,' the doctor said, folding the sheet back over her mother's belly. Edna's bruised legs were exposed, bare and white, spread with her knees raised. 'Come along now, Mrs Cross, a good big push… That's it, keep it up—it'll soon be over—'

Her mother gave a long grunting animal sound. With a rush, something red and fleshy and slimy appeared on the pile of sheets between her legs. Annie just had time to make out a tiny bulbous head and a minute arm amongst the mess before the doctor snipped something with his scissors, wrapped the thing in some of the sheeting and dropped it into the enamel bucket that Annie had brought up for him. Droplets of blood splattered over his white shirt-front.

'That's it, well done, Mrs Cross. Just the afterbirth now and we're done.'

Her mother was struggling to raise herself on her elbows.

'My baby—what was it?'

The doctor gripped her knee.

'Now then, Mrs Cross. The worst is over now. Soon you can have a good rest.'

'But my baby—'

Another shudder of pain went through her and more disgusting mess appeared on the bed. Again the doctor dealt with it swiftly, dumping the bundle in the bucket on top of the other one.

'That's it. Now, let's get you comfortable,' he said.

Edna reached out and clutched at his arm. Annie could see him wince under the fanatic strength of her fingers.

'Tell me. You must tell me—my baby—what was it?'

Dr Scott looked at her and for a moment his professional mask slipped.

'A boy, Mrs Cross,' he told her gently.

Her mother said nothing. She collapsed back on the pillow with a look of utter defeat on her face. Silent tears ran down into her wild hair.

Annie stared at her, and as she did, the full meaning of what had happened finally got through to her. It wasn't just a fall or an injury, or something terrible that her mother had suffered. The thing in the bucket was her baby brother. A human being.

Annie jumped up and ran out of the room and down the

stairs into the kitchen. She leaned over the sink and retched until there was nothing left in her stomach. Then she washed her hands, splashed her face with water and, with trembling legs, walked slowly up the stairs again to face whatever came next.

CHAPTER TWELVE

'COME on then, Tom lad, your mam'll have tea waiting.'

'What?'

Tom came back to the present, feeling totally disorientated. In his head, he had been sitting on the settee at Silver Sands with Annie. Her warm hand was folded in his. It was a shock to find himself leaning over the engine of a coach with a spanner in his hand. His father was looking over his shoulder.

'Home time, lad. You finished that yet? It's not a major job.'

'Oh—yes, that is, nearly—'

Tom tightened the last nut and shut down the bonnet. His father was standing there, jingling his keys in his pocket.

'Come on then, shake a leg. You've been away in cloud-cuckoo-land ever since you came back from that holiday of yours,' his father complained.

'Yes, right, sorry. I'll just put the tools away,' Tom said, gathering them up and hurrying over to the racks at the side of the repair bay.

They walked home past groups of black-faced men coming off shift. The pit was working full blast to keep up with the need for coal for industry. No more worries now amongst the colliers about unemployment. Quite the opposite, in fact.

There weren't enough men to fill the jobs. Past the rows of grimy cottages they went and up the hill to Amber Drive, where they lived in a solid semi with three steps leading up to the front door.

His mother had tea all ready on the dining room table. As they walked in the door, she poured the boiling water into the pot. Now that the men were here, the family could sit down to their meal. Tom didn't bother to take much notice of what was said around the table. A couple of times some-one had to say something to him twice before he heard them.

'Away with the fairies again?' his father said. 'You want to buck up, lad.'

'Hmm, well. Maybe it's not fairies we've got to worry about,' his mother remarked.

The edge to her voice failed to penetrate Tom's consciousness. But he did realise something odd was going on when his mother sent his sister off to play after the meal was finished instead of getting her to clear away the dirty pots. His father fiddled with his pipe—filling it, tamping it down.

'What's up, love?' he asked.

'It's Tom, that's what,' his mother said.

She set down her teacup abruptly, so that it rattled in the saucer.

'Oh, Tom, how could you do this to us?' she asked, her voice trembling with suppressed emotion. 'How could you be so deceitful? I was never so shocked in my whole life.'

'I don't know what you're talking about,' Tom lied.

Guilt and anger churned in his gut. She knew. His mam knew. Who had given him away? If he found out, he would kill them.

'What's our Tom supposed to have done?' his father asked, striking a match.

'There's no *supposed* about it. He's been lying to us. He never did go on that cycling tour. That was all a great pack of lies.'

His father remained calm. He drew on his pipe, trying to get it to light.

'Come on, now, love. He went off with all the others. We saw him go.'

'That's as maybe, but he didn't stay with them. Oh, no. He went off by himself, and I know where. To Wittlesham.'

'Wittlesham?' The match his father was holding burnt down to his fingers. He dropped it with a quickly suppressed curse.

Tom was almost as shocked. How did she know that? He had told nobody where he was going, only that he was off to visit a friend.

His mother fixed him with a resentful look.

'It's true, isn't it, Tom?'

His mind raced, trying to decide whether to deny everything or admit to it and let them do what they liked about it.

'Wittlesham?' his father repeated. 'What the heck were you doing there, lad?'

His mother reached into her skirt pocket. She slapped an envelope down on the table. Tom felt as if he had been kicked in the stomach. Even before his mother lifted her hand, he knew. It was a letter from Annie, the first she had sent him since he'd got back.

'That's mine,' he cried. 'You've got no right to open it.'

The thought of anyone else reading Annie's letters was horrible—horrible. It was like having his head opened up for everyone to see what he was thinking about.

'I've not opened it,' his mother told him with injured dignity.

Tom collapsed inside with relief. He snatched the letter and thrust it into his own pocket.

'Will somebody please tell me what is going on here?' his father demanded.

Tom said nothing. His mother took a deep breath in through her nose, pursing her mouth. Then she began.

'Tom wasn't the only person in this household to get a letter from Wittlesham today. I got one as well. From that nice Mrs Sutton—'

Tom went cold. Those flaming Suttons! There was no use denying it now. He had been dropped right in it.

He became aware of his mother looking at him, expecting a reply.

'Oh,' was all he could think to say.

'Oh, indeed,' his mother said. 'First I hear from Mrs Sutton that you've been having tea with them in Wittlesham when you should have been out over the Peaks somewhere, then *that* arrives from that girl, and it's easy to put two and two together, isn't it? You lied to us, your parents, and went off all by yourself to see her!'

There was a chuckle from the other end of the table. Tom and his mother both stared at his father. His eyes were twinkling.

'Well, well—been trekking halfway across the country to see a girl, have we? I hope she was worth it!'

His mother went scarlet. 'She is a nasty common little thing, which is why Tom had to deceive us in order to go and see her!'

That did it. Tom jumped up, knocking over his chair.

'She is not nasty or common. You're only repeating what that Sutton woman said to you. I knew you'd taken against her, I knew you wouldn't approve, that's why—'

He broke off. It was no use. They would never understand.

'That's why you went off without telling us,' his father stated.

'All right,' Tom said. 'All right, so I did go to Wittlesham instead of with the cycle club, and if I deceived you I'm sorry, but if I'd asked you, you'd've said no, wouldn't you? Because you treat me like a kid all the time, as if I haven't got a mind of my own and I'm too stupid to look after myself. But I'm not, see—'

'That's enough,' his father said. 'You're upsetting your mother.'

Tom looked at her. Her mouth was drawn down and she was dabbing at her eyes with a handkerchief.

'I'm only doing what's best for you,' she sniffed.

Tom was stopped short by guilt and exasperation.

'I know,' he said, trying to lower his voice, 'but if you will listen to what other people say—'

'That's no reason for lying to your mother,' his father said. 'Or me, for that matter. We expect better of you, lad. Why couldn't you tell us you wanted to go and see this girl—what's her name?'

'Annie,' his mother supplied. 'Annie Cross. She works on a farm.'

He hated hearing her say Annie's name like that, in that disparaging way.

'It's her father's farm,' he said. It went against the grain, bringing Annie's father into this and using his mother's snobbish standards, but he needed all the weapons he could get.

'Family firm, then,' his father pointed out. 'Nothing wrong with farming. Farmers are keeping the country fed.'

His mother saw the argument slipping away from her. She sniffed.

'We trusted you, Tom,' she said with a broken sob.

'I couldn't tell you because you wouldn't have let me go. You treat me like a kid,' Tom repeated.

'Are you going to let him get away with that, Bert?' his mother demanded of his father.

His father sighed. 'Of course not. You're gated till the end of the month, Tom. No going out except to come to work with me—'

'*What?*' Tom spluttered. 'That's so unjust—'

'That clear?' his father rolled on. 'And you'll apologise to your mother for upsetting her.'

His mother was sitting there looking martyred. Tom sighed. She always did that, whenever he did something wrong. She'd done it ever since he was a little kid. But he wasn't going to let her control him like that any more.

'I'm sorry I upset you,' he said with as much sincerity as he could muster. 'But I'm not sorry I went to Wittlesham.'

With which he walked out of the room before anything else could be said and went upstairs to his room.

Locking the door against all intruders, Tom flung himself on his bed and pulled out Annie's letter. He turned it over in his hands. Annie understood, even if nobody else did. His family might gang up against him, but he could always rely on Annie. He slit the top and drew out the sheet of paper. Only one sheet. He felt a slight sinking of disappointment. He lay on his back to read it.

Dear Tom,
How could you do it? I thought I could trust you.

He sat up abruptly. The words were such an echo of what his mother had just been saying that he could hardly believe what he was reading.

I've been having a really horrible time since you left, but I kept thinking, well, at least I've still got Tom even if he has gone back home, and then I went to meet Gwen after work and Beryl was there.

With a sudden horribly clarity, Tom realised what was wrong. Beryl had told her about his going to tea with her family. Why hadn't he admitted to it at the time? He might have known that she would find out. With doom pressing on his heart, he read on.

How could you go to her house and be all nice as pie to her horrible mother and her stupid brother? You know Beryl Sutton is my worst enemy. How could you say such nice things to her and promise to come back and see her again? How could you?

'What nice things?' Tom said out loud. 'I never said anything much to her at all.'

He thought back to that afternoon. The mother had gone on and on, questioning him, and he'd played with the little'un. But Beryl? He couldn't remember exchanging more than half a dozen words with her.

And then not to say anything to me about even seeing them, let alone going to their house. That was like lying to me. I just can't believe you did that. I thought you were my friend. I don't know if I can ever believe anything you say again. I don't know if I even want another letter from you. I don't know if I'll post this even. Yes, I will, because you ought to know how much I hate you.
Annie

'Oh, for God's sake!' Tom muttered.

It seemed as if all the women in his life were ganging up on him, and all because they didn't like other women in his life. Not that he counted Beryl Sutton as someone in his life. She was just a nuisance. But even so…what a fuss! What were they all getting in such a state for?

He heaved a great sigh and flopped back on the bed again with his hands clasped under his head. Roll on December, when he would get away from all this, from parents and girls and all this mess and join the RAF. Then he would have real work to do. He would be flying planes, shooting down Nazis. They would all get off his back then, all these stupid women. For a long time he lay there, picturing himself soaring through the skies, taking part in dogfights. Then he picked up Annie's letter and read it through again. She'd been having a really horrible time. That must mean her father. And he should have told her about how Beryl's old bat of a mother wouldn't take no for an answer. The anguish in the last paragraph seeped into his heart. She really was hurt. He hadn't meant to do that. She needed protecting, not hurting. *I thought you were my friend.* He *was* her friend. And the very last thing he wanted was to lose her.

He sat up and got a writing pad and fountain pen out of the drawer in his bedside table. He sat frowning at the blank page for a while, then he began to write.

Dear Annie,
I'm sorry, I'm sorry, I'm sorry…

CHAPTER THIRTEEN

July 1942

'WE'RE going to work all day Saturday from next week,' Gwen said. 'There's that much work on, we can't get it all done. Mr Sutton got us all together and asked us if we'd do the extra afternoon, for the war effort, like, and we all voted yes.'

She and Annie were sitting on the low wall outside Sutton's Bakelite, making the most of the summer sunshine before Gwen had to go back in for the afternoon session.

'Do you really want to work all that extra?' Annie asked.

'Well, it is more money. We can all do with that.'

'Yes.' Annie sighed.

For the umpteenth time she wished she had a wage like Gwen. It must be so wonderful to have money of your own. She worked seven days a week and all she ever got was what little her mother could spare from her dressmaking earnings.

'The only trouble is, Beryl's there as well,' Gwen said.

'Beryl?'

'Yes, she's sixteen just like us, isn't she? She's left school now. Doesn't half give herself airs. Just because she's in the office and we're on the floor. You'd think she was Lady Muck.'

'She always did think that,' Annie said.

'Yeah, but now she's worse. When we were at the elementary, it was like—school belonged to all of us, didn't it? Even though some of us come from richer families and some didn't. But Sutton's is her family's firm. Her dad's the boss, so she thinks she can say what she likes. It isn't just me, neither. She's awful to all of the girls. We call her Princess Peril.'

Annie laughed because it was expected of her but even the thought of all those girls giggling at Beryl behind her back didn't lighten her view.

'I'll never forgive her for trying to come between me and Tom—never,' she said. 'She nearly ruined it all, you know.'

'You shouldn't've gone flying off the handle at him. You might've known it was just her stirring it,' Gwen said.

There were times when Gwen was just too blooming sensible.

'He should never've gone to her house in the first place,' Annie said. That still rankled, even though it was nearly a year ago now. 'He knows how much I hate her,' she added.

'Oh, Tom, Tom, Tom—! We've been over all that a million times. Give it a rest, for Gawd's sake,' Gwen said. 'Or I won't give you something I've got for you.'

'You've got a letter? Already? Oh, Gwennie, darling, darling, Gwennie, give it to me now!'

'You got to promise to come to the pictures with me and the girls on Friday,' Gwen told her.

'The girls?' Annie said.

'Yeah, the girls from the factory.'

'Oh—I don't know—'

'Come on, Annie. You know most of them. We was all at the elementary together. What's the matter with you? You're like one of them what's-its-names—a recluse. You don't meet hardly anyone. What's the matter? Your precious Tom told you you got to stay in and be faithful to him?'

'Don't be daft.'

'What, then?'

'It's my mum. I don't like leaving her.'

Gwen cast her eyes up to heaven with exasperation.

'Oh, come on, Annie. You say she ain't ill. Surely she don't mind you going out every now and again? It ain't a lot to ask.'

'I know—'

Annie couldn't explain about her mother. Since the miscarriage, she seemed to be walking around within a blanket of fog. There was no spark of life in her face or her eyes and her voice was flat and expressionless. It was as if her body was still there—cooking, cleaning, sewing—but the essential person had gone. Telling Gwen that, though, would make it sound as if her mother was off her head.

'Right, then, so you'll come?'

'All right. As long as I can get away.'

'Promise?'

'Promise.'

'Outside the Toledo at half past six, then. It'll be good. We'll have a laugh.'

The other Sutton's workers, mostly older women and young girls, were hurrying back into the factory now. They waved and called to Gwen as they passed. Some of them, girls she had been to school with, spoke to Annie as well. She watched them with envy, aching for company her own age, for sheer cheerfulness.

'What about my letter?' she asked to distract herself. She might not have lots of workmates, but she did have Tom. Or Tom's letters, anyway.

'What letter?' Gwen said with wide-eyed innocence.

'You said you had a letter,' Annie protested. If this was one of Gwen's so-called jokes…

'I said I had something for you. I never said I had a letter,' Gwen teased.

'Gwennie…'

Annie pushed her, trying to get her off the wall. Gwen struggled back.

'Tut-tut. You're not fighting, I hope? Not on Sutton's premises.'

Annie and Gwen both whirled round. There was Beryl, glaring at them in disapproval just like a teacher.

'Ooh—it's Miss High and Mighty. I can do what I like. You can't tell me what to do. I don't work for Sutton's,' Annie told her.

'She does,' Beryl retorted, looking at Gwen.

If Gwen was worried about her job, she didn't show it. Instead, she shrugged. 'So what are you going to do about it?' she taunted.

'Yes, what are you going to do about it?' another voice chimed in.

This time all three girls looked round. There, grinning at them, was Jeffrey. Annie hardly recognised him at first. He wore long trousers now. He had grown taller than his sister and his face had sprouted a beaky nose and spots. But he was the same old Jeffrey, standing there with his hands in his pockets, ready to score points off whoever was around.

'Go away, Jeffrey. This is nothing to do with you,' Beryl cried. Her face had gone pink with anger.

'I work for the firm as well,' he said.

'Only in the holidays,' Beryl retorted.

'Ah, but when I do start full-time, I'll be doing a proper job, not just filing and addressing envelopes like some people,' Jeffrey told her.

That was too good for Annie to leave. 'Is that all you do, then?' she asked Beryl.

Beryl went from pink to scarlet.

'Of course not! He doesn't know what he's talking about. I have a very important job in the office.'

Jeffrey snorted. 'In a pig's ear,' he said, and sauntered off. As he went, he took one hand out of his pocket and raised it towards Annie and Gwen. 'Bye, girls!'

'Ta-ta, Jeffrey,' they chorused.

'Jeff,' he said. 'It's Jeff.'

The yard was empty now, except for the three girls. The sun beat down on the dusty ground.

Beryl recovered from her brother's interference. 'You're going to be late clocking on,' she said to Gwen.

'So are you.'

'I don't have to clock on. I work in the office.'

Gwen stood up. Clocking on late meant losing a quarter of an hour's pay.

Annie was seized with inspiration. 'Aren't you supposed to be setting a good example?' she challenged. 'Can't have the boss's daughter coming in late. Your dad wouldn't like that one bit, I'm sure.'

A flash of annoyance on Beryl's face showed that she had guessed right.

'I can do what I like,' Beryl told her. But she started walking towards the outside steps that led up to the office. As a parting shot, she added, 'I just can't be bothered to talk to you, that's all.'

'Ooh!' Gwen and Annie chorused, and giggled.

'I got to run,' Gwen said as Beryl started climbing the steps. 'Here—' She thrust a letter into Annie's hand.

A shaft of delight thrilled through Annie. 'Thanks a million, Gwennikins!'

'Remember, half past six Friday,' Gwen called as she raced for the main door.

'I'll remember,' Annie promised, but Gwen had already shot inside.

She smoothed the envelope, feeding on the familiar writing. Tom was still writing to her. Despite all the distractions of his new life—the flying, the hard work and fascination of learning to navigate, the new pals—still he wrote to her. He had almost got over his disappointment at being turned down for pilot training and had thrown himself into being the best navigator in his class, and it was Annie he wrote to and shared all his experiences with, good and bad. But soon he would be going on 'ops' as he called it. Active service.

Annie pushed down the fear that always niggled at the edge of her thoughts, slid the letter into her pocket and put her foot on the pedal of her bike. She still had three lots of alterations to deliver for her mother and the shopping to get. As always, the letter was a treat to look forward to tonight. Perhaps this one would tell her when he was coming to see her. He had promised he would, when he got his end of training leave, before he went on active service. She patted it as she cycled along. Soon, soon, he would be here in Wittlesham again.

...and so it looks like I shan't be able to come and see you after all. I can't tell you how sick I am about it, but I know you'll understand because you know what

*it's like to have your mother ill. I really can't not go
and see her this time, but I promise I'll come and see
you the very next time I get leave.*

*If you're not too angry with me, send your next let-
ter to the airfield. I'll be waiting for it.*
All the best,
Your friend,
Tom.
XXX

With grave misgivings, Tom folded the letter into the envelope and set it out ready to go to the post. It was only three
days since he had sent one telling Annie how and when he
was going to visit Wittlesham, and now he was forced to
write this. He couldn't guess how Annie was going to take
it. She was a great one for flying off the handle at him. But,
as he'd said in the letter, she did know what it was like when
your mother was ill, so maybe she would be understanding.
Not too understanding, though. He wanted her to be disappointed. After all, he was disappointed. There was so much
that had happened this year that he wanted to share with her.
Writing was not the same as telling someone and seeing
them react.

Two days later found him packing his belongings into his
kitbag and saying goodbye to his pals. For a few weeks they
had lived and trained together, suffered the same fears and
hardships and triumphs. Now they were all posted to different airfields. It was unlikely that they would meet again for
quite a while, if ever. Beneath the raucous cheerfulness and
backslapping, they all knew the rate at which planes were
being shot down.

The journey home was tedious and crowded. Tom had to

wait on hot platforms and unexplained sidings and all the tea stalls seemed to have closed down. It was early evening before he got into Mansfield station, and he was thoroughly fed up with travelling. But there, waiting outside, was a Featherstone's bus. The sight of it cheered him immediately. Home ground. There was nothing like it, after all.

His sister Joan opened the door before he could put a hand to the knocker and flung her arms round him.

'Tom! You're home!'

Her enthusiasm was infectious. He hugged her back, swinging her off her feet.

'Hullo, our Joannie. Yes, here I am, back to annoy you.'

He put her down and looked at her. His little sister wasn't a kid any more, he realised. She was growing up.

'Well, look at you. Quite the young lady,' he said.

Joan blushed and tossed her plaits back over her shoulders.

'I'm in charge of your tea,' she told him. 'Dad's gone to visit Mam in the infirmary. Come on in. It's all ready for you.'

He followed her in, dumped his kitbag in the hall and went into the dining room. The smell of home enveloped him. Everything looked exactly the same, from the rug by the empty fireplace to the plates on the table and the clock ticking on the mantelpiece. It was as if it had been frozen in time. So much had happened to him since he had last been here that somehow it seemed odd that home had not changed as much as he had. The only difference was that it seemed smaller. He was used to eating in canteens and sleeping in Nissen huts. Home appeared to close around him.

He followed Joan into the kitchen, where she was fussing importantly with the kettle and the teapot.

'How is Mam?' he asked.

'The doctor says she's poorly but improving. She's had

an operation and once she's over it she should be a lot better,' Joan told him.

'What sort of operation?' Tom asked.

Joan made a mystified face. 'You know what grown-ups are like. They don't tell you anything. All they'll say is it's women's troubles.'

'I see,' Tom said, none the wiser. 'But she is going to get over it?'

'Oh, yes,' Joan said.

She pulled the intricately knitted tea cosy over the big brown pot and carried it through to the dining room. The table was spread to make the food look more generous than it really was. There was a big plate of bread and butter, three types of homemade jam, Bovril and a tiny pot of fish paste, some tomatoes and radishes and a plate of rock buns. It was nothing to the glory of his mother's pre-war high teas, but it was a good deal more than the usual fare. Tom recognised that a big effort had been made to welcome him home with a decent meal.

'I made the rock buns,' Joan said proudly.

'I can see that,' Tom said.

Joan pouted. 'What do you mean? What's wrong with them?'

It was pretty obvious. They were more like paving stones than rocks, and slightly burnt. A year ago Tom would have teased her mercilessly about them. Now he just tweaked her plait.

'Nothing's wrong with them. I bet they taste really nice,' he said.

He was so hungry that he wolfed down plenty of everything, including two of the buns. They weren't too dry if you washed them down with lots of tea. Joan filled him in on all the local news.

'…oh, and best of all, there's a new family moved in next door. The Butterworths.'

'Really? Nobody wrote to me about that.'

'They only came last week. They've got three girls and Vera, she's the youngest, she's in my class and she's my best friend.'

'Another best friend?' Tom said.

'She's my *very* best friend. She wants to meet you. They all do. You can see them tomorrow if you like.'

'Right,' Tom said without enthusiasm.

He didn't have much choice in the matter. He spent the next day with his father at the bus yard, then went up to the infirmary to visit his mother, who looked frail but assured him that now he was home she would soon get better. When he and his father turned into Amber Drive, they saw two girls sitting on the front wall of their house.

'That'll be our Joan's new best pal,' his father said as the girls jumped down and came to meet them. 'Funny little thing, she is.'

It was easy to see what the attraction was. Joan, who always liked to be in charge, had found someone she could order around to her heart's content.

'You've got to meet the rest of the family too, hasn't he, Vera?' she said.

'Yes,' Vera agreed.

'Well, go and fetch them, then. Tell them my big brother who's in the RAF wants to see them.'

Vera nodded. 'All right,' she whispered and trotted off.

'Does she beg and fetch sticks as well?' Tom asked.

Joan glared at him. 'You'll like Moira,' she said.

Tom rather thought not. Not if she was like Vera. He got a surprise. As the Featherstones reached their gate, the entire Butterworth family came out of their front door to meet them. Mr and Mrs Butterworth were pleasant enough. Mrs B asked after his mother and Mr B invited him for a pint at the Brewer's Arms.

'Got to build your strength up, lad. You're the ones to go and give it 'em back, aren't you?' he said.

'That's the idea, Mr Butterworth.'

The middle daughter was nothing out of the ordinary, just a chubby fifteen-year-old, but the eldest caught his attention.

'Our Moira,' as her father introduced her, was a tall brunette maybe a year or so older than himself, with a stunning figure.

'He*llo*,' she said and smiled into his eyes as she shook his hand.

Tom found himself smiling back. 'Hello to you. Very pleased to meet you.'

'Moira doesn't know any young people round here yet,' her mother said.

'We'll soon put that right,' Tom said.

And for the remainder of his leave, he was as good as his word. He introduced her to those of his school and cycle club friends who were still in the area, and through them to their sisters. Moira was lively and chatty and fitted in right away. His leave turned out to be far more fun than Tom had anticipated. On the last evening, he went to see his mother at visiting time and promised her that yes, he would be careful and come back safe.

'I'm glad you've had that Moira Butterworth to go around with. Your father says she's a grand girl, and the family's nice. What I call nice, you know. Refined.'

'Yes, she's good fun,' Tom said.

His mother patted his hand. 'Sounds very suitable, dear.'

'Right,' he said. He wasn't going to argue with her on his last visit.

That evening he went to the Tennis Club with two of his old school friends and a bunch of girls. Moira, naturally, was one of the party. They walked back to Amber Drive together. At the corner of the street, where the front of the house was shielded by a high laurel hedge, she stopped.

'It's been lovely meeting all your pals,' she said. 'I thought I was going to hate it here, but now I think it's going to be fun.'

'Glad you like them. They like you,' he said.

Moira put her head on one side and looked at him. It was difficult to see her expression by moonlight.

'Do you like me?' she asked. There was a world of meaning in her voice.

'Of course,' Tom said. 'You're—very nice.'

'Nice? Is that all?'

Now she was offended.

'No…I mean…you're very pretty and…fun to be with… and…'

Moira moved closer to him. 'I think you're very nice too,' she breathed, and put her arms round his neck.

Tom held her warm body. Through her thin summer dress, he could feel her breasts touch his chest. Excitement coursed through him, urgent and hot. He pulled her closer, pressing her against him. He ran a hand down the length of her back and over her buttocks and heard her give a little gasp. He half expected her to pull away, to be offended, but she didn't. Instead, her lips found his, sweet and soft. First a testing kiss, then a deeper one, their mouths opening.

'Will you write to me while you're away?' Moira gasped, her hot breath mingling with his.

'Yes, yes of course.'

'Promise?'

In the heat of the moment, he would have promised anything, just to keep her there, in his arms.

'Promise.'

They kissed once more, long and searchingly.

Then Moira broke away and struggled out of his grasp. Before Tom could recover, she was hurrying away from him, up the street.

'Mind you do,' she called back, and then she was up her front path and inside her house, banging the door behind her.

In a daze, Tom followed slowly after.

CHAPTER FOURTEEN

Dear Tom,
I hope you're still all right and your pal who's in hospital is getting better. You know I always think of you when it's a moonlit night and I know you'll be flying.

Annie broke off from writing to look out of her bedroom window into the night. It was reassuringly dark—not only a new moon, but cloudy as well. They wouldn't send bombers out tonight. She focused on the close-written page again.

It's been much the same here. We've been lifting the potato field. Everyone has to grow potatoes if they possibly can because they're cheap and filling for people, and they break up the ground so you can grow other things. That's what the War Ag committee says, but I hate the things because I'm the one who has to pick up every single one and carry them to the side of the field and store them in the clamp. Some farms have people to help with harvests—schoolchildren or office workers or Boy Scouts or whatnot, but you know my dad, he won't let anyone on our land, so like I said it's all down to me as usual. I hate potatoes.

Gwen and I went to the pictures on Friday. We saw
Blood and Sand. *Have you seen it yet? It's ever so*
good. Gwen says she's in love with Tyrone Power. But
she was also saying (and I'm being serious now) how
she's fed up with her job and with Wittlesham. Beryl
is getting on her nerves because now her big brother's
gone and joined the army, Beryl thinks she's deputy
boss and she can go round telling everyone they're
doing their work all wrong. Or she looks over your
shoulder and says, 'You're really doing that quite well.
Carry on,' in a sort of teacher-y voice so that you want
to smack her face.

Annie could just hear Beryl saying that. But even having
to work with Beryl must be better than working on the farm
with her father. As Annie pulled the counterpane up over her
shoulders, she could feel the bruises from when he had hit
her with a broom handle the other day.

Gwen says she's going to join up as soon as she's
old enough. She says she can't wait to get away and
have some fun. I don't know what I'll do without her
to talk to. I've got other friends but I don't see them
much because I can't get out a lot and they're not the
same as Gwen. We've been friends ever since the first
day in the Infants. And what are we going to do about
the letters? I was really upset about it. She said I ought
to join up as well but how can I? I've got my mum to
look out for.

Gwen had argued with her for twenty minutes as they'd
slowly moved to the head of the queue outside the cinema.

Annie yearned to get away. She longed for it with a deep, constant ache. To be with girls her own age, to earn a real wage, to have some fun. Most of all, simply to get away from her father.

I dream and dream about getting away. I know you said I ought to as well. You said I ought to join the WAAFs. Sometimes I think, yes, I will, but I know I can't. Not really. So you've got to keep telling me about all the things you do so I can picture it and think about where you are and who you're with. I like to have something like that to think about when I'm out in the fields all day. Gwen says she's bored but at least she's got Music While You Work *on at the factory and people to talk to. So it's nice to hear about dances and things.*

Except that it wasn't unalloyed pleasure. She liked the window into his life just as she used to be fascinated by his cycle club trips and cricket matches in Noresley, but she was suspicious about what he didn't say. The town nearest to his airfield in Lincolnshire must be as full as Wittlesham was with young women and girls and they all wanted a boyfriend with wings on his uniform. Tom never mentioned any girls, but when he referred to 'a bunch of us' going to a dance or a social, she was gripped with the conviction that girls were part of the gang. After all, how could you have a dance without girls? Two girls could dance together when there weren't enough men to go around, but two men couldn't. She couldn't bear the thought of Tom waltzing with some girl in a church hall. Worse still was the thought of him walking her home. It tore her apart. What good were her letters to him when there were all those girls on his doorstep just dying to go out with him?

I hope you're behaving yourself, though, and don't forget all about me until my letters come. I think about you all the time. It seems like such a long time now since you were here. Every time I look across the fields to Silver Sands I remember how we got in the window and made it our little camp. Do you know when you'll be getting your next leave? It's such a shame you got posted to Lincolnshire when there are airfields much nearer to here.

If she could just know that he would be coming some day, then she would have something definite to look forward to, something to hold on to in her life. For between the bleak situation at home, the long hard days of work and the war that seemed to be going on and on, life sometimes felt very gloomy. She had her friendship with Gwen and her letters from Tom. They were the bright spots that kept her going. It was no use thinking ahead any further than some time when they might meet again.

Dear Annie
    Sorry it's been longer than usual since I wrote but it's been a bit busy round here.

Tom rested his head on the metal frame of the bed and stared at the ceiling of the Nissen hut. Busy. Yes. It did get a bit busy when flak was coming up at you and fighters homing in on you and the stupid bastards in the plane alongside you were ripping you up by mistake and the one in front of you was losing a wing and going down in flames and… But he couldn't write all that to Annie. She'd be worried sick.

The boys and I went down to the Red Lion yesterday evening for a drink and a game of darts. The beer was so weak a baby could have drunk it but the landlord said it was either that or go without so we had to lump it. On the way back Nev said all that feeble stuff made him feel sick and he needed a drink of milk to settle his stomach. Nev's the new boy, sent to replace Jimmy. He's from a farm, like you, and so he knows how to milk a cow. The next field we came to that had cows in it, he climbed over the gate, went up to the nearest cow and sort of talked to it a bit, then he put his tin hat on the ground under it and milked the cow right into it! Some of the boys wouldn't drink it, but I had a go—it tasted sort of funny but that might have been the taste of Nev's hat.

Nev was all right. He'd fitted into the team and now Tom wasn't the new boy any longer. He understood now the reserve he'd experienced from the rest of the crew at first. You remembered how the last man had died—Jimmy's brains had splattered all over the remains of the rear gun turret—and you weren't sure how reliable the new man was going to be. Once he'd proved himself with the first sortie, then it was OK, as the Yanks would say. You had to know that when it came to the crunch, everyone could count on everyone else doing their job and more. Nev had done that, just as Tom had managed to play his part on that first terrifying trip to Hamburg. They were both now part of the gang.

*We had a concert party come and perform in the
canteen last Tuesday. All the camp went to see them,
and a right mixed bunch they were. They were from
ENSA, who are supposed to have all the big names
playing for them, but I think they get sent to more important places than ours, because this lot were more
like the end of the pier show. There was a pianist, a male
and a female vocalist, a comedian and three dancers.
When we heard there were going to be dancing girls
we thought we were going to get something like the
Tillers, but these were doing all this folk stuff. And they
weren't exactly girls. More my mam's age, I'd say.
Anyway, the vocalists weren't bad. They did all the old
favourites and everyone joined in the choruses and the
comedian was quite funny in places. We all had a good
evening, anyway.*

Anything was useful to take your mind off what you might
have to face the next time you flew. Of all the personnel
gathered in the canteen that evening, it had been the air crew
who'd whistled and clapped and cheered and booed the loud-
est. You didn't think ahead. You just enjoyed each moment
as it came. After straining to get into the RAF, always having a goal ahead of him, it had taken Tom a while to adjust
to this new way of looking at life, but with six sorties notched
up now, he was finding that he too was just living for the day.

*We're lucky on our crew, because we've got Mike.
He's our bomb-aimer and he's been on more sorties
than anyone else here. He says he's safe as long as he
takes his lucky button with him and we know we're safe
as long as he's with us, so we're all right.*

They were all right, Tom repeated to himself. Even though he'd overheard someone from one of the other crews saying that Mike had survived so long that his number must be up and so he was unlucky for his crew. But that was just superstitious rubbish, and neither Tom nor any of the rest of his lot were going to believe that.

He glanced across the hut to where his best pal Alan was whistling as he polished his boots to a mirror shine. Alan caught his eye and grinned.

'Which one are you writing to this time, Romeo?'

'My mam,' Tom lied.

Alan laughed in disbelief. 'Oh, yeah? Pull the other one, mate. I know that look on your face.'

'Go stuff yourself,' Tom told him.

Alan just smiled and waved two fingers at him.

Tom concentrated on his letter.

I hope things are going well on the farm. It can't be much fun out in the fields in this weather. I thought of you the other day when it rained all day long and hoped you weren't out in it, but I expect you were. Have you seen anything of…

He was just about to write *the dreaded Beryl*, but thought better of it. Annie was so dead set against the girl. Well, not surprising really, she was pretty awful, and her mother—! Tom shuddered to think of Mrs Sutton and her domineering ways. He had nearly fallen out with Annie permanently over that time he had been forced to go to tea with them. So no mentioning Beryl. At least he didn't feel guilty about Beryl, whereas Moira—under no circumstances must Annie ever know about Moira.

For Moira was writing to him as regularly as Annie. Worryingly, there was a possessive tone to her letters. Just because he had taken her with him to meet his friends on his last leave, and they had all met up practically every day, she appeared to think she was his girlfriend. He should never have kissed her like that on the last evening. He had to admit that it had been very nice at the time, but it had given Moira quite the wrong idea. She seemed to be taking it for granted that he was going to go out with her on his next leave, which she assumed he would be spending at Noresley. On top of that, his mother and the rest of his family expected him to go home too.

His mother was as good a correspondent as either of the girls, telling him in minute detail everything that had been going on at home. Since the Butterworths had moved in, there was always a lot about them. She and Mrs Butterworth were now best friends and both of them were delighted that Tom and Moira had hit it off so well. Every letter brought some praise of Moira—what a lovely girl she was, so helpful to her mother, so kind to her younger sisters, what a splendid cook and housekeeper she was, how everyone at the office she worked at valued her. It was obvious which way his mother's mind was working.

Tom sighed and looked back at the letter he was writing. Annie expected him to go to Wittlesham on his next leave. What was more, he had promised her that he would. And he did want to see her again. There was something about Annie—something different, special. Nobody was quite like Annie. But it was such a long time now since he had last seen her that the clear image that he had once had of her in his mind was fading a little. Did she even still look the same as he remembered? He knew he had changed a lot. He certainly felt a hundred years older than the boy who had thought of nothing but joining up. So presumably she must have changed as well. What if they didn't recognise each other when they next met? But that was stupid. He would always be able to recognise Annie…

He was jolted out of his reverie by the wail of the siren.

'Raid!' Alan yelped as he, Tom and the others in the hut pulled on boots, grabbed coats and tin hats and made a dash for the door.

Outside in the damp night the station was alive with hurrying figures. Over their heads, the siren was still screaming as some personnel made for the shelters whilst others ran towards the planes. Already the searchlights were stabbing the sky and out by the hangars the first throaty roar of engines could be heard as crews raced to get the precious aircraft into the sky before they became sitting ducks. Pounding across wet concrete and weaving round other scurrying figures, Tom arrived to see the first plane already rolling out on to the runway while others were starting their engines. The air throbbed with noise and stank of aviation fuel and exhaust fumes. Tom raced to V-Victor and hauled himself on board just as the fourth engine fired.

'What kept you, Romeo?'

'Sure you can spare the time to join us?'

Other members of the crew were grinning at him.

'Hold tight, we're off!' the skipper shouted back to them.

'Where's Mike?' Tom asked as the plane started to roll forward.

'Sick bay.'

Tom felt slightly sick himself. He knew it was not like a sortie. They were only moving the planes out of the way and they didn't need a full crew. But all the same he felt exposed without bullet-proof Mike and his lucky button on board. The plane began to vibrate as it taxied towards the runway.

We had a bit of drama here since I started this letter. We got an air raid warning and had to scramble all the planes, but in the end it was a false alarm. The Jerry bombers must have been heading for the midlands. It was a good thing because we hardly had any fuel on board and we couldn't have stayed up for long. I was worried because Mike wasn't with us, but we got down again all right.

Tom tapped the pen against his teeth. It looked so bare on the page. *We got down again all right.* But how could he tell her about the lads who hadn't got down all right, about the plane that had unaccountably swerved on landing, clipped a storage building and burst into flames? The fire had been big enough to light half of Lincolnshire. It had lit the way for their landing wonderfully. If he told Annie about that, she'd be worried all the time. He knew how much she worried anyway, because she'd told him so enough times. What was more, he knew what it felt like, because he worried about her, stuck in that bleak farmhouse with that father of hers. Neither of them could do anything to help the other, except write these letters.

Don't go working yourself to death on that farm. I always think of it being summer in Wittlesham, but the wind must cut across your land like it does across the airfield here. Give my regards to Gwen and thank her for being such a good postlady. I'll try to get to see

Blood and Sand *when it gets up this way and then that will be something we've both done.*
Your friend,
Tom.
XXX

Annie sighed and gently folded the letter, slid it into its envelope and put it under her pillow. Tom was all right. He was safe. In fact, he didn't seem to be doing much flying at all. Visits to the pub, concert parties—it was all just one big round of fun. And to think that she had been imagining him up there over Germany. She smiled again at the story about the cow and the helmet. How puzzled the farmer must have been that one of his cows had suddenly produced less one morning. Lucky Tom. She was glad he was managing to enjoy himself, of course. But still she wondered what he was not telling her about. Was there a girlfriend at the airfield? Some WAAF who had caught his eye, or a girl in the village? He certainly wouldn't tell her if there was someone. If only they could get to see each other again, everything would be all right. She would know, the moment she saw him, if there was something he was trying to cover up. All she wanted was to hear that he had some leave and was coming to spend it here, with her, at Silver Sands.

CHAPTER FIFTEEN

'YOU got it, Mike?' Tom asked above the hubbub of conversation in the locker room.

Mike nodded and patted his breast pocket.

'Would I forget?'

''Course not, mate. I know I can rely on you,' Tom said.

But he felt reassured, nonetheless. They all carried mascots, even tough nuts like Mac, the top gunner, a wiry Glaswegian who kept a small toy rabbit knitted in Rangers colours in his trouser pocket. But of all of them, Mike's lucky button was legendary. Tom checked his socks, though he knew that they were inside out, and therefore all right, and made sure that his old school prefect's badge was securely pinned inside his flying jacket. Now he was ready.

All around him, men were struggling into their flying gear. Tom was sweating as he did up the zips and pulled on the bulky Mae West. It was warm in the locker room amongst the tight pack of men, but later on they would all be glad of the layers of clothing. He and Squiff, the radio operator, checked each other's parachute harness and lined up with the others to get the sandwiches and flasks of coffee, slabs of chocolate and barley sugar sweets that would keep them going for the long cold journey. Already the buses were arriving, and a corporal by the open door was shouting out the aircraft letters.

Out on the dispersal pans, the ground crew were making their final checks, while the air crew took a last leak before climbing on board.

'Make sure you zip it up safely, Romeo,' someone told Tom. 'You'll need it for all those girls of yours.'

Tom glanced up at V-Victor, to where the hand in a v-for-victory sign was painted on her nose alongside their tally of bombings.

'That's the girl I'm relying on tonight,' he said.

Mike reached up and slapped the Halifax's belly. 'She'll get us there and back all right. She's a tough old tart.'

There was the usual underlying tension as the engines were fired up and the plane taxied out to join the queue for take-off. Tom outlined the flight plan and climb instructions over the intercom. He breathed in the queasy smell of the aircraft as the vibration juddered through him, and unwrapped one of the barley sugars. Above the noise of their own engines, he could hear the roar of other planes taking off.

There was the usual hanging about, then Chip the skipper's voice crackled in his ears. 'Here we go, chaps!'

The engines powered up as Chip opened the throttles against the brakes, and then they were off, accelerating down the runway with Chip holding the nose down for as long as possible before finally hauling the big plane and its heavy load into the air. Tom felt himself relax a little as the motion smoothed and they began the slow climb into the night sky. The first hurdle was over. They were flying.

'Bearing, Romeo?'

Tom gave the course for the assembly point, picturing as he did the planes from other airfields setting out as they were now, all heading for the same point. Then it was navigation lights out and the flock of deadly birds made for Cromer. Even cooped up as he was in his curtained-off section, Tom could sense the other aircraft close around him in the skies. There was safety in the stream—the safety of the herd—but there was always the slightly uncomfortable feeling that someone else could get too close. Even now he could feel the disturbance in the air as another plane flew right over them.

As they crossed the coast, Tom tuned his new GEE set to a sharp picture while next to him in the cramped compartment, Squiff received messages and passed on information to him about wind speed and direction. Tom adjusted his calculations. A heavy head wind meant it was going to take longer to get to their target.

'Enemy coast ahead.'

That was Mike, up in the nose.

'Switch on oxygen.'

Tom threw in another barley sugar before covering his mouth and nose with the claustrophobic rubbery smell of the mask. The first lot of flak would be coming up now to welcome them to enemy territory. He sensed rather than heard it.

He gave Chip the course for the target and the new ETA, and then it was the long haul over Belgium and Germany, with the GEE becoming less accurate with distance. Tom backed it up with old-fashioned maps, bearings and calculations, just to make sure. Somewhere ahead of them the Pathfinders would be already on their way, ready to pinpoint the target. Over the intercom a game of 'get Nev' developed, a welcome antidote to the boredom and underlying fear. They all teased him over his alleged marathon session with twin sisters last weekend.

'Bet you wish you had them out there with you now, Nev. Keep you warmer than a Taylorsuit.'

'How did you manage with your little tart's hands, Nev? Did you use your feet as well?'

'It's easy for him—he's had all that practice servicing cows. Two girls at a time is nothing.'

Nev was laughing back at them. 'Don't you wish you had my stamina? All you can do is talk about it. Not the same as doing it. All night. Every way up.'

Which brought on a round of competitive boasting.

On across Germany they droned, an hour turning into two. Tom could feel the tension building inside him, bracing his jaw, locking his shoulders. It was all too quiet. They had steered clear of most of the possible anti-aircraft fire, but they should have been harried by night-fighters by now. He could only conclude that the enemy was saving up something nasty to throw at them.

Then Mac's voice came over the intercom warning of bandits, and the clatter of airgun fire rattled through the plane as the gunners tried to pick off the raiders. Tom could hear the scream of a single engine plane diving. He tried to concentrate on his maps. Beside him Squiff was listening to what was going on in the rest of the fleet. At times like this, he was grateful to be stuck in here, even if he couldn't see what was going on. At least he had Squiff for company. Mac and Nev were all alone, sitting ducks in their perspex turrets.

Above the steady growl and vibration of the plane, the sound of the higher pitched fighters and the clatter of gunfire circled round them. V-Victor held steady in the stream. With a bit of luck, they wouldn't be singled out. There were nearly four hundred others to choose from.

Tom took a new ETA. Just fifteen minutes to target. The reception committee was hotting up.

'Flak starboard,' came Mike's voice.

'D-Dog's caught it. Port engine alight. He's pulling out,' Squiff reported.

'Yow! Hole in one!' Nev yelled. 'Someone got the bandit!'

'Z-Zombie's claiming it,' Squiff reported.

'Nice one!' Tom said. Z-Zombie was Alan's plane.

The triumph was only seconds long.

'More bandits,' came Mac's warning. 'Corkscrew port, go!'

The whole crew braced themselves as Chip took evasive action, banking the heavy aircraft steeply to port, pulling the nose up, banking again, levelling out, heaving the unwieldy bomber around the sky so as not to be a steady target for the pursuing night-fighters. The airguns clattered and Nev's voice could be heard screaming, 'Take that, you bastards!' Tom felt rather than heard the rip of bullets through their starboard wing while in his ear Chip was talking to the plane.

'Come back, you cow, come back, that's it, good girl—'

He held his breath. Like all the Halifaxes, V-Victor had a rudder lock-over problem that could send her into a fatal deep stall. He hung on to his small table, jamming his back against the back of his seat. The plane was responding. Chip had not pushed her too far. More bullets slammed into the fuselage just above his head. Instinctively, he ducked and Squiff yelped just as Nev's voice came crowing down the intercom.

'Yeah! Gotcha!'

The big plane juddered round and levelled out just as another burst of fire was heard and Nev's triumphant yells were cut off in mid-stream.

'Nev?' came the skipper's voice. 'Come in, Nev. Nev, are you there?'

There was no reply.

Tom looked at Squiff. What he could see of his face was very white.

'Nev's bought it,' he said.

'Shit,' said Tom. 'Shit, shit—'

'ETA target?' Chip's voice cut in.

There was no time for Nev now.

'Eight minutes, Skip.'

They were level and steady now, lining up for the final run-in. The bomb doors were open and below them the city lay ablaze. Tom had to tear his mind away from imagining the searchlights probing the sky, the ack-ack aimed at them, the fighters circling for the kill.

'Right, steady, left a bit, left—' came Mike's voice, calm and cool as he talked them into position.

The plane rocked as a shell exploded right alongside them.

'Steady, steady—'

Spent shrapnel rained down on them. Up on top, Mac was firing away.

'Left a bit—'

Just as Mike said *'Now!'* and released the bombs, the plane reared up as the load fell away and part of a shell hit one of engines. Tom could hear Chip cursing as he fought to keep the plane straight and level while Mike took the aiming point photograph and checked that all the bombs had gone. It only took thirty seconds, but it was always the longest thirty seconds of the entire trip. If they hadn't released all the bombs, they had to go round and try again. If they had, then they could head for home. Tom found himself counting… Another shell exploded almost next to them and the plane bucked and juddered.

'Christ—' Squiff yelped.

'Bombs gone. Let's go!'

Slowly the damaged plane banked round and made to join the stream of homebound bombers. Tom braced himself for further attacks from fighters. They must be marked out as prey now that they had been hit. He could hear Mike cursing as he struggled to get the bomb doors closed. Something in the mechanism had jammed. Tom concentrated fiercely on the job in hand. What was their ETA for home? They had a tail wind for the return journey, but only three engines… He calculated one against the other ready for when Chip wanted the information, all the while trying to block out the sense that all was not well with V-Victor. She didn't feel right. She didn't sound right.

And then everything seemed to happen at once. There was the scream of a fighter and the rattle of gunfire and V-Victor slewed to one side. Through his headphones Tom could hear muffled shouts and cries from the cockpit, and then the flight engineer saying, 'I've got her, I'm holding her—' He had hardly a moment to guess that the fighter had shot up the cockpit before there was a ripping noise right behind him and a stench of cordite. A large hole appeared in the fuselage. Beside him Squiff cried out and slumped over his desk. The radio was sizzling and giving off the stomach-turning smell of an electrical fire.

'Squiff?'

As he reached out to help his mate he felt something slam into his shoulder with a pain like a hot wire and at the same time the plane lurched and threw him across the cabin bulkhead. They were dropping rapidly. V-Victor was out of control. The intercom went dead, but from the cockpit he could hear the flight engineer yelling, 'Bale out! Bale out!'

Tom crawled up the sloping floor to where Squiff was now flopping half off his seat. He grasped him under the arms.

'Come on, mate, come on—'

The radio burst into flames. By its lurid light, Tom saw that it was too late to save Squiff. Laying him down, he made for the bomb doors, mercifully still jammed open. The whole plane was screaming and rattling as it fell through the sky. Things fell on him. Smoke was billowing through the cabin. As he reached the bomb doors, Mike was there. Below them the black night was lit by the fires they had started. The city was burning. Streaks of flak were shooting up towards them. The rush of air buffeted them.

'Where's Squiff?'

'Bought it. Chip?'

'Him too. Get out, mate, now—'

Mike pushed him. He pitched forward into the emptiness. Something slammed into his side, taking his breath away. He was tumbling through the air with just enough sense left to count and pull the rip-cord before he passed out.

CHAPTER SIXTEEN

'ARE you sure you haven't had anything?'

'Of course I'm sure,' Gwen said. 'What d'you think I am, a liar?'

'No, of course not, it's just…' Annie said.

'Just what?'

'Nothing…well…I was expecting to hear from him by now, that's all.'

'That's the trouble with a boyfriend who's away. All you get are letters,' Gwen said smugly.

'Yes…' Annie agreed.

'Of course, Johnny's not in the RAF like some, but at least he's here. He can take me to the pictures on a Friday night, and dancing on Saturdays…'

'Yes,' Annie repeated.

She listened with half an ear while Gwen prattled on about the boyfriend she had acquired. Friendship required that she should appear to be interested in what Gwen was saying, but she was too worried to take in even part of it. Tom should have written to her by now. He had always been a faithful correspondent. Sometimes he would be a day or two late writing, but never this long. The cold well of fear that always lurked in the pit of her stomach began to rise.

Was there someone on or near the airfield who had taken him
away—some other girl? Or was there another, even more
sinister reason? On the news last week they had spoken of
a big bomber raid on Milan. Perhaps Tom had been on that.
Perhaps…but it didn't bear thinking about. She closed her
mind to the thought of all the planes that didn't make it back
home. Tom was all right. He was sure of that himself, just
as long as his plane had lucky Mike on board.

'So are we going to the pictures, then?' she interrupted
Gwen.

Gwen sighed. 'I *told* you, I'm going with Johnny,' she
said. Then, seeing Annie's disappointed face, added, 'Look,
when Tom's here, you go out with him, don't you?'

'Yes,' Annie admitted.

But it had been such a very long time since she had seen
Tom. And now he hadn't written…

'I don't think I'll be able to get into town till next week
now,' she said.

Another whole week to wait till she heard from Tom. She
didn't know how she was going to bear it.

'Tell you what,' Gwen said. 'If I get anything, I'll cycle
down to the sea wall and, if I can't see you, I'll leave it under
a stone or something on the veranda of Silver Sands.'

Annie flung her arms round her, tears pricking at the
backs of her eyes.

'Oh, thank you, Gwennie darling. You're the best friend
in the world, d'you know that?'

'Yeah, well—' Gwen said. 'You're potty, you are. Potty
about him, anyway.'

Three days dragged by and at midday and early evening
Annie kept looking across the flat fields towards the sea wall.
Sometimes people would appear and walk along it for a

while, often with a dog in tow, but none of them was Gwen. Each day she went and checked the veranda at Silver Sands anyway, just in case Gwen had been and she hadn't seen her, but there was nothing to be found but leaves and twigs blown into heaps and corners on the deserted chalet. A sick feeling of dread was slowly building up inside her. Something was wrong—something was dreadfully wrong for Tom to be silent this long.

On the fourth day it rained steadily all day, a thin grey rain that cut through all protection just as effectively as a downpour. Her father spent all afternoon tending a cow which was having a difficult birth, so Annie was left with the afternoon milking to do single-handed. When she had finally got through all the scrubbing down, she went into the barn, to find the new mother licking her calf clean. One look at her father told her that it was not good news.

'A bull?' she ventured nervously.

Walter grunted and picked up his old coat from the nail on the wall.

'What does it look like?' he growled.

Annie glanced at the calf. It was a bull. Bull calves were no use to a dairy herd.

'Let's—let's hope the next one will be a heifer,' she ventured. Another of their cows was due to calve in two weeks' time.

'What's the point of hoping? Won't change nothing,' Walter snapped and strode off towards the house.

Annie trailed unhappily behind. What was the point of hoping? But she couldn't help looking over the fields towards the sea wall before going into the house. In the gloom of the day, she could hardly make out where the land met the sky. She couldn't believe that Gwen would have cycled all the way down to Silver Sands in this, and yet…she could not quite give up.

Tea was a silent meal. Her mother, ever aware of her husband's moods, said nothing beyond asking whether he wanted more of anything. Walter chewed his way through his food as if he were eating a mortal enemy. Annie kept her eyes on her plate, her mind on Silver Sands. She pictured the veranda, the damp leaves, the big stone from the garden that she had left there on purpose. She pictured an envelope underneath it, an envelope with her name on it, in Tom's writing. Maybe if she believed in it strongly enough, it would happen…

At last she was free to tramp across the fields. She put on her sodden mackintosh and set out. She had walked this route so many times before. Last year when Tom had been waiting for her at the chalet, she had raced across the grass and hardly felt her feet touch the ground. Now her legs were heavy and every step was an effort. She dreaded finding the hiding place bare once again.

Silver Sands was a sad sight. It was three years now since it had last been done up and the paint was beginning to peel. Whoever it was that the Suttons had sold it to didn't seem to care about it at all. The brambles from the overgrown garden were reaching long tentacles on to the veranda and one of the bedroom windows was hanging open. The practical side of Annie's mind made a mental note to bring a hammer and nails next time she came to nail it shut. Once the weather got in, the place would be ruined. She rounded the corner of the veranda to the seaward side, where all thoughts of house maintenance flew out of her head as her eyes focused on the stone…

'Yes!' she cried out loud.

She ran, her feet slipping on the wet wood, and snatched the precious blue envelope. He had written, he had written, he...

Dread clutched at her heart. The writing, smudged from being under the damp stone, was not Tom's.

Annie stared at it. She felt cold and sick and clammy. Her breath came in short gasps. *Please*, she prayed, *please don't let this be it...*

With trembling fingers, she opened the envelope and drew out the one sheet of paper inside. For a long moment she stood holding it, wanting to delay the moment of knowing, wanting to hold back time. But in the end, it had to be faced. Slowly, she unfolded it. Already a terrible pain was beginning to wrap itself round her entrails.

Dear Miss Cross,

I'm very sorry that I have to write to you with bad news. I don't suppose you'll be getting an official notification, but I know Tom would want you to know.

We went on a big raid last night and ran into a very hot reception. Tom's plane was hit and went down. There was such a lot going on that I'm not sure exactly what happened, but I do know that I saw some of them bale out.

I'm really sorry to have to tell you this, Miss Cross. I haven't known Tom for long, but you get to know people pretty quickly in a place like this where you're living on top of each other all the time, and Tom is one of the best. Him and me hit it off straight away, and the rest of the boys liked him a lot too.

He didn't say a lot about you but I know he thought the world of you. He's a tough lad and if he did man-

age to bale out then he's got a good chance of surviving. I'm keeping my fingers crossed for him.

Again, I'm really sorry to have to be the one to tell you this.
Yours sincerely,
Alan Mitchell.

Annie's knees were shaking. Slowly, she crumpled the letter in her numb fingers and clutched it to her chest.

'No—' she whispered. 'No—no—'

She felt as if her body were being ripped apart and a huge piece torn away, leaving her bereft and defenceless. *Hit and went down—hit and went down—*the words whirled round and round in her head. No Tom, no Tom—how could she bear it? The strength seemed to have gone out of her legs. She slumped on to the wet veranda floor with its scattering of slimy leaves and doubled over, letting out a howl of anguish.

There was no one to share her grief. Her mother was too sunk in her own pit of despair to notice Annie's dark mood or, if she did, she was unable to reach out. Her father only remarked on it to criticise her.

'What's the matter with you? Cat got your tongue? Turn the milk sour, you will, with a face like that.'

And when Annie didn't answer, she got his heavy hand across her head for insolence.

She wasn't sure how she got through the next day, but in the evening she had a visitor. Gwen arrived at the kitchen door, shifting from foot to foot, her voice high with nerves, but there all the same.

'I've come to see Annie,' she announced, not quite meeting Walter's eyes.

A sob rose in Annie's throat. She jumped up and bolted

for the door, grabbed Gwen by the wrist and dragged her into the hay barn.

'What's—?' Gwen asked, but got no further. Annie leaned against her friend's solid frame and wept. It was such a relief to let go. Gwen's shoulder was warm and firm, her strong arms went round her and held her, rocking her gently and talking to her. At length, her words came through to her.

'Poor Annie, poor love, don't cry, Annie darling, please don't cry—'

It was a long time before she was able to stop, her eyes and face swollen, her throat sore, her breath coming in harsh sobs.

'Better now?' Gwen said hopefully.

Annie nodded, though it wasn't. Nothing was ever going to make it better. But the crying had helped. Gwen sat them both down on the warm hay. The sweet smell of it was all around them and it whispered as they shifted.

'I was worried it was bad news when I saw the writing. That's why I left you the note,' Gwen said.

'Note?' Annie managed to ask. She didn't know what Gwen was talking about.

'Under the stone. With the letter. Didn't you see it?'

Annie shook her head. She hadn't noticed anything but her letter.

'Was it—? I mean, is he—?' Gwen asked. She stopped, unable to put it into words.

'I don't know,' Annie told her.

'You don't know? But what—?'

It was difficult to get the words out. Annie had to force them, one by one.

'His plane…was…sh-shot down. S-some of them…baled out. They don't know…who…'

'Oh, Annie—' Gwen sighed '—I'm so sorry.'

Sorry. The gross inadequacy of the word set off a fresh rush of tears. Gwen stroked her head and rubbed her back and waited for her to stop. When she did, Gwen had something more to say.

'But look,' she said. 'It could've been him, couldn't it? He could've got out, and parachuted down, or whatever they do. He could be alive. Where was they when…when it happened?'

It was only then that it struck Annie that she didn't know. Nothing had been said in the letter. If Tom was alive, she didn't know where he was. It made her feel helpless all over again.

'Germany somewhere, I s'pose,' she whispered.

The very word sent a fresh chill through her. If Tom wasn't dead, he was in the hands of the enemy, deep inside their territory.

'Oh, Gawd,' Gwen said. 'But look, at least he'll be safe, won't he? He'll be a POW. My aunty's brother-in-law's a POW. He says at least he's not getting shot at no more.'

The small glimmer of hope wound itself around her heart. Annie nodded.

'Yes,' she whispered.

Maybe he had survived. Maybe he was safe.

'But how will I know?' she asked. 'They won't tell me. It was a friend of his what wrote. Would he know? How do I find out?'

'I think they only tell the next of kin,' Gwen said. 'But look—you could write to his parents, couldn't you? Ask them. They'd tell you, surely, if they heard anything?'

The hope grew a little stronger. Here was something she could actually do. It was so much better than just asking endless unanswerable questions of herself.

'Yes,' she said. 'Yes, I could. Oh, Gwen, you're the best friend anyone ever had. I don't know what I'd do without you.'

Gwen gave her a hug. 'Keep your pecker up,' she said.

Working out the exact wording of the letter became an obsession. Annie could think of nothing else. Whether she was tending the animals, working in the fields or helping her mother in the house, she kept going over and over the possible combinations of words. Sometimes it seemed too hard to do at all but she knew that she must get it right, put it down on paper and send it off. It was as if doing so was keeping Tom alive.

Finally, after writing, crossing out and re-writing half a writing pad, she managed a short polite note. She still wasn't happy with it, but she had to get something finished before her one chance in the week to get to the post box. She dropped it in and instantly regretted it. What were Tom's parents going to think? Would Tom disapprove of her writing to them? But it had to be done. She had to snatch at the only chance she had of knowing what had happened to him. Now all she could do was wait.

She went each day to Silver Sands, even though she didn't expect a reply at once. The weather cheered up and gave everyone a series of bright autumn days with misty mornings followed by blue skies and warm sunshine. In the evenings, Annie walked across the fields as the mist began to form again and sat for a while on the veranda of the wooden chalet or at the base of the sea wall. Nobody ever came by, so she was able to withdraw deep inside herself and remember her time with Tom. They had been so few, the hours they had spent together, and yet so intense that practically every minute was etched upon her memory. If she concentrated hard enough, she could practically sense his presence there with her, hear his voice and feel his arm round her shoulders. Sometimes it was a comfort, sometimes it just brought it home to her even more clearly just what she might have lost.

A week later, there was a letter under the stone. Annie let out a yelp of surprise. She hadn't thought she would get anything so soon. She snatched it up and stood looking at it. The writing was unfamiliar, but the postmark sent a thrill of painful excitement through her. Noresley. His town. For a long moment she hesitated. Was it good news or bad inside? She almost didn't want to open it at all, for while she still didn't know what had happened to him, there was still hope. She stuffed it in her pocket, then almost immediately pulled it out again, ripped it open and drew out the paper. She could hardly breathe.

> *Dear Miss Cross,*
> *Thank you for your note and your kind wishes. I have to say that I was a little surprised to receive it. We are all very shocked at the news about our son and do not expect to hear anything further yet, although of course we pray that he is safe and well. I have spoken to Tom's fiancée and we have agreed that when we do receive any information, we will let you know, as you have been such a regular pen-pal.*
> *Yours sincerely,*
> *M Featherstone (Mrs)*

For a long time she just stared at it, hardly understanding. Fiancée? Tom didn't have a fiancée. He wasn't engaged. She couldn't take it in. But gradually a terrible cold realisation crept over her. This was what she had feared. Ever since he'd joined up she had worried about girls at the airfield, girls in the nearby town. So now she knew. There was someone, but it was worse than that—much worse. He had asked this other girl to marry him and he had not even told her—his pen-pal.

That horrible word—*pen-pal*—jumped off the page at her.

So that was all she counted for. Just someone he wrote to every now and again. Someone that his mother felt should be told, along with all the rest of the cycle club and the cricket club and all those others he'd gone about with. Just one of the crowd of his pals.

'I thought it was special,' she whispered. 'I thought I was special. You were to me.'

She felt utterly betrayed.

CHAPTER SEVENTEEN

IN THE wide world beyond Marsh Edge Farm, a shift in the balance of power began to be felt. Though in Britain the bombing raids went on, rationing was harder and more people, especially women, were working towards the war effort than ever before, it seemed at last that the losses and the sacrifice were not in vain.

The first good news was the victory at El Alamein. Mr Churchill made his 'end of the beginning' speech of cautious optimism and on the fifteenth of November church bells that had been silent for two and a half years were rung throughout Britain in celebration. By the end of 1942, Axis forces were losing ground in both Asia and Europe, and then just a month later the German commander surrendered to the Russians at Stalingrad, a hitherto unheard-of act for a field marshal.

But while one dictator was starting to feel the opposition bite, in his small domain at Marsh Edge, Walter Cross now reigned supreme. Any spark of rebellion that Edna had once showed had been put out by her latest miscarriage and Annie simply kept her head down and plodded through the days, leaving Walter with nobody to clash with. Not that it stopped him from lashing out with tongue or fists, but hitting a soft target did not give him quite the same level of satisfaction.

Gwen tried her hardest to cheer Annie up, even after Annie had received a note from Mrs Featherstone informing her that she and Tom's fiancée thought Annie might like to know that Tom was being treated in a German hospital.

'That means he's still alive. That's wonderful news!' Gwen cried.

'Yes,' Annie said.

She was in such turmoil that she wasn't sure what she felt. It was good—more than good—to know for sure that he hadn't died with his plane on that raid. But part of her had always believed that he wasn't dead, maybe because she hadn't seen him for so long and she was used to his being far away. Which left the other cause for despair still intact.

'So why hasn't he written to me?' she asked.

'Well—I s'pose it's difficult. He can't get paper, or he's not allowed or something,' Gwen said. 'But he's alive, that's the main thing. Where there's life, there's hope.'

'Yes—for his fiancée. I bet she's had a letter from him. His mother doesn't even say where he is, so he can't have asked her to tell me,' Annie said.

Even Gwen couldn't think of an answer to that, until one day she came bouncing up to Annie with a great big smile all over her face.

'Look what I've got for you! I couldn't risk leaving it at Silver Sands so I've saved it to give to you. There—what did I say? He's sent you a letter.'

And there it was—her name in Tom's dear familiar handwriting, on strange coarse paper. A huge hand seemed to be clutching at Annie's chest, making it hard to breathe. At last, a letter for her.

'Thank you,' she whispered.

'Aren't you going to open it?' Gwen demanded.

Annie shook her head and slipped the precious letter into her pocket.

And there it stayed. Not because she was saving a pleasure, as she used to when everything was clear and open between them, but because she hardly dared read what was inside it.

For the rest of the day she guessed at what might be waiting for her. Her emotions took a roller coaster ride as different possible contents came to mind. At times she was euphoric as she dreamed of something along the lines of, *Don't take any notice of what my mother might say—I'm definitely not engaged because you're the only one for me.* But then she tried to prepare herself for the worst by imagining his writing, *I thought I'd better send you a line as my fiancée tells me you've been asking about me.* Either way, at least she had been kicked into feeling again. Even pain was better than the dreary mud of hopelessness she had been wading in all through the winter.

She hardly heard her father's bitter comments about the six o'clock news. She cleared away the plates and washed up without even knowing she was doing it. She fetched her knitting as usual to do as they listened to the wireless, but it stayed motionless in her lap. As soon as the bedtime cocoa was drunk, she took her candle and water jug and went upstairs.

The winter wind rushed across the marshes and flung itself against the house, whistling through the window frames in icy draughts. Annie undressed, washed, put on her nightdress and bedsocks and climbed into bed, pulling the quilt up round her shoulders. She sat holding the precious letter, staring at it in the dim yellow light of the candle, as if she might decipher what was inside it if she looked for long enough.

'If you don't open it, you won't ever know,' she told herself.
With shaking fingers, she slit open the cheap paper. And
there it was. His own thoughts for her.

Dear Annie,
I'm so sorry it's taken so long to write to you. I was in
a bit of a bad way when I baled out and spent a long
time in hospital, but I'm better now and in a camp.
Conditions (here something had been blacked out by
the censor) *but I'm with a lot of chaps from all three*
services and we keep each other going. We have to go
out on work detail (more blacking out) *keeps you from*
going mad.
I hope you are well and still enjoying your outings
with Gwen. I expect the farm and Silver Sands still look
the same. I keep thinking about the happy times we had
there. It all seems a very long time ago now.
A letter from you would be a real treat.
Always your friend,
Tom.
X

The swooping emotions of the day boiled up into one
great explosion of fury. Growling like a wild beast, Annie
tore the letter into tiny pieces.

How dared he? How dared he write like that, as if nothing had happened? *Your friend,* indeed! Not even a close
enough friend to say that he had got himself engaged. Not
a mention of it. Not even telling her what it was like for him
at the moment—just those flat statements. It could almost
have been a letter from anyone, male or female, to anyone
else. A letter from her would be a *real treat*, indeed! Did he

expect her to believe that? Well, it was a treat he was going to miss, because if he couldn't be honest with her, then he wasn't worth writing to.

She blew out the candle, turned her face to the pillow and cried herself to sleep.

Edna Cross was beginning to find that life was bearable again. She wasn't happy, but then she had given up expecting happiness a long time ago. Generally, the absence of pain and fear was enough. When Walter was out of the house, an oppressive weight lifted from her shoulders. She could find a small sense of satisfaction in a cake that had come out well, or a piece of sewing that looked pretty. The highlights of her life were visits from her customers, especially Mrs Sutton. She didn't count Mrs Sutton as a friend, for she had far too low an opinion of herself to think that such an important, well-off woman could possibly wish to befriend her. But she did look forward to her coming to the farmhouse. Or had, until the last miscarriage. That had left her foundering in a grey fog of depression that robbed her of any interest in living at all. Only her fear of her husband kept her getting up each day and going through the motions of existence.

But as the winter days started to lengthen, she found that the cloud was lifting a little. She found an extra brown egg in the barn and thought that it would be nice to be able to bake a cake now rather than scones. She devised a clever way of making a child's dress out of an old skirt and was touched by her customer's delight and praise. She stopped to listen to the blackbird's song.

When Annie came in from the yard at the end of a long rainy day, Edna looked at her properly for the first time in well over a year. Her little girl had grown up, she realised.

Not only was Annie taller than Edna now, she had a woman's face and figure. Racing after this discovery came the painful one that her daughter looked tired and unhappy. Her face might be rosy from the cold, but there was no youthful life to her. With a shock, Edna realised that this was more than just the effect of hard work and living with Walter. There was something else. Her baby needed her help.

It was difficult to find a time when they were alone together. Edna had to wait until Walter had, most unusually, gone to a War Ag meeting with some of the neighbouring farmers. Then she made a fresh pot of tea, opened the front of the range up to let out a nice blast of heat and sat down by the hearth with Annie to enjoy an evening without Walter. She pressed a cup of tea into Annie's hands and sat anxiously studying her. She was such a pretty girl, with her round elfin face and her big blue eyes and her fair hair with its natural wave, the image of what she had been at the same age. She wanted a better fate for Annie.

'You're looking peaky, dear,' she said. 'Are you feeling all right?'

'I'm fine,' Annie said.

'Are you sure? I thought… I've not been a good mother this last… I've not been looking out for you the way I should…'

'You've not been well,' Annie said.

Edna reached over and took Annie's free hand.

'You've been a good daughter to me. You've looked after me and I've not… The thing is, I've been…' She hesitated. It was hard for her to put into words how it had been for her since that night she'd miscarried. And then a biblical phrase came to her, and it seemed to describe it very well. 'I've been walking in the valley of the shadow of death. It's been…hard…'

'I know,' Annie said.

Edna hoped fervently that she would never know. She wouldn't wish that on anyone.

'But I'm coming out of it now, and I want to help you. You've had to manage for yourself all this time without a proper mother. There's something wrong, isn't there? You're not your usual self. You can tell me. Have you fallen out with Gwen? Is that it?'

Annie shook her head slowly.

'No, no—Gwennie's been a wizard friend.'

'What, then? Is it something to do with—with your father?'

Try as she might, she couldn't stop the squeaky note of fear entering her voice when she referred to Walter.

'No more than usual.'

'So—' Edna racked her brain. She knew so little about Annie's private life, such as it was. Most of the week she was here on the farm. One afternoon a week she went into town to do the shopping and pick up and deliver Edna's sewing work. One evening a week she generally went to the pictures with Gwen. Sometimes she went out for a walk by herself in the evening. Could she have met someone else? Could she—?

'It isn't—I mean—have you—is there a young man?'

The last words tumbled out apologetically. For surely Annie couldn't be courting, not at her age? When Edna tried to remember just how old her daughter was, she couldn't work it out immediately. It was a shock to realise that she was sixteen and a half.

Annie meantime had become very still. She was staring into the fire. Edna guessed she had stumbled on the root of the problem.

'You can tell me,' she said gently. 'Who is it? Isn't he treating you like he ought to?'

The thought of Annie suffering as she suffered at the hands of some man was almost too much to bear.

'He's—he's in Germany,' Annie whispered.

'He's a Jerry?' Edna squealed.

'No—' A brief ghost of a smile crossed Annie's face. 'No, he's an airman, a British airman. He was shot down.'

'Ah, poor lad. No wonder you're so upset. What a terrible thing to happen. And them so brave too, flying all that way in the dark. And to think that when we hear them go over, it might have been your young man up there—'

Edna's mind didn't know which way to go first. Annie's revelations opened up so many new thoughts, so many questions.

'How did you get to know him? There aren't any airfields near here,' she said. 'Or is he a local boy? Who is he?'

'He used to stay at Silver Sands,' Annie said.

'Silver Sands—the little chalet? The Suttons' place?'

Annie nodded.

Edna turned this over in her head.

'But it's been shut up for months. Ever since the Suttons sold it.'

'We got in a window. Nobody ever knew.'

Edna was about to say that they shouldn't have acted like a pair of burglars when something in Annie's voice stopped her. The girl's expression was soft now as she looked into the coals glowing in the range.

'For a whole week he stayed there, and I went to see him every evening. We were like Romeo and Juliet, you know? I went and borrowed the play from the library. Their parents didn't want them to be together, and in the end they died.'

Edna was not sure what she was talking about, but she did latch on to one certainty. She patted Annie's hand.

'He'll be all right though, your lad. He'll come home when this dreadful war is over, you'll see.'

'Yes, but…not to see me…' Annie's face crumpled and her voice rose rapidly into a barely controlled wail. 'He's getting married to someone else, and he never even told me—!'

Edna gathered her daughter into her arms and listened as the whole sorry story came out between bouts of crying.

'There, there,' she said soothingly, stroking Annie's head. 'How could he do that, now? All that time, and you waiting for him. It's not right.'

Her heart ached with pity and anger that some boy had hurt her dear daughter so cruelly. Her Annie was the sweetest, kindest girl and she'd been taken advantage of.

'He's not worth breaking your heart for. You'll get over it, you'll see,' she said.

Annie slipped down to kneel on the floor with her head in her mother's lap.

'I won't,' she sobbed. 'There's nobody else like him.'

There seemed to be no consoling her. Edna began to be concerned that Walter might be coming back. She took Annie up to bed like she used to when she was a little girl, and tucked her in with a hot water bottle. She kissed her goodnight.

'Maybe it will all look better in the morning,' she said.

But she knew they were empty words. If there was one thing that Edna had learnt, it was that where men were concerned, nothing was ever better in the morning or at any other time. What she didn't know was what to do about it.

The dreary cold days of the back end of winter dragged by and the problem still nagged at Edna along with a sense of guilt at not having seen earlier that Annie was so unhappy. It seemed to her that if she only knew a little more about this lad she might be able to help.

When Ivy Sutton next came to see her, bringing a dress
to be altered, it seemed the ideal opportunity. Edna made all
the right noises as she was treated to the usual long mono-
logue about how wonderful all four of the Sutton children
were. John had been made a lance corporal in the army,
Beryl was her father's right hand at the factory, little Timmy
was earning heaps of praise from his teacher at school and
Jeffrey—not a lot was said about Jeffrey, except that his father was looking forward to having him working in the family firm too.

Edna finished the pinning and marking and made tea
while Ivy dressed.

'Do you ever hear anything from that family you had
staying at Silver Sands?' she asked, passing a plate of freshly
baked cinnamon buns.

'Silver Sands? What, the Featherstones?' Ivy asked, taking a bun and biting greedily into the sweet spicy treat.

Edna nodded. 'The last ones you had there,' she said. She
didn't take a cake herself. They were needed for Walter's tea.

'Yes, the Featherstones. Such a nice family! So genteel
and such nicely brought up children. It was a pleasure to
have people like them staying there. Not all of the families
we had there were so pleasant, you know. Some of them
were very common. Left the place in a terrible state. It makes
you wonder how they live at home.'

'Mmm,' Edna agreed. 'Terrible. But the Featherstones
were nice, were they? Their—er—their boy, he was a decent
lad, then?'

Ivy swallowed, took a sip of tea and nodded emphatically.

'Young Tom? Oh, yes, charming boy. So polite. He went
into the air force, you know, became a navigator. Such a
worry for poor Mr and Mrs Featherstone. They were very

proud of him, of course. Well, who wouldn't be? We're all proud of our boys going to do their bit. But some of those aircraft do get lost. Not as many as the enemy ones we shoot down, of course, but even so—why do you ask?'

The question took Edna by surprise.

'Oh—er—my Annie heard he was a POW in Germany,' she said, unable to come out with a suitable lie.

'Your Annie did? How on earth did she know that?'

'He—er—he wrote to her,' Edna confessed.

'He wrote to your Annie? Well, I never. How extraordinary. Well, if you'll allow me to give you some advice, Edna, and you know I mean this kindly, but if I were you, I shouldn't encourage it. Firstly, Annie's far too young to be writing to servicemen, however nice their families might be. I certainly wouldn't allow my Beryl to do such a thing. Girls are growing up far too fast these days. The things you hear! Going and drinking in public houses and making exhibitions of themselves, and smoking in the street. I don't know what the world's coming to. I'm sure you wouldn't want your Annie to be thought fast.'

'Oh, no, of course not,' Edna agreed meekly.

Ivy reached for another bun.

'And secondly,' she said, carrying on her train of thought, 'the Featherstones are an important family in their town. Business people, you know. It would only end in tears, you know. These unequal matches always do.'

'Yes,' Edna agreed again.

She hadn't the heart to say that it already had ended in tears.

It only went to prove that Ivy Sutton was right about most things. It was for the best that Mrs Featherstone had told Annie about her son's fiancée. Otherwise poor Annie would have been living in a fool's paradise.

So when she found a strange letter in the post one day addressed to Annie with foreign writing on it, she whipped it into her apron pocket before Walter could see it, and presented him with the bill that had come with it. She hardly heard his tirade over the price of things as she debated with herself what to do.

It had to be from him, this Tom Featherstone. No one else ever wrote to any of them, and certainly not from abroad. There was no point in upsetting Annie all over again, Edna decided. The kindest thing would be to destroy it. She waited until she had the house to herself again, opened up the door of the range and thrust the letter into the flames.

'There,' she said out loud. 'That's the end of you. Now you can't hurt my little girl no more.'

CHAPTER EIGHTEEN

AROUND him, Tom could hear the familiar snoring and grunting of a hut full of men. Bright moonlight was flooding through the windows, illuminating the hunched bodies beneath their grey regulation issue blankets. Life was not so grim now that summer was here. The nights were no longer penetratingly cold. The rations were slightly better quality. Even the guards seemed better tempered.

Tom raised his head and looked through the window. It was practically clear as day out there—silver light and thick shadows. You could read a newspaper, if by some miracle a newspaper could find its way here. The forest was still black and menacing, though. He hated that thick wall of trees. It seemed to lean in on him, imprisoning him more surely than the barbed wire.

'Bombers' moon,' a voice whispered close to him.

It was another airman, a Canadian named Douglas in the next bunk. Tom got on well with Doug, at first liking him simply because he had had such a good time in Canada doing his crew training, and later because he was good company.

'They'll be out on ops tonight,' he agreed.

He pictured the planes lumbering through the cloudless skies, keeping close formation in the stream, bearing their full loads towards the target for the night. Europe would be lying silvered and wide open beneath them, but they in turn would be clearly seen against the moon and the stars. Perhaps even now they were lining up for the final run, while the enemy flung everything they had at them. Even in the silence of the forest, he could hear the noise, feel the tension. His weak leg ached in sympathy, the nerves jumping and twitching uncontrollably. Silently, he sent a message of luck to his colleagues in the night sky.

'Lucky bastards,' Doug said. 'Wish I was still there with them.'

'Yes. At least they'll be getting a pint when they get home.'

It was the acceptable response, and he genuinely longed to be out of the dreary limbo that was prison camp life, but just a part of him, a small voice of honesty, was glad simply to be safe. He was lucky to be alive, he knew that. Lucky to be in one piece. It had been touch and go. On top of the bullet and shrapnel wounds, he had smashed his leg up badly on landing. The doctors at the German military hospital could have amputated it rather than going to the trouble of fixing it. The continual dull ache was a small price to pay.

'They're flying. They're doing something. They're not cooped up here day after flaming day,' Doug was saying.

Tom merely grunted in reply. His mind was still on his last op. He had no idea if any of the rest of the crew had survived. He hoped that at least some of them were sitting out the war in other Stalags.

'This place is getting to me. I'm going to go mad if I have to stay here much longer. I'm a man, not a flaming farm animal,' Doug said.

His voice had risen above a whisper. There were grumbles from nearby bunks. They all subsided into silence again.

Tom was too wide awake to go back to sleep. He lay on his back and thought about the letters that must be due to arrive soon. His mother, his sister, even his father wrote regularly, telling him about all the things that had happened back in Noresley. He read them over time and time again, for even the most boring little details were welcome as a reminder of home. In his mind he could open his front door, walk down the street, buy a paper at the corner shop. Simple things, taken for granted once but impossible now that they were nothing better than caged animals, as Doug would have it.

Moira wrote even more faithfully than his mother. Her letters were always lively and chatty. Better still, she always told him how much she was missing him and promised to prove it the moment he came home. It was enough to fire up a whole chain of wonderful fantasies.

The one person who did not write was the one he most wanted a letter from. Annie. He had sent letters to her, via Gwen and direct to the farm, so he was almost certain that at least one of them must have been received. But not one note had he got in reply, not even a Dear John. It was as if she did not exist. He couldn't understand it. Sometimes he thought that she must have met someone else and was no longer interested in him, even as a friend. At other times he worried that something terrible had happened to her. A stray bomb might have fallen on the farm, or her father might have completely lost control and beaten her to death. The worst of it was not knowing. Annie had been a big part of his life ever since the day they had met. He couldn't bear to think that he would never see her again. Perhaps the next batch of mail would be the one that would bring that long awaited letter from her, explaining everything.

As the long hours of the night passed, Tom thought about that week he had spent at Silver Sands. When he finally fell asleep, it was Annie he chased through his dreams. At least he knew it was her, though he couldn't see her. She was a phantom figure in a swirling mist, always just ahead of him, for ever out of reach.

The next day brought a break in the deadly routine. Right after *Appel* one of the men tried to make a break for it by hiding in a supply truck, but was discovered in a routine search. The first Tom knew of it was a sudden flurry of activity by the gates. Men were shouting, guard dogs barking, all the drums and boxes on the truck were dragged out and thoroughly searched, and then a man Tom recognised from the next hut was marched off towards the Commandant's office.

'Hard luck, mate!' Tom called out.

'Good try!' someone else shouted.

Others joined in.

'Better luck next time!'

'Don't let the bastards get you down.'

The guards rounded on them, trying to disperse them. The prisoners refused to be dispersed.

Tom felt a hand touch his shoulder. Doug was speaking urgently in his ear.

'Cover for me.'

Tom did not look round. Instead, he redoubled his efforts at shouting, taunting the guards so as to distract them. It worked. One of them came over and jabbed a rifle in his chest, then motioned with it that he should move.

'You. Come. Now.'

Tom spread his hands in mock innocence.

'Why? What's the problem?'

Around him, other men protested.

'What's he done?'

'Leave him be!'

And then there were more shouts behind him in German and a clatter of machine gun fire. A sick feeling sank through Tom's guts. The prisoners fell silent and turned as one man, each of them knowing what had happened. Just feet beyond the open gate, Doug lay dead in the dust, blood still welling from the bullet wounds in his back.

Their outburst of protest was quelled in minutes. They were all confined to their huts for twenty-four hours. There were heated arguments in Tom's hut as opinion divided sharply between those who admired Doug for attempting a break and those who thought he had been just stupid to do it on the spur of the moment like that, when he hadn't a hope in hell of succeeding.

When they were let out again, the Commandant had them all lined up and lectured them for half an hour in his slow, heavily accented English on the futility of trying to escape.

'Yeah, but it's worth it just to rattle you lot, ain't it?' the man next to Tom muttered under his breath.

'Not when you're dead, it isn't,' Tom replied.

As an extra punishment, the mail that had arrived while they had been confined was not given out for a further twenty-four hours. The loss of his friend made Tom long even more for news from home. This was going to be the one, he decided. This time he would get a letter from Annie.

His name was called. He went forward. Two letters were handed to him. Eagerly, he scanned the handwriting, only to be disappointed. One was from his mother, the other from Moira. Anger came to his aid. Annie didn't care for him. So he no longer cared for her. He wasn't wasting precious thoughts on someone who couldn't be bothered to write one single line to him. Unlike Moira. Moira never missed a chance to let him know that he was always in her heart. Moira was waiting faithfully, just for him. He opened her letter first.

CHAPTER NINETEEN

March 1945

'WHAT'S that?'

Annie paused in her job of heaving the churns of milk on to the roadside platform from which they were collected each day. She looked down the Wittlesham road to where the traffic noise was coming from. There were vehicles in the distance.

'What's what?' Walter growled. 'Get on with it, you useless girl. Shift y'self.'

Annie did as she was bid, but kept half an eye on the road. It was usually so quiet that anything coming along was of interest.

'Looks like a convoy. It's certainly something military,' she said.

Her father just grunted.

The road ran in a gentle curve round the old coastline and as the Marsh Edge Farm land was so flat and there were no trees or hedges in the way, Annie could see for some distance. There was definitely a short line of lorries and armoured vehicles approaching, led by a Jeep with a flag fluttering from its bonnet.

'They're Yanks!' she cried, unable to control her excitement even though her father was beside her. 'Look, you can see the Stars and Stripes.'

'Useless airy-fairy lot,' Walter snorted.

'They're helping us win the war,' Annie dared to contradict.

'Ha. Only come in when they were forced to. Like last time. Let us take the worst of it, then come along and claim all the glory. Got no time for 'em.'

Annie didn't try to argue further. It would only invite a clout round the ear. But she did pretend not to hear her father when he told her to come along. She wanted to see them go past.

The small convoy swept by, all five vehicles packed with sharp-uniformed GIs. Annie just had to wave. She couldn't help herself. Rushing along the road like that, they seemed to embody the optimism that everyone now felt. Soon the war had to be over. Everything was going our way.

The GIs waved back, grinning with their strong white teeth. One of them had red hair, Annie noticed. She only just stopped herself from wondering out loud whether they had any gum or nylons to spare. She'd heard all about nylons. They were like silk stockings only stronger and even more glamorous. If you wore a pair of them, you felt like a film star.

'They must be from that new camp,' she said.

Her head swayed and her ears rang as her father caught her with the back of his hand.

'Stop acting like a bitch on heat,' he growled. 'And with them lot too. Only come here to go over and do the mopping up.'

Annie turned away. She knew when it was time to obey.

Today life seemed brighter than usual. The farm looked fat and prosperous, a far cry from the place it had been at the beginning of the war. Her father had been forced to adopt modern farming methods, the quality and quantity of their crops and milk yields had increased tremendously and everything they produced was bought at a fair rate. Not that Annie got any credit or any profit out of it, but at least she felt that she had done her bit towards winning the war. People might have been on short commons but there had been enough food to go round. The farmers of Britain had managed to feed the population.

And now winter was coming to an end, the war was coming to an end and she was going out dancing tonight. Annie flew through her tasks, ate her tea, did the evening chores and raced upstairs to change. What to wear was a great problem. Even if she had something suitable for a dance, she couldn't have worn it since she couldn't possibly admit to her father where she was off to. He had never been keen on her going to the pictures with a girlfriend, so he certainly wouldn't hold with her meeting with young men. Annie wasn't even going to risk asking. She knew what the answer would be.

She put on her only smart skirt and blouse, both made by her mother so they fitted beautifully. Then she got her one pair of summer sandals out of the cupboard, brushed her hair and fixed it up at the sides with combs and looked at herself in the tiny spotted mirror. The skirt and blouse showed off her small waist and full breasts nicely and, after all, very few girls had proper dance dresses these days. More than a dress, she longed for nylons and high heels. She had good legs, but nobody could look glamorous in lisle stockings and flat sandals. Still, it would just have to do. She bundled the sandals into a shopping bag together with the combs from her hair, a brush and her precious lipstick that she had bought eighteen months ago and used only for special occasions. Then she put on her sensible lace-up shoes and her mac. Nobody would know that she was going dancing.

Before she left, her eyes were drawn to the window and the view beyond, across the flat fields to the sea wall, the water—and Silver Sands. Once she had got ready like this, but ten times more breathless and bubbling with excitement, to run across the fields to meet Tom. However much she told herself that if he didn't care for her, then she didn't care for him, still the mere sight of the little wooden chalet never failed to stir her. She had been so happy then. Those had been Technicolor days, full of wonderful possibilities. For the umpteenth time she wondered where Tom was now. What if the part of Germany where he was imprisoned was nearer to the advancing Russian army than the Allied troops? Would he still get home all right?

'That's for his darling fiancée to worry about,' she told herself out loud, and tried to push the niggling worry away.

Half an hour later she met a group of girls from Sutton's outside the Palais. It wasn't the same since Gwen had been called up, but at least she had someone to go out with.

They were all in a state of high excitement.

'Annie, Annie!' they shrieked. 'The Yanks are here! Come on, we're missing all the fun!'

Eyes bright, lips parted, the girls were ready for the night of their lives. After years of all the young men disappearing the moment they were old enough to join up, of having to quickstep with other girls and make do with the army rejects, now they had a glut of men. And not boring local men, but big, virile, glamorous Americans. They were beside themselves.

Annie was caught up in group hysteria.

'The Yanks? At our dance?'

'Dozens of them! Enough for everyone!'

'Oh, she doesn't need one. She's keeping Little Jeffy with his tongue hanging out.'

'I am *not!*' Annie shrieked. 'I can't get rid of the silly boy.'

Jeffrey Sutton was one of the minor plagues of her life. He was always hanging around, asking her to dance.

'He's only got eyes for you—' one of the girls sang.

'Oh, stop it!'

'Come on,' another girl interrupted, 'all the best ones will be gone.'

Squealing and giggling, they pushed their way into the cloakrooms, did each other's hair and passed around scarce lipsticks and powder, each girl eyeing all the others up to assess just where she stood in the pecking order. At last, they were ready for the fray.

The dance hall was full. Its pre-war splendour was fading and peeling now, but still it had a magic about it, with its blue and cream decor, ornate lighting and sprung floor. Up on the stage, a five-piece combo was struggling to sound like a full dance band as it belted out 'Goodnight Irene'. On the floor, a widely assorted crowd was waltzing. There were older men and adolescent boys in suits, a few women in dance dresses, a lot more women of all ages in whatever finery they could lay their hands on, and a sea of uniforms. That was all much as usual. What was different was the proportion of males to females. For once, there were hardly any women left sitting round the edges of the room on chipped gilt chairs, the sad wallflowers watching the others enjoy themselves, for there were more than enough men to go round.

'Wow!' Annie breathed.

For there in front of them were what looked like hundreds

of GIs in their smart uniforms, with slicked-down hair and eager expressions. Most of them were already dancing, but there were still plenty hanging about in groups, at the bar or at the edge of the dance floor, obviously looking for partners.

'Hold on to your hats, girls! We're in for a whoopee time,' said one of Annie's friends.

In as many seconds as it took to walk on to a dance floor, the girls were surrounded by gorgeous young men, all of them meticulously polite and all speaking in that glamorous accent that the girls had only heard at the pictures before. One of them, Annie noticed, had red hair, but he was already speaking to one of the other girls.

'Good evening, miss,' a tall boy with a crew cut said to her. 'Would you be so kind as to have the rest of this dance with me?'

'Dairnse' he pronounced it. Annie was enchanted.

'Thank you, I'd love to,' she gasped, and was whisked on to the floor.

Her partner was called Brad, and he whirled her round to the remaining bars of 'Goodnight Irene', never once treading on her feet. After him, she danced a quickstep with Howard, a foxtrot with Bernard and a waltz with Sammy. They were all good dancers and all had excellent manners. Annie felt as if she was being treated like a film star. And then the band leader made a surprise announcement.

'In honour of our American guests, the next number is a jitterbug.'

There was a wave of squeals, groans and applause from the audience. Annie found herself being addressed by the redheaded GI.

'Excuse me, miss, do you jitterbug?'

'I don't know,' Annie admitted. 'I've never done it.'

'Then now's the time to try, miss. I'm an expert. Just follow me and you'll do real dandy.'

How could she refuse? The band launched into a fast syncopated number with more enthusiasm than skill, and Annie's new partner led her on to the floor.

'I'm Bobby Joe,' he introduced himself. 'And you're the prettiest little lady on the floor.'

'I'm Annie,' said Annie, dazzled.

'It's my lucky day, Annie. I feel it in my bones.'

After that, she had no breath left for talking. Bobby Joe whirled her round, back, under his arm, in and out, into his arms for a few moments, then back spinning round again. Annie squealed and gasped and found she could trust him. She only had to have the correct hand out to be grasped and he would catch her and send her skipping and whirling round again. The room and the people around her became a blur. There was just the music, the excitement and Bobby Joe, playing her like a child's toy.

When the number ended, he swept her into his arms for a last turn, while around them people were applauding their performance. Annie was pink-cheeked, breathless and pulsing with the wild thrill of it.

'That was wonderful!' she gasped.

'You were wonderful,' Bobby Joe told her. 'Are you sure you've never done that before?'

'Quite sure.'

'I'd never believe it. You're a natural.'

He gave her waist a squeeze and released her. Annie felt a sudden drop of disappointment.

'You were right. You are an expert,' she said, to hold his attention.

'That's not the only thing I'm an expert at,' Bobby Joe

told her as he put a hand under her elbow to take her to a seat at the side of the room. 'Save me another for later?'

Out of the corner of her eye, Annie spotted Beryl. She was gazing at her with naked envy. Annie's happiness was complete.

'You bet,' she said.

Bobby Joe laughed. 'You're a doll,' he said, and went off into the milling crowd.

Annie had hardly sat down before she was approached by one of the local boys.

'Are you free for this one, Annie, or do you only dance with Yanks now?'

Behind him, Annie could see Jeff Sutton coming over with a hopeful expression on his face. Jeff, this one, or one of the Yanks? Such riches, to have a choice of men to dance with! Annie was feeling so warm towards the whole world that she agreed to dance with the man who had just asked her, even though he didn't have any of the allure of the Americans. She soon regretted it. Her partner complained throughout the entire number.

'You girls were all happy enough to dance with us before, but now these Yanks are here we don't get a look-in,' he told her. 'I'd heard what it was like when they arrived in a place— all the women going crazy for Yanks and running off with them. Married women too! Now I know it's true. And what's so wonderful about them anyway? That jitterbug, I ask you, what sort of a dance is that? More like something out of the jungle if you ask me.'

'It was fun,' Annie maintained. 'Smashing fun. The best thing I've done in ages.'

Her partner snorted. 'The Yanks might be good at that sort of thing, but you can't beat a civilised dance.'

Annie couldn't agree. The slow foxtrot might be civilised, but it didn't make your heart beat and your blood rush like the jitterbug.

'You're just cross 'cause you can't do it,' she said.

'I wouldn't want to do it,' her partner assured her, treading on her toes.

They shuffled through the rest of the number in silence. Annie looked over his shoulder at the rest of the couples, trying to see who Bobby Joe was dancing with. She spotted him foxtrotting with one of the gang from Sutton's. He caught her eye and smiled. Annie felt that deep stirring that had lain dormant ever since Tom had gone away and knew that she was alive again.

She got away from her partner the moment the number ended and was grabbed by one of the Sutton's girls.

'Ooh, Annie, isn't this fun? I'm having the time of my life here. Aren't they super dancers? That Brad is just so handsome. I think I'm in love.'

'You were in love with Jimmy last week,' Annie teased her.

'Jimmy, ha! He's got two left feet. It's Brad for me now. Here—where did you learn to jitterbug? I didn't dare.'

'Bobby Joe says I'm a natural,' Annie told her.

'Ooh! So Bobby Joe's the one, is he?'

'Not necessarily,' Annie said.

But her eyes were scanning the room for his red head, and her breath came a little faster as she saw him coming towards her across the floor. Two more GIs appeared and asked the girls to dance and Annie hastily accepted. As Bobby Joe came up to her, she stepped on to the floor with her new partner, giving Bobby Joe a regretful smile. She was fizzing with excitement. For the first time in her life, she was playing the flirting game and it was intoxicating.

She allowed Bobby Joe to catch up with her for the last dance before the interval. Feet flashing in perfect unison, they quickstepped round the floor to 'Chattanooga Choo-Choo'.

'We were told we'd have a real good time at a British dance. Now I know it's true,' Bobby Joe said, fishtailing slickly round a slower couple.

'The band's pretty awful,' Annie said.

Bobby Joe didn't deny this. 'But the company makes up for it,' he said.

'How long are you boys here for?' Annie asked, for surely this abundance wasn't going to last for ever.

'Who knows? Until they send us over to Europe, I guess. Until then, we're all out to enjoy ourselves.'

Until they were sent to Europe. Annie shivered, despite the heat of a room full of dancing bodies. For a moment, she thought of Tom, somewhere in Germany waiting for the Russians to come.

'Why so sad? I thought you were a girl who liked fun,' Bobby Joe said.

Annie gave herself a mental shake.

'I am,' she said with her brightest smile.

At the end of the number, he led her into the bar and managed to get drinks by way of a buddy of his who had got to the front of the queue. He handed Annie her lemonade and looked doubtfully at the contents of his glass.

'This is beer? It's warm,' he said, taking a cautious sip. 'Tastes like—well, I shan't say in front of a lady. My idea of a beer is something ice-cool and pale.'

'You're lucky to get that. They often run out,' Annie told him.

Bobby Joe shook his head in amazement.

He wasn't particularly handsome. He had very pale skin with a dusting of freckles across his snub nose, ice-blue eyes and a wide American smile. It was the total effect of him—so big and broad-shouldered and confident—that overwhelmed Annie. He was a different type of male altogether from the ones she had been used to.

'Smoke?' he asked, bringing out a packet of Camels.

Annie shook her head.

'Mind if I do?'

'No—you go ahead.'

He flicked at a lighter.

Annie was fascinated. 'I've only ever seen one of them at the pictures,' she said.

'The pictures?' Bobby Joe looked puzzled. 'What pictures—? Oh, you mean the movies. Are you a fan?'

'Oh, yes,' Annie breathed. 'I go as often as I can.'

They discussed films and stars. Bobby Joe had seen features that hadn't even come to London yet, let alone Wittlesham. Annie drank it all in. He was so sophisticated, so worldly-wise.

'I feel like a country bumpkin,' she said.

Bobby Joe leaned forward and closed a hand over hers.

'You're a cute little English rose,' he said.

After that, neither of them danced with anyone else. Foxtrot, tango, quickstep, waltz, then another fast and furious jitterbug. Bobby Joe and Annie showed everyone else how it should be done. Annie was walking on air.

She made a bolt for the ladies before the last waltz. Beryl was in there applying powder to her shiny nose.

'You want to watch it,' she said to Annie.

'Watch what?' Annie said.

She looked at their two reflections in the mirror. Beryl had not lost any weight as she'd grown up but she did now have her hair in a more becoming style. With a surge of triumph,

Annie confirmed what she had always known—that she was by far the prettier of the two. It wasn't just that Beryl didn't have such nice features, it was her expression. All hoity-toity. It must put the boys off.

'Those Americans,' Beryl said. 'You can't trust them an inch. They're only after one thing.'

'What's the matter? Didn't any of them ask you to dance?' Annie said. She applied a smear of her precious lipstick.

'I wouldn't want to. I value my reputation. I don't want to be known as a little tart. Someone who does the jitterbug.'

Annie smiled at her reflection. A flushed, excited face smiled back at her.

'That was such fun,' she enthused.

She knew Beryl was just jealous.

'Got anyone nice lined up for the last waltz?' she asked.

'Of course. A decent English fellow.'

'Oh, hard luck. Hope your toes don't get too trodden on. Those Americans are such gentlemen, such perfect manners,' Annie told her. 'Must fly!'

And she skipped off back to Bobby Joe.

The last waltz was a romantic dream of swooping melody and the two of them in perfect unison. As the last notes died away, Bobby Joe took Annie's hand.

'Will you let me take you to the movies tomorrow?' he asked.

Annie had never been let out for two evenings on the trot. But she wasn't going to let that stop her.

'Depends what we're going to see,' she said, deliberately offhand, though her heart was thumping with anticipation.

'There's *Love Story* on in town,' Bobby Joe said persuasively. 'You said you wanted to see that.'

'Oh, well—all right, then,' Annie agreed, as if conferring a huge favour.

She had not felt so feverishly, dangerously happy since that last summer before Tom had joined up. At last, her life was opening up. She had a chance to have fun. It might not last very long, and she was going to wring the last ounce of enjoyment out of it.

CHAPTER TWENTY

'YOU'RE going out again? He won't like it.'

Edna put down the scrubbing brush and sat back on her heels. Her face creased into an even more anxious expression than usual.

'I'm only going to visit one of the Sutton's girls,' Annie lied. 'Vera. You know, Vera Thomson. I was at school with her.'

It was best, she judged, not to tell her mother anything. She worried enough as it was.

'It's a pity little Gwen went away. She was a nice friend for you,' Edna said.

'Yes,' Annie agreed. 'I really miss Gwennie. She's having a wonderful time in the WAACs.'

But for the first time since her friend had left Wittlesham, Annie didn't envy her a bit. Gwen might be in the Women's Auxilliary Army Corps but she didn't have Americans camped near her.

Edna gave her a watery smile. 'I'm so glad you never got called up, dear. I don't know what I'd do without you here.'

This time, Annie didn't go through the familiar loop of regret, envy, guilt that the thought of leaving Marsh Edge Farm brought on. With her date with Bobby Joe beckoning that evening, she was glad she had stayed at home.

'Oh, well, I couldn't of stood all that marching,' she said.

'You're such a good girl. Listen, we've got some extra eggs; I'll do you a nice boiled egg for your tea. How'd you like that?'

'That'd be nice,' Annie said absently. She was running through the contents of her wardrobe in her mind yet again and trying to decide what to wear for Bobby Joe.

'He likes a boiled egg. That'll put him in a good mood. You're not really going out this evening, are you?' Edna asked.

'I'll get all my jobs done first. He won't have anything to be angry about,' Annie said.

Edna looked doubtful. They both knew that Walter could find fault even when everything had been done perfectly.

'He won't like it, though,' she said.

'Then he'll have to lump it,' Annie said.

Nothing, not even her father, was going to stop her from being outside the Roxy to meet her big American.

Edna looked frightened. 'I wish you wouldn't, dear.'

Annie tiptoed over the washed area of floor and kissed her mother on the top of her head.

'Don't worry, Mum. It'll be all right. After all, I'm only going to see an old schoolfriend.'

There would be hell to pay if her father found out, but for once she was glad that he hated all the other farmers and never talked to anyone unless he had to. It meant that there was very little risk of him hearing about what she was up to on the grapevine.

Just as Edna predicted, Walter did not like the idea of Annie being out two nights running, but he was in what for him was a good mood and didn't actually forbid her to go. He made it as difficult as possible and she missed the bus, so that she had to cycle like a woman possessed to get into town anything close to on time. As she flew up the High Street, standing on the pedals, she could see Bobby Joe in his smart uniform standing waiting outside the cinema. Cheeks scarlet, lungs pumping, she swerved down a side street before he could catch sight of her. She flung her bike against a wall, took out her comb, tidied her hair and tried to steady her breath and her pounding heart. Then she made herself walk slowly round the corner.

Immediately, Bobby Joe saw her, waved and came hurrying up to meet her.

'Hey, am I glad to see you! I was beginning to think you'd blown me out,' he said. 'Here, these are for you.'

He held out a box of chocolates.

Annie gasped. 'For me? What—the whole box?'

Bobby Joe laughed. 'Well, I won't say no if you offer me one,' he said.

Annie went bright red. 'I don't mean— Of course they're for sharing—but—a whole box! There must be at least a pound in there.'

Annie gazed at the gift in wonder. It was not just the excess of chocolates. The box itself was so luxurious. It was made of thick gold-coloured card and had a picture of a bouquet of flowers on the top, and it was tied up with pink satin ribbon. Annie ran her fingertips over it.

'No one's ever given me anything like this before,' she said.

Bobby Joe shook his head in disbelief. 'It's only a box of candies,' he said. 'Shall we go in? The first picture's about to start.'

'Oh! Yes, I'm sorry I'm late. It was a bit difficult to get away,' Annie explained. 'My dad—'

'Got a strict poppa, have you?' Bobby Joe asked, all sympathy.

'A bit,' Annie said, pushing the truth.

'I guess he just wants to look out for his little girl. My pop's the same with my sister.'

'You've got a sister?'

It was strange to think of his belonging to a family.

'Sure have. But she's not as cute as you.'

Cute. Nobody had ever called her cute before. Annie shivered with delight. Every anxious moment of getting away from home was worth it for this. She looked up at Bobby Joe. Here she was, Annie Cross, walking along Wittlesham High Street with a real GI, carrying a monster box of chocolates. She hardly needed to go to the cinema. It felt as if she had stepped into a film herself.

Bobby Joe bought the most expensive seats. They settled down and Annie opened the wonderful chocolate box. The rich aroma of cocoa rose and enveloped her. She breathed it in, her mouth watering, then reached for the tray. As she prised a huge delicious sweet from its moulded nest, Bobby Joe's fingers brushed hers, sending quivers up her arm. Rich, velvety chocolate caramel melted in her mouth, oozed over her tongue and slid down her throat.

'Mmm—' she purred, savouring every last particle.

'You like them?' Bobby Joe asked.

'They're wonderful, just wonderful.'

Nothing as luscious as this had ever passed her lips before. Even before the war and rationing, even at Christmas, a box of chocolates had never been found at Marsh Edge Farm. She had occasionally been offered one when round at Gwen's house and had agonised for ages over her choice, but those ones had not been as delicious as these, and now she had a whole tray to share with just one other person. The pleasure was almost too much to bear. She ran her fingers

over the different shapes—long, round, smooth, textured—
which one to have next? It was such a gorgeous dilemma.

When the lights came up, Annie realised that she had hardly
noticed the first feature, beyond its being an old comedy.

'I saw that one back in Illinois,' Bobby Joe told her.

'Illinois—' Annie repeated.

It sounded the most exotic place in the world.

'Is that where you come from?'

'Sure do. Town called Fourways, on account of it was
built where the highway crossed the railroad.'

'Is it in the Wild West?' Annie asked. She had no idea
where in the U.S. the state of Illinois was to be found.

Bobby Joe laughed out loud. 'What, do you mean do the
cowboys and the Indians shoot it out round the wagon train?'

'Sort of,' Annie muttered, embarrassed. Her only knowledge of what his country was like came from films.

Bobby Joe patted her arm. 'You're just so cute. No, it's
just a regular town, honey. Got everything in it a town should
have, just like your Wittlesham.'

'Wittlesham's boring,' Annie said.

She was sure that Fourways was a hundred times more
interesting than Wittlesham.

'Not when it's got you in it, it ain't,' Bobby Joe said.

Annie glowed with pleasure. He must like her! This exciting soldier from the glamorous town of Fourways, Illinois
liked her, Annie Cross, from Marsh Edge Farm.

The lights dimmed again and the newsreel came on,
showing the tanks and the infantry of the U.S. First Army
entering Cologne. There were cheers and applause from the
audience. Annie was filled with pride. She was sitting right
next to a GI like those storming across Germany.

'Nothing can stop us now, honey,' Bobby Joe told her.

She believed him completely. The Americans were invincible. Soon the war would be won.

The main feature started. Lush music filled the auditorium, the titles rolled, Annie settled back in her seat. But the usual magic didn't work. The whole point of going to the pictures was to get lost in the story. She generally got so involved with the heroine that she completely forgot herself. For an hour and a half, she became someone else. It was the perfect escape from the dreary reality of her life. But this time it was quite different. Instead of losing herself, she became more and more aware of her body and of Bobby Joe's, so close to her in the dark. The scent of the chocolates left in the box wafted round her and those she had eaten lay rich and heavy in her stomach. Bobby Joe's elbow touched hers on the shared armrest, then his leg fell against hers as well. Rushes of pleasure ran up her thigh and into her groin, exciting and disturbing. She knew she ought really to move her leg away, but it seemed very unfriendly and perhaps he hadn't put his there deliberately. He was a tall man and took up a lot of space. But then he gently moved his knee against hers and she knew it was entirely deliberate, but so nice that she didn't want it to stop.

Bobby Joe shifted in his seat and, in what seemed like a innocent move, stretched and rested his arm along the back of hers. She could feel the warmth of it, just a fraction of an inch away from her. It made all the nerves down the back of her spine tingle. She sat staring at the screen, not taking in a thing that was happening, not daring to steal a glance at Bobby Joe, not daring to move. For what seemed like an age his arm just lay there, so close and yet not touching. Then his hand slid on to her shoulder and his thumb caressed the hollow above her collar-bone. Annie caught her breath.

Sensation shot through her breasts and over her belly and down between her legs, a pleasure that was almost a pain, exciting and dangerous.

The rest of the film passed in a blur. Bobby Joe gradually drew her closer to him, until they were head to head, shoulder to shoulder, knee to knee, with only the hard ridge of the armrest keeping them apart. Annie was in a ferment of indecision—if he tried to kiss her, would she let him? The girls from Sutton's were very clear about the rules. You never kissed on the first date. A man would think you cheap. Annie did not want to be thought cheap, but she did desperately want to be kissed. Maybe with Americans the rules did not apply. She did not know whether she was relieved or disappointed when the closing credits rolled and he had not made a move. The National Anthem played and they stood with the rest of the audience. Her body felt exposed and lost not to be touching his any more.

Bobby Joe picked up her coat and held it for her to put on. Annie was enchanted. She really was being treated like a lady.

'Did you enjoy that?' he asked as they shuffled out between the seats.

'Oh, yes!' Annie enthused.

'Margaret Lockwood was great, wasn't she? I've seen all her movies. I think she's wonderful.'

'Wonderful,' Annie repeated.

They emerged from the gilded womb of the cinema into the chill drizzle of a March night. Bobby Joe turned up his collar.

'This sure is a damp country,' he commented. 'Can I walk you home?'

'Oh—no. No, I live quite a way away. Out in the country,' Annie said.

The last thing she wanted was her father seeing her arrive home with a GI. The very thought of it made her go cold with fear.

'All the more reason. How are you going to get back? Is there a bus?'

'Yes—no—' Annie could feel herself blushing with embarrassment. 'I—er—I've got my bike.'

It was just so humiliating to have to admit to something so unsophisticated as cycling to meet a boyfriend. She was sure that it was unheard-of in America.

But Bobby Joe sounded really impressed.

'You cycled here? Say, that's just so cute. You British girls are something else, d'you know that?'

Annie collapsed inside with relief. It was all right. He didn't think she was a country bumpkin.

They walked round the corner into the side street, Annie very conscious of the small space between them. Once or twice his arm brushed against hers. She wanted to put her hand into his, but did not dare. She found she was chattering nineteen to the dozen just to cover her uncertainty, and when they reached her bike she grabbed it from where it was leaning against the wall so that both her hands were occupied. Bobby Joe rested one of his on the handlebars.

'Are you sure you're OK to ride home from here?' he asked.

'Oh, yes, I do it all the time. It's quite safe,' she assured him.

'I've sure enjoyed this evening,' he told her.

'So have I,' Annie said.

She saw his white teeth gleam as he smiled in the dark.

'Does that mean you'll come out with me again?'

It was amazing. This man from across the Atlantic with his boxes of candies and his worldly-wise ways wanted to see her again. But it would be difficult. She didn't have to act her hesitation in order to make herself seem hard to get. Getting away would be a real problem.

'I…don't know,' she said.

'I thought you said you enjoyed yourself,' Bobby Joe said.

'Oh, yes, I did, but…I don't know. I've already been out two nights running…'

They debated it to and fro until Bobby Joe put a huge hand over hers.

'Just say you will. Just for me. I could be going over to Europe next week and then I might never see you again.'

Never see him again! The world suddenly seemed a bleak and dull place. She couldn't let that happen.

'I'll try,' she promised.

'You're a doll,' Bobby Joe said. 'How about Wednesday? Seven o'clock outside the Toledo? Say you'll be there.'

'I'll be there,' Annie said recklessly.

She didn't know how, but if she had to move heaven and earth, she would do so.

Bobby Joe squeezed her hand and let go.

'You're the cutest little thing I ever did see,' he said.

Annie rode home in a dream.

The cutest little thing he ever did see! Her, Annie Cross!

But as she bounced up the track to the farm, reality kicked in. If her father found out, there would be hell to pay. She could imagine his cutting words if he knew she was seeing a GI. Worse still, his actions. Her body recoiled from the imagined blows. Her stomach, unused to the quantity and richness of the chocolates, rebelled. She rode into the yard, stumbled off her bike and doubled over, throwing up until there was nothing left.

CHAPTER TWENTY-ONE

'WHAT'S happening? This is the third bloody day without a proper meal. It's against the Geneva Convention, that is.'

'So what's new? We ain't had decent meals for months.'

'This is a prison camp, mate. Not the bleeding Ritz.'

Tom stared down at the food in his mess tin. Four boiled unpeeled potatoes. It wasn't a lot to sustain a man who had been digging ditches all day. Not that they had been exactly breaking their backs over the work. They'd all learnt how to pace themselves through the long days, how to go through the motions, pretending to work when in fact they were doing hardly anything.

'It's got to mean something,' someone was saying.

'Means they're bleeding starving us, that's what.'

'Too true, mate. What I wouldn't give for a plate of ham and eggs. Ham, eggs and sausages, with a big fried slice. No, make that three fried slices.'

'Fish and chips, that's what I dream of. Dream of it, I do, night after night. Cod and chips, to be precise, with a nice pickled egg.'

'Boiled eyeballs.'

'What?'

'Boiled eyeballs, that's what me and my kid brother used to call 'em.'

The conversation ran along a well-oiled track, as favourite meals were brought forward. A more developed form of it was the café menu, when they debated the best selection you might hope to find when sitting down at a café table. That one could last for hours sometimes, while its exact make-up was decided upon, together with what the waitresses should look like and what other services might be offered…the fantasy went on and on.

But today Tom couldn't raise the will to take part. He felt weak and ill and demoralised. How long had he been here now? He had long since given up recording the days, now that they had run together into weeks and months and years. Sometimes he wondered if he would ever get out of here. It was nearly a year now since the last consignment of prisoners had arrived, bringing them news of how the war was going. It had sounded fairly hopeful, with Allied troops fighting their way up Italy and rumours that the invasion of Europe was imminent, but since then they had heard nothing reliable, and who knew what might be happening out there? Maybe the invasion had failed. Maybe the Nazis were even now tramping through India and China. Maybe they were going to fight on and on until they took over the world. Which meant that he could be in here for the rest of his life.

'You know, this could be a good sign,' someone was saying.

'How d'you mean?'

'It could mean that the Jerries are losing. If their people are on short commons, they're not going to give stuff to us lot, now are they?'

Several men looked cheered by this thought.

'Or it could be a bad sign. It could mean that the Nazis are so well in power that they don't give a damn about the Geneva Convention or the Red Cross any more, so they're treating us how they like,' Tom said.

'You're a right little ray of sunshine, you are,' someone commented.

'Yeah, we can do without thoughts like that,' someone else put in.

'So when did we last have any Red Cross parcels?' Tom asked.

They all considered this.

'Too bloody long.'

'There you are, then,' Tom said.

He ate his potatoes very slowly while the debate went on round him. He wanted to be proved wrong, but he had been here for so long now that he could hardly imagine being let out. He looked at the men around him. None of them were in good condition. It had been a long, cold winter, the standard of the food had been going down steadily and there had been an outbreak of sickness and diarrhoea recently. They all looked pale and gaunt, and any sores or small wounds they had healed very slowly. It had been some time since there had been any serious attempt at an escape. They still talked about it, but the fanatical edge had become blunt.

That night Tom dreamed he was on the other side of the wire, but he didn't seem to be glad. On the contrary, he was lost and bewildered, running on and on through the pine forest on legs that were as heavy as lead with something or someone pursuing him, while nameless dangers lurked in the dense shadows beneath the trees. He knew he had to get somewhere, but he had no idea of the way. He was relieved to wake and hear the familiar sound of snores and grunts and shifting bodies around him. They were his brothers now, these men in the hut—his security. Sleeping, eating, working together every day as they did, they knew each other better than some married couples did. Like married couples, they sometimes loved and sometimes hated each other. Tom shivered in the chill of the small hours and pulled his thin blanket more closely round his shoulders. He knew he had to make the effort to reach out, otherwise he would sink into believing that the Stalag was the universe and the real world outside was just an illusion.

Morning brought a change in the usual routine. After roll call, the Commandant announced that there was to be no work detail that day. The men cheered. Tom felt deflated. He liked going outside the gates, even if it was just to dig all day. The man next to him in the line elbowed him.

'Good, eh? A whole day off. What's got into Fritz? Is it his birthday?'

'God knows,' Tom said.

Whatever the reason, it couldn't be a good one.

On the Commandant's order, an NCO bellowed at them to be quiet.

'You will return to your huts. There will be no fraternising. Your rations will be brought to you at midday. That is all,' the Commandant told them.

'Return to our huts? No bleeding fraternising? What's all that about, then?'

Around Tom and all through the assembled ranks of men, there was a rumble of discontent. A day off was no use if they weren't allowed out in the compound. Their Commanding Officer immediately asked for an interview with the Commandant, but in the meantime the men were escorted back to their huts and locked in. For a while Tom's companions debated the meaning of this break from routine. As usual there were those who thought it was a good omen and those who disagreed. Nobody had any real grounds for their opinion, but it passed the time to give it all a good airing. After that, they drifted into their usual occupations, mending their clothing, cobbling their boots together, playing cards and chess.

Tom lay on his back on his bunk and reread all his letters until he had conjured up a clear picture of home. The pit and the men with their blackened faces, the town and its streets of terraced houses, the corner shop, Amber Drive, his house. His mam doing her knitting, his dad tamping down tobacco in his pipe, his sister Joan thumping out scales on the piano. So far, so good. It all gave a secure feeling of everything going on as it should do, real life, away from the grey routine of the Stalag. But then he turned to the letters from Moira—the girl he had only known for the space of one leave. The girl who referred to 'we' and 'us' all the time, meaning him and her. The girl whom his mother said was not going out with anyone else even though she had plenty of offers. Sometimes he was very flattered. After all, she was a pretty girl and he had been away for a long time now. She certainly didn't have to save herself for him. But part of him felt trapped. There was a huge weight of female expectation hanging over him.

He sighed and sat up, and searched for his last stub of pencil and scrap of paper. For a while he just stared at the small grubby corner. He wanted to create a sense of space, a landscape totally different from the looming pine forest that surrounded the Stalag. The windswept height and rocks and heather of the Peak…or the wide salty expanse of the marshes. He could see it clearly now—the wide horizon where the sky met the sea, the silvery luminous quality of light reflecting off mud and water. He could smell the seaweed and the shellfish. He could hear the curlew. He was standing on the sea wall, with the sun on his face and the wind at his back.

He lifted the pencil. There was not enough paper for him to record all that. Instead he began to draw a small wooden chalet with a veranda all round it. With infinite care, he detailed every shingle, every window-pane, the sunray pattern of the veranda rails. Sitting on the steps was a girl with fair curly hair. Annie. Whom he had not seen since she was sixteen. Who was a young woman now. Who had not answered his letters and probably never even thought of him any more. And yet…and yet she was more real to him than the faithful Moira.

'Hey, Tom! Get off your arse and take a hand here. We need another player.'

Tom put the tiny picture with the pile of letters and went to join the card players. There was no point, after all, in dreaming of the outside. They were probably stuck here for ever.

That night the searchlights went on as usual. Tom, who slept fitfully, heard the sound of vehicles leaving, but as their hut was on the far side of the compound from the main gate, he did not see what was happening. In the morning, there was an eerie silence.

'Here, look at this!' one man called. He was looking out of the window at the perimeter fence.

'What?'

Some of the others crowded round. Tom looked out of the window nearest to him.

'Christ!' he breathed.

The man from the bunk below his stood up.

'What's up?'

Tom nodded towards the wire. 'There's no one in the goon-tower,' he said.

'Where? What?'

All of them were staring now. There were no guards in either of the towers they could see from their hut. Then there was a frantic banging on their door.

'Come on! Come out! They've gone!'

'*What?* What's that bleeding lunatic on about?'

'They've gone. The Krauts. Left. Scarpered. We're free, mate, free!'

From across the compound, they could hear a new noise—that of men yelling and cheering. Then there was a crowd of them round their hut, all shouting the same thing. Their captors had stolen away in the night. They were prisoners no longer.

'Stand clear.'

The largest and strongest man in the hut strode up to the door, paused, then crashed his shoulder into it. The screws round the lock creaked but held. The man tried again. This time something splintered. Two others joined the task. With a crash, the door flew open and the men fell out to rousing cheers.

Tom and the others in the hut crowded out, dazed at the turn of events. It was true, Tom found. All the guards had gone. Everything was still locked up, but there was no one to keep them in. They could just swarm under the wire and go.

Some did just that, packing up their belongings and disappearing into the forest. Others, Tom amongst them, argued that this must mean that the Germans were losing the war and they should march out of the main gate in good order, like a proper fighting force. Others still were for staying right where they were and awaiting further events.

A search of the guards' quarters found a hacksaw that had not been packed up and taken away. They were almost through the second chain holding the gates when above the sound of excited shouting there could be heard the sound of heavy vehicles approaching. The men fell silent.

'It's a fresh lot of bleeding Krauts,' someone said, voicing the fears of all.

The chain fell away, but they kept the bar across the gate and stared through the chainlink at the rutted road leading out into the forest. A small convoy came bouncing round the bend—just an armoured car and two trucks.

They didn't look like German ones to Tom. Then he saw the red stars.

'It's the Russians!' he shouted. 'The Russians! The Russians have come to set us free!'

His cry was taken up and repeated. The bar was pulled back and the gates thrown open. Cheering and waving, the men lined the way as the Red Army swept into the compound.

CHAPTER TWENTY-TWO

'HERE, honey, I got your favourites—'

Bobby Joe passed a paper bag over to Annie. She peeked inside.

'Ooh—doughnuts! Yum*mee*—'

Annie dived into the bag and took out a glorious sweet confection. Chewing gum she had never really seen the point of, but doughnuts were another thing. Doughnuts were heavenly. She bit into the soft ball, savouring each mouthful, carefully licking every scrap of sugar off her lips.

'Mmm, *de*licious.'

Bobby Joe watched her as he drove the Jeep, one arm draped negligently over the steering wheel. He smiled as her pink tongue washed her cheek.

'You sure do like your food, honey.'

'You don't know what it's been like with rationing for all this time. All this sugar—it's just wonderful.'

'You missed a bit.'

He wrapped his spare arm round her shoulders and pulled her to him, licking the corner of her mouth. Annie turned her head so that her lips met his. They kissed until the Jeep ran off the road and Bobby Joe had to wrench the wheel round and get them back on course. They both yelled with excitement as the vehicle bumped and bounced along the verge before hitting the tarmac again.

'Hey, honey, you get me so hot I don't know what I'm doing,' Bobby Joe said.

Annie laughed. She felt wild and abandoned. She was a new person now—a girl who rode around in a Jeep with a GI, a girl who wore nylons and went out three times a week. She even let Bobby Joe pick her up at the end of the track, so they could steal an hour or so together.

'You don't sound too unhappy about it,' she said.

'Unhappy? Not as long as I can do something about it. Say, where can we go to—you know—be on our own a little? Seeing as I gotta get you back home again so soon.'

They were approaching the unmade road that led down to the holiday chalets. Fleetingly, Annie considered Silver Sands, and almost instantly dismissed it. Silver Sands belonged to her and Tom. It was special—too special even to share with Bobby Joe. But he was ahead of her.

'Did I see some old shacks down that track there?' he asked.

'Those—oh no, that's no good. They've got squatters in them—people who've been bombed out,' she said. It was true enough, most of them did have families in them, but the ones in Silver Sands had disappeared only last week.

'Pity. They looked just the job. Kinda private.'

Bobby Joe put a hand on her knee.

Annie squealed. 'Stop it!' she cried, smacking his fingers.

'Why? Don't you like it?'

She did. It sent quivers of excitement running up the insides of her thigh.

'Just stop it.'

'You do like it.'

He slid his hand a little further up, massaging with his fingers. Annie suppressed a moan of pleasure and used both her hands to remove his. She liked it too much. That was the trouble.

'Tease,' Bobby Joe said. 'C'mon, where shall we go?'

'I must be back by nine.'

'I know, I know, you told me. Because your poppa's only out for a while. Look, what about this?'

He swung the Jeep off the road by a church and into a side turning that ran along the back of the graveyard. It was dim in the last grey of twilight and a high hedge hid them from the road. Bobby Joe cut the motor. The silence rang loud in Annie's ears. Her whole body was pounding with fear and excitement.

'Here, have one of these with me,' she said, thrusting the bag of doughnuts at Bobby Joe.

He took it from her and dropped it on the floor.

'I can have them any day. What I want is you.'

He reached across and wrapped his arms round her, his mouth fastening greedily on hers. Annie opened up in the way he had taught her, letting him invade her with lips and tongue, kissing him back until they finally broke apart, gasping for breath.

'Jeez, but you're a bombshell,' Bobby Joe breathed, kissing her throat, working down to the base of her neck. 'Feel what you do to me.'

He took her hand and pulled it towards him, pressing it over his crotch. Annie felt something like a rod beneath the fabric of his trousers. She gasped and snatched her hand back.

''S all for you, honey. C'mon—'

Bobby Joe tried to grasp her hand again but she resisted.

'Aw, c'mon, there's nothing wrong in it, it's only natural. You like French kissing now, don't you? And you like this—' He cupped a breast in his hand and began fondling and squeezing. 'That's nice, ain't it? You like that?'

'Yes—' Annie gasped.

It was painful and pleasurable, exciting and frightening all at the same time, and when he kissed her as well, it was almost too much to bear. She wanted it to go on and on. She hardly noticed the way angular bits of the Jeep were pressing into her when the rest of her body was aching to be touched. Bobby Joe's fingers were scrabbling with the buttons of her blouse. She knew she ought to protest, but when his hand found its way inside her bra the effect of his thumb against her nipple was so electric it was all she could do to bite back a groan.

The small part of her brain that remained detached was ringing alarm bells. She shouldn't be doing this. It was getting late. Her father would be back soon—

'No, no—' she pleaded. 'I've got to go—'

She struggled out of Bobby Joe's arms and back on to the passenger seat.

'I must be back home before my dad.'

'You make him sound like a damned ogre,' Bobby Joe complained. 'Hell, honey, you can't leave me like this. I don't believe all this about your pop. You're just making it up to play hard to get.'

He thumped the dashboard. She could feel anger emanating from him.

'I'm not, I'm not,' she protested. 'You don't know him. You don't know what he'd do to me if he knew—'

Something in her voice must have convinced him.

'All right, all right. Shut up, will you? I'll take you home if that's what you want.'

Bobby Joe started up the Jeep and crashed it into gear.

Revving it up, he shot backwards down the track, swung it round in the road and roared back towards the farm without saying a further word. He jammed on the brakes as they reached the turn-off into Marsh Edge land.

'Are we still going to the Palais on Friday?' Annie asked in a small voice.

She knew she ought to jump out and run all the way back home, but she couldn't leave things like this, with Bobby Joe not talking to her.

A long moment stretched her nerves to breaking point. Then Bobby Joe made a resigned noise in his throat.

'Yeah, yeah, we'll go to the Palais on Friday. I'll see you there, right?'

Relief surged through her.

'Right,' she agreed.

She hurried back to the farm, the cold air cooling her flaming cheeks. Her lips felt bruised, her body was throbbing and aching, but it was all right. Bobby Joe still wanted to see her, even though she hadn't done all the things he wanted. It was so hard, but the girls from Sutton's were very clear about the rules. Boys were only after One Thing, and nice girls didn't let them do it. Not if they had any sense, that was. You didn't let a boy touch anything below the waist until there was an engagement ring on your finger, and you didn't let him go all the way until you were married. Although, when it came to that, everyone seemed to know someone who'd had an eight-month baby, but that was just about all right as long as it didn't show before the wedding. But the worst thing that could happen to a girl was being left pregnant and unmarried. She was despised by everyone.

The Friday night dance was safe. It was romantic and exciting and wonderful and very public. The GIs arrived and left en masse in transports and Annie and the rest of the girls made their own way home afterwards, so there were no problems with being alone with Bobby Joe in a Jeep.

As a bonus, she had a bit of a set-to with Beryl and came out very decidedly on top. It happened as she and a couple of the girls from Sutton's Plastics, as it was now called, were going into the cloakroom, all three of them shrieking and giggling. When they saw Beryl they fell silent for half a beat, then all burst out laughing together.

Beryl put on her most repressive expression. 'Good evening, girls,' she said.

As one, the three of them put on high, little girl voices.

'Good evening, Miss Sutton.'

If it upset her, Beryl was not going to let them see that.

'Chasing Americans, are you? I'd be careful if I were you,' she told them.

'Why? Want one for yourself?' one of the girls taunted.

'Fat chance!' said the other.

'Oh, leave her alone, poor thing,' said Annie.

Now that did annoy Beryl. Annie Cross sticking up for her, Annie Cross feeling sorry for her, was unbearable.

'Poor?' she retorted. 'I'm not poor. My father's richer than all yours put together.'

The friend she had with her caught hold of her arm.

'Come on,' she hissed. 'Leave them. They're not worth it.'

Annie and the other two just laughed.

'So what?' one of the works girls said. 'Bet you haven't got nylons like Annie. Here, give us a feel, Annie. Ooh! Ain't they lovely? All silky and smooth.'

The two of them concentrated on Annie's legs, stroking the nylons and asking about how well they wore and completely ignoring Beryl. Beryl's friend pulled at her arm.

'Come on,' she insisted.

But Beryl just could not leave it.

'I suppose they came from a Yank,' she said, loud enough to be heard over the high-pitched chatter of the pack of young women in the room. 'What did you have to do to get those, then?'

A hush fell over the crowded cloakroom as the insult registered. Heads turned to look from Beryl to Annie, greedily anticipating trouble.

Annie smiled sweetly back at Beryl.

'I didn't have to *do* anything, Beryl Sutton. Anything I want, my Bobby Joe will get for me, because he thinks I'm the cutest thing he's ever seen.'

She turned to her two friends. 'Come on, leave her be. The poor thing can't help it. She's never had a boy look twice at her.'

And she walked out with the others in tow, leaving Beryl staring after her, speechless.

The rest of the evening was sheer pleasure. She and Bobby Joe danced almost every dance together and slipped out in the interval for a bit of necking in the alleyway alongside the dance hall. She did have to control his hands a bit then, but it was easy enough to stop it by saying it was time to go back and dance again. She met Beryl as they emerged from the alleyway and was treated to another of her disapproving stares, but she was far too happy to care what Beryl or anyone else thought.

Saturday night was another matter. To start with, Annie's mother seemed even more anxious than usual when she was getting ready. She even made an excuse to go upstairs and sit on the edge of Annie's bed while she was dressing.

'What d'you think, Mum—this or this?' Annie asked,

holding up her two blouses. 'I can't decide. I wore this one last week, but it is very pretty—'

'I don't know, dear. You look nice in either of them,' her mother said.

'I think that one. But then I did wear that the week before—'

Annie gazed at her choice with a misty smile. She had been wearing that when she'd met Bobby Joe. She slipped it on and did the buttons up.

Her mother picked at the corner of the faded eiderdown.

'Annie, pet, you're not going round to your friend's, are you?'

Guilt and anger lurched in Annie's stomach.

''Course I am,' she lied.

But, even as she did so, she knew it was no use. She might have known she wouldn't get away with it for ever. How had—? And then she realised what had happened. Too late it occurred to her that it might have been a good idea to be nicer to Beryl.

'You've been talking to that Mrs Sutton, haven't you?' she said.

Her mother's voice rose in a defensive squeak. 'She only means to warn you, dear. She's got your best interests at heart. She said so. But, sweetheart, is it true? Are you see-ing—' she dropped to a conspiratorial whisper '—*an American boy?*'

Should she keep lying, to stop her mother from worry-ing? Annie looked at her anxious face. She wouldn't believe her, not if Mrs flaming Sutton had told her. What Mrs Sutton said was like the Word of God.

She did up the last button. They were pretty pre-war ones, little discs of mother-of-pearl.

'It's all right, Mum. He's very nice. He's called Bobby Joe and he's from Illinois.'

'Illinois—' Her mother repeated it, as if it were the moon. Her eyes locked with hers, pleading. They were still bright blue, the only thing about her that hadn't faded. 'Oh, darling, do be careful, won't you? Only Mrs Sutton said you were—'

'Were what?' Annie demanded, more sharply than she meant to.

'Well, you know what they say about these Americans—'

Annie knew.

'Don't worry,' she told her mother. 'I'll be all right. I promise.'

After all, a girl only had to keep saying no.

Later on that evening, it didn't seem quite so straightforward. Bobby Joe and a small bunch of his buddies had come into town in a Jeep and met up with their girlfriends in various places.

'Our luck's in, honey. We drew straws and I got to keep the Jeep,' Bobby Joe told her, grinning all over his face. 'Where'd you like to go?'

'There's Noel Coward on at the Roxy,' Annie said.

Bobby Joe snorted. He didn't think much of English actors.

'We can go to the movies when we haven't got transport. C'mon, honey, jump in. We'll go to one of your British pubs and then we'll see what comes up.'

He laughed as if at a joke and opened the door. Annie climbed in and squealed with alarm and excitement as he accelerated up the High Street and swerved between a pair of cyclists and a bus. Bobby Joe laughed again, showing his strong white teeth.

'Hold on tight! You like a bit of fun, don't you?'

They bounced out of town and stopped at a pub in the first

village they came to. Annie asked for a shandy, since she knew Bobby Joe wouldn't listen to her request for a lemonade.

'Shandy! What kinda drink is that? The beer's got hardly any guts in it even without mixing it.' Bobby Joe enlisted the landlord's help. 'What kinda drinks have you got for a lady?'

The man suggested port and lemon. Annie found she rather liked it. She drank one, and stopped worrying about her mother. She drank another and stopped worrying about anything, and giggled at everything Bobby Joe said. Bobby Joe downed his second pint, made a face and stood up.

'Shall we try somewhere else?'

Annie could feel the disapproving eyes of the locals on her as she left, but didn't care.

'Somewhere else' turned out not to be another pub, but a lay-by under trees in a quiet lane. Bobby Joe turned off the engine and produced a flat bottle from his pocket. He undid it and passed it to Annie.

'Here, try this, honey.'

'What is it?' Annie asked. She could smell the strength of it.

'Southern Comfort. It's nectar, honey. Try it—you'll love it.'

Annie took a little sip. The fumes made her nose prickle, but the liquor slid down her throat, warming and golden.

'Nice,' she said.

'Go on—have some more.'

Obediently, she took a larger sip. She could feel it glowing in her stomach, making her whole body limp and fuzzy. She handed it back to Bobby Joe, who took a swig and gave it to her again. Annie shook her head.

'Tell me about Fourways,' she said.

So he told her about the drugstore and the diner and the

movie theatres. Everything in the U.S. sounded bigger and brighter and more exciting than anything Wittlesham had to offer. Annie sighed with longing.

'It sounds wonderful,' she said.

Bobby Joe's arm was round her shoulders. He offered her more drink. She swallowed some. She was feeling very odd.

'It's nothing to Chicago,' Bobby Joe said. 'Now there's a place. You should just see Chicago.'

And then his mouth was on hers and his hands were all over her and Annie was powerless to resist. Need fed on pleasure fed on need, surging through her body, so that she didn't even notice when two of the precious mother-of-pearl buttons burst off and were lost beneath the seat of the Jeep. She only made the feeblest of protests when his hand went up her skirt, and when he touched between her legs she groaned out loud.

'You like it, don't you? It's good. You want more, baby?'

A tiny part of her knew she should say no, but somehow it came out as yes, and when Bobby Joe took her hand and closed it round himself, this time she didn't draw back. It was his turn to groan.

'Oh, baby, you drive me crazy—come in the back, honey? C'mon—where it's more comfortable—?'

Danger signals at last got through to her.

'No—we mustn't—'

'What's the problem? It's better in the back.'

'No, no—'

This was what all the warnings were about. Even in her drunken state, Annie knew that stretching out in the back was what Nice Girls didn't do. As long as she stayed in the passenger seat of the Jeep, it was only necking, and that was all right.

'Ah, c'mon, honey,' Bobby Joe coaxed. 'I won't do anything you don't want. You know I love you, baby. We'll get married. You can come to the States with me.'

'America? Really?'

A vision of perfect happiness opened up in front of her. She would stop being Annie Cross, unpaid farmhand and drudge, and turn into Mrs Bobby Joe Foster of Fourways, Illinois.

'Yeah, why not? What do you say? You love me, don't you?'

Right at that moment, she was convinced that she did.

It was like a dream come true.

'Yes—' she breathed. 'But—we'll really go to America?' She couldn't believe it. Things like this didn't happen to her.

'As soon as the war's over,' Bobby Joe assured her. 'You and me. I'll take you to Chicago. Now, come on, baby, you know I'm dying for you. Come in the back with me, yeah?'

Dazzled, Annie agreed.

It was all over very quickly. They had hardly laid down in the cramped well of the Jeep before Bobby Joe had her skirt up and her knickers off. And then he was inside her and it hurt, and he was pumping and grunting and it wasn't hot and exciting and delicious any more, but painful and uncomfortable. Bobby Joe cried out and collapsed on her, telling her he loved her, then, to her amazement, he fell asleep.

Annie was squashed and bruised and unsatisfied. Something warm and sticky was trickling out of her. But it was all right. Bobby Joe had said he would marry her. She was going to fly over the rainbow. She was going to the Emerald City.

CHAPTER TWENTY-THREE

AT FIVE to three on Tuesday the eighth of May, Walter, Edna and Annie Cross gathered in the kitchen of Marsh Edge farmhouse. It was a quite unprecedented occasion. Annie couldn't remember ever having been allowed an afternoon break before. But today was different. Mr Churchill was due to make an announcement at three o'clock. They all knew, or hoped they knew, what it would be, but still they had to listen to it. Walter turned on the wireless, waited for it to warm up and tuned it to the *Home Service*.

They stood frozen as the rich voice of the Prime Minister flowed out of the fretwork front of the set, explaining what had happened.

'The German war is at an end,' he concluded. 'Advance Britannia! Long live the cause of freedom! God save the King!'

'Oh, thank God!' Edna cried.

Of one accord, she and Annie turned to each other and hugged. Great sobs of joy and relief tore from Annie's chest. Edna was weeping too.

'No more dreadful bombs. Those poor people! Those awful doodlebugs! It's all over.'

'Ha,' Walter grunted. 'Given those bastard Huns what for

again, then. Better make sure we wipe them out completely this time. Make sure they'll never try it again.'

'And all those boys will be coming home. There'll be some happy mothers today, and wives too. All their menfolk will be safe now.'

Tom would be safe. But Tom would be going home to his fiancée in Noresley.

'They can send all them flaming Yanks back where they came from, for a start,' Walter said.

Hope flared in Annie's heart. Bobby Joe would be back. He hadn't even said goodbye. She had heard from somebody else that the Americans had left camp and were on their way to Europe. She'd sent him a letter, addressing it to him at his regiment, but she had had no reply. She had comforted herself with the thought that he must be far too busy to write. The trouble was, other girls had heard from GIs, girls who hadn't even been proposed to. Soon, she told herself. Now that it was over, she would hear from him.

In Noresley, Amber Drive was alive with people. Chairs and tables were being hauled into the street, flags were being hung from windows and lampposts, precious rations that had been hoarded over the last few weeks were being turned into fare for a party to end all parties.

'Isn't it wonderful?' Moira enthused. 'It's all over at last. I can hardly believe it!'

'Wonderful,' Tom echoed.

He had hardly believed it, at first. Could hardly believe anything—that he was still alive, that he was out of the Stalag, that the Russians had handed him over, that he was back home. Back home. Really home now, in Amber Drive, with his family around him and Moira thrilled to see him and everybody happy.

And today, finally, the war in Europe was officially ended. At three o'clock the whole street had been silent as families gathered round their wireless sets to hear Mr Churchill make the announcement.

Moira clung to Tom's arm with both hands, pressing her breast against him.

'Now you're really safe. You'll be de-mobbed in no time and back for good.'

'Wonderful,' Tom repeated.

He wished he felt as ecstatic as Moira sounded. All that time in the camp, all he had wanted was just to get back to England. Now he was here and, of course, nothing was as simple as it had seemed from a distance. England wasn't just a dream, it was real life starting up again, with all the dilemmas that brought.

'Best go and help,' he said.

As one of the very few younger men around during the day, he was needed to do the heavy lifting, so everything would be ready for when the workers came home. His own father would not be back until the last bus had run and the garage was locked up.

Moira gave him one last squeeze.

'You're right,' she agreed. 'Let's get those chairs organised.'

He watched her as she arranged the seating. She was attractive, capable, strong, good fun—excellent wife material. She had, according to her and everyone else who knew her, been waiting faithfully for him ever since the day his plane had gone down. And he was fond of her. But... But there was something missing. It wasn't like he remembered it with Annie. There was no magic. She didn't make a simple walk along the street special, the way Annie had. Maybe that was just part of growing up, maybe you only felt like that when you were a kid who knew nothing about life. Maybe he was reaching for a fairy tale. He didn't know.

'Wake up, lad, you'll have us over!'

The man on the other end of the table he was lifting, a gunner on leave, was trying to manoeuvre the heavy carved legs round the railings at the side of the steps.

'Sorry, mate.'

He gave his attention to the job in hand. The man grinned at him.

'Plenty of time for that later, lad.'

The words were oddly comforting. Plenty of time. He didn't have to make his mind up yet. He wasn't committed to anything. Reassured, Tom concentrated on making sure the party was one to remember.

Several hours later, all the sandwiches had been eaten, the toasts had been drunk, all the old favourite songs had been sung and the last drop of beer had been drained. Young children were in bed, older ones were still racing round taking advantage of the grown-ups' lax attention, and the adults were either flopped on chairs with cups of tea or dancing to the gramophone. As the record finished, Moira pulled Tom out of the circle of light thrown by lanterns and hurricane lamps to the protection of a solid privet hedge. She wrapped her arms around him and sighed deeply.

'Hasn't it been the most heavenly day?'

'Mmm,' Tom agreed.

He was pleasantly drunk and it was getting on for heavenly having Moira's shapely body pressed against his. She nestled her head on his shoulder.

'Are you happy?'

'Of course.'

He couldn't not be, could he? Not when six years of war had come to an end. Not when he had a lovely girl in his arms.

'You don't sound very certain.'

There was arch disappointment in Moira's voice.

'I am. It's just—'

He was lucky to be alive, he knew that. Bloody lucky. Alive with nothing worse than a slightly misshapen leg and anaemia. A lot of his old oppos were in a far worse state. A lot of them were dead.

'Just what?' Moira prompted.

'I was thinking of the others,' he said.

'Ah—' Moira sighed in understanding. 'Of course. But, darling, you can't do anything about them, you know. Being sad about them doesn't help. You've got to look to the future now. Now the war's over we've got all the rest of our lives to look forward to.'

She raised her face so her lips were just a fraction away from his. He could feel her warm breath.

'That's something to celebrate, isn't it?' she whispered, and kissed him before he could reply.

Her soft mouth was irresistible. Kissing her, running his hands over her luscious body drove away all thought. Tom gave himself up to the pleasure of the moment. Moira gave every sign of enjoying it just as much as he did. It was only when he tried to get his hand under her skirt that she gave him a playful slap.

'Naughty! That's not allowed till later.'

'Later?' Tom questioned.

'You know,' Moira said.

He knew. And he was not going to be cornered that way.

'We've just won the war. We're celebrating,' he coaxed, sliding his hand down her thigh.

She had the most gorgeous long legs.

'That's as maybe,' she said, moving his hand and placing it in the small of her back.

Tom put both hands on her buttocks and pulled her towards him. This she didn't object to.

As they surfaced from another long kiss, Moira sighed with pleasure.

'It's so wonderful that you're here for this. Aren't we lucky? There's nobody else I'd rather be with today.'

Tom knew what she wanted to hear. He was supposed to tell her that he felt the same. But he couldn't quite do it.

'We're very lucky,' he said, and stopped any further questions with a kiss.

The bonfire on the spare building plot behind the holiday chalets was dying down, the drinks were long since gone and the mood had subsided from euphoric to nostalgic. Earlier, they had all been singing and dancing—*Knees Up, Mother Brown, The Hokey-Cokey, The Lambeth Walk.* Now everyone was sitting round, looking into the last flames and the glowing ashes and the song was one from the last war, the yearning notes of 'There's a Long, Long Trail'.

They were a mixed bunch. There were squatters from the holiday chalets, families from the nearby streets, one or two guest house owners—and Annie. Normally, the regular families and the squatters disliked and mistrusted each other, but tonight everyone was friends, joined in the joy and relief of the war's end.

Annie was sitting with a couple of the Sutton's girls who lived in the last terrace of houses before the chalets began.

'Did you say Gwen was getting married?'

'Yes, I heard from her the other day,' Annie said. 'She's marrying this Reggie she met six months ago, and they're going to live near his parents in London. I'm going to miss her.'

It had been quite a blow, hearing that from Gwen. Annie had been counting on her best friend coming back to Wittlesham once the war was over.

'But you'll be off to the States with your Bobby Joe now, won't you?'

'Yes,' Annie said.

She wished she'd never said anything about it. She had only mentioned to one girl, as a strict secret, that Bobby Joe had asked her to marry him, and now the whole town seemed to know.

'All that chewing gum and doughnuts and nylons! Bit different to here. Still, my Sid'll be home soon, and then we can get married and all. Mind you, we'll have to stop at his mum's for a bit, till we can get a place. His mum's a bit of an old Tartar, but what can you do…?'

Annie wasn't really listening. She hugged her stomach. She was feeling sick again. She hadn't had any of the beer because it made her want to throw up. She hoped she would feel better when she had started the curse, as she and her mother always called it. She always felt ill before that, all bloated and out of sorts, and this month it was much worse. Her breasts were horribly tender and there was this sickness. She supposed it was because it was so late starting. As her friend chattered on, Annie tried to work out just how overdue she was, and was shocked to discover that it must be over three weeks.

'So where's your Bobby Joe now?'

Annie jerked her attention back.

'Oh—in Germany. You know—liberating people. Mopping up, that sort of thing,' she improvised.

The truth was, she had no idea. But the war was over now. Bobby Joe would have time to write to her. Soon, he would get round to telling her when he was coming back and she would start the curse and everything would be all right.

The last notes of 'There's a Long, Long Trail' faded away. Annie took a breath deep into her chest and started to sing her favourite song—'Somewhere Over The Rainbow'. All round the bonfire, people joined in, murdering the high notes but putting their all into the spirit of the song. Annie's voice faltered towards the end as tears rose in her throat. She couldn't go on. Her friend put an arm round her. She wasn't the only one. There had been plenty of weeping that evening, along with the laughter and the celebrations.

'What's the matter, Annie?'

'Oh, nothing, everything—you know—'

Annie hardly knew herself. It was all just too much. She got up and stumbled away from the party.

It was chilly once she was out of range of the fire. Still brushing away tears with her fingers, Annie hurried up the unmade track, past the chalets, past Silver Sands, till she reached the sea wall. Scrambling up, she reached the top and slid down the far side till she was sitting with her feet on the sand, staring through the barbed wire. She knew now what she was crying for. It was for those far-off magical days when Tom had sat here with her.

CHAPTER TWENTY-FOUR

IT WAS Edna who first noticed, but she was so horrified by the thought of all that it would mean that for a month she tried to convince herself that she was wrong. By July, though, she could ignore it no longer. She braced herself to speak to her daughter.

Annie was cleaning out the hen house when she saw her mother coming across the yard. She knew just by the way she held herself that the moment had arrived. It was a relief in some ways. She put down her brush and straightened up. Edna stopped a couple of paces away from her, her eyes drawn to Annie's belly. Automatically, Annie tried to suck it in.

'Hello,' Annie said, to fill the silence.

Her mother pressed a hand to her face, her fingers spreading over her mouth.

'Annie love, there's something… I mean, I couldn't help noticing…it's just…well, you haven't had the curse for a while, have you?'

There was a pause, in which both women took in all that this meant. Around them, the life of the farmyard went on. Hens scratched for food around the steaming midden, the pigs rootled and grunted in their sty, a duck led a line of ducklings towards the cart shed.

'No,' Annie agreed.

'How many have you missed?'

'Three—or four, really, if you count this month.'

Edna closed her eyes briefly and sighed. 'And—you were feeling sick, weren't you?'

'Yes—but that's better now. I'm fine, not sick at all,' Annie said in the vain hope that this would change everything.

It didn't. Her mother merely nodded.

'It doesn't usually last more than two or three months.'

The feeling of doom that had been hovering over her for weeks settled in Annie's entrails.

'Oh,' she whispered. It was all she could think of to say.

So it was true, what she had suspected. The worst thing that could possibly happen to a girl had happened to her. She looked at her mother's face and felt crushed by the weight of what she had done. For now she had made her mother's burden ten times worse. They were both going to be for it when—

Her mother glanced fearfully over her shoulder. 'What are we going to tell *him?*' she asked.

Annie shook her head. The impossibility of it haunted her night and day. Soon her father would see for himself, like her mother had.

'I don't know,' she said.

Edna gave a little moan. 'Was it—I mean—it was this American, was it? The—the father, I mean?'

The father. Now it was really out in the open. Bobby Joe was the father of her child.

'Yes,' she admitted.

'Oh, my word.' Edna looked appalled. 'An American, coming to take you away. What's he going to say? What's he going to do? What am I going to do without you?'

Annie was bombarded with conflicting emotions. Guilt,

fear, resentment, but, most of all, desperate hope. For though her mother seemed to assume that Bobby Joe was coming back to take her home with him, Annie was not at all sure that this was going to happen. Bobby Joe had answered none of the five letters she had sent to him.

'You could come too, Mum,' she said in answer to her mother's last question. 'You could come with me.'

Her mother stared at her in utter amazement.

'Me? Go to America? I couldn't do that.'

'Yes, you could. Why not? You could get away from *him*.'

It was as if she had suggested that her mother should sprout wings and fly.

'Oh, no. I couldn't do that, dear. I couldn't leave him.'

'It'd serve him right. When there was no one to look after him he might get to think what he was missing, instead of just hitting you all the time.'

For a moment Annie almost believed it could happen. Bobby Joe would come rolling up to the farmhouse door in a Jeep and take her and her mother away from Marsh Edge for ever.

'I can't just leave him, dear. That's against the wedding vows. And anyway, he only hits me when I deserve it. I'm clumsy. I do things wrong.'

They were back on familiar territory. Tears of frustration rose in Annie's eyes.

'He shouldn't hit you! He shouldn't! You say wedding vows—hitting isn't in the vows, is it? I thought you were supposed to love and cherish. Hitting isn't cherishing.'

Edna shook her head sadly.

'Wives have to obey, dear. You'll learn that when you marry your American. It will be soon, dear, won't it? Because you'll start getting a lot bigger soon. People will notice.'

Annie didn't have the heart to disillusion her.

'I expect so,' she said.

After all, it could still happen. Bobby Joe had said he would marry her. He might be on the way back to her right now.

Her mother put her hand to her mouth again.

'Oh, dear,' she said. 'What is he going to say when he finds out?'

'I don't know,' Annie said.

As it happened, they didn't have to tell him. Somebody else did the job for them. A few days later a letter was delivered to Marsh Edge Farm. It was in an anonymous brown envelope and the address was typed. It looked like a business letter. Edna put it by Walter's plate for him to open when he came in for midday dinner.

Annie was helping her mother bring the food to the table as her father opened it. There was silence as he scanned the contents. He was a slow reader, needing to run his finger along the page under the words. Annie picked up a dish of potatoes and started carrying it across the room. There was a roar of anger from her father and the next thing she knew, his hand crashed into her face.

'You bitch! You filthy little bitch!'

Annie squealed with shock and pain. The dish slipped from her hands and smashed on the stone floor of the kitchen.

'Now look what you've done—that cost good money, that did!' Walter yelled.

Edna scuttled across the kitchen and began picking up the pieces. Walter's foot sent her sprawling.

'What do you know about this, eh? Eh? You been keeping it from me, have you? Been making a fool of me so's I don't know what's going on in my own home?'

'No—' Edna shuffled along the floor to the shelter of a fireside chair. 'No, I never—'

'You leave her alone. It's nothing to do with her,' Annie screamed.

Behind her, she half heard her mother gasp with horror at her outburst.

Walter rounded on her.

'You, you shameless little whore—you dare talk to me like that when you're standing there bold as brass with a Yank bastard in your belly? I'll show you who's master round here. By the time I've finished with you, you'll never give me lip ever again!'

He swung at her, but Annie dodged round the big table. She held on to the edge, her eyes on her father, ready to move as soon as he did. She had to stand up to him, for the sake of the child inside her—Bobby Joe's baby.

'You come back here. I'll make you wish you'd never been born,' Walter threatened. 'Bringing a bastard into the family—!'

'It's not a bastard. He's going to marry me,' Annie yelled back at him.

'Marry you? A Yank? You stupid little whore—he'll do no such thing.'

Walter's harsh voice dripped scorn. Try as she might to withstand it, Annie couldn't help but shrivel inside. Those unanswered letters seemed to mock her.

'He will. He said so. He promised,' she insisted. She needed it to be true so badly. She was speaking to convince herself even more than her father. 'He'll come back and marry me, and then I'll go to America and you'll have to get someone else to slave for you.'

There was a whimper of fear from her mother. Out of the

corner of her eye, Annie caught sight of her terrified expression. The moment's distraction gave Walter his chance. He lunged across the table and caught Annie on the side of her head. The blow made her ears ring, but she bit back a cry.

'Coward,' she hissed. 'That's all you can do, isn't it? Hit us. Just you wait. I'll go to America and I'll take Mum and all and you'll be left all alone. You won't have no one to take it out on then.'

The moment the words left her mouth she regretted it. Now she had turned his attention back to her mother, and that was the last thing she wanted to do. Already, her father was swinging round to look at her mother as she cowered behind the frail cover of the chair.

'You—you thought you'd leave me, did you? You need teaching a lesson—'

Edna cringed away from him, retreating into the corner.

'No, I never— I wouldn't leave. I never said—honest—'

Annie raced from the dubious safety of the table to grab his arm.

'Leave her alone! I want her to go but she won't!'

Walter's other arm whipped round to hit her on the jaw. Her teeth cracked together, catching her tongue, bringing tears to her eyes. Her head was swimming and her mouth was full of the salt taste of blood. Confused, Annie let go of him and staggered back. Immediately, Walter was after her, raining blows on her head and body, calling her every name he could fling at her. Instinctively, Annie's arms wrapped round her belly and she made for the door, wrenching it open and slamming it behind her, then stumbling across the yard. Desperately, she cast about for a refuge. There was nowhere, nowhere... He would get her wherever she went. Her father was behind her, coming out of the back door, yelling.

'I'll get you, you harlot—giving me cheek like that. I'll make you sorry—'

Annie caught sight of her bike, propped against the upright of the old cart shed. With terror driving her, she darted across the yard, scattering squawking hens, and grabbed the handlebars. One foot on the pedal, a push with the other and she was off. Walter uttered a curse as he grabbed at the back mudguard and missed, and Annie wobbled away, out of the mercifully open gate and down the track, her knees shaking, her head reeling, but safe. Somehow, she cycled till she was off Marsh Edge land. Her legs gave way as she got off the bike. She collapsed into the long damp grass of the roadside verge and wept.

There were further humiliations in store for her. When she went into Wittlesham the following Thursday, still bruised and aching, her first stop was at the grocer's where they were registered customers. She pushed open the door with its jangling bell and stepped into the cool shop with its tiled floor and its mingling smells of bacon and cheese and coffee. The three assistants were in their usual places and there were half a dozen customers either being served or waiting their turn. All of them were women whom Annie had met in there before and knew well enough to pass the time of day with. As she entered the shop, one of them saw her and nudged her neighbour, who turned to look. They both stared at Annie for a moment, then turned away without saying a word. The shop fell silent. The only person to greet her was one of the assistants, and she only gave a curt nod. Annie was left with the smile dying on her face.

Cringing inside with hurt and loathing, Annie wanted desperately to walk out and never come in the place again, but she couldn't. There were provisions to buy and their ration books would not be accepted elsewhere. So she just had to stand there and pretend she hadn't noticed the atmosphere as she made her purchases. With relief she put the last blue paper wrapped parcel into her basket and made for the door. As she went out, animated talk broke out behind her. She knew just what they were saying, and it wasn't pleasant.

It was the same story at the butcher's when she went to buy their tiny allowance of meat—the stares, the turning away, the silence. Expecting the same treatment, she went into the fishmonger's, and was pathetically grateful to find that news of her disgraced state had not yet reached there. The cheerful owner joked with her as usual. Revived a little, Annie went to deliver a skirt that had been altered to one of her mother's customers. The woman looked her up and down as she stood on the doorstep, and sniffed.

'Well, I wonder you have the gall to show your face. Your poor mother. How she can bear it, I do not know. Wait there.' She shut the door in Annie's face and came back a minute or so later with an envelope, which she held out to Annie as if not wanting to contaminate herself. 'I think your mother will find that is correct. I won't be using her services again.'

Flabbergasted, Annie was left staring at a closed door again. She finally found her voice. 'It's not my mother's fault!' she yelled at the stained-glass panel. 'Don't take it out on her!'

Swallowing back tears, she got on her bike. In need of comfort, she made for the road to the back of town. Her errands were done now, and she had time to catch the Sutton's girls before they started their afternoon shift. The only problem there, of course, was that Jeff might turn up. He had a habit of doing that—standing there talking to her in front of all the factory girls, so that they teased the life out of her when he went.

'Ooh, our Mr Jeffrey's soft on you!'

'When are you going to be Mrs Sutton, then? That'll put Princess Peril's nose out of joint.'

'Can we all be bridesmaids?'

But with a bit of luck, he wouldn't be there, and the girls would cheer her up.

A group of them were sitting on the wall, waiting till the last minute before going in to work. Annie waved as she approached and called out. Her heart sank as she saw there were no answering waves. As she got nearer, she heard the mocking remarks.

'Oh, look who's here, the dirty cat.'

'We know what *you've* been up to.'

'Or what's been up you.'

'Didn't take you long to get your knickers off, did it?'

She almost cycled off again without waiting, but something made her stop and challenge them.

'Is it you lot who've been spreading lies about me all over town?'

'Lies, is it?' one girl said, staring at Annie's stomach. 'So what's that under your jumper? A cushion?'

The others sniggered.

Annie felt herself going hot. 'You got no right to go gossiping about me. I thought you were my friends,' she said.

'We're not friends with little tarts,' she was told.

'Not with unmarried mothers, we're not.'

Annie wanted to fly at them and scratch and bite and hurt them as much as they were hurting her, but there were six of them and one of her, and a sense of self-preservation honed by a lifetime of living with her father held her back. She got back on her bike.

'You'll see—he's coming back to marry me. You'll be

laughing on the other side of your faces when he takes me with him to live in America,' she flung at them, and cycled off.

Mocking laughter followed her down the road.

'In a pig's ear!' somebody called.

Annie stuck her head in the air and did not reply.

She would show them, she told herself. They would be so jealous when they heard she had gone off to Illinois to be a real American wife with a car and a refrigerator and a front porch. They'd all want to be her friend then and she would tell them where to get off.

She had to believe it, because the alternative was too dreadful to think about.

CHAPTER TWENTY-FIVE

'Do YOU think your father will make you manager now you're back for good?' Moira asked.

'We've got to discuss it,' Tom said.

'Yes, you have. I mean, things are very different now, aren't they? Before the war, you were still at school. Now you're an adult, and perfectly able to help him run the company.'

An adult, went the silent line, soon to have responsibilities of your own.

They were sitting by the river. It was a lazy August afternoon of blue skies and puffy white clouds. The air was warm and buzzing with insects and a slight breeze stirred the leaves of the trees along the river bank. A perfect English summer's day, and here Tom was with a pretty girl by his side. It was everything he had dreamed of during those long freezing nights in the Stalag. And yet...

'Tom?'

Moira was expecting an answer.

'Yes, you're right,' he said.

'Of course I'm right. And your father's not in the best of health, you know. He could really do with someone to take the load off his shoulders.'

'I know,' Tom said.

She was right, there was no doubt about it. He had been shocked at how much older his parents looked. His mother had been through that major operation and, though she had recovered well, she didn't seem to be the woman she used to be. And his father looked tired and worn as well. But then everyone did. Six years of war had taken its toll. They had won, thank God, but the end of the fighting hadn't brought instant ease and abundance. Now there was the peace to be won, and it needed the young and fit and enthusiastic to get started on it. People like himself, and Moira.

'And I could come and help in the office, if you like. I'd sort out all your systems in no time. I'd really enjoy it,' Moira volunteered.

'That's really sweet of you, darling, and I'm sure you'd be wonderful, but we couldn't sack Iris, not after all the faithful service she's given,' Tom said hastily.

He could just imagine what his father would say to having his right-hand woman replaced. Iris ran the office like her private kingdom.

Moira sighed. 'Yes, I suppose you're right, darling. You're so loyal. That's one of the things I love about you.'

She laid her head on his shoulder, and Tom put an arm round her. She was a lovely girl, and devoted to him. He was a lucky man.

'Isn't it wonderful that it's really all over at last?' she said.

'Certainly is,' Tom agreed, glad to have the subject changed. 'Terrible thing, that A-bomb. They say people are still dying of the effects. I'm glad I never had to drop anything like that.'

'They deserved it, the Japs,' Moira said.

'Mmm—' Tom said. There were some terrible stories circulating now about how prisoners of war had been treated in the Far East. They made the Stalag seem like a summer holiday.

'And now everybody's going home,' Moira said, neatly sidestepping any discussion about bombing. 'You know that evacuee family my aunty Winnie had in her cottage? They're off back to London next week. The woman wants to get their house ready for when her husband comes home, she says, but she doesn't know whether she'll be able to get any builders to do it. They're like gold dust down in London, apparently. But anyway, that means my aunty Winnie will be looking for new tenants…' She paused, looking sideways at Tom to gauge how he was taking this piece of information, then added, 'She'll not be asking much for the rent, but she does want someone who'll take care of the place. Someone responsible.'

'Mmm—I expect she does,' Tom responded.

He stared at the brilliant turquoise damsel flies darting and hovering over the brown water of the river. He knew the cottage Moira was talking about. It was a nice little place— a bit damp, and it had an outside toilet and only one cold water tap inside, but houses were in short supply and most young couples would jump at it. Most young couples. That was the sticking point. He just couldn't quite make the jump to seeing himself and Moira as a couple, a proper engaged-to-be-married couple.

Beside him, he could feel Moira's disappointment that he hadn't taken the cue and suggested that they go and see the cottage together.

'Isn't it amazing,' he said, nodding at the damsel flies, 'the way they spend all that time underwater as larvae or whatever, and then they just emerge for a few hours to mate and die?'

'Fascinating,' said Moira. There was a definite edge of sarcasm to her voice.

That night, Tom lay awake for hours, mulling over the situation in his head. Everyone expected him to marry Moira—his friends, her friends, their two families and, most of all, Moira herself. She would have that cottage spick and span in no time, she would be an excellent mother and a great support to him in running Featherstone's Coaches, plus he found her attractive and exciting and good company. But. He came constantly back to that big But. Moira wasn't Annie. Moira didn't seem like the other half of himself the way that Annie had. The sensible part of him told him that it had just been a boy-and-girl thing, that Annie had never written to him in Germany and had probably forgotten about him, but still he couldn't let go. Some time in the early hours of the morning, he came to a decision. He would go to Wittlesham and see Annie. He felt an enormous sense of relief. If he could just see Annie, then he would know which direction his life ought to take. His way clear now, he went to sleep.

And so he found himself retracing the journey he had taken down to Wittlesham all those years ago when he should have been on the cycle club tour. The trains were no more frequent than they had been in wartime, and certainly no cleaner or more comfortable, but one thing was different. The English seemed to have gone back to their old habit of not looking at, let alone speaking to strangers. The wartime spirit of camaraderie had evaporated with the peace.

Tom bought a newspaper but couldn't concentrate on it. He spent his journey looking out of the window at the scenery and wondering what was awaiting him at Wittlesham. It was late afternoon before he arrived at the seaside station and he could not help leaning out of the window as the train drew in at the platform. Last time, he remembered, he had hoped Annie would be there to meet him and had been horribly disappointed not to see her there waving at him, but then, just as he'd thought he was going to have to wait till she was able to get away from her father, there she had been at the ticket barrier. It had been a wonderful moment.

Wittlesham was much as he remembered it. A lot shabbier, of course, as was everywhere, but lively with holidaymakers. A lot of the shops and cafés had reopened and people were out to enjoy the first holiday of peace-time before what threatened to be a long, hard winter. Tom walked to the bus stop and found that luck was with him. There were only ten minutes to wait until the Brightlingsea bus came in. He had decided not to pussyfoot around trying to contact Annie without her father finding out. If there was still a chance for them, then Mr Cross would have to like it or lump it. Tom was not going to let that evil old man get in his way.

The bus trundled through Wittlesham, past rows of small guest houses and through an area of workshops and small factories. Standing out from the rest was a big brown brick building with peeling blue paintwork and a large sign by the front gate—Sutton's Plastics. Tom looked at it with interest. So that was where the dreaded Beryl worked.

Out into the country they went, and soon Tom could see the chalets at the edge of the town across the fields. He thought he could make out the roof of Silver Sands. And then there at last was the track to Marsh Edge Farm, with the wooden platform by it for the milk churns. Tom rang the bell, stopped the bus and jumped down. It was very quiet, after sitting in the rattling bus, just the sound of the wind in the sparse hawthorn trees, and, in the distance, the plaintive cry of the curlew. Tom began to walk up the track towards the grim group of buildings where Annie lived. He stopped trying to guess how she was going to react. He just set his mind on finding her.

And there, ahead of him, as if conjured out of his own head, was a small familiar figure perched on a grey tractor. She was coming down the track towards him.

'Annie!' Tom called, though he knew she wouldn't be able to hear him above the noise of the tractor engine. He waved frantically. 'Annie, Annie! It's me!'

The figure in the driver's seat waved back, but half-heartedly. She hadn't recognised him, Tom realised. She could hardly be expecting to see him there on her land. He stood still, waiting for her to come to him, watching as she became clearer—still the same Annie with her fair curls. He caught the moment when she recognised him, staring at him in astonishment. The tractor stopped with a jolt and she just sat there, holding on to the steering wheel, looking stunned. Tom started into action then, walking and then running— running to meet her.

'Annie!' he shouted. 'It's me—I'm back!'

She didn't jump down from the tractor as he approached, just shut off the engine and sat there, staring at him. A small worm of doubt entered Tom's guts. She didn't look overjoyed to see him, just bewildered. He slowed down to a walk again, taking her in, trying to judge how they stood. She looked much the same—older, of course, a woman now rather than the girl he remembered, and rounder in face and figure but the clear blue eyes and the elfin nose and chin were unchanged. What was not there was the delight he had hoped to see. He had the sudden horrible conviction that this had not been a good idea. He stopped by the front wheel of the tractor and looked up at her.

'Hello, Annie,' he said. 'Surprised?'

She nodded very slowly and swallowed.

'Why?' she asked. 'Why did you have to come now?'

To his horror, there was a catch in her voice. Far from being delighted to see him, she appeared to be dismayed. Unable to accept this, Tom tried to laugh it off.

'Why? I've come to see you, of course. And you haven't even said hello yet.'

'Hello,' she said automatically.

He shouldn't have come, he could see that. But still he couldn't give up, not after coming all this way.

'Won't you get down, Annie?' he said.

She nodded again, pulled on the handbrake and climbed down from the tractor. She was wearing a checked shirt with the sleeves rolled up under a pair of dungarees and, as she turned to face him, Tom realised why she had been reluctant to move from her seat. She wasn't just rounder, she was expecting a baby.

Now it was his turn to stare, astounded.

'Whose—I mean—when did—?' he stuttered.

All this time he had been wondering about her, and she was already married to someone else. He felt sick and angry and betrayed.

'Who's the lucky man?' he managed to ask.

She looked horribly embarrassed. His eye went to her left hand. She saw him looking and flushed. She was not wearing a wedding ring.

'He's coming back for me,' she said defiantly. 'When he's finished his tour of duty in Germany.'

'I see,' he said.

His throat felt dry. He wanted to get out of this impossible situation, and yet even more he wanted to find out what had happened.

'Is that why you didn't write to me, Annie?' he asked. 'Were you courting him even then? I was stuck in that prison camp longing for a letter from you and not one did you send me.'

'I couldn't. I didn't know where you were. Your mother wouldn't tell me,' Annie said. She spoke gruffly, avoiding his eyes.

'But you did know. I wrote to you.'

'Once!' She looked at him now, a flare of anger in her eyes. 'And what a letter. So stiff and cold. As if I was just anyone. I thought we had something special. It always felt like it to me. But it was different for you, it seems.'

'No!' Tom reached out and took hold of her upper arms. She flinched, but he did not let go. 'I thought we had something special, Annie. I wrote to you three times, via Gwen and direct to the house. You never answered me at all. You might have told me you had someone else. At least I would have known why you cut me off.'

'Well, hark who's talking!' She was really angry now, her blue eyes hot with unshed tears. 'You who was engaged to be married without telling me.'

'Engaged?' Tom was bewildered. 'What do you mean, engaged? I wasn't then and I'm not now.'

Not yet, anyway, said the voice of honesty inside him.

'Your mum said you had a fiancée. She said her and she had agreed to let me know what had happened to you because I'd been such a *faithful pen-pal*.' Her voice was loaded with venom.

Tom gazed into her flushed face.

'But—I wasn't engaged. I didn't—I don't have a fiancée,' he repeated.

There was a long moment of silence while Annie took this in.

'That's what your mum said,' she insisted.

Tom remembered the fuss when his mother had found out about his last trip to Wittlesham. She never had liked Annie. But to put her off with a deliberate lie like that, that was downright wicked.

'My mam's got some explaining to do when I get home,' he said.

But, even as he said it, he knew it was futile. From the moment he had seen Annie's condition, he had known the whole thing was finished. He had just been putting off admitting it. He let go of her.

'It's all too late now, anyway,' he said.

The words seemed to reverberate in his head. *Too late, too late, too late*. He could almost hear a door clanging shut on his past life, and Annie was the wrong side of it.

Annie glanced down at her stomach. 'Yes.'

She blinked back the tears. Then suddenly she flung her arms round him and held him with frantic strength.

'Oh, Tom, Tom, I wish it was different.'

Tom held her dear familiar body. She felt so sweet, so right in his arms. But pressing against him was a firm little lump—another man's child growing there in her belly.

'So do I, sweetheart, so do I,' he said.

He cupped her face in his hands and kissed her gently.

'Goodbye, Annie,' he said. 'I hope it all goes well for you.'

And he walked off down the track to the road, not daring to turn round and look back.

CHAPTER TWENTY-SIX

IN THE week following Tom's visit, Annie went round in a state of shock. She couldn't eat, couldn't sleep, couldn't think of anything but Tom. Every time she drove down the track to the road, she saw him there once more, experienced again the see-saw of emotions. Sometimes she was angry, sometimes regretful, sometimes despairing. She raged at Tom's mother for telling her lies, at Tom for writing such a cold letter, that she had not seen through those lies, but most of all she raged at herself. If she had written back, even a note saying she never wanted to hear from him again now that he was engaged, then the mistake would have been cleared up. And then how different everything would have been.

For seeing Tom again had made her realise that what she had felt for Bobby Joe had not been love. It had been something animal, to do with the excitement and glamour the GIs had trailed. She had been in love with the idea of America, and escaping. She had behaved like a mare in season. It made her go hot with shame.

If she had written back to Tom...if she had not given in to Bobby Joe... The road she might have travelled tantalised her with its wonderful possibilities.

But she had made the wrong choices, and now there was

no changing them. Tom had said goodbye, and she was left with a baby growing inside her. Every day it was getting a little bigger, until the time came when it would push its way out of her in pain and blood. There was only one path forward.

Slowly she came out of the paralysis that Tom's visit had induced. One evening, bending down to wash a cow's udders, she felt a strange fluttering inside her. At first she thought it was just wind, but it was a different sensation from that. When it happened once more as she lay down at night, and then again as she dressed in the morning, she realised what it was. The child was moving inside her. It was not just a bump, a miserable problem, it was a living thing and she was its mother and responsible for it.

She thought a lot about Joycie, a girl in her class at school. Joycie had no father. A few other children were without fathers, but theirs had been killed in accidents or had died of illness. Joycie had never had a father. In the playground, Annie had heard the other children repeating what their parents had said about Joycie, the names they had called her. Love-child was the kindest expression. If anyone wanted a soft target to tease, Joycie had been there. You could catch her in the toilets, or dance round her in the playground, chanting those bad names. Annie stroked the bump. Would other children dance round him or her, calling out those horrible, hurtful things?

She had to do something about it. However much she might wish that things were different, however much she loved Tom and knew that she always had loved him, the plain fact was that she was carrying Bobby Joe's baby, and it needed a father. She had to get him to answer her letters, to acknowledge what he had done. It was no use talking to either of her parents about it. Her father would only rage at her and her mother would cry. None of her so-called friends in Wittlesham were speaking to her. The only person in the world she could confide in was Gwen. So it was to Gwen she wrote, asking for advice.

Gwen did not let her down. Instead of writing about her new life and her job in London and her plans for the future with Reggie, her fiancé, she offered a plan of action:

> *I asked my Reggie about it. I hope you don't mind, it being so personal and all, but Reggie and me talk about everything and he says you sound like a really nice person and a good friend. Anyway, what he said was, you should write to Bobby Joe's regimental commander. Like, his colonel. He said, if you can get the colonel's name it's better but, if not, it will still get there. You've got to tell him what the problem is and ask him to speak to Bobby Joe. And, he says, mark the envelope Private and Confidential, and then it won't get opened by some secretary.*
>
> *Good luck, Annie. I'll be thinking about you and keeping my fingers crossed for you. Be sure to let me know what happens.*

As she read the words, hope woke painfully inside Annie's heart. Here was something she could do, someone in authority to appeal to. She kissed the letter and hugged it to her chest.

'Good old Gwennie,' she said out loud. 'What would I do without you?'

All that day as she worked, she had something new to involve her mind. Instead of plodding the endless treadmill of regret, she was planning the exact wording of this crucial letter. It had to be short and to the point, she realised. Colonels were important men, they did not want to be bothered with girls rambling on about their problems. She went over and over it until, by evening, she was reasonably happy with what she had formulated. After supper, she wrote it out carefully in her neatest handwriting, addressed it and put on three stamps to make sure it covered the foreign postage.

'Just going out to the post box,' she said as she passed through the kitchen.

Her mother looked up from the sock she was darning.

'You sending back to Gwen already? You only got one from her this morning,' she said.

'Yes—well—it's something she asked me that she wanted to know quickly,' Annie lied. She wasn't going to admit what she was doing to her father.

'Good for nothing little bitch,' Walter muttered from behind the Sunday paper that he took all week to read. Whether he was referring to Annie or Gwen was unclear. Either way, Annie ignored him. If all went well, if the colonel spoke to Bobby Joe and Bobby Joe took her to America as he had promised, then soon she would be out of Marsh Edge and never have to listen to her father again.

Two weeks went by. The post brought bills, a catalogue, a small part for Edna's sewing machine, but no official-looking envelope postmarked American forces mail, Germany. The hope that had been born with Reggie's suggestion began to die slowly of suffocation.

And then it arrived. It was Edna who handed it to Annie.

'What's this, dear?' she asked, holding it with two fingers as if it might explode. 'It's from Germany. It's not from *him*, is it?' She lowered her voice to a whisper and looked significantly at Annie's bulge.

'No,' Annie said. 'At least— No.'

She reached out to take the letter with shaking fingers. She felt sick. So much was riding on this; she wasn't sure if she could bear it. Her mother was saying something but she couldn't hear it through the buzzing in her ears. She ran upstairs to her room.

The letter was as short and to the point as the one Annie had sent. The writer regretted to inform Miss Cross that Private Robert Joseph Foster was a married man and the father of three children. If Miss Cross wished to pursue her claim, she could ask for blood tests to be performed after the birth of the child, but she should bear in mind that this would not provide definite proof of the child's paternity. Until then, nothing more could be done and nothing gained by any further correspondence.

Annie sat staring at the piece of paper. The print blurred before her eyes. There was a sinking feeling in the pit of her stomach, as if she were falling into a black abyss. This was the end. There was no escape, for her or for the baby. She was doomed to stay at Marsh Edge and be bullied by her father for ever.

But, before self-pity could rise up and overwhelm her, she was saved by a surge of anger. She tore up the letter into tiny pieces, flung them on the floor and stamped on them.

'Married!' she raged. 'Married! You pig, you low-down lying swine! I believed you—I trusted you—you filth! All that about going to Fourways and Chicago, all that about loving me and wanting to marry me—all lies, lies, lies!'

She flung herself about the room, thumping the walls, kicking the door, screaming her hatred and sense of betrayal until it all seemed to fall on top of her, and she collapsed on the bed in a storm of weeping. For no amount of railing against him or against fate was going to change a thing.

It was some time before she became aware of a hand stroking her head, a soft voice speaking soothing words, the weight of another body sitting beside her on the narrow bed.

'What is it, my pet? You can tell me—'

The offer was irresistible. Annie turned to her mother and was folded in the comfort of her arms. She cried on her shoulder and was rocked and soothed against the softness of her slight body until the tears gave way to racking sobs.

'Better now?' Edna asked. 'What was it that upset you so? What was in that letter?'

'Oh, Mum—he—he's—'

At first, she couldn't get the words out. But gradually, prompted by Edna, she told the dreadful news. It was such a relief to be able to talk to someone at last, to be the one supported by her mother, instead of the other way round. Edna stroked her back, patted her shoulder.

'It's all right, my pet. We'll survive. We'll get through it, you'll see. That man don't deserve a lovely girl like you. Leading you on! We'll be fine here together, you and me. It'll be lovely having a dear little baby about the place.'

In her raw emotional state, it took Annie a while to fully understand what her mother was saying.

'You mean—you don't mind?'

'Mind? Well—you didn't ought to have done it, that's for sure. It was a very wicked thing, and I was shocked when I found out. I mean—my daughter. I always thought—well— that you were a good girl.'

Edna paused, and Annie felt the weight of her disapproval hanging about her heart.

'Oh, Mum,' she croaked, 'I never wanted to upset you. I know I shouldn't have let him. I don't know what got into me—it's spoilt everything—'

Edna squeezed her shoulder.

'What's done's done. We got to think of the baby. This is my grandchild we're talking about. We'll look after it together, you and me. I've been making things for it already. Lots of things—nighties, matinée jackets, bootees. They're so sweet. I was going to surprise you with them, but I think it's better if I show you now. I've been enjoying myself so much doing them. Wait—I'll fetch them.'

Annie sat on the bed. She felt drained. It was all too much. She just waited for the next thing to happen.

Her mother came back into the room carrying a large gingham-lined basket. Out of it she tenderly took an assortment of exquisitely made baby clothes, all in white, the sewn garments pintucked and embroidered, the woollen ones knitted in intricate lacy stitches. She spread them out on the bed, her face more animated than Annie had seen it in years.

'Do you like them?' she asked anxiously.

Annie touched the tiny mittens, the soft bonnets. She smoothed the silky ribbon ties.

'They're beautiful—' she whispered.

There was a catch in her throat. Tears were threatening again. Her mother had done this in secret for her—for her and the baby.

'We'll be all right, you and me and the little one, you'll see,' her mother insisted.

'Will we? People are already giving me the cold shoulder. Some of your customers are staying away. What'll they do to the baby? They'll call it a—'

'Stop!' Edna sounded almost fierce. 'Don't say those ugly names. It doesn't matter what anyone says. We'll love it. We'll be together, you and me. That's all that matters. You'll be here at Marsh Farm with me.'

It did matter, of course. It hurt when she went into town and old friends cut her and disparaging remarks were made within her hearing. It hurt when nurses at the clinic made a point of calling her Miss Cross in a tone of voice that distinguished her from all the married women. It hurt to hear other expectant mothers chatting to each other about their husbands painting cots and mending prams ready for the new arrivals.

The baby gave Walter a wonderful weapon to use against her. But even he wasn't as bad as she had feared. Gradually, she realised why. Just like her mother, he needed her there at Marsh Edge Farm, even though he would never admit it. The baby might be a disgrace, but it had tied her to them for ever.

In the early hours of the morning, a week into the new year of 1946, Annie was woken by pains in her back. She got up as usual and made tea for her father and herself before they went out to do the morning milking. The pains were reaching round her stomach now and felt similar to monthly ones, except that they came and went. She stopped to hold on to the side of a stall as one gripped her.

'What are you hanging about for? There's work to be done,' Walter growled.

'I think…it's the baby…' Annie gasped.

But already it was fading again. She straightened up.

'You get this job finished. You got hours yet. Plenty of time to finish the milking and get the cleaning done. No need to be lying on your back because of that little Yank bastard.'

In a way, he was right. It was nearly midnight before the baby was dragged into the world in an excruciating forceps delivery.

'It's a boy,' the midwife declared.

She washed him in an enamel basin, wrapped him in a

towel and placed him in Annie's arms, where she lay, torn and exhausted, in her lumpy bed.

'Ah—' Edna sobbed, 'isn't he just the little darling?'

Annie gazed into the baby's cross little face. He had pale blue eyes and on his head was a fluff of gingery hair. There was no mistaking whose son he was.

'Hello, baby,' she whispered, amazed that she should have produced this tiny, perfect human being.

She named him Robert Joseph, after his father, since he was never going to have his father's surname.

'Don't you worry, baby,' she told him. 'He might not be here, but I'm going to look after you and love you better than any baby with two parents.'

CHAPTER TWENTY-SEVEN

March 1952

'Mum*MEE*!'

Bobby flung himself into Annie's arms and clung to her with frantic strength.

Annie held him and kissed the top of his hot little head.

'What is it, sweetheart? What's the matter?'

Though she knew already. She had known the moment she'd seen him tearing down the road towards her, his face flaming and his coat torn. The other children had been ganging up on him again. Pain twisted within her, that her child should be made to suffer so.

'I had to fight them,' Bobby burst out, raising his face to look at her. There was an odd mix of defiance and fear in his pale blue eyes. 'They were calling you nasty names.'

That made it even worse. Annie felt helpless. She wanted desperately to keep him from harm, but did not know how.

'What did the teachers say?' she asked.

'They told me off for fighting. They said I started it, but I didn't! I didn't, Mum, honest. They was picking on me, the big boys, so I had to hit them, didn't I?'

Annie didn't know what to say. Turning the other cheek

had done no good. But then lashing out didn't seem to be working either.

'You're a brave boy, Bobby, and I'm proud of you,' she told him, avoiding the question. 'We don't care about those bullies. We know they're just stupid.'

'Yes,' Bobby said, but he didn't sound convinced.

Annie racked her brain for something else to suggest. She had tried speaking to Bobby's class teacher, but had got nowhere.

'Just a little harmless playground ragging, Miss Cross. Good for them, toughens them up. It doesn't do to be overprotective, you know.'

Far from being overprotective, Annie felt she was failing to protect him at all.

'We don't need them, we've got each other,' she told him.

She swung him up to sit on the seat of her bike. He was too big now to sit in a child seat on the back.

'Let's do something nice together,' she suggested. 'We'll go down to the beach before we go home.'

'All right.'

The dull acceptance on Bobby's face hurt most of all. She was his mother and should keep him safe, but already Bobby knew that she couldn't stop the bullying any more than he could. They were both powerless.

Annie put a foot on the pedal and scooted the bike down the last road out of town between rows of prefab houses and on to the unmade one that led out towards the chalets and the sea wall. Bobby hung on to her shoulders, his feet jammed against the frame of the bike. They bounced over stones and shot through puddles, the chill air of early spring making their cheeks and ears pink. Bobby let out a squeal and Annie's spirits rose with his.

For a while, they were free and able to enjoy each other's company.

Some of the chalets now had permanent tenants, others were let to holiday-makers in the summer and families in the winter—large, unkempt groups with fierce dogs and hordes of children. The last time Annie had come this way, Silver Sands had just been emptied of a family that had kept goats and donkeys in the big garden.

'I wonder if there's anyone new in Silver Sands?' she said to Bobby.

They rounded the last corner.

'Oh!' Annie cried out loud.

For there, on a post by the gate, was an estate agent's notice.

'For Sale,' Bobby read out.

'Well done,' Annie said. At least they were teaching him something at school, even if he was unhappy there.

'I used to dream of living here,' she told Bobby.

The little boy nodded. She had told him this story before.

'You wanted to run away and be here all by yourself. An' then you met a nice boy called Tom who painted pictures. He painted him and you on the v'randa.'

'Yes—'

Annie looked at the neglected chalet and the trampled garden. It was hard now to picture how it had been the year Tom and his family had first come here. Silver Sands had suffered from being empty during the first years of the war and from being occupied by a series of tenants since. It was badly in need of someone who would take pride in it— somebody like herself.

'Let's go in,' she said to Bobby.

The boy scrambled down and Annie leant the bike against

the wobbly fence. The gate had sunk on its hinges and needed lifting to get it open. Annie heaved it aside and, hand in hand, she and Bobby walked into the garden and up the veranda steps. She peered in at the windows.

'Poor house needs an awful lot of work doing on it,' she said.

Her fingers itched to take a hammer and nails, sandpaper and paint to the place. Its current owner had never really taken much care of it. She remembered the last time it had been for sale, and how her father had refused to buy it. He had more money now, of that she was sure, but there was no point in even raising the subject with him. He just would not see why he should branch out into anything outside farming.

'Do you like it?' she asked Bobby.

'Yes,' he said, but she could tell that he was only saying it to humour her. To him it was just a damp wooden hut surrounded by a rough piece of land stripped of nearly all vegetation by the previous inhabitants' goats.

Annie sighed. People wanted holidays again. If her father were, by some miracle, to buy Silver Sands and do it up, families would pay good money to stay here. There was even enough space to build another couple of chalets on the garden. But it was no use dreaming. Some other person would buy it and make a business out of it. At least it made a piece of news to put in her letter to Gwen.

'Come on,' she said to Bobby. 'Let's go and play on the beach.'

Over the next week she would often look across the fields to where the chalet stood under the sea wall and wonder about who might buy it. She hoped that at least it would be someone who would look after it properly, for if it wasn't repaired soon it was going to start rotting away. Salt air found every weakness in the woodwork. She couldn't bear it if her last link with Tom were to collapse into a sad heap of timbers.

And then Gwen's regular fortnightly letter arrived.

Gwen's life had not turned out quite as she had imagined. Her marriage to Reggie was everything she had hoped it would be, but the children they had assumed they would make had never arrived. Gwen had grown bored with her job now that it was not just a temporary thing until she became a mother, and Reggie was impatient with the restrictions of working for the council. Living in their London suburb was no more exciting than living in Wittlesham, except that it was easier to reach the attractions of central London. For some time they had been talking about moving out and starting a business of their own. The only problem was that they were not sure just what that business should be.

Gwen enthused on to the page:

Your letter has changed everything, It was like turning on a light. My Reggie saw it straight away. Silver Sands, he said, isn't that a holiday chalet? And I said yes, it was the last one before Marsh Edge Farm, right by the sea wall and a big garden all round it. And he said, how much garden? You see, we've been talking lately about running some sort of holiday place, only not a guest house like my aunty's. Reggie says guest houses have had their day. All that having to leave at ten in the morning and not being let in again till teatime, people won't stand for it like they used to. Anyway, you remember we went to that caravan at Southsea for our last holiday? Something like that was what we thought. A caravan site. Only we'd have to start small because we've got some money saved and we could go to the bank but still we haven't got a lot. So when you said Silver Sands was for sale, it seemed like the ideal place. What do you think? We could live in the chalet and put caravans in the garden and we could both still go to work during the winter and then in the summer I could run the site. What do you think? Best of all, it would mean I'd be just across the fields from you! Isn't that marvellous? We're coming to Wittlesham on Saturday to look at it and find out how much it is.

Hope to see you then.

Lots of love,

Gwen.

Conflicting feelings swirled inside Annie. If Silver Sands had to go to someone, then it was better that it went to her best friend, especially as that best friend had a husband who would get it back into tiptop condition. But she could not help an ugly stirring of jealousy. Gwen had always been the lucky one, having a nice family, going away to join the WAACs, then marrying Reggie and being so happy with him. Now she was going to live in the place Annie had always dreamed of owning. It really wasn't fair.

'Fair doesn't come into it,' she told herself severely.

She read the letter again. Gwen was right. The best thing was, her friend would be just across the fields. At last she would have someone other than her mother to talk to, to laugh with, to share problems with. It was like coming out of a long dark winter and seeing the spring sunshine again.

Immediately she saw it that way, a new worry arose—Gwen and Reggie might not buy Silver Sands after all. They might think it was too dilapidated, or too expensive, or not big enough for the number of caravans they wanted to put in the garden. By the time Saturday came, she had gone through a cycle of will they, won't they a dozen times. She longed to rush out and do something to improve the look of the place, but knew that nothing she could achieve in the small amount of free time she had would make any difference. All she could do was to wait and see what Gwen and Reggie decided.

It was a cold, miserable day. Walter had saved a job for Annie and Bobby to do together.

'That hen house needs a good cleaning,' he told them over breakfast. 'Get all the muck out and scrub it down with carbolic. And mind you do it proper. No skimping. I'll be along to see what you're up to.'

Annie looked at her hands. They were roughened and callused from heavy work, the nails trimmed right back and black round the rims despite twice daily scrubbing. By the end of the day they were going to be red and sore as well. Then she looked at Bobby. It wasn't right. He was having a rotten time at school. He shouldn't be forced to do such a horrible job on a Saturday.

'I can do it by myself. Bobby can stay and help Mum,' she said.

Helping his grandmother would consist of a bit a light dusting before embarking on a pastry-making session. She knew how much Bobby enjoyed rolling and shaping the dough.

Walter snorted. 'Stay in doing women's work? What d'you want to do—turn him into a Nancy boy? You, boy!' He rounded on Bobby, who started and gasped. 'Go and fetch my boots.'

Bobby was out of his chair almost before his grandfather stopped speaking.

'Yes, Mr Cross,' he muttered, and scuttled across the room.

'He'll only be in the way. I'll do it much better on my own,' Annie said.

But it was no use. Walter had decided, and that was that.

'He's got to learn,' he insisted.

So the two of them spent a cramped, smelly day labouring in the hen house. Whenever they emerged into the yard, Annie looked over towards Silver Sands.

'I wonder if they're there yet. I wonder what they're saying.' She speculated. 'It's ages since Gwennie last saw the place. It's gone downhill a lot since then. It'll need an awful lot of work to make it look like a nice place to spend a holiday.'

'What's a holiday like?' Bobby asked.

For a moment, Annie was stumped.

'Well, I don't know really, because I've never had one. But it must be lovely, mustn't it, to just do what you want all day long, with no one ordering you around?'

'Just playing?' Bobby asked.

'Just playing,' Annie agreed, thinking of Tom's cousins with their tents in the garden and their games of cricket and 'he' and hide-and-seek. She didn't want a holiday for herself any more. She was used to the continual grind of labour. But she did long for Bobby to be allowed a small piece of carefree childhood.

They had just finished afternoon milking when a frenzied barking from the bad-tempered dog warned of visitors. Without even asking Walter's permission, Annie shot out into the yard. There were Gwen and Reggie, muffled up in their overcoats and scarves, glowing with excitement. She only had to take one look at them to know.

'You've done it!' she squealed, and threw herself at Gwen.

'We did, we did—we thought it was just right!' Gwen cried, hugging her back. 'Isn't it thrilling?'

'It's wonderful! I'm so pleased!' Annie said.

She broke away from Gwen to give Reggie a kiss on the cheek.

'Congratulations, Reggie—I'm sure it'll be a huge success.'

Reggie squeezed the top of her arm. 'Thanks, old girl. I hope you're right, 'cos we're going to sink every penny we've got into it. But Gwennie's got her heart set on it, so what more can I do?'

'You liked it as well. You thought it was a good idea,' Gwen insisted.

'What's all this row?'

Walter's harsh voice cut across the euphoria. Both girls went quiet, but Reggie extended a polite hand.

'How do you do, sir? Reggie Smith, and I think you know my wife, Gwen. We're going to be your new neighbours at Silver Sands.'

Walter ignored the outstretched hand. 'Flaming idiots,' he growled. 'Must be off your heads.'

Coming to Silver Sands was absolutely the right move for Gwen and Reggie.

'You always used to say this place was magic. I thought it was just you being daft, but you're right,' she said to Annie. 'There is something very special about it.'

It needed a touch of magic the day they moved in. It was raining and the roof leaked in several places, making the damp interior a whole lot damper. But, like a couple of kids in a Wendy house, they ran about putting buckets and bowls under the drips and making a camp in the driest room.

From then on they worked all the hours they could, first

making the chalet weatherproof, then doing up the outside so that it looked welcoming. Builders were hired to construct a small toilet block. Next the fences had to be repaired, the garden tidied and a swing and a see-saw installed. And then they were ready for their great enterprise to begin. Five six-berth caravans arrived—not new, but in very good condition. Gwen and Reggie cleaned and polished them until they were the shiniest on the whole east coast. That was at the end of May. On the first Saturday of June, their first customers arrived—a family from London who had seen their advertisement in *Dalton's Weekly*. A week after that, Gwen went to the doctor's. She came home walking on air.

It just so happened that Annie came visiting that evening. Gwen flew down the veranda steps, flung her arms round her and burst into tears.

'What is it?' Annie asked. 'What's happened? What's the matter?'

'Nothing's the matter,' Gwen told her when she could speak. 'Oh, Annie, it's happened at last—after all this time! I was beginning to think it never would!'

A slow smile spread over her friend's face.

'You're not—are you?'

'I am, I am!' Gwen hardly knew herself whether she was laughing or crying. 'I'm expecting a baby! And you're the first person we've told, Annie. We haven't even been to see my mum and dad yet.'

'That's wonderful news,' Annie said. 'Congratulations, both of you.'

Gwen looked over at Reggie, who hadn't stopped grinning since she had made her announcement. 'No more nasty digs about pencils and lead now, eh? It was just waiting till it could be born here, in our little wooden hut.'

'That's right. Now we'll be a proper family,' Reggie said, coming to hug her and Annie together.

In their emotional state, neither of them noticed that Annie was a bit quiet.

As the summer progressed, along with Gwen's pregnancy, the only thing that worried her was Annie's situation. She often talked it over with Reggie.

'She always did have a horrible time there with that father of hers, but at least she used to get out and enjoy herself every now and again. Now everyone's turned against her because of—you know— It's even worse. I think I'm the only person who's still friends with her. It's really horrible, the way people behave.'

'A lot of girls had their heads turned by the Yanks,' Reggie said.

'He promised to marry her, you know! The dirty swine. She wasn't to know he was already married. But people don't think of that, they just treat poor Annie like she's some good-time girl, and she isn't.'

'No,' Reggie agreed. 'She's a really decent person. She's bringing that boy of hers up really well.'

'She is. He's a smashing little boy, is Bobby. But people don't see that, they don't see how hard she's trying. They just call her all sorts of names. I mean, I'm not surprised at that blooming Beryl Sutton. She always did hate Annie, and they're living over there on the North Cliff now and she's Lady Muck with knobs on. But the others—! You'd think they were all plaster saints, and I know for a fact that they weren't. That lot that used to work at Sutton's, they'd run after anything in trousers, but Annie, the only boys she ever went out with were her Tom and that blooming Yank.'

Gwen sighed.

'I wish I could wave a magic wand and change your life,' she often said to Annie.

And Annie would laugh and hug her. 'Just stay being my friend,' she said.

At the end of their first summer as caravan site owners, they still had a huge bank loan, but they did have plenty of customers who wanted to come back next year and who said they would tell their friends. They cleaned out the vans for the last time and shut them up for the winter. Gwen gave up her job at the rock factory with relief and settled down to knit bootees and wait for the baby.

On the last day of January, the wind howled across the low-lying fields and battered against the walls of the chalet. It found its way through all the cracks and made the fire blow back and fill the little living room with smoke.

'It's going to be a bad night,' Reggie said. 'I'll go and check on all the vans before we settle down.'

They listened to the weather forecast, which wasn't very cheerful.

'What a good thing we had the electricity put in,' Gwen said. 'It feels safer somehow when you can see properly.'

'Silly old thing,' Reggie said. 'Want to listen to *Saturday Night Theatre?*'

It took them both a while to get off to sleep that night, what with the wind shaking the little chalet and Gwen finding it difficult to get comfortable. It seemed to Gwen that she had only just managed to drop off when Reggie shook her awake.

'What? What is it?' she slurred.

'We're flooded,' Reggie told her. 'Quick, get dressed. We've got to get out of here.'

'Flooded? How?'

Gwen sat up in bed. She realised that the blankets were all wet. Thoroughly awake now, she put a hand over the side of the bed and met with cold water.

'Oh, my God! What's happening? Put the light on.'

'In all this water? Don't be daft. Come on, we can't just sit here.'

They waded about the room in the thick darkness, trying to find clothes. The wardrobe doors wouldn't open and only the top drawer of the chest of drawers was above water level.

'Come on, leave it, it's getting deeper. We've got to get out.'

Gwen whimpered with fear. 'I don't want to go, Reggie. I don't want to leave the house.'

The water was cold and stinking. The outside was a frightening place. The chalet was her home.

Reggie got hold of her wrist. 'It's nearly up to the windows. Come on, you've got to. I'll help you.'

Clumsy and ungainly with her big bump in front of her, Gwen had to be pushed through the window. She landed up to her waist in water on the veranda and shrieked with terror, for here there was a strong current and it was trying to carry her along. She grabbed hold of one of the veranda posts while bits of flotsam jostled past, knocking into her.

'Reggie!' she cried. 'Help! Quick!'

The cold and the dark were terrifying. The current was like a live thing, clutching at her with strong arms.

'It's all right. I'm with you.'

Reggie was there beside her, but she could tell that he was frightened too.

'What are we going to do?' she wailed.

'We got to get out of the water,' Reggie said. 'The roof!'

We got to get on the roof and stick it out until someone comes to rescue us.'

'The roof? I can't! I can't, Reggie!'

Gwen felt huge and helpless. Even without the nine months' lump in front of her, the thought of climbing on to the roof in the dark was a nightmare.

'You must,' Reggie insisted. 'I'll help you. Come on, get yourself up on the rail.'

Somehow, Gwen managed to heave herself up so she was standing on the fancy balustrade. She was above the water now, but her nightdress clung wetly to her legs and the wind was buffeting her. She felt chilled to the bone. She clung to the post while Reggie clambered up and stood beside her. He bent down and got his shoulder under her buttocks.

'Ready?' he gasped. 'Now!'

He slowly straightened, and Gwen found herself rising up until her head and then her shoulders were level with the roof. She scrabbled to get a purchase on the guttering. Still Reggie was pushing her. She pitched forward in the darkness and spread-eagled from the waist up on the slippery shingles. The wind was much worse up here. She pressed her face to the roof.

'Hold on, I'm changing my grip—' Reggie grunted.

Gwen felt his reassuring presence beneath her backside fail, and screamed.

'Reggie! Hold me!'

'Don't panic. For Christ's sake, don't panic.'

She had never heard him swear before. It silenced her. His hands were under her now.

'Get your knee up, Gwen. Get your knee up and heave.'

Somehow, she did what he said. With a knee in the gutter, she managed to get her whole body on to the roof. Her muscles trembled uncontrollably with the effort.

'Hold on,' Reggie told her.

Whimpering, Gwen lay on the roof, trying to grip with her fingers and toes. After what seemed like an age, Reggie hauled himself up beside her.

'Made it,' he gasped. 'You all right?'

She was so far from all right that she nearly laughed.

'Yes,' she squeaked.

'Good girl. Now we'll try to get up on the apex, then all we've got to do is hang on. Someone will come and get us as soon as it's light.'

The words were hardly out of his mouth when they both heard a roaring sound above the noise of wind and water. A shudder seemed to go through the fragile chalet, releasing a clawing fear deep in Gwen's gut.

'What was that?' she gasped.

Reggie was edging his way up to the apex. Up here, there was some moonlight to see by. Gwen could see him peering into the distance along the sea wall.

'Oh, my God!' she heard him gasp. 'Oh, my God. Gwen, hold on! Hold on for all you're worth.'

CHAPTER TWENTY EIGHT

'DAD!'

At Marsh Edge Farm, Annie was clinging to the tree trunk, horrified at what she had just done.

Her scream was snatched from her lips. There was no answering shout, only the howl of the wind. She stared into the night, but could see nothing except the glint of moonlight on water. One moment her father had been there, the next he had gone, swept away by the force of the tide. The black waters swirled round her shoulders and pulled at her body, threatening to wash her away too, to turn her into one more piece of flotsam carried along in the flood. Storm-whipped waves broke over her head. There was no time, no space in her mind to consider what she had done. It was a fight for survival. She peered up into the tangle of branches, blacker against the night sky. The tree was only a twisted hawthorn, prickly and dense, but the branches were well within reach. If she could just pull herself up a little way, get her body out of the water…

She stretched out, her fingers touched the first branch, settled round it, gripped tight. The force of the flood tugged at her feet. The level was still rising. It was up to her neck now. She had to get higher. Slowly, fearfully, she let go of the trunk—and the current lifted her off her feet, trying to rip her away. Desperately she scrabbled for a hand-hold, found another branch, pulled. Her bulky wet clothes were pulling her down, her arms were leaden, but terror lent her strength. She heaved, lunged up and forward, flailed her legs and she was there, gasping, choking, sobbing, but with the upper part of her body clear of the water. For a while she just lay there exhausted, still clinging on for dear life. Then she became aware of thorns and sharp twigs sticking into her stomach, her face, her head. She was soaked to the skin, her legs were still in the water and there was an icy gale blowing. She began to pray, recklessly promising God anything and everything if He would just spare her for her Bobby's sake. The cold ate into her.

After a while, her mind became as numb as her body, and life narrowed down to one essential task: to hold on. It was some time before it got through to her that the water level was falling, that the flow was reversed. The tide was going out. When it finally sank into her dull consciousness, Annie wept with relief. With the first grey light of the dawn, she saw a strand of barbed wire running clear of the water below her. That would be about waist level. It was safe to get down.

It was almost as much of a struggle as getting up had been. Her body was stiff with cold. The thorny twigs tore at her. She felt hair rip out as she pulled free. Slowly she got to the point of balance, then slithered down with a rush. Her legs gave way as her feet touched ground, and she collapsed into the water.

She hardly knew how she made it to the farm. An overwhelming instinct for survival took her home, slipping and staggering, forcing her numb limbs to wade through the mud and the water until at last she fell over the threshold of the farmhouse.

Then there was a confused blur of faces and voices, of hands attending to her, of softness and dryness and rubbing and slowly, slowly, stealing over her like a blessing—warmth.

'Mum? Mum, are you awake?'

Bobby's excited voice penetrated the thick blanket of exhausted sleep. Annie surfaced slowly, reluctantly. Something was very wrong, but she could not remember what it was. Her body ached all over and throbbed in places. She focused on her son's face.

'Mum, there's a man outside with a Jeep and he's going to rescue us.'

'What?'

Her brain felt fuddled. It did not help that she appeared to be in the wrong room. Instead of lying in her own narrow bed, she was tucked up in her parents' one.

'A man with a Jeep. He says he's come to get us.'

It started coming back to her. The flood, the tree, something else, something terrible...

'Oh, my God!' She sat up in bed and clutched at Bobby's arm, startling him. 'Bobby, where's D—Mr Cross? Has he come home?'

'No. He's not here. Grandma doesn't know where he's got to. Mum, there's water all round the farm.'

Annie got out of bed and tottered over to the window, her legs wobbling beneath her. A scene of desolation spread out before her. Down below in the farmyard, a huddle of cows stood knee-deep in muddy water, surrounded by the corpses of several of their fellows, a lot of dead chickens and a flotsam of straw, timber, seaweed, bottles and nameless muck. At the open gate there was indeed a man in a Jeep, up to its axles in water. Beyond that, where there should have been green fields there was nothing but angry grey-brown waves with only fence posts and the odd hawthorn tree sticking out to remind her of how it should have been. The water went all the way to the Wittlesham road, which ran along the old coastline. The sea had reclaimed all its former territory.

Annie gaped at it all, appalled, until a quirk of the mind brought the memory of looking out of her own window last night, looking towards Silver Sands…

'Gwen!'

She flew out of her parents' room, slipping on the bare floorboards in the two layers of socks her mother had pulled on to her frozen feet last night. She burst into her own room and skidded over to the window.

'Oh, my God,' she repeated, but this time she whispered it, her hand flying to her mouth. Horror crawled queasily through her guts. The black line of the sea wall that had not been high enough to save them stood between the grey sea and the brown flood, a big gap knocked in it, through which the water was now draining away. At its feet, the cheerful pastel-coloured caravans lay scattered and smashed like a spoilt child's toys. Worse, much worse than that, Reggie and Gwen's chalet had been lifted right off its supporting piers and was tilted amongst the wreck of the caravans, lapped by the flood waters. There was no sign of life anywhere.

'Oh, no,' she moaned. 'Oh, no. Oh, God, let them be safe. Please let them be safe.'

'Mum—?'

Bobby's small arm went round her hips. Annie hugged him to her, hungry for the comfort of his warm, wiry body, pulsing with life.

'Mum, are we going with the man?'

Decisions. She had to make decisions because her mother wasn't up to it and her father—her father was missing.

'I don't know. I'm not sure. We'll go and talk to him.'

She went back into her parents' room and forced open the window. Bobby put his head through too and they waved at the driver. He stood up and waved back. He was a dependable-looking middle-aged man in a roll-necked sweater and duffel coat. The cinema fan in Annie could imagine him at the wheel of a ship crossing the Atlantic in convoy, cool in the face of attack by submarines.

'Do you need help?' he called. 'Is anyone injured? I can take you to safety.'

Annie considered. If the tide was going to flow in and out twice a day for however long it took them to mend the sea wall, then they could not hold out here. But what was going to happen to the animals, or what was left of them?

'Wait a minute,' she said.

She pulled on some clothes and went to find her mother.

Edna was downstairs, surveying the wreck of her kitchen with a look of bewilderment on her face. It was still a foot deep in filthy water. When she saw Annie, she fell on her.

'Oh, I'm so glad you're awake. I didn't like to disturb you, but there's a man in the yard—'

'I know. I think we'd better go with him, but I don't know what to do about the stock. I'm going to go and have a word with him.'

Edna was horrified.

'We can't leave. What will your father say when he comes back and finds we're gone?'

Guilt churned in Annie's guts. When he comes back. *If* he comes back.

'We'll leave a message. We can't stay here, Mum. Look

at it. The water's not going to go away. There's a great big hole in the sea wall and this'll stay flooded until it's mended.'

She found a pair of wellingtons and waded out to meet their visitor. He assured her that the animals would be seen to. Their nearest neighbour on the dry side of the Wittlesham road had volunteered to take them up to his farm and look after them for as long as was necessary.

'We'll go, then,' Annie decided.

They gathered some personal belongings together, climbed into the Jeep and set off down the track. Annie recognised the tree that had saved her. The fear hit her all over again. Bobby was bouncing up and down beside her. His nose was still running, but the drama of the situation seemed to have cured the worst of his cold.

'Look at all the water. We're making waves see! It's like being in a boat.'

She fought to stop the darkness invading her mind. She stared at Bobby, at his small eager face, pink with the excitement of the journey.

Ann! Help me!

She held her head, digging her fingers into her scalp.

'Mummy? Mum, what's the matter?'

Bobby was pulling at her arm. She took a shuddering breath and forced a smile. She had to pull herself together. She couldn't give way; she had Bobby and her mother to look after.

'Nothing. I'm all right. Look! There's seaweed right up in that tree.'

They were absorbed into the rescue system that had sprung up overnight to deal with the disaster. They were driven into Wittlesham, where Bobby's school had been converted into a rest centre. Here they were treated with the utmost kindness by people who had been very cool towards Annie ever since Bobby's birth. WRVS ladies—the women's voluntary service—and the Salvation Army bustled about providing soup and tea and sandwiches, the Red Cross was there ministering to injuries and illness. Clothes and bedding, children's toys, even a gramophone and some records were coming in by the minute from individuals wanting to 'do their bit'. Annie spotted Mrs Sutton and Beryl arriving with their arms full of blankets and Lady Bountiful smiles on their faces. She looked away before they could make eye contact. They were the last people she wanted to talk to.

Everyone commented that it was 'just like the war', as if the war had been the best thing that had happened to them. But in a way they were right, for disaster did bring out the best in everyone. There was a post-blitz atmosphere about the rest centre. The volunteers spoke of being rushed off their feet and hardly able to cope with the volume of problems, but underneath the grumbles they were secretly delighted to be part of this emergency and proving to be up to the job.

For the survivors it was all still recent enough for them to be high on having cheated death. They sat around the school hall in animated groups, swathed in blankets and borrowed clothes, swapping narrow escape stories.

Like most other communities on the stricken east coast that day, they did not yet know that this was not just a local disaster. Even the BBC was largely unaware of what had happened, so they heard nothing about the flood on the news. Central government had shut down for the weekend, so from Lincolnshire down to Kent local services and volunteers were struggling to rescue families clinging to chimneys and rafters and to cope with the hundreds of homeless who had escaped with nothing but their nightwear. All night and into the morning, unsung heroes had taken boats from pleasure lakes and winter storage and rowed them down the streets to ferry shocked and frozen refugees to where strangers opened up their homes and gave them warmth and tea and blankets. For many, help came too late. Just along the coast at Jaywick, a village of holiday chalets like Silver Sands, thirty-seven people were drowned, while Canvey Island in the Thames Estuary was completely inundated, with the loss of fifty-eight lives, mostly the very young and the elderly.

For Bobby the extraordinary day was turning into a treat. He ran off to join a group of children playing a rowdy free-for-all game with beanbags. Annie tried to settle her mother in a deckchair that someone had brought in, but Edna refused to sit down. She stood, clutching at Annie's arm and looking around at the groups of people talking and smoking and drinking tea. The big assembly hall was crowded. The sea had come right up to the edges of the town, making refugees of the inhabitants of the new prefabs and washing through two streets of older houses. 'I can't see him. He must be here, mustn't he? Somewhere?'

For the first time in her life, Annie longed to see her father. Maybe he had fetched up against a tree as she had. Maybe he had reached the Wittlesham road but hadn't been able to get back. Maybe—but she knew it was unlikely. The moment she closed her eyes she could see again that great wave, feel its terrifying power. It had all been so quick. She recalled the feeling of helplessness as it had carried her along. She saw her father's face, saw his hand, just inches from hers. Had she really refused to reach out to him? It had all been over in a matter of seconds. First he had been there, then he was gone, swept away into the roaring darkness.

'He could be at the hospital or something,' she said, but her own doubt sounded in her voice.

The words were hardly out of her mouth before one of the teachers appeared, a worried-looking middle-aged man in a tweed jacket. He had an exercise book in which he was recording all those who arrived at the school. Her heart thumping, Annie told him that her father was still missing. She found she was holding her breath. The teacher consulted his list, shook his head, looked grave. Then he drew her to one side where they could not be overheard by her mother or Bobby.

'I have to tell you that there is a man of about your father's age at the hospital, Miss Cross. He was found washed up near the Wittlesham road and there was nothing on him to identify him. If you're feeling strong enough, do you want to see if—? Or perhaps your mother had better—?'

For a moment, Annie was confused. Wild hope surged through her. He was not dead.

'At the hospital? You mean he's—?'

Then she realised. The man did not mean that her father was recovering in bed in hospital. He was in the morgue.

'Oh, no,' she whispered. 'Oh, no.'

She had known it all along, really.

She glanced at Edna. The last thing she wanted was to take her mother with her.

'No, I'll do it,' she said.

But Edna had been watching them and interpreted the signs. She grabbed Annie's arm. 'What is it? What's happened? Have they found him?'

Annie explained. Her face felt stiff, her voice seemed hardly to be her own. Edna nodded very slowly. Her anxious expression settled into hard, bleak lines.

'I want to see him,' she said.

'Mum, you don't have to. I can go.'

'I want to see him,' Edna insisted.

'It might not be your husband, Mrs Cross,' the teacher said. 'He could be sheltering somewhere else. I only have a list of those who have come to this rest centre.'

'It's him. I know it,' Edna said.

'I'll come with you, then,' Annie said. But first there was another enquiry to make. She wasn't sure if she could take more bad news, but still she had to know.

'Have you—have you got the Smiths on your list? Reggie and Gwen Smith from Silver Sands?'

The names were not in the exercise book. Annie felt sick.

'Who else would know? The police?'

'Possibly. But—' The teacher hesitated. 'Are the Smiths relatives of yours?'

'No. They're friends. Very good friends.'

'I see…' The man appeared to be considering what to say. 'Of course, there's a good chance that they were rescued and they're now being looked after in someone's house.'

'Yes,' said Annie, eager to grasp at any hope. 'Yes, of course.'

But part of her was not convinced. She had seen the devastation the flood had caused at the caravan site.

A WRVS lady took them down to the hospital in her car. She kept up a steam of talk about the events of the night, how many people had been rescued, what had been done to help them, how long all the volunteers had been on their feet. Annie glared at the back of her head. She hated these jolly, bossy women. This one was enjoying every minute of the crisis. It was making a nice change for her, a break from her usual routine. In contrast, her mother was perched on the edge of the car seat, hanging on to the strap for dear life and saying nothing.

'Some people have lost everything in this flood, you know,' Annie said.

Edna came suddenly to life, looking at her in alarm and hissing, 'Annie!' at her. People like the WRVS lady were not to be spoken to like that.

But their chauffeur was oblivious to the criticism in her voice.

'Oh, I know, my dear. Those poor folk in the prefabs. Quite washed away. So tragic. There was one family…' And she was off again, an unstoppable flow of information and opinion.

Annie was relieved to get to the cottage hospital.

There were six bodies laid out in the sterile chill of the morgue. Only one was still to be identified. Annie put an arm round her mother's shoulders, concentrating on her rather than on the shape laid out beneath the cover. How thin her mother felt, her bones sharp even through the layers of shapeless cardigans she was wearing. She gave her a squeeze. Edna was stiff, braced physically as well as emotionally for the ordeal.

'Ready, Mum?' she asked. Her voice came out cracked and croaky from a dry throat.

Edna gave the smallest of nods.

The cover was drawn back. Annie felt rather than heard her mother's sharply indrawn breath. She stared at the face on the table. He looked smaller in death. Smaller, but just as inflexible, even with grey stubble softening his jutting jaw. There was the tyrant who had ruled all their lives with his sour temper, who had made all of them feel constant failures, unable to achieve the unrealistic amount of work he'd expected from them. She could not remember one word of praise from him, one look of affection. The only time he'd touched her as a child was to hit her. Nothing had ever been right for her father. And now—now he was gone. Dead because she had refused to hold out a hand to save him.

'Yes,' she said to the attendant, 'that's my father. Walter Cross.'

Beside her, there was a low moan. Annie looked at her mother. Edna's face was stricken, her eyes bewildered.

'Oh, Annie,' she whispered. 'What are we going to do? How are we going to manage?'

Annie ran a dry tongue round drier lips. It was down to her. She was responsible, she had to say something. She forced some words out.

'Don't worry, Mum, you still got me. We'll be all right. I'll see to it all.'

Quite how, she had no idea.

Outside, in the grounds of the cottage hospital, the storm wind was still blowing. It howled round the corners of the low building, whipping through the bare branches of the young trees by the gate and bending the shrubs planted to cheer patients looking out of the windows. The WRVS lady's car was waiting for them at the entrance. Something drew Annie's eye beyond it to a park bench by what in summer was a fragrant rose bed. A solitary figure sat there—a young man in a beige duffel coat, hunched over and rocking with grief.

'Reggie!'

Annie was torn in two. Beside her, her mother clung to her arm like a lost child. She could not leave her, but neither could she ignore her friend's need. Gently, she steered her mother over to the bench and sat her down. Reggie seemed hardly to notice they were there until she laid a hand on his arm.

'Reggie, it's me, Annie. What is it? What's happened? Is Gwen—?'

Slowly, he turned a ravaged face to her. For a long moment he appeared not to recognise her. Then he collapsed into the arms she held open to him.

The words came out raggedly between harsh sobs.

'I couldn't save her, Annie…the water…it was like a great tidal wave…I had her in my arms…we were on the roof…but the wave…it took her away. I couldn't hold her, Annie…'

Annie wept with him, rocking him as if he were Bobby, offering him what small comfort she could in the face of such overpowering loss. She felt helpless. Nothing she could say could make a difference, for nothing would bring Gwen back.

Over the next few days, Annie spent hours listening to Reggie. Together with two of the families from the prefabs, they were given temporary accommodation in one of the smaller sea front hotels. While her mother retreated into a shell of silence, Reggie needed to keep talking. Endlessly he spoke about Gwen, about how they'd met, their courtship, what a wonderful woman she was. Endlessly he went over their last terrifying minutes together. Annie tried to convince him that he had done all he could, that nobody could have saved her from the forces of nature, all the while asking herself what she could have done to save her father and knowing that, unlike Reggie, she had plenty to be guilty about.

The funerals were very well attended. The disaster touched the hearts of the people of Wittlesham and they turned out in force to pay their respects to the victims. Gwen's in particular attracted people who had never known her in life. The death of a young woman about to become a mother was especially tragic, and the sympathy for Reggie deep and genuine. But nothing could even begin to heal his pain.

'I can't stay here, not without her. I can't face going back there to Silver Sands alone,' he told Annie the evening after Gwen's funeral.

The practical side of Annie's mind knew that every last penny of their savings had been sunk into the caravan site and that their insurance did not cover flood. They had been covered against most other eventualities, but the premium for flooding had been just too high.

'What will you do, Reggie?' she asked. 'Where will you go?'

'I don't know. I don't care. Anywhere. To my brother's, maybe. All I know is, I can't go back there without her.'

'Don't worry, Reggie,' she heard herself saying. 'I'll buy Silver Sands off you. Then you can make a new start somewhere.'

Reggie took her hand.

'You're a true friend, Annie. I don't know how I would've got through this without you.'

So after that she couldn't back down.

CHAPTER TWENTY-NINE

IT WAS a Sunday like any other for Tom. To start with, there was Moira's discontent to deal with.

'Don't forget Mother's expecting us at half past twelve for Sunday lunch, not one o'clock,' she reminded him over breakfast.

Tom shook salt over his poached egg. 'I'd better meet you there, then,' he said.

He could almost see the hackles rising.

'What do you mean, you'll meet me there?'

'I've got to go in to the yard and see a couple of coaches out.'

'On a Sunday morning? You never told me.'

'Of course I did. I told you last week,' Tom said, though in fact he wasn't sure whether he had.

'Mikey come too?' a small voice broke in.

Tom smiled across the table at his little son. ''Course you can, Mikey-boy. We'll make sure it's all shipshape and Bristol fashion, eh?'

'Bisto fashion,' the child chanted happily

'You most certainly did not tell me,' Moira insisted. 'And that yard is not a suitable place for a child. It's dangerous.'

Tom jabbed the egg with his fork. It was perfectly done—

the white set, the yolk runny. No one could accuse Moira of not being an excellent cook.

'Rubbish. I'll keep a tight hold of his hand,' he said.

'I don't see why you have to go up there just to see a couple of coaches out,' Moira persisted.

'Somebody has to be there, and you're the one who's always pushing for me to take over the management side from Dad. You should be glad I'm not out driving.'

Moira liked to tell her friends that her husband ran a coach hire company. It annoyed her no end when one of them happened to see him out driving a party to the seaside or a football match. Being a coach driver's wife was not the same at all.

Moira tightened her lips. 'I suppose you're paying them time and a half for Sunday work,' she said, changing her means of attack. 'It's ridiculous what these people expect.'

'It stops their wives from nagging them for missing their Sunday lunch,' Tom said.

'I am not nagging,' Moira told him.

'Nobody said you were.'

He escaped as soon as he had finished his breakfast, taking Michael with him on the crossbar of his bike. Moira was dead keen for them to buy a car, but Tom didn't see the necessity. If he needed a car, he could always borrow his father's. They had a nice little semi now that he was buying on a long mortgage, he had had a telephone installed and had bought a television, the first one in their street. That was enough for Moira to swank about for the time being.

Once at the yard, he put the stresses of home behind him. Michael trotted happily up and down the aisle of one of the coaches and sat on the driver's seat pretending to drive, while Tom talked to the men who were going out that day and made sure they knew where the pick-ups were and which routes they were taking.

'He's a fine little lad, that,' one of the men said, nodding at Michael.

'Yes, he is that,' Tom agreed.

Michael was the best thing to come of his marriage.

'Giving the missus a break, are you?'

'That's right. Let him see where his bread and butter comes from.'

Though looking after Michael was no chore. He loved being with his son.

'Right chip off the old block, en't he?'

They both smiled as Michael sat on the driver's seat with his small feet sticking out in front of him, hanging on to the steering wheel and making engine noises.

'I'll have him driving round the yard as soon as his feet reach the pedals,' Tom boasted.

He and Michael saw the coaches off and locked up the yard. There was still an hour to go before they were expected at his in-laws' for lunch. It was a cold, raw day with the remains of last night's high wind still blowing, not the most inviting of days to be outside, but still he didn't much want to go home. He looked at Michael. The boy was wrapped up warm enough in an overcoat and leggings and woolly balaclava.

'How about we ride up Gough's Hill before we go to Grandma's?' he said.

'Ride like the wind?' Michael asked.

'Ride like the wind,' Tom agreed.

By the time they arrived at the Butterworths', they were rosy cheeked and laughing, and glad to be in out of the winter cold. Moira, though she gave him an icy look, was as nice as pie to him in front of her parents and sisters. She was a great one for keeping up a front.

Later on, they all went next door to have tea with Tom's family. They had just about finished when the wireless was turned on for the six o'clock news. The measured voice of the news-reader rolled round the crowded room.

'Gales during the night caused abnormally high tides and widespread flooding along the east coast of England, from the Thames Estuary to Yorkshire…'

Tom went cold. He leaned forward, listening intently.

'There has been loss of life; agency reports put the number of dead at between fifty and sixty. Many other people are missing. Sea walls were breached at various places and huge seas swept inland…'

'Dreadful thing—those poor people—' Mrs Butterworth commented.

'Shh,' Tom hissed, straining to hear.

'Tom!' Moira exclaimed, scandalised.

'Quiet!' Tom insisted.

'In Essex, there was widespread flooding in the Clacton-on-Sea area, and at least six people are known to have drowned…'

Tom felt clammy with fear. Six drowned in the Clacton-on-Sea area. That would include Wittlesham. And there was nothing but low-lying fields between Marsh Edge Farm and the sea wall. Was Annie still living at the farm? Or was she with the father of her child, safe somewhere miles away? He had no way of knowing.

His mother, who was sitting next to him, dug him in the ribs.

'Wake up,' she muttered fiercely.

He became aware of talk going on around him.

'…knew it was stormy last night but I never thought it was that bad,' Mr Butterworth was saying.

'Of course, it's very low lying all along that coast. You were there the first year of the war, weren't you, Margery?' Tom's father said.

'We were right by the sea wall,' his sister Joan butted in. 'Do you think those chalets are all right? Poor Silver Sands! That was a lovely holiday.'

A great ball of anxiety filled Tom. If Annie was still at Marsh Edge, or still anywhere in the coastal area, then she might be amongst those terrible statistics quoted on the news.

'How awful to have your house flooded in the middle of winter like this,' Mrs Butterworth was saying.

Moira was sitting across the table from him. She was staring at him in surprise.

'What is the matter, Tom? You've gone quite pale.'

'Oh…nothing…'

Tom tried to pull himself together. He had never told Moira anything about Annie, although she did know that he had met a local girl when on holiday with his family at Wittlesham. He had certainly not told her that he had gone down to Wittlesham just before he'd proposed to her, saying instead that he was visiting an RAF friend. Moira, however, was still looking at him suspiciously.

'I—er—it's like Joan says, it's sad to think of our holiday home being flooded. That was the last family holiday we had together.'

'I suppose so,' Moira said.

'I shouldn't think there was anyone in the chalets. Not at this time of year,' his mother said.

'No. They didn't say anything about Wittlesham on the news, did they?' Joan agreed.

Talk drifted on to a more general discussion of holidays. Tom let it flow on without him, while he tried to think of a way to find out more. The police, he decided. The police at Wittlesham were the best people to contact.

'…Tom, as you went out this morning.'

His mother nudged him again. 'Tom, your father's talking to you.'

'Sorry—what?' Tom asked, aware that he sounded stupid.

His father laughed. 'You were well away with the fairies, weren't you? I've not seen you go off in a dream like that since you were a lad. I said, I'll go and see the buses in as you went out this morning.'

Tom jumped up immediately. If he went up to the yard, he could use the phone there. Otherwise, he would have to wait till the morning.

'No, that's all right, Dad. You stay here. I've got my bike with me.'

'Tell you what, we'll both go in the car,' his father offered. 'If you don't mind hanging about in the yard for a bit, Moira, you and Mikey can come too and I'll run you all home.'

Moira smiled prettily.

'Thank you so much. That's so kind of you. It's a cold night out there.'

Which put an end to Tom's hopes of a phone call.

'Just come upstairs a minute before you go, Tom, dear,' his mother said. 'There's something I want to show you.'

Puzzled, Tom followed her. His mother shut the door of the front bedroom behind her and folded her arms over her chest and fixed him with a determined look. It felt freezing in the unheated room.

'Now, just you be careful, son,' she said.

'About what?' Tom said, though he knew. It was as if he

were seventeen again, caught out in his lie about the cycle club tour.

'That's a lovely girl you've got there for a wife, and now you've got a splendid little boy too. Don't you go doing anything to spoil it,' his mother warned.

Tom spread his hands in innocence. 'And just what am I supposed to have done?'

'I saw your face,' his mother said, sidestepping the question. 'And so did poor Moira. What's she supposed to think when you're so keen to hear about those floods that you're rude to your mother-in-law? I don't think Moira knows anything about That Girl, because she certainly hasn't heard anything from my lips, but anyone could see that you were acting very strangely.'

She was right, of course.

'You're talking rubbish, Mam,' he said. 'You're reading a whole lot into something that means nothing at all. Talk about a mountain out of a molehill! The last time I saw Annie was—when?—in 'forty-one, the summer before I joined the RAF. That's nearly twelve years ago, for heaven's sake!'

His mother ignored this. 'You do know she's an Unmarried Mother, of course?' she said, lowering her voice to a stage whisper for those two shameful words.

Tom felt as if he had been kicked in the guts. *'What?'* he said.

He could see Annie so clearly in his mind's eye, telling him that the father of her child was coming back to marry her.

'Some American, I believe. At the end of the war. I'm not surprised. I always thought she was flighty. Not your sort at all.'

'Not—?' Tom was still struggling to come to terms with this news. 'How do you—? Oh—Madam Sutton, I suppose.'

It was all becoming clear. His mother had known this for

years and had kept it from him. He did not trust himself to pursue it any further.

'I've got to go,' he said brusquely. 'Dad's waiting.'

All the way over to the yard this new information about Annie buzzed round his head, making it hard for him to concentrate on what anyone else was saying. One thing stood out—this meant that Annie was almost certainly still living at Marsh Edge Farm. His own words to his mother came back to him—that he had last seen her twelve years ago. It wasn't that long, of course, but it was nearly eight years ago. A considerable time, and a lot had happened to them both since then. He couldn't understand himself, why he had felt such a strong reaction on hearing the news of the flood. The rational part of him knew that he shouldn't even try to find out more, but the need was too pressing to deny.

He lay awake worrying most of the night and hurried off to get to work early in the morning. As soon as he got in, he found out the number for the Wittlesham police station and tried to book a trunk call, only to be told that the lines to Wittlesham were still down. That only increased his anxiety. He asked to be put through to Colchester central police station and after a number of delays finally got hold of someone who knew what was going on.

'I'm very concerned about a family on the marshes near Wittlesham,' he explained. 'I can't contact them or anyone in the town.'

There was a long rigmarole of name-taking.

'And what was the name of the family, sir?'

'Cross. Of Marsh Edge Farm.'

He could feel a pulse beating in his throat. It seemed to be affecting his breathing.

'Ah, yes, sir.' The same bland tone, giving away nothing. 'And are you a relative?'

'Yes,' Tom lied, knowing he would get nowhere otherwise. 'I'm a—nephew. Of Mrs Cross.'

Nothing was going to induce him to claim Annie's father as a relation, even as a lie.

There was a slight pause, then the official voice softened just a fraction.

'In that case, sir, I'm very sorry to have to inform you that Mr Walter Cross was drowned on the night of the flood.'

'Oh—'

Her father was dead. It took him a moment to take it in. That wicked old bastard who had made her life a misery was gone.

'I'm very sorry, sir.'

'Yes—right—' Tom gathered his thoughts. 'But the rest of the family—they're all right?'

'No one else by the name of Cross on my list, sir.'

'Right—er, thank you—goodbye.'

Tom put the phone down, feeling stunned. Annie was safe—that was the most important thing, and for that he was immensely relieved. But he was nothing like calm. A deep part of him wanted to get in his father's car and drive straight to Wittlesham to see what he could do to help her.

He sat with his elbows on the desk and his fingers dug into his scalp. In front of him was a photograph of Michael taken a year ago on his birthday, with a Featherstone's Coaches driver's cap set lopsidedly on his head. Tom picked up the picture and stared at it. He was a married man with a son. He couldn't go chasing after rainbows. But still he could see that sea wall snaking across the landscape, with nothing but dead flat land between it and Marsh Edge farmhouse. Annie was not amongst the drowned, but things might still be pretty desperate for her. He couldn't just leave it. He had to find out.

He reached for a sheet of Featherstone's Coaches headed notepaper. If he was going to do this, he certainly mustn't risk a reply coming to the house. And, as he decided that, he realised that if he didn't want Moira to know, then he was admitting to this being more than an enquiry from one human being to another. He ran over a form of words in his head, knowing that it had to be short, concerned but distant. There were so many ifs and buts that he hardly knew what to do. Should he mention his own situation, or would doing so imply that she would take this letter the wrong way? Should he indicate that he knew what her situation was, or pretend that he still thought she was married? Should he mention her father?

When he finally put pen to paper, it was like a floodgate opening. The first stilted sentence melted into a rush of worry about her, a long reminiscence of their times together and a potted version of all that had happened to him since last they'd met. He was telling her all about Michael when the office door opened and his father came in.

'That's what I like to see, someone hard at work.'

'Oh—'

Tom was so engrossed in his letter that it took him a moment to come back to reality.

'I—er—just jotting a few ideas down. Easier when you put it on paper, isn't it?'

'Never found that myself, but each to their own. I'm just going to look at that loose door.'

'Right you are.'

Tom went limp with relief. That had been a very close call. He looked at the sheets of paper he had covered and knew that there was only one place for them—the bin. He tore them up into very small pieces, took a clean sheet and wrote:

Dear Annie
I heard about the flooding on the news last night and
wondered how you had all fared there in Wittlesham.
I trust that you and yours are safe and well.
Yours sincerely,
Tom Featherstone.

He addressed it simply to *Annie, c/o Marsh Edge Farm*, sealed the envelope and slipped it into his inside pocket, ready to be posted at the first opportunity.

CHAPTER THIRTY

ONCE the country became aware of the terrible flood all along the east coast, help began to arrive, disaster funds were set up, gifts of food and clothing and furniture were sent to the stricken areas. The first priority was to mend the broken sea walls before the next spring tide. The armed forces, the unemployed and a host of volunteers laboured for a fortnight in wintry conditions to close the gaps with sandbags. Then began the clearing up and drying out.

It was a depressing job. At Marsh Edge Farm the tide had flowed in and out for ten days before the sea wall was fixed. When it finally drained away, Annie went back. Her mother had wanted to come too. Her mind had become fixed on the need to go home. She felt lost and uncomfortable at the hotel, imagining that people were wondering what she was doing there and wanting her gone.

'I want to sit by my own fire,' she kept repeating.

'Let me get the fire lit first, Mum,' Annie insisted. 'You stay and be here for when Bobby comes in from school, eh?'

As she trudged up the lane to the farm on a bleak February day, she was thankful not to have her mother beside her. The bare fields that should have been green with winter pasture were covered with grey silt, topped with a crust of salt. The land looked dead.

She was aware of the hawthorn tree on the edge of her vision. Try as she might not to look at it, to keep her eyes on the dreary fields, she could not avoid it. She tried to set her mind on what she had to do today. Air the house, clean up, rescue anything that could be used again. But as she came up to the tree she could hold the memories at bay no longer. The black water came rushing back. She could smell it and taste it. It roared in her ears. Her father's face bobbed in front of her, his voice cried out.

'Ann, for God's sake—'

'No—!'

Annie put her hands over her ears and ran, head down. She did not stop until she came to the farmyard.

She stopped a few feet inside the gate, appalled. The devastation here was enough to jolt her mind back to the present. A team had been round to remove the larger animal carcasses and destroy them, but otherwise the place was untouched. The flood had left behind a disgusting layer of slime mixed with a flotsam of rotting vegetation and ruined household goods. A smell of decay hung over everything.

'Oh, my God,' Annie said out loud.

She could not even begin to think where to start. She picked her way slowly across the yard. Odd gloves and wellingtons lay amongst the mud, a wooden spoon, a filthy rag that on closer inspection proved to be one of her mother's precious crocheted jug covers. It was several minutes before Annie realised what was also wrong. It was the silence. Their neighbour was still looking after what was left of the stock, so except for the wind whistling through a broken window and rattling loose boards, there was no sound but for her footsteps squelching through the mire. No clucking of hens or snorting of pigs or lowing of cows. No human voice. It was oppressive and strangely eerie. She almost found herself wishing for her father's hectoring tones. Then she heard a scrabbling sound. She turned sharply towards it and caught sight of a rat running into the hay barn. Squealing with disgust, she picked up a scrubbing brush that lay in a heap of straw and seaweed at her feet and hurled it after the creature. Then she went into the house.

The smell there was worse. Food in the larder was going off. The rag rugs that she and her mother had made together on winter evenings were sodden and muddy. The table linen and tea towels in the dresser lay mouldering in their drawers. The horsehair-stuffed sofa and chairs in the parlour were still wringing wet. And over everything was a slimy grey-brown deposit of mud, salt, soil and excrement. As Annie wandered, horrified, from room to room, the only thing she could be glad of was that her mother wasn't here to see it all. She had suffered enough. To see her home ruined like this would be too much.

It was all so dreadful that it was difficult to know where to start. There was so much that just needed to be thrown out. Annie propped the kitchen door open, then decided that fresh air was what was needed and forced open the front entrance, which was only used for important visitors and funerals. Then she tried to open all the windows, but that wasn't easy as the frames had swollen and many of them were stuck. She was about to start taking up the rugs when she heard a car arriving at the farm. Surprised, she went outside.

A stately maroon and black Riley had come to a standstill just outside the yard. Two middle-aged ladies in tweed coats and wellingtons got out of the front, and three younger women in dungarees and overalls climbed from the back. The lady who had been driving gave a cheerful wave when she saw Annie and marched across the yard to meet her.

'Hello, my dear. You must be Annie Cross. Molly Selby, how do you do? We're here from the Wittlesham Flood Committee to see what needs to be done. We went to see your mother, poor soul, and she told us that you had come out here. Now, what can we do to help? We're calling ourselves the Mrs Mop Brigade, and that's what we're here to do—mop up.'

Without waiting for an answer, she called across to the rest of the women, who were busy getting cleaning equipment out of the boot.

'Come along, let's get going! Plenty here to keep us out of mischief, I'm sure.'

Annie was flabbergasted. 'But—I—' she stammered.

'Now, then, my dear,' Molly Selby interrupted, 'no standing on foolish pride. You can't possibly do all this by yourself, now can you? And we're all more than glad to pitch in for emergencies like this. I'm sure you would do just the same if it was one of us who had been flooded out.'

Even if Annie had wanted to refuse, it would have been impossible. Molly was as unstoppable as a tank, though a kindly one. She could not resent her as she had done the WRVS lady in the car on the day after the flood.

Annie found her house invaded by the team. There was Molly's friend Joan, who was as silent as Molly was talkative, and the three younger women, Jenny, Sheila and Glenys whom she knew already by sight. They all had children at the same school as Bobby. Together, they set about putting the farmhouse to rights.

At first, Annie couldn't understand why people who had been very cool to her in the past were now going out of their way to be kind. Gradually, clues emerged. As they worked together, sweeping and hosing and scrubbing and disinfecting, she realised that she was no longer regarded as a scarlet woman. She was now a brave survivor. Being deceived and abandoned by Bobby Joe was still seen as being her own fault, but the flood was a terrible tragedy and she was one of its victims, with her father drowned and her home and living ruined. Now they were pleased to be of use to her.

On the second day of clearing up, Jenny asked what was happening to Bobby after school.

'He goes back to my mum at the hotel,' Annie told her.

'But I thought you said your mum was—well—not coping very well with it all.'

'That's right.' Annie sighed. 'I hoped it would help, having to see to Bobby. You know, it cheers you up sometimes, doesn't it, having a kiddie chattering on? But yesterday Bobby said that his grandma didn't want to listen to him. She just tells him to go and play.'

She could not understand why her mother was quite so grief stricken. It had been a miserable marriage. She had never seen any sign of love or even affection between her parents. Yet her mother was totally obliterated by her loss. The very roots of her life seemed to have been torn up. And each sigh, each tear was a reproach to her, the daughter who had reached out too late.

Jenny shook her head. 'Poor lady. How long were your parents married? Thirty years? You don't get over that in a hurry, do you? Look, why don't you send Bobby back with our lot? We're taking it in turns to look after all of them after school while we're doing this.'

Annie was amazed. Bobby had never been invited to anyone's house before. It was as if he was contaminated.

'That's really kind of you. If you're sure—'

''Course I'm sure.' Jenny called through to the next room. 'That's all right, isn't it, Sheila? Young Bobby can come and play with our lot after school each day. Then Annie won't have to worry about him.'

Sheila stopped scrubbing the parlour floor and sat back on her heels. 'Yes, good idea. It's my turn today. He can stop and have tea.'

A resentful voice inside Annie wanted to ask if they really wanted her Bobby playing with their whiter-than-white offspring, if they were sure something nasty wouldn't rub off him, but she silenced it. It would be so nice for Bobby to have some friends.

In an odd way, Annie began to enjoy herself. It was a gruelling job, scrubbing out, hard on the back and the hands and the arms, working always in the cold and the damp, with the smell of wet and mould in your nostrils. But the sense of purpose kept the guilt penned up. Sometimes she felt that if she could just scrub hard enough, she would clean the guilt away as she did the material filth from the flood.

The band of women were cheerful and practical and hard-working. Jokes and stories were thrown back and forth as they laboured, advice was handed out, agreed with or contradicted. Together, they dragged the furniture out to air, cleaned the walls and floors, washed the curtains and rugs.

On the third day the postman arrived, offered his condolences and enquired how things were going.

'I've been keeping these for you until I was sure you'd be here,' he said, handing Annie some letters.

As he drove away, Annie glanced at the envelopes. There were two official-looking things for her father and—her heart seemed to stop for a moment as she instantly recognised the writing on the third letter.

'Tom!' she gasped.

She tore open the envelope and scanned the short letter. The fact that it hardly said anything did not matter. Tom had thought about her. Despite everything, Tom was concerned enough to write and find out if she was all right.

'Thank you,' she whispered, smiling at his signature through tear-filled eyes.

She put the letter carefully back in the envelope and slipped it into her pocket.

She hardly had time to adjust to this turn of events when three men seconded from neighbouring farms arrived and started clearing up the yard, sweeping and hosing out the barns and outhouses, sorting out the usable feed and straw from the ruined stuff and getting the milking parlour scoured and functioning. Annie could hardly believe it. It would have taken her weeks to achieve all that on her own.

As she worked inside the house, Annie tried to think what she should do about Tom's letter. She wasn't sure whether she should even answer it and, if she did, how much she should say. She turned the question over and over in her mind, but could come to no satisfactory answer. Sometimes she even felt a faint resentment that he had written at all, as it had stirred up all those old feelings that she'd thought she had got the better of. She tried to put the matter out of her head and concentrate on the job in hand.

There was great satisfaction in bringing it all back from the edge of ruination. On top of this, for the first time in her life Annie was part of a team. She still wasn't quite ready to believe that she was accepted, but it was very nice while it lasted. She could even put up with Molly's well-meant interference. Not content with just cleaning up, Molly wanted to make sure that Annie and her mother were provided for.

'Now, my dear,' she said as they all sat round having one of their many tea breaks, 'have you done anything about claiming insurance? Or probate? Did your father leave a will?'

'I—I don't know. I don't think so. He didn't trust banks and solicitors and the like. He said they were all thieving sh—oh!' Annie broke off as she realised what she was saying. Molly's husband was a solicitor. 'I didn't mean—'

Molly waved away her embarrassment.

'Lots of country people think like that. Misguided, but there you are. Now, where would he have kept his papers?'

'I'll have to ask my mum,' Annie lied. There were some things that she did not want Molly Selby prying into.

That evening, before squeezing into the Riley with the others, she took the tin deed-box from on top of her parents' wardrobe and hid it in the basket she used to carry her flask and sandwiches.

Her mother was not at all eager to open the box.

'He never let me look in it. Said it wasn't my place to know,' she said, looking at the box as if it were an unexploded bomb.

'But we've got to see what's there, Mum. Otherwise we won't know who the farm and everything belongs to.'

'I don't know, Annie—'

'Don't worry, Mum. You won't have to see to any of it. I'll deal with everything,' Annie reassured her, wondering as she said it just what she was going to do. She knew as little as her mother about legal matters.

There was not much inside the box. There was her own and her parents' birth certificates—not Bobby's, which she had in her own safe place—her parents' wedding certificate, the mortgage agreement for the farm and—a will. Not a solicitor's will, but one written on a printed will form from Woolworth's. It was short and to the point, leaving everything to 'my son if I have one, or else to my wife, Edna Cross'. It had been witnessed by the neighbour who was caring for their animals.

'Look at the date—two months before I was born,' Annie said.

'He hoped you was going to be a boy,' her mother said.

'Well, that was tough luck for him,' Annie retorted.

Her mother's eyes filled with tears.

'Annie! Don't speak ill of the dead.'

'Sorry.'

She frowned as a new thought struck her.

'Did you want me to be a boy?'

'It would have made him happy.'

The pain of it silenced her. She got up and went to the window, staring out at the night sky. She was as unwanted as poor little Bobby. She should have been a boy. He shouldn't have been born at all.

'Well, you'll have to put up with me. Is there anything in here that looks like insurance papers?' she asked, covering her feelings with a Molly-like briskness.

There wasn't. But there was a mysterious message. It was written in pencil on the back of a feed bill, in her father's handwriting.

By the fireplace in the back bedroom.

'What does this mean?' she asked.

Her mother shook her head. 'I don't know, dear.'

Annie put the paper in her pocket. The rest she bundled back into the deed-box. It was so difficult. If only she knew about these things. If only she had been allowed to stay on at school, then she might understand more. There was only one thing for it—she was going to have to ask Molly. Molly in turn insisted that she speak to her husband.

Mr Selby turned out to be a quietly-spoken serious man, several years older than his energetic wife. He shook his head over the will, but said that it was valid as a legal document and that he would oversee the business of ensuring that everything was transferred to the widow. Like his wife, he was concerned about how Annie and her family were going to live. There were no insurance policies to claim on. There was talk of compensation for farmers, but that might take months and in the meantime how were they going to survive?

'You say that if there had been a bank book, it would have been in here. But I would have thought there would have been something put by in the way of savings. Ask your mother. She might know where your late father might have hidden a store of bank notes. Under the mattress is a popular place.'

Annie thought of the message on the feed bill.

'I'll ask her,' she said.

'You do that,' Mr Selby said. 'You will need something to tide you over. If your mother wishes to keep the farm, that is. She may want to sell it, though I have to say that she will be unlikely to realise very much on it in the condition it is in at the moment. In fact, I very much doubt if anyone would want to buy it.'

Annie thanked him for his advice. Mr Selby rose as she left the room and opened the door for her himself. He held his hand out and, as Annie shook it, took hers in both of his.

'It has been a great pleasure to be of service to you, Miss Cross. My wife is very impressed with you, and I am inclined to agree with her. But you have some difficult times ahead of you. I will be in touch with you in the matter of the will, but if there is anything else about which you need advice, remember that I am here to help.'

Annie was stunned. Nobody in authority had ever spoken like that to her before.

'Th–thank you—' she stammered.

As she left the office, she wondered if the flood had worked some sort of magic on the people of Wittlesham, making them all kind and helpful.

On Sunday, Annie took Bobby for a walk. She asked her mother to come too, but Edna insisted she was too tired. Annie did not persist. She needed to think—about Tom's letter and about what they were going to do with the farm. Somebody had to make some decisions, and she supposed that somebody was her. It was a blustery day and Bobby had on the brown balaclava and matching gloves that she had knitted for him. Glad to be out of the gloomy atmosphere of the hotel, Annie raced him along the clifftop road until they were both red-nosed and out of breath. Annie found herself laughing. Already she felt much better.

'Where are we going, Mum? To the pier? Can we go up the pier?'

'No, I thought we'd go and look at Silver Sands.'

'But that's a long way.'

'I know, but we can do it.'

At first, Bobby scampered ahead, chasing seagulls and pretending to be an aeroplane. Then after a while he came and walked by Annie's side, slipping his woolly paw into her gloved hand.

'Aunty Gwen died, didn't she?' he remarked matter-of-factly.

'Yes, she did.' Annie's throat ached. It was hard to keep her voice steady.

'I liked Aunty Gwen. She was nice.'

'Yes, she was.'

'Is she coming back?'

'No, darling. When people die they never come back. They go and live in heaven.'

They had a long discussion about heaven which lasted them until they were out of the town and striding along the sea wall. Annie could see the exact spot where she had first met Tom. Such a lot had happened to them both since then, so much had been lost through misunderstandings. Annie felt the clouds of indecision lift from her mind. Tom had stretched out a hand of friendship. They had known each other far too long for her to reject it. She would write back, and in the same style that he had written to her—a short, friendly note.

With that decided, she felt strong enough to face the devastation at Silver Sands. The fences were torn away, the caravans were smashed and turned over, the chalet tipped off its piers and leaning drunkenly sideways. The only thing that appeared to have survived the storm unscathed was the brick-built toilet block. Annie stared at the chalet, imagining Reggie trying to pull Gwen up on to the roof in the wind and the rain, and then the sea wall giving way, and Gwen being washed out of his grasp by the massive wave… Tears slid down her face as she felt his desperation.

'Mummy? Why are you crying?'

Annie brushed her sleeve across her face. 'I'm not crying, darling. It's just the wind making my eyes water.'

'It's not very nice here any more. Where are the swings?'

'I don't know. I suppose they're in a heap here somewhere with everything else.'

Reggie and Gwen had such plans for this place. She had heard them enthuse about it for hours. Once they had paid off their loan, they were going to buy more caravans, and then, if they could buy the chalet next door, which also had a big garden, they would expand the whole enterprise, but never have the vans crowded too close together. They were going to carry on the job they had started in making the place look pretty with flower beds and trees. They were going to add to the swings and see-saw and make a big children's playground with every sort of ride.

'After all, if the kiddies are happy, the mums and dads are too,' Reggie pointed out.

Their favourite plan had been to open up a café serving teas and ice creams and meals.

'After all, it's not much of a holiday for Mum if she still has to cook,' Gwen said.

'We might even be able to get a licence, run a bar for the men in the evenings,' Reggie said, raising cries of protest from Gwen and Annie.

'Why not the women as well? They like a drink sometimes, 'specially if they're on holiday.'

'If you put all that in, they won't need to leave the camp at all,' Annie said.

Reggie grinned. 'That's the idea,' he said.

It was very hard to picture happy people enjoying their holidays here now. The place was a desolate wreck. And she had promised to buy it from Reggie. She shoved her hands into her pockets and hunched her shoulders against the raw wind. She couldn't possibly keep her promise. They had no money, nothing but a damp house and a flood-damaged farm with hardly any stock and eight years of mortgage still to be paid. Unless...

'Come on!' she called to Bobby. 'We're going home. There's something I want to look for.'

Molly and her Mrs Mop Brigade had done a wonderful job. The house was clean and orderly, and the furniture that could be saved had been polished. But, despite having the wind blowing through it day and night, it was still running with damp and not fit to be lived in.

Bobby walked in cautiously, as if he was expecting his grandfather still to be lurking there.

'It's funny in here. It sounds funny and it smells.'

'I know, that's because we had to throw lots of stuff out. But when it's dried out, Mrs Selby says the Flood Committee will find us some things to replace them. Come on.'

They went up to the back bedroom, a dark little room with only an iron bedstead and a pile of old newspapers in it. There was very obviously nothing by the fireplace. Annie knelt down pulled out the dusty grate. Nothing but some fallen soot. She felt cautiously up the chimney. More soot trickled down, making her cough.

'What are you looking for, Mum?'

'I don't know—'

She stared at the floorboards, frowning. That note must have meant something. Then she noticed that one of the boards had been sawn across, making a section only about a foot long. She pressed it and it moved very slightly. Her heart began to beat faster.

'Bobby, run down and get me a knife from the kitchen.'

Bobby was back in a flash. Annie prised up the board and felt around in the space between the joists. Her fingers met with a parcel wrapped in sacking.

'That's it!'

'What, Mum?'

She pulled it out. It was quite light and covered in dust. She opened it up and caught her breath. Bobby let out a long whistle.

'It's treasure. Hidden treasure!'

It was all in notes—bundles of ten shillings, one pounds, white fivers, all neatly done up in rotting rubber bands. She counted it and counted again, unable to believe her eyes.

The old skinflint. He'd kept them all without a decent coat or a smart pair of shoes, he'd never let her mother have anything new in the house, they'd had to scrimp and save, make do and mend, and all the time there was a fortune under the floorboards.

'Whose is it, Mum? Who put it there?'

'Your grandfather. So it belongs to your grandma.'

'Is Grandma rich, then?'

'Richer than she ever thought she'd be, yes.'

What was her mother's reaction going to be? At a guess, she was going to find this much money a worry. She would not know what to do for the best. At the moment, she could hardly decide which of two skirts to put on of a morning. Still holding a bundle of five-pound notes, Annie wandered into her own bedroom and over to the window. She stared out across the fields at what was left of Silver Sands.

It was up to her to make the decision. She felt sick with the responsibility. She had never had to make her mind up about anything to do with money before. Her father had always held the purse-strings and given the orders. There had been no choices. She and her mother had to do as they were told.

Bobby came in and joined her at the window. He put his hand in hers.

'What are you doing, Mum?'

'I'm thinking—about this money. You see Silver Sands? I don't know, but I think we could buy it.'

If only she knew something about land and prices. The weight of her ignorance was dragging her down.

'But it's all broken.'

'I know, but it could be fixed, and much sooner than the farm. The land's all salty and nobody seems to know how long it will take till it's usable again. Some people are saying it's going to take years. But if we could get Silver Sands going, we'd be able to keep the wolf from the door. Perhaps even more than that. Reggie was always sure he was going to be rich one day…'

But Reggie was a man and knew about business. She was a farm girl who had missed a lot of her schooling because her father had needed her to work. How could she possibly make a go of it? She wouldn't know where to start. Then she found herself remembering the night of the flood. If she had not fetched up against that tree, she would have been washed away. She would be dead now, drowned, like Gwen and her father. She'd not survived that just to go on living like a drudge for the rest of her life. This was her chance. She had thought her big chance had come when she'd met Bobby Joe, but she had been wrong. It was now, and it was up to her to make something of it.

'Come on,' she said to Bobby. 'Find me a bag to put all this money in. I've got to go and do some sums.'

CHAPTER THIRTY-ONE

THE money changed everything. Annie couldn't believe how different it felt to know that she had all that amount at her command. Her confidence rose, she began to look ahead with pleasure and excitement, she even held herself straighter and walked with a spring in her step. As she had suspected, her mother looked on the hoard as one more thing to worry about, and was more than willing to let Annie deal with it. And deal with it she did. Together with Reggie, who came back to Wittlesham for the day, she went to see Mr Selby. He had consulted contacts at a bank and an estate agent and sorted out a fair price for Silver Sands. As soon as it was agreed, Reggie left. He couldn't bear to stay in Wittlesham a moment longer.

Annie and Reggie hugged as they stood on the station platform.

'I still can't believe you're doing this for me, Annie. All your nest egg!'

'Not all of it. And anyway, I'm not doing it just for you— it's what I want. I've always longed to own Silver Sands,' Annie told him.

The guard blew his whistle. Reggie kissed Annie on the cheek.

'Bless you, Annie. You've been a wonderful friend.'

'You and Gwennie were the very best of friends to me. You stuck by me when nobody else did. Now, get on board. It's about to go.'

Reggie climbed on to the train and leaned out of the window.

'Best of luck, Annie. And thanks for everything!'

The engine tooted its whistle and started up with a snorting of black smoke. Annie stood and waved till she could not see Reggie any longer, then watched the back of the guard's van pass out of sight. Tears ran down her face. Another part of her past was gone for ever.

'Be happy again one day, Reggie,' she whispered.

Her next task was to move back into Marsh Edge. She knew her mother would never even start to be herself again until she was in her own home. Since the Mrs Mop Brigade had left, she had been keeping the kitchen range going all the time so that room at least was nearly dried out. The solid old wooden furniture had survived its soaking, though the doors to the dresser were warped. Most of the crockery and utensils were all right. Most important of all, her mother's sewing machine had been cleaned and oiled and pronounced none the worse for its ordeal. The ruined parlour furniture hardly mattered, since they never used the room anyway.

Edna wept as she entered the house. For all the efforts of Molly Selby and the clean-up gang, it still smelt damp and looked forlorn.

Annie fetched a heap of folded curtains and pushed it into her mother's arms.

'The Flood Committee gave us these, Mum. They're very pretty, but they don't fit our windows. Do you think you can do something with them?'

Reluctantly, Edna shook one out and held it up.

'I suppose so,' she said, 'but—'

'I've bought some matching thread, and the machine's working perfectly. Why don't you get going on them? It's ages yet till we need to get a meal on.'

The task was just what Edna needed after the long days of inactivity at the hotel. She had always been if not happy, then content when working at her sewing.

Bobby was delighted to be back home, and with friends to play with at school now and no one making his life a misery at home, he was happier than he had ever been.

The greatly reduced dairy herd was brought back to the farm, though they had to be kept in pens in the yard as the fields were ruined. Chickens ran about clucking and scratching once more. Marsh Edge had come back to life. Annie looked at it with satisfaction, but knew that the money from the small amount of milk and a few eggs was not going to go anywhere near keeping them. If Silver Sands was to be their future, then she had to get it up and running ready for the summer season.

With the last of her money, she had the site cleared and bought two caravans.

'That's not going to be enough,' she said to Bobby as they watched the men manoeuvre the vans into place.

'You've got to get the swings back and the see-saw. And a slide too,' Bobby told her.

'You're right,' Annie agreed. 'And that all takes money. We'll have to go and borrow some.'

'How do you do that?' Bobby asked.

'You go to a bank.'

It was easy enough to say, but a lot more difficult to do. On the morning of her appointment, Annie paraded in front of her mother.

'Do I look all right?'

She was wearing an assortment of clothes. There was a sunray-pleated grey skirt and a navy jacket that had come from the Flood Relief Committee, a white blouse her mother had made some years ago and new navy court shoes she had bought herself. For an outfit of hand-me-downs, it really looked very good.

'Very nice, dear.'

It was said in the same flat tone that her mother used for everything. Annie could see that she was trying to sound approving, but that the effort was just too much for her.

'Do I need a hat and gloves? It doesn't look complete without a hat and gloves, does it?'

'Well—I suppose it doesn't really matter.'

'But it does matter, Mum. I'm going to see the bank manager. Our future depends on this!'

The all too familiar bewildered look came over her mother's face. 'Do you really think this is a good idea? All that money—'

Annie sighed. 'It's the only way, Mum.'

It was no use trying to make her see. The thought of borrowing money frightened her.

'Well, it'll have to do,' Annie said, going back to the problem of her appearance. 'I got to go, Mum. Wish me luck!'

As she clip-clopped down the track in the new shoes, part of her could hardly believe that this was happening. She, Annie Cross, was the owner of a business and going to see a bank manager. It was exciting and terrifying. She held tight on to her handbag, where she had the notebook in which she had worked out all the figures. It was a bright May morning, but here in the fields there was still little sign of life. The salt no longer sparkled on the surface, but it had penetrated the soil. The only things that were growing were salt-loving marsh plants whose seeds had been left behind by the flood-water. There were government plans for rehabilitating the ru-ined land, but it was all going to take years. Annie hardly cared about that now. She had her eyes on a better scheme.

She had only been inside the bank once before—when she'd made the appointment to see the manager. It had not been a pleasant experience, having a snotty clerk question her about why she wanted to speak to the great Mr Everard. She looked up at the stone-faced building with its heavy oak doors, determined not to be intimidated. She had as much right as anyone else to be here, she told herself. She took a deep breath and walked in.

She spoke to a different clerk this time, a chubby young man with a severe short-back-and-sides. He gave her a look of veiled surprise when she said she had an appointment to see Mr Everard.

'Really? If you would just wait a moment, I'll go and enquire.'

He was soon back. 'If you would like to come this way, Miss Cross.'

There was a faint but definite emphasis on the 'Miss'. Annie clenched her teeth. Wittlesham was such a small town. Sometimes she felt as if she had a placard round her neck saying 'Unmarried Mother'.

She was left to wait on an uncomfortable chair in a lobby outside the manager's office. It was all right, she told her-self. She had spoken to a solicitor so she could speak to a bank manager. There was nothing to it.

The clerk reappeared, knocked on the door and opened it.

'Miss Cross to see you, sir.'

Annie walked in.

Mr Everard was not like nice Mr Selby. He did not smile encouragingly or tell her she was doing splendidly or give her good advice. He was a stony faced man with a shiny bald head and a belly that strained beneath his waistcoat. Instantly and instinctively, Annie disliked him. His eyes flicked over her as she entered the room and registered faint disapproval. He nodded at the straight-backed chair set in front of his big oak desk.

'Sit down, please, Miss Cross.'

Annie sat. He made the nerves all down the back of her spine tense. If she had been a dog, her hair would have been standing on end.

'And you are—a hairdresser? A dressmaker?'

He did not sound particularly interested in either possibility.

Annie looked steadily back at him. 'I own the Silver Sands Holiday Park,' she told him. It came out rather more loudly than was necessary.

'Indeed?' Mr Everard looked as if he did not quite believe her. 'And why do you wish to see me?'

Battling with the feeling that she was on to a loser before she had even started, Annie launched into her prepared speech. Mr Everard sat staring at a point somewhere beyond her shoulder, appearing to be hardly bothering to listen to her ideas. He nodded vaguely when she said she wanted to start small and expand a bit each year, but she was sure he did not take in a word about her wanting to give the holiday-makers everything they needed without stirring outside the site. He hardly glanced at the figures she'd slaved over for so long. Annie felt as if she were talking to a mattress. She wanted to smack his hand like her schoolteachers used to do, to wake him up and make him take notice of her.

When she finished, he put down the pencil he had been fiddling with and folded his hands over his paunch.

'I'm sorry, Miss Cross, but it's absolutely out of the question.'

He did not sound sorry, just bored.

Annie could not believe he had said that. She glared at him. 'But why?'

Mr Everard gave a sigh. He spoke with exaggerated patience. 'Miss Cross, this bank is here to provide financial support to viable businesses, not to pipedreams.'

That was it. Annie snapped.

'But it's not a pipedream! I can do it, I know I can! I just need a bit more money to get it all going.'

'I don't think so, Miss Cross. Now, if you don't mind, I do have other clients to see—'

He reached for the bell on his desk.

Annie could see everything slipping away. It was so unfair.

'I bet if it was Mr Smith what used to own it sitting here, you wouldn't say that. You'd listen to him.'

Mr Everard was unmoved. 'I don't think so, Miss Cross,' he repeated.

The clerk came in, summoned by the bell. He stood with the door open, waiting for her to leave. Annie ignored him. She took a deep breath, trying to steady the shaking inside, trying to control the impotent fury. She leaned forward, concentrating all her efforts on the manager.

'But don't you see, it was starting to be a success last summer. Mr Smith was making a go of it. He was going to expand this year. He only left because his wife was drowned in the floods.'

'That was last year, Miss Cross, before the floods and when the site had six vans on it. Things are very different now. I'm afraid that is all I have to say on the matter. Good day.'

Annie was furious. Tears of anger and disappointment stung her eyes. She blinked them back. She was not going to let this horrible man and his sidekick see her cry. She jumped up.

'You'll eat your words one day, just you wait and see!' she shouted, and marched out of the office and out of the bank.

Behind her, she could feel them casting their eyes up to heaven, then dismissing her from their minds. She was just a silly young woman. Emotional. Not to be regarded.

Annie stumped the length of the High Street, blind and deaf to everything in her path. She came to a stop at the sea front and thumped both fists on the iron railings.

'Stupid, stupid, stupid man! I hate him! Why can't he see—? I could make a success of it, I know I could—'

Somehow, she would show him. She'd make him eat his words. She imagined him in ten years' time, looking at her holiday camp with its rows of gleaming caravans and its café and play area and swimming pool and clubhouse, looking at the hundreds of people there spending their money.

'You were right, Miss Cross,' he'd be saying. 'You were right and I was wrong, so wrong. This is the most successful camp in Essex. It's even bigger than Butlins.'

And then he'd say how he'd been sacked and he was desperate for a job, and would she consider him for anything, anything at all, even toilet cleaning? For several happy minutes, Annie debated whether it would be more satisfying to turn him away or give him a truly horrible job and watch him having to be grateful to her day after day. She decided on the latter.

In the meantime, she realised she was shaking with cold

and anger. She needed a cup of tea. She found a café already bravely open and sat down in a window-seat and ordered. She put three spoons of sugar into her tea and stirred fit to wear the cup away. But as she sipped her hot brew, her fury subsided, leaving room for bleak reality. By the time she had finished it, she had to face the next problem. What was she going to do now? She had a caravan park with two vans on it, a farmhouse that was still not fully dried out, fields of ruined grassland and no income. There was the compensation money… Annie leaned her elbows on the table and stared out at the sea. It looked blue and friendly today, sparkling in the spring sunshine. People from cities would love to be here today, staying in her caravans, strolling by that sea. The compensation money was supposed to be for supporting farmers until their land was productive again, but if she spent it on getting more caravans, surely that was a better use for it?

She pondered over the idea for a long time. Mr Everard's dismissal of her ideas as pipedreams undermined her. Supposing he was right? He was a man, a bank manager, he was supposed to be an expert in business matters. What did she know, after all? She always had imagined things. Stupid things—kid's dreams. Bobby Joe, he'd been a dream, or rather the idea of being married to him and living in America had been. Her vision of how Silver Sands was going to be seemed so real, but was that all pie in the sky too? If only there was someone she could talk it over with. She thought of the women of the Mrs Mop Brigade, secure in their homes with their husbands to support them. Why wasn't there someone for her? It seemed as if she had always been alone—an only child and now an unmarried mother. Perhaps she should give up on Silver Sands before she threw all their precious money away.

She paid for the tea and went outside. A short way along the clifftop was the hotel they had stayed in after the flood. They'd survived that, and gone back home. Down the coast, where the land dipped down to sea level, she could see Silver Sands and her brave new caravans, all two of them.

'Blow you, Mr High-and-Mighty Everard,' she said out loud. 'I'm going to do it if it kills me. Reggie thought he could make a success of it, and so do I.'

The decision refuelled her fighting spirit. She squared her shoulders and took several deep breaths of sea air. She would use the compensation money to buy more vans. Right. But in the meantime, how was she going to support her family?

The hard truth was that she was not qualified for anything. She knew about farming and she could keep house, and that was just about it. She had to get something that gave her time to look after her mum and Bobby, and see to the caravans, so it was no good going for a shop job or something at Sutton's. There was only one thing for it. It had to be a cleaning job.

By the time she went home she had three jobs lined up. It wasn't at all what she had hoped for when she'd set out that morning, but it had served to focus her purpose. She was going to make a success of Silver Sands, come what may.

CHAPTER THIRTY-TWO

EVERY morning as she cycled through the entrance, Annie looked at the new sign: *Silver Sands Holiday Park—Wittlesham-on-Sea—Prop. A and E Cross.* Every morning without fail her heart lifted with pride. Her holiday park. Her baby. There wasn't much to it yet, but with the compensation money she had been able to buy three more vans. Now there were five caravans, a toilet and washing block and a couple of swings and a slide, but it was hers, proof that she was Somebody, not just an Unmarried Mother from a poor farm.

It was September and the last week of the school holidays. Next week she was only half booked, but now all five vans were occupied. She looked at the bathing suits hung out on the lines outside the vans, at the balls and buckets and spades abandoned by the steps and was glad that the holiday-makers were having such good weather. She loved seeing pale city children arrive, looking as if they had never seen the sun, and brown, tousled children leaving with precious stones and shells and paper flags to remind them of their happy time at Silver Sands.

She was halfway through cleaning the toilets when a very pregnant young woman came in with a howling toddler. She looked apologetic when she saw Annie.

'Oh, dear, you haven't finished, have you? I'm ever so sorry, I don't want to mess it all up again, but he's got the runs—'

Annie assured her it was quite all right to use the toilets, that was what they were there for.

'Oh, that is nice of you. There's no rest when you've got little uns, is there? On the go all the time. But at least they can run about here and get dirty and it don't matter. We went to this boarding house last year and the landlady fussed about the mess all the time. I don't think she liked children...'

She chattered on as she saw to the smelly child and left trailing a dripping nappy. Annie cleaned up after her. Years of living with her father had trained her to listen, look polite and keep her thoughts to herself. If the young mother felt really welcome here, she might be back next year, she might recommend Silver Sands to her friends. Annie finished off the floor, packed away the cleaning things and made a mental note to mow the grass that afternoon.

After scouring out the toilets at Silver Sands, she went back to the farm to get Bobby off to school, feed the chickens and pigs and see that her mother was all right. Then she usually whizzed down to the site again to make sure everyone was happy and there were no complaints before pedalling over to get to whichever house she was due at by ten.

Once there, there were no problems to be solved and the work was easy. The houses she was employed at had always been kept in tip-top condition and it was only a case of cleaning off the surface dirt and dust and doing the polishing. There were even vacuum cleaners to use that went over all the carpets in a trice and got them ten times cleaner than a stiff brush would ever do. It was all so different from the farmhouse, which had always been hard work to keep clean and was now ten times worse, with damp and salt still sweating out of the walls.

So the part-time work was not a problem, and the money kept their heads above water. What she didn't quite know how to deal with was Jeff Sutton. He seemed to be turning up at the site far too often.

'What are you doing here?' she asked the first time he appeared.

'Skiving off,' he admitted, smiling disarmingly.

Annie's attention was only half with him. She was walking round the site, making sure everything was all right. Jeff tagged along.

'Why aren't you at work?' she asked.

Jeff shrugged. 'Oh—work. It's such a bore.'

'But won't you be missed?' Annie persisted. She knew all about trying to sneak a bit of time away from work before her father had noticed.

'Missed? Oh, yes. Like a hole in the head.'

Jeff's handsome, boyish features drooped into a discontented pout. 'They're glad to see the back of me. I mess up everything I do. At least, that's what my father says, and he's the boss. He built it all up from nothing as he's for ever telling us, so he knows best, as he's also for ever telling us.'

'It's not easy working for your father,' Annie said with feeling. 'I should know. Mine—'

'You're so right,' Jeff interrupted. His voice became conspiratorial. 'It's so nice to speak to someone who understands. I knew you would. It's no use trying to explain to Mother, she never listens to a word I say. And as for Father, well, I can never do a thing right as far as he's concerned.'

'My dad was like that as well. It makes you feel sort of useless,' Annie sympathised.

With a jolt, she realised just how much better things were now. She was working hard, yes, but then she'd always had to work hard. She had the full weight of responsibility for providing for and looking after her mother and Bobby. She had the headache of doing all sorts of things she'd never done before at the caravan site, like writing letters and taking money and keeping accounts and advertising. She had the constant worry that Silver Sands was not going to pay its way and they were all going to be paupers. But at least she was doing it herself. If she made mistakes, there was no longer the dread of her father finding out. And the atmosphere at home was so different, even though her mother was still grieving. It was like having a lead weight taken off her spirit. Yes, the days were much better than before. It was only at night that her father came back to haunt her, pleading with her out of the swirling black water so that she woke trembling and terrified and racked with guilt.

'…always been the favourite, of course. That's the trouble with being the middle one,' Jeff was saying.

'Yes, of course,' Annie said, with no idea of what he was talking about. She glanced at her watch. 'Heavens, look at the time! I'll be late for my job.'

'I had better let you go, then,' Jeff said reluctantly. 'It's been really nice talking to you. You're such a good listener, Annie. But then, we've always been good friends, haven't we?'

'I suppose so,' Annie said. She wouldn't have said Jeff was a friend, exactly.

'We could be even better friends.'

'We'll see about that,' Annie said.

Which only served to encourage Jeff. He seemed to find the time to turn up at the site a couple of times a week, roaring up the track in his red MG. Today was one of those days.

Annie could hear the sports car as soon as she arrived from seeing to the chickens and pigs at the farm.

'Are you here again?' she said.

He really was a bit of a nuisance.

'I just wanted to see you. I've got to take my horrible little brother out for a game of tennis this morning,' Jeff explained.

'That's nice,' said Annie.

Tennis. Now a tennis court would be a good thing to have on the site. When she had more vans, of course. Maybe the year after next.

'No, it isn't. Tim's so spoilt. He always sulks when he loses.'

'Well, it must be better than being cooped up in an office on a nice day like this.'

'I suppose so.'

Jeff loped after her as she greeted the holiday-makers. He was wearing tennis shorts and a white V-necked sweater. His legs were tanned and muscular.

'I bet there's some nice girls at the Tennis Club,' Annie said.

'Not as nice as you,' Jeff answered.

At that moment, the young mother with the smelly child waved at her. 'He's much better now. We're going down the beach in a minute.'

'Oh, good. Have a nice time,' Annie responded.

One of the other mothers came to speak to her. Still Jeff hung about.

'Hadn't you better go?' she said to him. 'Your brother will be waiting for you.'

Jeff gave an exaggerated sigh. 'Oh, all right. I know my place, I'm just an unpaid nanny.'

'For heaven's sake!' Annie snapped. 'Just go. I expect it'll be fun.'

She had better things to do than sympathise with him when he had such an easy life.

It was only later on when she was washing some dishes that she wondered if she had heard Jeff right. She hoped not. She liked Jeff well enough, but that was as far as it went. No, he couldn't have said it. He had all those posh girls at the Tennis Club and the Little Theatre Club and the Young Conservatives to choose from. She started drying the first draining board full of china. Would there ever be anyone for her? Probably not. Who was going to look twice at a woman with an illegitimate child in tow? She was the sort of person who was held up as an object lesson by the mothers of rebellious young girls. 'Don't you go staying out after half past ten with that boy, or you'll end up like that Annie Cross.'

She stood with her hands in the warm soapy water. End up like Annie Cross, with an illegitimate child, cleaning other people's houses. But Annie Cross had Silver Sands. Annie Cross would show them all. And she would make sure that Bobby had more than she ever did.

At three o'clock she set off for home. Wittlesham was bright with the last rush of summer visitors as she cycled back through the town. Families trailed about licking ice creams, girls in cotton dresses flirted with young men in open-necked shirts, pensioners sunned themselves on benches. Down on the beach, mothers in straw hats and fathers with knotted handkerchiefs on their heads sat in deckchairs knitting and reading the papers while children dug holes and made sandcastles and rushed, screaming, in and out of the waves. All along the promenade and the cliff top road, the cafés and ice cream kiosks and souvenir stalls were doing a roaring trade.

It must be nice to have a holiday. It must be nice to go

somewhere far away from your own home for a week. One day she would take Bobby and her mum and they'd go somewhere lovely and stay in a real hotel and have other people wait on them. With this happy thought in her head, she freewheeled down the slope out of town and bumped up the track to Silver Sands, where Bobby was waiting for her at the swings.

Cutting the grass was hard work with only a hand mower. Soon, she told Bobby, they'd have a big petrol-driven one like Jeff said the Suttons had. Had Jeff really said that? she wondered. *Not as nice as you.* If he had, then he was just pulling her leg. She pushed the thought out of her head.

They rode home with Annie standing on the pedal scooting and Bobby on the saddle holding on to her shoulders and both of them squealing and laughing as they bounced over the potholes in the track. The fields on either side were white now with the gypsum that was being spread on them.

'See that?' Annie said, as they flew along. 'Next year the grass will grow again, according to the government boffins. That white stuff will take away all the salt.'

Should she rent out the fields then, get rid of what was left of the dairy herd and put all the money into Silver Sands? If she bought more caravans—a lot more caravans—and started using the field next to Silver Sands to put them on, then they would bring in more money than the farm ever did, even if she was buying them on the never-never. If they were fully let, that was. They'd only been fully let the six weeks of the school holidays this year. They couldn't live on that. She still needed the cleaning jobs to keep them going.

'Mum?' Bobby's voice was loud in her ear, his hands tight on her shoulders.

'What, darling?'

'It's nice when you're home.'

'I know, darling. I'd like to stay at home with you, you know that, but I have to go and earn some money.'

'Other mums stay at home.'

'Yes.'

People like Jenny and Sheila and Glenys.

'It's because I haven't got a dad, isn't it?'

Oh, God. Annie's knuckles whitened on the handlebars. She was glad she wasn't looking him in the face. She couldn't bear that, the hurt look he had when he spoke of his father.

'You have got a dad, Bobby. He's in America.'

They bumped through the gate and stopped in the yard. Bobby climbed down. He mumbled something.

'What?' said Annie. 'What was that?' Even though she knew she wouldn't like it when she heard it.

Bobby looked away. His lip trembled. 'It's no use having a dad in America,' he growled and ran off.

Annie followed him slowly. She parked the bike against the barn. All the brightness had gone out of the day. Whatever she did, even if Silver Sands was a great success and she ended up very rich, Bobby would never have a proper father.

They were nothing but trouble, men, she reflected as she walked into the house. Bobby Joe had deceived her, Jeff might well become a nuisance if he carried on saying silly things like he had this morning, and Tom—well, Tom was part of the past now. That letter he'd sent after the flood had been nice, it had shown he hadn't forgotten her, but that was all. He had his own life up in Nottingham.

It wasn't till the evening, after she had finished the chores and put Bobby to bed, that Annie sat down at the kitchen table to deal with the post. There wasn't a lot now that the season was almost at an end, just four letters. She sorted through them, then caught her breath. Tom. One was from Tom. She ripped it open.

Dear Annie,

I just thought I would write and ask how you are all faring after everything that happened to you in the floods. I was so sorry to hear about Gwen. She was a good friend to both of us, looking after our post as she did. You must miss her terribly.

I'm not sure what to say about the loss of your father. What is happening to the farm now? I don't even know if you are still there. How did your mother take it all, and how are you managing?

You might like to know that I am helping my father run the coach company now and I have a son, Michael, who is three years old and the most wonderful little boy in the world. I expect you feel the same about your child.

It would be really nice to hear from you, just to know how you are, but I shall understand if you would rather not reply.

Yours sincerely,

Tom Featherstone.

All through that night, and on and off for days afterwards, Annie thought about the letter and tried to come to some conclusion about the meaning and the intention behind the wording. But, right from the moment of reading it, part of her knew that of one thing there was no doubt—eventually, she would write back.

CHAPTER THIRTY-THREE

'YOU'RE home early,' Moira said as Tom came in through the door of their small house on a freezing January day.

'There's nothing more to be seen to today. It's always quiet for a while after Christmas,' he said, hanging his hat on the hall stand, unwinding his scarf.

Moira stood in the doorway through to the kitchen and watched him, her arms folded across her chest. When they were first married, she used to come hurrying to the door to meet him. Even a year or so ago she might have planted a dutiful kiss on his cheek when he came home. The vacuum was filled by Michael, who came rushing in from the back garden, his cheeks red and his knees dirty.

'Daddy!' he cried, flinging himself into Tom's arms.

Tom scooped him up and kissed him.

'Mikey! How's my best boy? Have you been good today?'

The child nodded happily. 'I been playing with David.'

'That's nice. You like David, don't you?'

Tom looked over the boy's head at Moira, who was just turning away.

'You've been round at the Butlers', have you?'

Moira immediately became defensive.

'So what if I have? I'm entitled to some time out of the house, aren't I?'

'Of course you are,' Tom said, perplexed by the attack. 'I was only asking. When have I ever complained about you going to visit people?'

'It's all very well for you. You're out all day, doing things and meeting people. I'm stuck here with no one to talk to but a four-year-old.'

It seemed to Tom that she was out most days. There was the church Young Wives group one afternoon and a gathering of ex-Young Conservative mothers on another and in between days, like today, she visited friends or relatives or had them round for tea and cakes while the children played.

In his arms, Michael had gone very quiet. Tom looked down at the child's face and saw with dismay that he had gone pale and wide-eyed. Michael knew the signs. He could tell that a row was brewing.

'Did you have a good game with David while the mummies were talking?' Tom asked him.

'Mummy went out. I was a good boy and didn't cry at all,' Michael told him.

Tom couldn't help looking at Moira again with a question in his face.

Moira flushed. 'Joan Butler minded him for ten minutes while I went to the shops. You're not going to complain about that, I hope?'

'Of course not,' Tom said.

He set Michael down on the floor and hung his coat on the stand.

'Come on,' he said, 'we'll go and lay the table for Mummy while she finishes getting tea ready.'

'Don't expect anything yet. You're so early, I've hardly started,' Moira told him.

'I'm only fifteen minutes early,' Tom pointed out.

'Oh, I see. I've got to be on time like one of your coaches now, have I?' Moira retorted, and slammed into the kitchen.

Tom did not make the point that it was usually Moira complaining that he was not on time and telling him that he upset her routine if he was not home on the dot to eat what she had prepared. Instead he squatted down and helped Michael undo his buttons and belt.

'We'll go and make up the fire then, shall we?' he suggested.

After the jollity of Christmas, he began to notice other changes. Where Moira used to encourage him to take more of the management tasks over from his father, now she was all in favour of his being out driving the coaches, especially in the evenings.

'Those drivers are out for all the overtime they can get. It's much better if you do the evening and Saturday work. I'm sure your father would appreciate it,' she said.

'I thought you didn't like me working at weekends,' Tom said. 'You're always saying how I don't take Michael off your hands enough.'

'He can always go to one of his grannies. And we must put business first,' Moira told him.

At first Tom was glad of what seemed to be a loosening of her rigid attitudes, but then odd little discrepancies occurred. When he mentioned a film, Moira corrected his understanding of a point in the plot as if she had seen it, then covered herself by saying that a friend of hers had told her all about it. One of the drivers happened to say that he had seen her in a café in town one afternoon, but Moira denied all knowledge, saying the man must have been mistaken and implying that he was a troublemaker. There was sometimes a whiff of cigarette smoke about her clothing, when neither of them smoked.

None of this would have added up to anything much if it had not been for a far more important matter. Before they had even married, they had agreed that of course they would have two children, a boy and a girl preferably, but certainly two children. Both of them had been brought up with sisters and thought that only children missed out on a lot of the fun of family life. Michael was now four, but when Tom said he thought they ought to be thinking about having another, Moira turned the idea down flat.

'Oh, I can't be doing with all that baby stuff again,' she stated.

'But we agreed that Michael should have a brother or sister,' Tom said. 'And even if you fell for one almost at once, there's going to be nearly five years between them now. That's already a bit too much of a gap for them to play together well.'

'I told you, I don't want to go through all that again—broken nights and boiling nappies and teething and all the rest,' Moira repeated, picking at an imaginary piece of fluff on her jumper.

'But—' Tom was flabbergasted. 'You mean—you don't want to have any more children? Not ever?'

'I didn't say not ever, just—not yet,' Moira said, avoiding his eyes.

'But—I thought we agreed on this. We wanted Michael to have a brother or sister. We didn't want him to be an only child.'

'Oh, Michael, Michael, Michael—that's all you ever think of,' Moira flared. 'What about me? I'm the one who has to carry the baby for nine months, getting all fat and ugly and breathless and ruining my figure, and then I'm the one who has to look after it and feed it and clean up after it. Me, not you. It's all very well for you to talk, but I'm the one who has to do all the hard work.'

'But—I thought you wanted another child,' Tom said, utterly baffled.

'Well, you thought wrong, didn't you?' Moira retorted and walked out of the room.

Tom was left reeling. He had known for some time that things weren't too good between them. He had never suspected they were that bad. And then he remembered all the other little things, along with the frequency with which she turned away from him when he wanted to make love. A nasty little worm of suspicion started up in his mind and, once there, it was almost impossible to eradicate it.

There was nobody whom he could turn to for advice. It wasn't the sort of thing he could discuss with his friends or his father, and his mother and sister were bosom pals with the Butterworths. There was only one person he knew who had always listened with sympathy to everything he had to say, and that was Annie. Driving along the dreary trunk routes, or up over the breathtaking moorland roads, he would compose letters where he opened his heart to her. He never sent them, restricting himself to the friendly monthly newsletter that they had fallen into the habit of sending each other. But in his mind he told her just how much he had longed to hear from her when he had been in the prison camp, how shocked and desperately disappointed he had been to find her pregnant and waiting to marry the child's father, how Moira had always been second best, how he'd tried to be a decent husband but seemed now to have failed.

It wasn't as good as really writing it all down and sending it to her. It certainly wasn't as good as telling her face to face. But it helped. And he was grown up enough to know that, even if he did tell her, Annie couldn't wave a magic wand over his situation. It was up to him to find a solution.

Then, one evening early in February, he had a job driving a choir over to a church hall in a neighbouring town. The concert they performed in ended rather earlier than expected and Tom was home twenty minutes or so before he had told Moira he would be back. He was surprised when he opened the front door, to find the house silent. Moira generally liked to sit and watch the television in the evening, whatever the programme might be.

'Hello?' he called softly as he stood in the narrow hall.

There was no reply.

He opened the door to the front room and looked in. The light was on, but it was empty. He tried the dining room and the kitchen. He supposed she must be in the bathroom and in a mood, so she wasn't answering him. He ran up the stairs two at a time and tapped on the bathroom door.

'Hello—I'm back,' he said, then stopped.

Not only was there no reply, but there was no light showing under the door. The only answer was that Moira was unwell and had gone to bed early. He put on the landing light and carefully opened the bedroom door. She was not in there either.

A terrible fear gripped his heart. Had she left and taken Michael with her? A weight seemed to be crushing his chest.

'Not my son,' he muttered out loud. 'Not Michael.'

Hardly knowing what to expect, he went into the back bedroom. In the dim light creeping in from the landing, he made out a dark shape in Michael's bed. There was a sigh and a rustle of bedclothes as the child turned in his sleep. The rush of relief was so strong that he only just stopped himself from scooping his son from the bed and clutching him so close that he would never let him go. Instead, he stood and gazed down at the boy. As his eyes grew accustomed to the half light, he could make out the dark tufts of his hair, the sweep of his long lashes on his soft cheek, the baby roundness of his chin. He loved him so much that it hurt. Whatever happened, he realised, it didn't matter just as long as he still had Michael.

In the still of the house, he heard a rattle. It was the back door. Tom raised his head and listened as the door clicked to again.

'Tom?'

Anger coursed through his body. Moira had gone out and left Michael and anyone—anyone at all—could have come in and injured or abducted him. He crept out of the boy's room and ran down the stairs and into the kitchen.

'Where the hell have you been?' he demanded.

Moira was holding her coat closed at her throat, but though her arm was across her chest, it did not quite disguise the swift rise and fall of her breathing. Her pupils were still dark and dilated from being out in the night.

'I—had a headache,' she said.

'A headache?' Tom repeated. 'You went out and left our son all alone because you had a headache? Anything could have happened. A murderer could have got in. At the very least he could have woken up and found nobody here. How could you? Call yourself a mother and you go out and leave him!'

Moira's face hardened. 'For heaven's sake! I had a headache and I went out for five minutes to get some fresh air.

Five minutes! I checked before I went and he was fast asleep. And is he fast asleep now?'

'That's beside the point,' Tom said.

'No, it isn't. I went out for five minutes and there's no harm done, so what's all the fuss about? Anyone would think I'd committed a major crime.'

Tom stared at her, trying to see past her hot denial, trying to read what was going on in her head. For he did not believe her.

'If you've only been out for five minutes, how come I didn't see you as I came down the road?' he demanded.

'I—went to the corner and back. The bottom corner,' Moira said.

He noticed the slight hesitation. She was lying—he was sure she was lying—but he couldn't see how to prove it.

'You shouldn't have gone out at all,' he persisted.

'All *right*. So I shouldn't have gone out. I won't do it again. Happy now?' Moira demanded.

'No,' Tom said.

'Well, tough luck,' she said and pushed past him.

He heard her hang her coat up in the hall, then go into the front room. There was a click as the television was switched on, then a pause while it warmed up and finally burst into life. A plummy BBC accent filled the silent anger of the house.

Tom stood staring out at the darkness that was the back garden.

She had not gone away and taken Michael with her, that was the main thing. But something here was terribly wrong. Though caution told him that it might be better not to find out, still he had to know just what was going on.

He took to coming home when she wasn't expecting him, or saying he was going to be out on a driving job, then at the last minute telling her it had been changed or cancelled, but though he never caught her out, he seemed to see a challenge in her smile as he came in each time. In front of their friends and their family, they both carried on as if nothing was amiss. They even kept the pretence going in front of each other. They were both playing a game and neither of them was admitting it. Tom wondered how much longer it could go on. Maybe if they pretended for long enough, then it really would be all right again. Maybe this was just what people called a bad patch.

The first Saturday of March, a fishing club booked a trip to Lowestoft to try their hands at sea fishing. It was to be a long day, starting at the crack of dawn, in order to give them a decent amount of time out on the boats. The prospect of going to the East Anglian coast made Tom's mouth go dry and his heart beat faster. He checked the distances on the map. It was quite a long way further south to Wittlesham. It would make for a big distance altogether in one day. But it was worth it. If he could just see Annie once more, he reasoned, he might be able to put everything into perspective. Talking to her face to face was so much better than a letter. He wouldn't warn her. He'd just turn up and see if she was pleased to see him. If she wasn't—but he didn't put that possibility into words.

The day started badly, with driving rain. The fishermen grumbled as they got on board, as if he had personally arranged the weather. The standing water on the roads meant that he did not make good time and had to cut down on tea stops. Again the fishermen grumbled. It was still raining when they arrived, but not so hard now. The fishermen cheered up reluctantly and milled about getting their gear organised. Tom could hardly wait to throw them all out of his coach. Then he headed south.

Through clearing showers he drove down the A12 through pretty Suffolk villages and market towns, his spirits rising with each one passed. Why hadn't he done this before? he wondered. It was so simple. Just to see her, talk to her, would make everything brighter. It wasn't too much to ask, and it wasn't as if he was expecting anything other than her friendship, so he wasn't cheating on Moira in any way. He began to sing. Ipswich was clogged with traffic. So was Colchester. He crawled along the narrow, crowded streets, grinding his teeth with impatience. Eastwards, and now he was getting close. Wittlesham featured on the signposts. He caught sight of a distant gleam of the sea across flat fields. Then there was the town sign. *Welcome to Wittlesham—pearl of the Essex coast.* Tom cheered out loud.

There was a small painted sign on the road now, pointing down the track to the chalets: *To Silver Sands Holiday Park.* The track itself had not improved. Tom bounced down it with scant regard for the coach's suspension. A few potholes were not going to slow him down now that his goal was in sight.

He pulled up by the sea wall and leaned on the steering wheel, staring. Even though he'd known that the chalet had been washed away in the floods, still it was a shock to find it gone. All that was left of Silver Sands as he knew it was the shape of the boundary. Instead of the pretty wooden chalet and the big unkempt garden there was a neatly mown space with five caravans placed about it like the spokes of a wheel, a brick building that looked like a toilet and a play area. So this was the project that Annie wrote about with such enthusiasm. In the grey winter light, it all looked pretty dismal. It was difficult to imagine people enjoying holidays here.

With a jolt, Tom realised what was missing from the

scene—Annie herself. Too late, he saw that he should have gone straight to the farmhouse but, now that he was here, he felt he just had to go to the top of the sea wall. For old times' sake.

He stood with his back to the land and the damp wind in his face and gazed along to where a raw new section marked the place where the water had broken through. So much had changed since last he had been here. Then he scanned slowly round, taking in the gleam of light in the mudbanks, the snaking creeks amongst the saltmarsh, the far grey of the horizon. That was still the same. It was as wild and open as he had imagined it when he'd been cooped up in the Stalag, and the sky was just as huge. The smell was the same too— salt and seaweed and rotting crustaceans. He breathed in deeply, taking it right down to the bottom of his lungs, feeling it invigorate his sluggish blood. Overhead, seagulls arced and, in the distance, faint but still piercing, he could hear the haunting cry of the curlew.

'Hello.'

He spun round, catching his breath.

'Annie!'

There she was, at the bottom of the sea wall, looking up at him. Her round face was framed by a blue woolly hat and her fair curls escaped round the edges. His heart seemed to turn right over. And then he scrambled and slithered down the steep grass slope of the wall to stop in front of her. His hands reached for hers and they stood, smiling and smiling into each other's eyes.

'Are you my daddy?'

With a start, Tom realised that there was somebody else there. A boy of about seven or eight was standing at Annie's side, staring up at him with unnerving intensity.

Annie flushed with embarrassment and put a hand on the boy's shoulder.

'Bobby! I'm sorry, Tom, he doesn't understand—this is my son, Bobby,' Annie explained, flustered. 'Bobby, you mustn't—this isn't—this is my old friend Mr Featherstone.'

The boy looked down, disappointment written all over him.

'I wish I was your daddy,' Tom said with total honesty. 'But I'm not. I have a son of my own at home. His name is Michael.'

The boy sighed. He scraped at a stone amongst the grass with the toe of his wellington boot. 'My daddy's got a son of his own in America. That's why he can't marry my mum.'

Tom ached for him and for Annie. He squatted down so that Bobby was now taller than he was.

'I know,' he said. 'And it must be pretty rotten for you. But just remember that you have got the very best mam in the world.'

Bobby glared at him for a moment. Then he looked up at Annie and a smile broke on his pinched little face. He slid his mittened hand into hers.

'Yes, I have,' he said. Then he broke away and picked up the bike that lay against the slope of the sea wall. 'Look!' he said, his voice overflowing with pride. 'I've got a bike. It's all mine. My mum gave it to me for my birthday.'

'It's a very fine bike,' Tom told him. 'How fast can you go on it?'

'Super-fast! Look—'

Bobby swung a leg over the crossbar and pushed off. Soon he was pedalling round the caravans yelling, 'Look at me!'

'You must be a good dad,' Annie said, watching her son.

'I hope so,' Tom said. 'It must be hard for you, on your own. But you're doing a grand job. He's a fine boy.'

'I think so, but then I would, wouldn't I?' Still watching Bobby, she asked, 'Why did you come?'

All sorts of answers flashed through Tom's head. The only honest one was—because he needed to see her. Instead he said, 'I was coming as far as Lowestoft and it seemed like a good chance to look you up.'

Which, even as he said it, sounded lame and bland.

'Ah,' Annie said, carefully neutral. 'It's quite a way from Lowestoft.'

'Yes, well—'

He hesitated. He knew he should stick to being bluff and friendly. That was the safe path. That was the loyal path. Loyal to Moira.

'I thought it would be nice to meet up again,' he said. 'Letters aren't quite the same, are they?'

'They're not,' Annie agreed. 'It was just such a surprise to see you, that's all.'

'A good surprise, I hope?'

'Oh, yes. Very good. I often think of you when I'm here. At first, when I saw you standing on the sea wall just where we first met, I thought I was seeing things. That's why I thought there might be some—some reason why you came.'

Moira loomed between them—silent, invisible, but a presence nonetheless. Tom saw with sudden clarity just how feeble it would sound if he voiced his reason out loud. His wife might be up to something, but he didn't know what, so he had come running to Annie for—what? He hardly knew.

'Does there have to be a reason? You've told me so much about Bobby and the caravans and all the rest, I wanted to see it for myself.'

'Oh—well—' Disappointment showed in her face, hastily masked.

Tom reached out a hand, was just about to tell her how much he missed her, when she took a step away.

'You'd better come and look round, then. There's not much to see at this time of year, but I've lots of plans for the future…'

She led him round the site, showing where she intended to fit more vans in, then waved an arm at the next field, at present part of the farm, and told him all about what she would like to do if she had the money.

'Just think what a lot I could do on just one field, let alone expanding into any of the others. If I can get this going, I'll let the rest of the farmland and just concentrate on Silver Sands—'

Listening to her, Tom was amazed at how much she had changed. The downtrodden young girl had been transformed into a confident businesswoman.

'It all sounds very exciting,' he said. 'And you're doing it all by yourself—I really admire that. I always knew you were someone special, Annie.'

She shrugged. 'Yes, well—I don't know about that—' She busied herself with speaking to Bobby.

When the boy went off again to play on the swings, Tom leaned on the fence and looked across the fields to the farmhouse.

'The floods changed everything, didn't they? Now you haven't got that father of yours making your life a misery, you're a new person.'

Annie was silent. For a moment Tom wondered whether she had heard him. She was gripping the fence as if she might fall down if she did not hang on to it, and her face had gone deathly pale.

'Annie? What is it? What's—?'

'I killed him,' she said, in such a low voice that he only just caught her words.

'*What?*' he said. 'You don't mean—? I thought he was drowned.'

'He was, but—I could have saved him. I was holding on to a tree and he was being swept past and he called out to me… He begged me, begged me to help him…but I didn't and then…then he was washed away and I tried to reach him but it was too late—'

She stopped, her voice rising in a sob. Tom reached out and took her shoulders, turning her round to face him. There were tears standing in her eyes.

'It's all right,' he said, trying to think, trying to imagine how it had been. 'It was dark, right? And he was being swept past you? It must all have happened very fast—you could have been swept away too—you might not have been strong enough to hold the both of you.'

'I know—I know—but I didn't try. I should have tried.'

To Tom's mind, Walter had only got what he'd deserved.

'If you had've tried, you could've been drowned, and Bobby would have been an orphan. You're not to blame, Annie. It was the work of a moment, and you had to save yourself. Think of how it would be for Bobby if he was alone in the world except for your mam.'

'I know, but—I can't get it out of my head, Tom. It keeps coming back to me, and there's no one— You're the only person I've ever told—'

'Oh, Annie—'

He drew her to him and held her as she wept on his shoulder. All the old feelings of tenderness came sweeping back—that need he had to protect her from Walter. He had thought

that she was free of the man, but now it seemed the old bastard was haunting her still.

'What are you doing to my mummy?'

He had forgotten Bobby. The boy was standing a yard or
so away from them, his face pale and his eyes fierce, frightened but ready to stick up for his mother.

'It's all right,' Tom said. 'I'm not hurting her. I would
never hurt her.'

Annie raised her head and held out an arm to Bobby.

'I was upset, darling. Mr Featherstone is being kind.'

Bobby lunged forward and hugged her round the hips,
and the three of them held on to each other until Annie broke
away. She found a handkerchief and dried her eyes and blew
her nose.

'I'm sorry, making all that fuss.'

'It wasn't a fuss, and I'm glad you did,' Tom assured her.
He felt privileged that she should have confided in him.

She nodded and put the handkerchief back in her pocket.

'I feel better now, better for telling you.' She looked down
at Bobby's worried face. 'It's all right. I was telling Mr
Featherstone about something and remembering it made me
sad. It was nothing he did.'

With a jolt, Tom realised that the only man Bobby had
lived with was Walter. He expected men to hurt women and
make them cry. Tom put a hand on his shoulder.

'You're a good boy, Bobby, sticking up for your mam like
that. A brave boy. I'm glad she's got you looking out for her.'

There was much for him to think about on the way back.
Nothing had been solved and nothing had outwardly
changed, yet everything felt different. It was as if a kaleido-
scope had been turned and all the pieces had shifted and fallen into a new pattern. Going home was going to be ten times

more difficult now, for he had come to see what he had known all along—that Annie Cross was the one woman for him. He had never stopped loving her.

CHAPTER THIRTY-FOUR

SEEING Tom again stirred all manner of painful feelings. Annie almost wished he had never come. Speaking to him, having his arms round her, had only served to remind her just how much she had lost. And now he had gone again, back to his wife and his son, leaving a ragged hole in her life.

She was wrapped up in thoughts of him when she met Jeff Sutton in the High Street. As usual, he tried to start up a conversation. As usual, she asked him why he wasn't at work.

'Oh, they won't miss me,' he said. 'Look, why don't we have a pot of tea and some cakes? I don't see anything of you now you're not down at Silver Sands every day.'

She tried to resist but in the end she was feeling so lonely that she agreed. Delighted, Jeff steered her into a teashop, ordered the best of everything and set about telling her all his woes. His chief complaint was that, with Beryl getting married in the summer, the whole house was wedding crazy. Annie listened with half an ear. She'd heard about Beryl's triumph via her mother and Mrs Sutton, who was still coming to her for alterations. It just went to prove that Beryl always got what she wanted, even if, as in this case, she had to wait quite a while for it.

'Mind you, I think he's a bit of a nancy boy,' Jeff said.

'What?'

'You know—bats for the other side.'

Annie didn't know. She had no idea what he was talking about.

'As long as Beryl loves him—' she said.

'Yes, but really—'

'Oh, do stop moaning,' she told him. 'You're just jealous because Beryl's getting all the attention. You're like a spoilt kid.'

Jeff looked chastened. 'Sorry—I was going on a bit, wasn't I? Tell me about what you're doing at the site these days.'

'Not a lot at the moment,' Annie said. She made an effort to brighten up and put Tom out of her head. 'I go and air the vans out every few days so that they don't get damp and musty. And I've been teaching myself touch typing from a book I got from the library. I'm getting quite quick at it now, so that'll be useful for doing the paperwork this summer. What I have to do is start putting some adverts in for this year's bookings. I'd really like to get some families in earlier. Everyone wants to go on holiday in August, but that's only four weeks, or six if you count the end of July and the beginning of September, and I can't make anything like a living out of that.'

Jeff considered this. 'Would they come earlier if it was cheaper then? Better to let the vans cheap than not at all.'

'Oh, yes, I've thought of that. But Reggie always said how people are very set in their ways, and he was right. There's a time and a place for everything, and holidays are supposed to be in August.'

'Hmm…' Jeff frowned, thinking. 'It's a tricky problem. Perhaps if you made a big thing of it in your advertisements? Sort of drawing the public's attention to the fact that it's cheaper at other times? I mean, what do you usually put at the top of your adverts?'

'I only put a few in last year. Because Reggie and Gwen had a dozen caravans and I've only got five, I filled quite a lot of space with people who were coming back for a second year,' Annie told him. 'The ads I did do said where we were and about clean modern vans and how much they were.'

'Well, how would it be if you made the cheap price a feature? Made that the headline, so to speak?' Jeff suggested.

Annie turned it around in her head. Amazingly, Jeff was talking real sense.

'Bargains, you mean? Like a sale?'

'That's right. Something to catch the eye. You might get people who wouldn't be able to afford a holiday normally. A whole new market. My father's very keen on new markets. And we're all supposed to be New Elizabethans now, remember. New holidays for New Elizabethans.'

'You're right,' Annie said. The idea caught light. She could see that it would work. 'New holidays—early holidays—early holidays for early birds. Yes! Early birds catch the worm! They get the cheap weeks. Jeff—you're a genius.'

Jeff flushed with pleasure. 'Oh, well, I don't know about that.'

'You are. You made me think about it a different way. That's what it needs. I was stuck in a rut, just like the August people. I'm going to start writing a new advertisement the moment I get home.'

Jeff's face was bright with enthusiasm. 'Why wait till then? Let's do it straight away.'

'But I haven't got a form with me,' Annie objected.

'Where do you place your adverts?'

'Daltons Weekly.'

'Right, I'll go and get one from the newsagents right now.'

'You're mad! You should be at work.'

'This is much more fun,' Jeff said. 'Don't move—I'll be back in two ticks.'

Leaving Annie to finish the last iced fancy cake, he dashed out of the teashop. In no time he was back with a *Daltons Weekly* and a notebook and pencil.

'Here we are. Now, let's get to work.'

Together they argued over the best heading, then honed it down to the correct number of words. Annie balked at having a semi-display layout. It seemed a lot of money to her.

'You've got to speculate to accumulate,' Jeff told her. 'People are impressed by a bigger advert. It makes them think that your holiday park is better than the ones with the small ads. Silver Sands is the best. You've got to make them believe that too.'

'I see what you mean,' Annie agreed. 'But it's so expensive.'

'It'll be worth it when it brings in the custom.'

'Yes—'

It was all right for him; he had plenty of money.

'Look, let me pay for it,' Jeff said, as if he had read her mind. 'It's my idea, so I'll back it. I'll write you out a cheque.'

'No!' Annie was horrified. 'You'll do nothing of the kind.'

Jeff tried to get round her, but she was adamant. In the end, he had to give in.

'All right, but promise me you'll send it off like that.'

Annie agreed. 'You've been ever so kind, helping me like this. It's really nice to be able to talk to someone about it. My mum just gets worried if I try to share any of my ideas with her.'

'I've really enjoyed it,' he told her. 'Honestly. It's funny, isn't it? I just can't get excited about the factory. My father is. He goes on about it all the time. Give him a new machine or a new process and he's happy for weeks trying it out, but it leaves me cold. I just don't care about it. But this—it's different. It's—an adventure. Yes, that's it. An adventure. Something new. It's fun.'

'It might be fun for you. It's the difference between being a cleaner and being a businesswoman for me,' Annie told him.

But it had lifted her spirits considerably, so that when he suggested they met at the teashop again next week, she agreed without much of an argument. Soon it became a regular thing. She almost looked forward to it.

On top of that, the advertisements appeared to be working. Bookings were coming in for June and July, and a few for September. Things were looking up, and she had to admit that it was partly due to Jeff. So when he asked her to go out with him for an evening, she agreed.

Her mother was very suspicious at first. 'You're going out? Where? Who with?'

Annie had considered saying she was going to the pictures with a girlfriend. One of the mothers at the school, perhaps. But she knew her mother wouldn't swallow it. And besides, there was nothing wrong with going out with Jeff. They were both single. Unlike Tom. Yet again she pushed the thought of him away and adopted a casual air.

'Actually, it's Jeff Sutton.'

'Jeff—? You're going out with Jeffrey Sutton? Mrs Sutton's son?' Edna was utterly astounded.

'Yes. The very same.'

'But—but— When did you—? I mean, you hardly— How did he come to—?'

'I've met him a few times in the High Street. Besides, I've known him for years. There's no harm in it, is there?'

She tried to keep very calm. It was difficult when her

mother was looking as if she didn't know whether to be terrified or delighted.

'Dear me—Jeffrey Sutton— Such a lovely family… Oh, but, Annie, love, do his parents know? Do they approve?'

'I very much doubt it,' Annie admitted.

Her mother put a hand to her face. 'Do be careful, dear. You don't want to go upsetting the Suttons. Perhaps you'd better not go.'

'Too late now, Mum, I've agreed. And I'd better go and get changed, 'cos he'll be here soon.'

In fact she was only half dressed when Jeff came bouncing into the yard in his MG. Her mother let him in and, by the time she came down, he had her twisted round his little finger. Both of them turned to look at her as she came into the kitchen. Both of them were astonished at the transformation. With her best outfit on, her face made up and her hair brushed into a fashionable style, Annie looked a very different person from the woman who went out cleaning.

'Wow! Who's this film star? I think I've come to the wrong address,' Jeff said.

Annie smiled. It was nice to get dressed up, nice to be going out, even if it was only with Jeff.

The evening was unlike anything Annie had ever experienced before. Off they went in the little red sports car, all the way to Colchester. They pulled in at the most expensive hotel, where Jeff had booked a table for dinner. In the hushed atmosphere, surrounded by crisp white napery, sparkling glasses and a bewildering array of knives and forks, they worked their way through three courses, coffee and—wonder of wonders—a bottle of real French wine. Jeff was excellent company, treating her to a hilarious account of the preparations for Beryl's wedding.

It was only as she tottered out of the entrance and collapsed into the low seat of the MG that Annie began to feel anxious. Was this going to be Bobby Joe and the Jeep all over again? She need not have worried. Jeff was the perfect gentleman, running her straight back to the farm.

'Oh, it's been such fun. Thank you so much,' she said, reaching for the door handle.

'Thank you for coming. I don't know when I've ever enjoyed myself more,' Jeff told her. He got out, walked round the car and opened the door for her. 'I hope we can do this again,' he said.

'Well—'

'We could go dancing. You like dancing, don't you? Please say you will, Annie.'

In the end, she agreed.

'Wonderful!' Jeff leaned forward and kissed her on the cheek. 'How about Friday?'

'But— that's only three days away!'

'Three whole days. I don't know how I'll get through them. Till Friday, Annie.'

And so she found that she was going out with Jeff twice or even three times a week. They never went anywhere in Wittlesham and, when Annie challenged him about this, Jeff admitted that he hadn't told his parents about her.

'It's none of their business,' he insisted. 'They try to rule everything else I do. I'm not letting them spoil this.'

Because she was fond of him and he was so nice to her, Annie let Jeff have a kiss and a cuddle at the end of each date, but beyond that she did not go. She had learnt her lesson the hard way. However often he said he loved her, she slapped his hands away. Jeff, because he was so desperate to please her, was far easier to manage than Bobby Joe. She only had to threaten not to see him again and he fell into line.

Going out with Jeff was now an established part of her life, but it was a part that got mysteriously left out of her letters to Tom.

CHAPTER THIRTY-FIVE

ANOTHER summer was fast approaching. All the caravans were booked for the school holiday period and most of them for July and even the end of June. Annie and her mother gave them all a good clean out ready for the first holiday-makers of the season and Annie added a see-saw and roundabout to the children's playground and painted the inside of the toilet block. Then she hit a problem. The advertisements were too successful.

'But that's wonderful!' Jeff cried when she told him she was actually having to turn people away. 'I told you that ad would work, didn't I? Who's the genius, then?'

'It isn't wonderful, it's heartbreaking,' Annie said. 'All that money I could be making if only I could afford to buy even a couple more vans.'

They were sitting in the restaurant of an old coaching inn, a place full of black beams, hunting prints and shiny brass. Jeff waved an arm in an expansive gesture.

'Then buy a couple more vans. Like I said before, you've got to speculate to accumulate. I was right about the ad, wasn't I? You didn't want to spend on a semi-display and it's paid off in bucketloads.'

'Caravans are a lot more expensive than a few ads, even

if I get them on the never-never,' Annie pointed out. 'And nobody's going to lend me money to buy them outright.'

Jeff put his glass down, reached across the table and took her hands in his.

'I'll lend you some. I've got a bit, and I could sell the car. That'd buy some vans.'

Annie was appalled. 'Oh, no, I couldn't possibly let you do that!'

Jeff looked hurt. 'Why ever not?'

Because she did not want to be beholden to him, that was why. But she didn't want to hurt him by saying that.

'It—it would spoil things—' she said feebly. 'You shouldn't lend money to friends; it makes things…different—'

Jeff only held her hands tighter. He looked into her eyes, his face alight.

'But if we were more than friends, if we were married, then it would be all right, wouldn't it? Then all of mine would be yours.'

Annie stared at him, not sure whether to believe what she had just heard.

'*What?*'

'Oh, Annie, say you will. It would be wonderful. Just think, we could be together all the time. I could leave the beastly factory and come and work with you at Silver Sands. We could do it together, you and me. We'd be so happy.'

'But—'

Her head was reeling. Jeff Sutton was asking her, Annie Cross, to marry him.

'You're joking,' she said.

'Annie—!' He looked profoundly shocked. 'I was never more serious in my life. You know how much I love you. I've got it all worked out. My father's giving Beryl the deposit on a house for her wedding present. He'd have to do the same for me, but we needn't spend it on a house. You've got a house already. We could live at Marsh Edge and invest the money in Silver Sands. And then you know it would be much easier to borrow money. Banks are much happier to give loans to well-financed businesses.'

He meant it, Annie realised. He really meant it. Jeff, whom she had always thought of as being an overgrown baby, had thought it all through and come up with a really sensible plan.

But it was quite out of the question.

'Jeff, it's really sweet of you, but I can't—'

'Oh, Annie, please don't say that. I can't live without you. I've thought about it so much. You've been so brave and clever all these years by yourself, and now I want to take care of you. I'm no good on my own, Annie, but you make me want to make something of myself.'

Jeff's face was alight with excitement at the thought of this wonderful future. He let go of her hands and waved his about to emphasise his words.

'I know that if I had you I could *be* something. Together we could be a real success. We could show everybody that they were wrong. My parents, who think I'm useless, and that beastly bank manager who turned you down—we would show them, Annie darling, we'd show them that they were wrong. We could do it together.'

Annie stared at him as the idea danced before her, tempting in its simplicity. Against all the odds, someone loved her enough to want to marry her, despite her past. And not just anyone, but the son of one of the richest men in Wittlesham. She could be a respectable married woman. No more snide remarks, no more disparaging looks. Bobby would have a father. Well, a stepfather, anyway. And she could really start to make Silver Sands into the place she wanted it to be… She brought her thoughts to a shuddering halt. It was madness. She was beginning to think that it was actually possible, when clearly it wasn't. She didn't love him.

'I can't, Jeff. You know I can't,' she said. She teetered on the edge of telling him the real reason, but his whipped puppy-dog look stopped her. Instead, she prevaricated. 'Your parents—they'd go mad—'

Jeff waved this aside. He clasped her hands again, shaking them slightly as he spoke, gazing into her eyes as if hoping to hypnotise her into agreeing with him.

'I don't care about them. We don't need their permission. We're both over twenty-one. We could get married straight away. We don't have to wait for anything. We can just get married and be together. I'll work so hard once we're together, Annie. I'll look after you, you'll see. I'll look after everything.'

That just tipped the whole situation over into comedy. Jeff looking after her? Jeff doing a full day's work? As far as she could make out, he was out of the factory more hours than he was in it. It was only because he was working for his father that he got away with it. Any other employer would have sacked him years ago. Annie had to press her lips together to stop herself from laughing.

'No, Jeff. It's lovely of you and I'm flattered and all that, but no. It won't work.'

'It will,' Jeff insisted. 'It will work. I'll make it. I won't take no for an answer, Annie. I'll ask again. I'll keep on asking till you say yes.'

Annie pulled her hands free and picked up her knife and fork. 'You're going to have to wait a long time, then,' she said.

'I'll wait for ever,' Jeff declared, 'but you'll say yes in the end, you'll see.'

After a long wrangle, she had to insist that they drop the subject.

'All right,' Jeff agreed, the sulky boy expression settling over his face. 'But I'll ask you again another day. I'll keep on asking until you see sense.'

It was a tense journey home. For the first time since they had been going out together, Annie was glad to get home.

She found it impossible to sleep. The events of the evening chased round her brain. Jeff Sutton had actually proposed to her! Her, Annie Cross the Unmarried Mother. She imagined what the Suttons' reaction would have been if she had said yes. Mrs Sutton would be coldly furious. Beryl would hit the roof. To have her as a sister-in-law! She could even have threatened to have the wedding before Beryl's, and steal the thunder from Beryl's Big Day with the scandal of having a fallen woman marrying into her family. She smiled to herself, thinking of just how incandescent Beryl would have been.

But then the cold reality began to dawn. She would have to stop going out with Jeff, which was quite a shame, really. She enjoyed going to all those nice places and, when he wasn't being spoilt and sulky, he was good company. But she couldn't carry on letting him pay for all those outings now that he wanted her to marry him and she had no intention of doing so.

And that was the end of the matter.

Except that it wasn't. Because the alternative was lurking there in her head, and it wouldn't go away. What if she were to become Mrs Jeffrey Sutton? She could be respectable. She could build up Silver Sands. She could be a

Somebody in Wittlesham. But it always came back to the same thing. She didn't love him. She didn't love him the way she loved Tom, had loved him from almost the moment she'd met him, and loved him still. She didn't even feel for him the way she had for Bobby Joe, which had been a sort of madness, an animal need, a wild bid for escape into all things American. She liked Jeff. He was fun to go out with. But she didn't even respect him, so it was out of the question that she should marry him.

'You look pale, dear,' her mother remarked over breakfast the next morning. 'You're not sickening for something, are you?'

'No, no—you know me, I'm never ill,' Annie said, imagining what the reaction would have been if she'd announced her engagement to Jeff. Her mother would have been absolutely flabbergasted. To be connected with the wonderful Suttons was beyond her wildest dreams.

'I'm never ill either,' Bobby said, tucking into his scrambled eggs and bacon.

'That's right. You're growing into a big strong boy,' Annie said proudly.

What would Bobby have said? He was never very happy when she went out for an evening with Jeff, but that was just because she was going out, not because she was with Jeff. He'd not really seen much of him. He would have got used to it all right. There was nothing about Jeff for Bobby to dislike, really. He'd almost be a big brother to him.

Throughout the day, and the most of the following days, and a good deal of each night, she worried and worried at the problem until she felt hollow and jagged and didn't know which way to turn. It was such a big decision. She could totally change the course of her life. And as usual there was no one to turn to, no one to advise her. It was her choice alone. She dreaded seeing Jeff again and avoided all the places where she might run into him, but she couldn't avoid the caravan site, and it was there that he waited for her.

'Annie, Annie—' He came bounding up to her and hugged her. 'Have you changed your mind yet? No, no, don't say anything, just listen. I've got such a good idea. It came to me this morning, when I was at the golf club. How about a crazy golf here? Or at least, not here, but in the field next door there. When we've got the new vans, that is. Can't you just see them, all lined up across the field? And we could build that clubhouse you're always talking about. Everyone will be flocking to Silver Sands! We'll be bigger than Butlins.'

She let him ramble on. Anything was better than having to put him off again.

At last he looked at his watch and yelped. 'My God, look at the time! I was supposed to be picking the sprog up from school and taking him to the dentist in Colchester. Mother will have my guts for garters. She can't do it because she's doing some wedding stuff with Beryl. Oh, darling, just think how wonderful it would be not to be at her beck and call any more! Now, listen, you are coming out with me tomorrow, aren't you? It's our regular night, after all. You won't let me down, will you?'

Tomorrow evening. In a way, that made it better. If she had a deadline, then she would have to make her mind up and not keep going over and over it until she thought she was going mad. She would see him tomorrow evening, and she would tell him once and for all.

'All right,' she agreed.

'Darling Annie!' Jeff hugged her again and kissed her. 'I

love you so much. I can't live without you, you know that, don't you? Till tomorrow! I'll pick you up at seven. We'll go somewhere special!'

Annie watched him as he roared off down the track in the MG, bouncing over the potholes. One small corner of her mind noted that she would have to get the holes filled, even if she couldn't afford to have the whole thing properly surfaced.

That night she lay sleepless again. How were things going to be if she sent Jeff packing? Much the same as they were now. She looked down the long years ahead with no husband and little money, and no way to provide a better future for Bobby. For, however hard she worked, without investment the site was only ever going to grow very slowly. It would be years and years before it got anywhere near the vision she had for it. She wanted Bobby to have everything she'd never had, but at the moment he had less, for at least she had been born of parents who had been married. Nobody had called her those horrible names that poor Bobby had to endure. If she had money, that would make all the difference. People respected money, and they respected the Suttons. If she was one of them, Bobby would be drawn in as well.

Unable even to lie down any longer, she pulled on her dressing gown and padded downstairs. There was still some warmth in the range. She opened the front and sat down in front of it, notebook on her knee. She drew two columns—For and Against. The Fors made the most sense.

It was getting light. Annie walked through to the parlour and looked across the fields. In the half light the caravans were silvery against the darker grey of the sea wall. The sea wall that had burst to kill Gwen and her father. The sea wall where she had met Tom, where she had last seen Tom, where she had realised that she loved him now and for ever. But Tom was married, just like Bobby Joe.

She made her decision.

CHAPTER THIRTY-SIX

'I SUPPOSE you're working this evening *again*,' Moira said.

She was standing in the tiny kitchen, her arms folded across her chest, an expression of contained exasperation on her face.

'As a matter of fact, I'm not,' Tom told her. 'I'm letting the new man do it. So we can go out if you like. Is there anything on at the pictures you'd like to see?'

'Oh, well, you're a bit late telling me, aren't you? I'd assumed you'd be working, so I've already arranged to go to the pictures,' Moira said. She turned away and started stacking the dirty breakfast things prior to washing them up.

Tom felt irritated. He had especially organised it so he could have Saturday evening off, thinking that if they went out together more like they used to, then things might improve between them.

'Who are you going with? Joan? If they could get a baby-sitter, then we could go as a foursome with her and George,' he suggested.

'No—not Joan. Someone from the Young Wives. You don't know her. Her husband's away a lot and she doesn't get out much, so I can't let her down,' Moira said, running water into the sink. The rising steam made her face flush.

'Well, there's no need to change it, she could still come along with us. It's not as if we're a courting couple any more,' Tom said.

Moira clattered plates around. 'No, no, that's no good. She doesn't know you and she's quite shy. She'd be embarrassed. No—I'll just run over and tell our Vera we don't need her to babysit, and you can stay in with Michael. You're always saying you don't see enough of him.'

'You're always saying we don't go out enough,' Tom pointed out.

'No, I'm not. I never complain if it's work,' Moira retorted. 'Don't you go making me out to be a nagging wife.'

'I'm not,' Tom said.

He picked up the tea towel and began drying the plates. He tried to remember when last they had been out together other than to visit his family or hers and realised that unless he arranged it well in advance, Moira was always reluctant to go. It all added to his general unease about just what she was up to while he was out of the way.

'In fact,' Moira said, interrupting his thoughts, 'if you want to take one of these weekend trips you and your dad were talking about, I shan't mind. It's not as if it will make much difference to Sundays.'

'Right,' Tom said. 'I'll bear that in mind.'

He set off as usual for work, accompanied by Michael on his trike to the end of the road. It was a beautiful summer's morning with a real promise of warmth in the air. Roses glowed in the flowerbeds of the neat front gardens and rival blackbirds were singing on the chimney pots, but they failed to raise Tom's spirits. He kissed his son goodbye at the corner and paused to watch him pedal back towards home, his head down and his little legs pumping round as if he were racing for a gold medal.

'That's a grand little lad you've got there,' an elderly voice remarked.

It was the lady who lived opposite them, a widow who kept her eye on everything that was going on in the street. Her equally elderly Pekinese dog glared at him with its bulging eyes from the shopping basket on wheels that it travelled in.

'Thank you,' Tom said, his foot on the pedal ready to go. He didn't want to start a conversation.

'Takes after his daddy, riding his tricycle like that.'

'Yes, he certainly does. Must get off to work. Mustn't be late.'

His neighbour fixed him with a stare as uncompromising as that of her dog. 'It doesn't do to spend too much time at work, young man. Remember that other people are at home when you're away.'

Tom went cold. He did not want to know what she was on about, and yet he had to ask. 'What do you mean?'

The woman pursed her lips and looked at a point somewhere over his shoulder. In the tree above their heads, a robin sang.

'Just that you should be careful, that's all.'

And that was all he could get out of her.

'I'm not a gossip, Mr Featherstone. Other people's business is their own, that's what I always say. Good day to you.'

And she went off down the road, trundling the basket before her.

Tom was left in a state of confusion.

When he got to the yard, he was disappointed to find that yet again there was nothing from Annie. He hadn't heard from her for three weeks now. He dashed off a quick note to her, asking if she was all right, but even that hardly distracted him from the suspicion that gnawed at him. He had

to settle it once and for all, he decided. It was no use simply confronting Moira. He had to prove it. The process sickened him, but he put it into motion all the same. He had to know if there was something going on behind his back. If he was just imagining it, then he would make an extra effort to put things right between him and Moira. If he was right...
He did not let himself think about that. The implications were too enormous.

'I'm taking that trip to Scarborough,' he told Moira when he came home that evening. 'I hope that's still all right with you? Only it'll save us a fortune if I do it.'

'Oh—right—yes. Well, I said so, didn't I?' Moira said.

There was a continual belligerence about her these days, it seemed to Tom. Whatever he said, however trivial, seemed to get the same aggressive response. Now, however, she was too intent on getting out to make an issue of the matter. She disappeared upstairs to get ready, leaving Tom crawling round the dining room floor with Michael putting the train set out.

'I'm off. Don't wait up,' she called from the hall.

Tom heard the front door open and hurried Michael out into the hall to say goodnight. A waft of perfume met him. Moira had a light mac on so he couldn't see what she was wearing, but her hair and make-up were perfect. There was an air of suppressed excitement about her.

'You look nice,' he said.

'Just because I'm going out with a girlfriend, I don't have to look a frump,' Moira told him. 'Night-night, Mikey.'

She bent down and touched Michael with her lips, leaving a bright red mark on his cheek. Then she was off out of the door and away.

Tom found it hard to settle. He kept Michael up way beyond his bedtime, but that still left plenty of time to fill. The television failed to hold his attention. He tried to go over some of the drivers' rotas but couldn't concentrate. He made cocoa and scanned the newspaper but the print blurred before his eyes. Was Moira really out with this mystery girl-friend? When she arrived home, at exactly the time it took to get back from the last showing in the town centre, he studied her face. Her cheeks were glowing from the cool air outside. She did not have a hair out of place and her lipstick was still fresh.

'You smell of cigarettes,' Tom said.

'People were smoking all round us. It gets in your hair,' Moira said, and added with heavy sarcasm, 'Did you have a nice time, Moira? Yes, thank you, Tom. The film was a bit feeble, but my friend enjoyed it. I think I'll go straight up.'

Tom was left none the wiser.

The next few days went far too fast. The knowledge of what he had put into motion weighed heavily on him. It was not a pleasant thing to set a trap for your wife. Part of him hated himself for doing it. The other part had to know the truth. On top of this, there was still no word from Annie. He was worried that she might be ill. He could think of no other reason why she would not write to him for so long.

On Saturday morning, Moira handed him the overnight bag she had packed for him. 'Drive carefully,' she said, and actually kissed him on the cheek.

Tom hid the bag beside a filing cabinet and went through the motions of working. Several times, people had to speak to him twice before he heard them. His father asked him if there was anything wrong. Tom assured him that he was fine, and hoped that it was true. In the evening, he ate tucked away in the corner of a café then whiled away the time at the pictures. He left before the end of the main feature.

He felt sick as he walked along his street. It was nearly half past ten and there were some lights on in upstairs windows as people prepared to go to bed. He glanced at the house over the road from his and thought he saw the curtain fall back. His own house was in darkness. With feet that seemed to be weighted with lead, he trod soundlessly up the front path and slowly, carefully, let himself in.

He stood in the hall, listening.

At first the house was silent. If he had not been so suspicious, he would have thought that Moira had simply decided on an early night.

Then he heard it—a soft, low laugh from Moira and the deeper rumble of a man's voice. Anger exploded through him. He snapped on the landing light, pounded up the stairs two at a time and flung open the door to the front bedroom, reaching for the switch. Everything happened at once. Light flooded the room, Moira screamed, a naked male figure came charging straight at him, head down, flattening him against the wall and making a break for the stairs. In a split second, Tom was after him. With Moira's cries ringing in his ears, he raced down the stairs and caught his rival as he tried to open the door. He got him by the throat and slammed him into the corner. The desperate crimson face that confronted him was that of the young man who lodged with the people a few doors down.

'What the hell do you think you're doing?' Tom shouted.

'It's not—what you think—' the man managed to croak, raising his hands in submission.

'You mean you weren't in bed with my wife?'

'Yes—no—'

'I'll have your bloody balls off!'

The man was sweating now, his eyes staring with fear. 'No—please—'

Vaguely, Tom registered that Moira was pleading with him to stop. He drew back his fist and slammed it into the mouth that had kissed hers. There was a satisfying crunch as teeth gave way. Blood flooded from a split in the lower lip and dripped down the chin and on to the naked chest. Moira wailed. He felt her snatching at his arm and shook her off.

'Not so pretty now, are you?' Tom taunted. 'Thought you'd knock my wife off while I was away, did you? I'll show you!'

'Daddy!' A thin cry of terror cut through his fury. He glanced behind him, to where Michael was standing at the top of the stairs, white-faced and clutching his favourite teddy. Moira's lover seized his chance and wrenched open the front door. Tom turned back and aimed a ferocious kick at his backside, sending him sprawling on the front path.

'Go—and don't you ever show your face here again!' he yelled, and slammed the door shut.

He leaned against the door, his chest heaving. Moira was crouched on the bottom step of the stairs, sobbing. She had her dressing gown gripped tightly about her. Her bare feet looked oddly vulnerable. He looked beyond her to where Michael was still standing staring down at them, tears of fear trickling down his face. The anger drained away, leaving him hollow inside.

'It's all right, Mikey. It's all over now,' he said, and was surprised to hear an almost normal voice come from his mouth.

He walked past Moira and up the stairs. His body felt stiff and difficult to control. To his horror, Michael cowered away from him. He felt deeply ashamed. The boy should never have witnessed this. He should have handled it differently.

He sat down on the top step and spoke gently to Michael, coaxing and reassuring until the boy came forward and allowed himself to be hugged. Two small arms went round his neck and held on tight while Tom rocked him, taking comfort from the small warm body. He stroked Michael's dark hair, smoothing the tuft that stood up at the back. This was real, this was solid. Whatever else happened, he still had his son. Leaving Moira still weeping below him, he picked Michael up and took him back to his room. He lay down beside the boy on the narrow bed and stared sleepless into the darkness as he listened to Michael settle back into the deep sleep of childhood.

Some time later he heard Moira come slowly up the stairs. Her footsteps stopped outside Michael's room for some time, but she did not come in. Tom was relieved. He did not want to speak to her now. He did not know how he felt about anything. He wanted only to lie in the dark and say nothing. From the front bedroom he could hear the sound of muffled weeping.

In the grey light of dawn, he went downstairs and made tea. He stood looking out at the garden as every bird in Nottinghamshire seemed to be singing its heart out from the surrounding trees. The kitchen door opened behind him.

'What are you going to do?' Moira asked.

'I don't know,' he said.

It was true. A whole night's turning it over and over in his mind had got him nowhere. He knew he didn't love Moira and she didn't love him. But divorce was such an extreme step. Ordinary people like them didn't get divorced. They put up with things. They carried on for the sake of the children. Of all the people he knew, there was only one divorced couple, a hasty wartime marriage that would never have happened under other circumstances. People of his mother's generation referred to them with lowered voices and significant looks. Their children were objects of pity. He couldn't do that to Michael. And yet he knew he couldn't carry on with things as they were.

'How long has it been going on?' he asked, still staring blindly into the garden.

There was a slight hesitation.

'A bit,' Moira said.

He had to turn round. He couldn't make out the sincerity of her words without seeing her face.

Moira stood in the doorway. She looked pale and strained and her arms were wrapped defensively round her, but there was still a faint belligerence about her. She did not look down, but met his eyes with defiance.

'How long's a bit? A month? Six months?' Tom persisted.

Moira shrugged. 'Does it matter?'

Tom realised that it didn't, not really.

'I just want to know,' he said.

Moira said nothing. Tom thought of the warning he had received last week.

'Who else knows?'

'No one.'

'Mrs Thing over the road told me, so that means the whole street knows.'

Moira did look shaken at that, but she recovered herself. 'I expect the whole street does know now, after the row you made last night. Yelling out of the door like that! They must have all heard every word.'

'So what was I supposed to do?' Tom said. 'Ask him politely to leave?'

'You shouldn't have gone for him like that. Attacking him like—like a wild animal. Getting him by the throat and hitting him. It was horrible. How could you do that? How could you hurt him like that?'

Moira's white face was flushed now. Tears were standing in her eyes. Tom stared at her, appalled.

'So you care more about him than about how I feel?'

Moira said nothing, but she no longer met his eyes.

'Are you going to give him up?' Tom demanded.

Still Moira said nothing.

Tom closed his eyes briefly. He took a long breath through his nose.

'Do you want us to stay married?'

'Do you?' Moira asked.

'I think it's best for Michael,' Tom said.

Moira cast her eyes to the ceiling. 'Oh, well, there's no more to be said then, is there?' she said, and walked out of the room.

The day was the longest and most miserable Tom had spent in his civilian life. They went to Sunday lunch with his parents and attempted to keep up the appearance of normality. Tom's mother was not fooled, and took him aside to ask what the matter was and give him a pep talk. Tom was sorely tempted to tell her everything, but did not. He still hoped to keep everything together. Being with his family had brought it home to him just how many people would be affected if he and Moira were to part. It wasn't just him and her and Michael. It was her family and his. They would all be hurt.

If Moira would just promise him that it was all over with her boyfriend, if she would tell him that she really wanted their marriage to work, then it would be worth trying.

That evening, she went up to bed early. Worn out by the emotional stress of the day, Tom followed soon after. He found the door locked.

He rattled the door gently, not wanting to wake Michael. 'Moira?'

The voice that came back was a hiss of hatred. 'Go away.'

Tom spent yet another sleepless night, this time on the sofa.

He went to work early. The yard and the everyday problems to be solved seemed a haven of peace after the minefield that was home. He was glad when one of the drivers phoned in sick. That meant he had to go out on the road and not face his father's trying to question him, for he was sure that his mother would have asked him to have what she called a quiet word. His father's attempts at quiet words in the past had been embarrassing for both of them.

It was past seven when he got back. His father was waiting in the yard, looking apologetic.

'I'm sorry, lad, but I'm going to have to ask you to go out again. It's a last-minute thing, a favour. I didn't like to turn it down. I'd do it myself, but it's Lodge night—'

Tom nodded his understanding. After years of faithful Masonic membership, his father was rather hoping to be made Master next year.

'It's all right. I don't mind,' he said with masterly understatement. He was delighted to delay his return home.

So it was gone half past ten before he had to face going back to Moira. Even then, he went into the office, knowing that the later he got back, the more likely it was that Moira would have gone to bed. He sorted through the papers in his in-tray. And there it was. Just when he had almost given up waiting for it, just when he most needed it.

A letter from Annie.

A shaft of sheer delight went through him. Annie had not forgotten him after all. He tore open the envelope.

Dear Tom
I'm sorry it's been so long since my last letter, but a lot
has been happening and I wasn't sure how to tell you.
  Tom, you know how hard it is for me managing on
my own, and how difficult it is for Bobby, what with
him not having a father and everything, so the thing
is, I'm going to marry Jeff Sutton.

'What?' Tom said out loud. 'You can't do this, Annie! You
can't do this to me!'

He scanned the rest of the letter, first swiftly, then with
more attention, looking for clues. Nowhere could he find any
reference to loving Jeff Sutton, only lots of reasons for making a sensible choice.

'Sensible!' he said to the letter. 'Sod sensible! Look where
that got me.'

He had to stop Annie from making a disastrous mistake.

'Why aren't you on the phone?' he demanded of the letter.

He looked at it again to make sure of the date of the wedding. Tuesday. Tomorrow! Tomorrow was Tuesday! There
was only one thing for it. If he couldn't speak to Annie on
the telephone, then he would go and have it out with her face
to face. He locked up at top speed, jumped on his bike and
cycled round to his parents' house. Not wanting to have to
tell a pack of lies to his mother, he waited outside for his father to arrive back from his Lodge meeting. As the car pulled
up, he got into the passenger seat.

'Dad, I need to borrow the car. Right now. I'll bring it
back by tomorrow evening.'

Mr Featherstone tried to take it in. 'Now, hold on, son.
What's all this about? Where's the fire?'

Tom tried to sound reasonable. 'I've just had a letter from

a friend of mine, one my RAF oppos. He needs help. I must be there tomorrow, and it's down south. I've got to set out now, Dad. It's imperative.'

It took a bit more persuasion, but five minutes later Tom was on the road. He felt alive again. He had purpose again. He was taking control of events instead of being pushed along by them. As he turned on to the A1 he found himself smiling for the first time in days.

CHAPTER THIRTY-SEVEN

'I DON'T want to go to the wedding,' Bobby protested.

'Don't be silly, dear. Of course you're going to the wedding. We all are,' his grandma told him. 'Now stand still and let me comb your hair.'

Annie sat hunched over a cup of tea as her mother smoothed Brylcream over Bobby's hair and slicked it neatly back. The smell made her feel queasy. So did Bobby's outthrust lip and mutinous expression. She knew just how he felt. She didn't want to go to the wedding either.

'There!' Edna said, turning Bobby so he could see himself in the mirror. 'Don't you look smart? You'll be the smartest boy there.'

He certainly looked a different little boy from the child who played about the farm. Edna had made him a real suit with a properly tailored jacket. His new shirt was gleaming white and he was wearing a red bow tie.

Edna sighed with pleasure. 'All you need now is your buttonhole,' she said.

'Don't want to look smart. It's stupid,' Bobby growled, and put both hands to his hair and mussed it up.

Edna and Annie both squealed with dismay.

'Bobby! Your grandma's gone to a lot of trouble for you,'

Annie cried, though part of her wanted to do just the same and rip the rollers out of her hair and go running off over the fields to the sea.

'Now you just stand still and let me do it again, and then I'll give you a cherry bun,' Edna coaxed.

'Don't want a cherry bun,' Bobby muttered, but eventually he submitted to the inevitable and let himself be combed.

Edna settled him at the table with a new colouring book.

'Now,' she said to Annie, 'you take those rollers out of your hair while I get dressed, and then we'll get you ready.'

Annie couldn't get over the change this wedding had made in her mother. She had never seen her so animated, so happy. In the years of her marriage to Walter, she had always been fearful and often depressed, and since he had died she had sunk into a state of apathy. She had been pleased when Bobby was born, but in a furtive, anxious way. This was quite different. She had positively bloomed. The prospect of having Annie married but staying at home and, what was more, marrying one of the Suttons, was like a dream come true for her. She'd busied herself in an orgy of dressmaking, putting off customers' orders to make the suit for Bobby, an outfit for herself and two for Annie—one for Beryl's wedding and one for her own. As a family, they had never before had so many new clothes all at once.

'Isn't it exciting?' she said now, giving Annie's shoulders a squeeze. 'I still can't believe it's really true.'

'Neither can I,' Annie said miserably.

She listened to her mother running up the stairs. Ever since she had agreed to Jeff's proposal, a feeling of doom had been growing in her. She knew she was doing the wrong thing, and yet she felt paralysed, unable to stop the juggernaut that now carried her along.

It was not too late, she told herself, looking at Bobby gouging the paper with his coloured pencils. She could run down to the telephone box and call Jeff and tell him that it was all off. Then she would be free.

But upstairs, her mother was actually singing as she got changed. And over at the Suttons', Jeff would be getting ready, also in a state of high excitement. At the Grand Hotel, lunch was booked for both families and the cake would be waiting, and Mr Sutton had already paid for the honeymoon.

'You do like Uncle Jeff, don't you?' Annie asked Bobby.

'No, I hate him,' Bobby said.

He got hold of a black pencil and scribbled all over the picture he had been colouring.

'He's always nice to you,' Annie said.

She could hear her mother's voice in her own, coaxing and appeasing.

'I hate him,' Bobby repeated.

But it was partly for Bobby that she was doing this. When she was Mrs Jeffrey Sutton, people would no longer treat her like dirt because she was an unmarried mother, and Bobby would no longer be bullied for having no father. A stepfather was a whole lot better than no father at all. For the first time in his life he would be part of a proper family.

'But why do you hate him?' Annie persisted.

Bobby shrugged. 'He's stupid. Not like Mr Featherstone.'

The very sound of Tom's name made Annie's insides tie themselves in knots.

'Tom,' she whispered.

He must have got her letter by now, telling him that she was going to marry Jeff. She had put off writing to him for ages, ignoring the increasingly urgent notes he'd sent to her, asking if anything was wrong. She wondered what his reaction was going to be. Perhaps he would send a telegram of congratulations to the reception. She wasn't sure whether she could bear that.

A car could be heard pulling into the yard. Bobby jumped up and ran to the door.

'Oh,' Annie heard him say. 'It's only the stupid flowers.'

The delivery man stood in the doorway with a large and a small flat box in his arms.

'Would you be the blushing bride?' he asked Annie.

The queasiness rolled over her again.

The bride. She was the bride.

'Yes,' she said.

'Lovely day for it. Where do you want them?' the man asked.

'Er—better put them in here,' Annie said, opening the door to the scullery. 'On the draining board.'

The small box contained a rose and gypsophila corsage for her mother and a rose buttonhole for Bobby. In the large box was her bridal bouquet. It was fashionably enormous, a great mass of pink roses, cream lilies and clouds of gypsophila designed to trail down to her knees. The chilly little room was filled with exquisite perfume. Annie's stomach churned.

The man, seeing her pale face, patted her arm kindly.

'Pre-wedding nerves, love. You'll get over it.'

Annie doubted it. She managed to thank him and send him on his way.

Edna came clattering downstairs.

'Is that the flowers? What are they like? Are they all right?'

'They're lovely,' Annie assured her.

Edna went into raptures.

Annie watched her as she raved over the bouquet, then tenderly lifted the corsage and held it to her shoulder.

'And this must be for me. Mmm—smell—it's so pretty—'

'You're the one who looks pretty, Mum,' she said.

Edna had changed into her wedding costume, a navy silk suit with a navy and white spotted blouse, and she was actually wearing lipstick and powder. Nothing could erase the effects of years of hard labour and abuse from her face but, glowing as she was with excitement and happiness, her natural beauty shone through.

Edna actually blushed. 'Oh—get away with you! Me? Don't be silly. Now come along upstairs and get ready. The car will be here before we know where we are.'

'I think I'm going to be sick,' Annie said.

She rushed into the lavatory and threw up the very little she had had to eat that day. Her head began to throb. She stayed there for a long time, wishing she could just lock the door for ever and hide there.

There was a tap on the other side.

'Annie, love? Are you all right?'

Annie wanted to say no.

'I suppose so,' she admitted.

'Well, come on out and I'll make you a nice cup of tea. And then we'll get you ready.'

There was no escaping it.

Annie sat down at the kitchen table again, the tea cooling in her hands while her mother took out the rollers and brushed her hair. Then she was chivvied upstairs and supervised while she put on her make-up, then made to step into a petticoat made of layers of starched net.

'So far, so good,' Edna said, nodding her satisfaction. 'Now for the dress…'

Her dress for the wedding was hanging under a cotton wrap in her mother's wardrobe. Edna lifted it out and removed the wrap. A classic virgin white wedding dress had been out of the question, of course, but this was just as beautiful in its own way. It was a silk dress in cream with a sprinkling of tiny pink hearts, made with a sweetheart neckline, tight bodice and tiny waist, flowing out to a wide, calf-length skirt that floated over the stiff petticoat. Over it went a pink silk bolero jacket with tight three-quarter length sleeves and a stand-up collar.

'Perfect—' Edna breathed.

Annie did not dare look at herself. Instead she stared out of the window. She could see the hawthorn tree where she'd fetched up in the flood.

'Ann! Help me!'

She gasped.

'What's the matter?' Edna asked. 'What is it?'

'Nothing—nothing—'

Annie was shaking. There was no escape.

Edna gave her a little kiss.

'You're just suffering from nerves, dear. It's only natural. Now—'

She fetched a shoe box and took out a pair of pink satin court shoes and placed them on the floor for Annie to put on.

'Just think,' she said, sitting back on her heels, 'you're going to be one of the Suttons! I still can't hardly believe it. All these years I've known Mrs Sutton, ever since you and Beryl was born, and I never dreamt that one day you'd be marrying into their family. You and Beryl are going to be sisters-in-law.'

'Yes,' Annie said, because an answer seemed to be required of her.

Once, she would have thought it hilarious that Beryl

would be forced to accept her as a relation, would have revelled in all the new opportunities it was going to give her to score points over her old enemy. Now it all seemed rather petty and childish. She had outgrown their rivalry.

Edna got down a hat box from the top of the wardrobe. Inside was a little cream hat with a tiny spotted net veil.

'You'll be able to go to all those lovely things that Beryl does,' she said. 'Tennis Club dances and Conservative dinners and all that. I'll have to make you lots of pretty dresses. You'll have such fun. You deserve it. You never had much fun when you was growing up.'

The thought of going to a Tennis Club do with Jeff and Beryl and Beryl's creepy husband made Annie feel even more nauseous than she was already, but if Edna noticed, she only put it down to nerves. Still chatting happily about the wonderful life Annie was embarking upon, she settled the hat on her daughter's head and arranged the veil so that it just covered her eyes. Then she fastened the pearl necklace that Jeff had given Annie only yesterday. Misty-eyed, glowing with pride, she gently turned Annie round so that she was forced to look in the mirror.

'There,' she said.

Annie looked at the stranger in the glass. A film star figure gazed back at her—elegant, ladylike, beautiful, dressed in the height of fashion. Ready for her wedding. She panicked.

'Mum, I can't go through with it,' she cried.

'Can't what—? Not get married, do you mean? Why ever not?' Edna stuttered. She looked appalled.

'I don't love him,' Annie stated.

'But—but—' Edna cast about for something persuasive to say. 'But he's a charming young man. Lovely manners. And he adores you. You've only got to see the way he looks at you. I mean—why did you say—? You must be fond of him, surely, or else why—?'

'I'm fond of him, yes—'

That was why she had agreed to all this in the first place. That was why she hadn't backed out already. She couldn't face the hurt it would cause if she said she had changed her mind, especially when he had stood up to his family and defended her from their insults.

'But is being fond of someone enough?' she asked.

She didn't need her mother's reply. She knew the answer already.

'You'll grow to love him,' Edna said. 'People do, you know.'

Annie didn't ask whether this had been the case with her mother and Walter. She looked out of the window again. There was a black car coming up the track. Coming to take them all to the wedding. Panic gripped her again.

'I can't do it, Mum! It's all wrong, I know it is. How can I get married when it feels wrong?'

Edna wrung her hands.

'But you've got to! You can't stop now; it's all arranged. What would the Suttons say? There's the register office and the lunch at the hotel and the honeymoon—I couldn't face them, Annie, if it was all put off— You don't mean it, do you? Not really? Everyone feels like this, darling. It's only natural. It's a big step, getting married. Everyone feels nervous. But they get over it. You'll get over it—'

Annie hardly heard her. She was watching the car come through the open gate into the yard. Part of her observed that it didn't have white ribbons fixed to it and that when the driver got out, he wasn't wearing a uniform, but all she could think was that it was coming to take her away, and that she desperately didn't want to go.

Voices could be heard downstairs—Bobby's high-pitched one and a man's deeper tones.

'No,' she said out loud, 'no, no, no—'

Bobby's small feet came pounding up the stairs. He burst into the bedroom.

'Mum, Mum! Mr Featherstone's here! He wants to see you.'

'Mr Featherstone?' Annie repeated.

She felt very cold. There was a ringing in her ears. A long way away, her mother and Bobby were talking. She shook her head and tried to focus her eyes. She grabbed Bobby.

'What do you mean? Is he here, in this house?'

Bobby stared at her as if she was mad.

'Yes. He's downstairs, in the kitchen. He wants to see you.'

Annie tottered out of the room and across the landing. Hanging on to the handrail like an old lady, she wobbled down the stairs in her pretty new shoes. At the kitchen doorway, she paused. There was Tom, standing in the middle of the room, gazing at her.

'Annie—' he said. 'You look beautiful.'

Annie steadied herself on the doorframe.

'How did you get here?' she asked.

'I drove all night,' he said. 'I got your letter yesterday evening. I would have been here earlier but I nearly ran out of petrol and had to wait for a garage to open this morning. I was so afraid I was going to be too late.'

'Too late?' Annie repeated stupidly. Nothing was making sense.

Tom stepped forward and took her hands in his.

'Annie, you don't really want to marry Jeff Sutton, do you?'

It all slipped smoothly into place. Tom understood. Tom always understood.

'No,' she said. 'I don't.'

'Then don't do it, Annie. Please. You'll regret it for the rest of your life.'

It was as if she had stopped swimming against a strong current. The relief was enormous. She felt quite limp.

'I know,' she said.

'It's not too late, then. You don't have to go through with it. You can phone, or send a letter—anything. Don't marry him just because it seems sensible. Please? I married Moira because everyone seemed to expect me to, most of all her, but it hasn't worked. Don't make the same mistake, Annie.'

Her brain was beginning to work again, taking in all the consequences.

'My mum will be so upset. She's set her heart on it,' she said.

'It's not your mam who's getting married,' Tom pointed out.

'And it's all arranged—'

'It can be unarranged.'

Annie found herself smiling at him.

'It can, can't it?'

'Of course it can.'

'I knew I shouldn't be doing it. It felt all wrong.'

'It is all wrong.'

Bobby was tugging at her arm. 'Mum, Mum, there's another car in the yard.'

'Oh, my God,' Annie said. She looked out of the kitchen window. This time the car did have white ribbons and the driver was in uniform. And he was walking towards the door.

'Tell him to go away,' she said to Tom.

Now it was Tom's turn to smile. 'You bet,' he said. 'But first you'd better write Jeff a letter, and we can ask the driver to deliver it. It's the least you owe the poor devil.'

It was the hardest thing Annie had ever had to write. While her mother begged her to think again, Tom made conversation with the wedding car chauffeur and Bobby wandered round demanding of everyone what was happening, Annie hurried off three garbled pages of apologies. None of it, she knew, was going to make Jeff feel any better.

'I feel dreadful,' she said as the chauffeur drove out of the yard. 'Poor Jeff. I've let him down and I've made him look a fool in front of his horrible family. He'll never forgive me.'

'No, he won't, and what will the Suttons say? How can I face them again?' Edna wailed.

'You've done the right thing,' Tom said.

Bobby stamped his foot. *'What's happening?'* he yelled. All three adults fell silent and looked at him.

'Oh, darling—' Annie swept him into her arms. 'I'm sorry. It's all such a dreadful muddle. We're not going to the wedding. I'm not going to marry Uncle Jeff after all.'

'Good.' Bobby's small face switched magically from the sullen anger he had worn all morning to his normal cheerfulness. 'Can I put my other clothes back on now? These are stupid.'

Annie kissed the top of his head and let him go. 'Yes, darling. Then you can go and play outside.'

She sat down at the kitchen table. She felt weak and shaky all over.

'Look at me,' she said. 'All dressed up and nowhere to go. I suppose I'd better go and change too.'

Edna was crying quietly. 'It was all going to be so wonderful, and now it's all spoilt. I might have known it was all too good to be true.' She looked resentfully at Tom. 'You're the airman, aren't you? The one in the prison camp? You hurt her before.'

'It was all a mistake, Mum. A stupid mistake. But this

time he's stopped me from making an even bigger one,' Annie told her.

She could see that there was going to be no convincing her mother. In Edna's eyes, nothing compared with marrying into the Suttons.

'Why don't you put the kettle on, Mum? I'll be down in a minute.'

She hung the beautiful dress back in her mother's wardrobe, put the hat and shoes back in their boxes and changed into her everyday trousers and shirt. Tom smiled at her when she came downstairs again.

'You still look just as beautiful,' he said. 'I don't know about you, but I think I could do with some fresh air.'

'Good idea,' Annie said.

Outside, the summer sun shone down on fields that were growing green once more. They didn't have to consult as to where they were going. Automatically, they set out for the sea wall. Their hands found each other as they fell into step.

'Are you all right?' Tom asked.

'Never better,' Annie told him. 'You stopped me just in time. I'm not sure whether I would have been strong enough to do it if you hadn't arrived.'

'You didn't love him,' Tom said.

'No, I didn't,' Annie agreed.

'Just like I didn't love Moira when I married her.'

Through all the turmoil of her own broken engagement, Annie realised that something had happened to Tom.

'What's the matter? Is it Moira?' she asked. She found it hard to even say the woman's name.

'Yes.'

For several long moments, Tom said nothing.

'Come on,' Annie prompted. 'Tell.'

'I'm going to get a divorce,' Tom told her. 'I decided on the drive down here. Moira's been having an affair with one of the neighbours. At first I thought I could live with it, for the sake of Michael and our families, but thinking over it all, I saw that we were never going to be happy. She probably turned to somebody else because she knows deep down that I don't love her. It's always been you, Annie. There's never really been anyone else.'

Above her, Annie was aware of a skylark singing its joyful song high in the clear blue sky.

'There's never been anyone else for me, either,' she said. 'Jeff, and Bobby Joe—I only ever looked at them because I thought I'd never have you.'

Tom dropped her hand and put his arm round her shoulders instead, drawing her close against him. Annie slid her arm round his waist. It felt so right.

They walked past Silver Sands, with Annie's shiny caravans and their groups of happy families, scrambled up the sea wall, slid down the long coarse grass and tarred stonework the other side and sat down on the warm sand at the foot of the wall.

'Remember how we sat here and looked through the barbed wire?' Tom said.

'We wondered if the Germans were going to march in over the farm. And your little cousins came and stared at us.'

'Yes—my horrible little cousins. They're quite civilised now. Meanwhile, we've survived war and floods and broken promises.'

'And here we are still,' Annie said, laying her head on his shoulder.

She felt the warmth and weight of his head against hers.

'Will you wait for me a bit longer, Annie? It's not going

to be easy, this divorce business. If they know I have somebody else in my life, I might not get custody of Michael.'

Annie rested her hand on his knee. They weren't kids any
more. They had responsibilities.

'You know I'll wait as long as it takes,' she promised.

WHAT WOULD YOU SACRIFICE FOR LOVE?

Overnight, Jewish eighteen-year-old Emma Bau's world is turned upside down when Germany invades Poland. And after only six weeks of marriage, her husband Jacob, a member of the Resistance, is forced to flee.

Escaping the ghetto, Emma assumes a new identity and finds work at Nazi headquarters. As secretary to the charismatic Kommandant Richwalder, Emma vows to use her unique position to gather intelligence for the Resistance – by any means necessary.

Kommandant's Girl is the poignant story of one woman's struggle to survive one of the darkest periods in human history.

MIRA

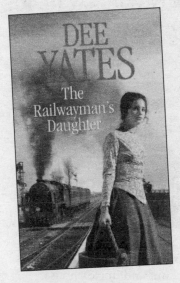

**In 1875, a row
of tiny cottages
stands by the
tracks of the
newly built
York – Doncaster
railway…**

Railwayman Tom Swales, with his wife and five
daughters, takes the end cottage. But with no room to
spare in the loving Swales household, eldest daughter
Mary accepts a position as housemaid to the nearby
stationmaster. There she battles the daily grime from
the passing trains – and the stationmaster's brutal, lustful
nature. In the end, it's a fight she cannot win.

In shame and despair, Mary flees to York. But the pious
couple who take her in know nothing of true Christian
charity. They work Mary like a slave – despite her heavy
pregnancy. Can she find the strength to return home to
her family? Will they accept her? And what of her first
love, farmer's son Nathaniel? Mary hopes with all her
heart that he will still be waiting…

Mollie
on the Shore

How Maisie Gibbs met Daniel Adams, and it all began ...

ELIZABETH
JEFFREY

A past shrouded in mystery, a future full of uncertainty...

After her mother's death, Mollie Barnes finds herself in her aunt and uncle's house. Then one day, her aunt spitefully reveals the shocking truth about Mollie's parentage.

Every day, Mollie works by the shore, under the shadow of the big house. Now she knows that the master of that house, James Grainger, is her real father, she vows that one day she will sit at his table.

But her dreams of finding acceptance are shattered as she finds herself the unwilling object of her half-brother's affections...

A compelling North-East saga in the bestselling tradition of Catherine Cookson

Born the day of the great mining disaster at Jane Pit, Merry Trent is brought up by her only surviving relative, her feisty grandmother Peggy, and lives in stricken poverty. Times are hard, and when an unwelcome visit from the ruthless mining agent, Miles Gallagher, leaves her pregnant, she tells no-one.

When Merry begins training as an apprentice nurse she attracts the attention of dashing young doctor Tom Gallagher, Miles' son, and Merry falls pregnant again. She loses her job and accommodation at the hospital, and her future looks bleak as she faces a tough choice: a marriage of convenience, or destitution and the workhouse…